SHAKIR RASHAAN

SAGEBORN

This book is a work of fiction. Names, characters, places, and incidents are the product of the author's imagination or are used fictitiously. Any resemblance to actual events, locales, or persons, living or dead, is purely coincidental.

NEBU Publishing, LLC
Fairburn, GA

Edited by SK Lawrence
Cover art and design by Sophia Chunn
https://sophiachunn.com/portfolio

Hardcover ISBN 979-8-9866688-1-9
Ebook ISBN 979-8-9866688-2-6

Printed in the United States of America
First Edition October 2025

1 0 9 8 7 6 5 4 3 2 1

MORE FROM SHAKIR RASHAAN

The Nubian Underworld

The Awakening
Legacy
Tempest
Samois

Kink, P.I.

Obsession
Deception
Reckoning

Standalones

Love, Lust & Beautiful Liars
Unthinkable
In Service to the Senator
The Devil's All-American
Queen of Cambridge

The Phenom Chronicles

A Deal Inked in Blood
A Fate Forged in Fire & Ice

All magic comes with a price…

~Rumpelstiltskin

For babygyrl:

Daddy loves you.

SHAKIR RASHAAN

SAGEBORN

Chapter Zero

Johari Salah awoke to a series of urgent knocks at her front door. She found it odd that someone would come calling in the middle of the night. Considering she was the "resident wiccan" in her Southwest Atlanta neighborhood, Johari had grown accustomed to these types of unannounced visits.

Little did she realize this visit would drastically change the course of her life.

The thunder in the distance should have been a dead giveaway, an ominous sign that she would have been sensitive to under normal circumstances. As she ambled down the stairs leading to the door, a flash of lightning lit up the windows that flanked the entrance to her home. It didn't scare her; very few things in this world rarely did anymore. Nothing would prepare her for what would be on the other side.

Johari went through her usual sequence, unlocking the series of deadbolts and latches before opening the door, coming face to face with a gentleman she hadn't seen since she'd buried her beloved husband. His chestnut brown eyes were sad, lending to the tingling sensation in the base of her spine and the tightening around her heart. In his arms, sleeping peacefully, was her grandson.

She couldn't believe how big he'd gotten. The last time she'd seen him in person, Yasir was a toddler. Seeing him now, remembering that he'd turned six over the winter months, Johari wondered how the mysterious man had been able to gather all the long limbs to even carry him to the porch.

Still, Johari feared asking the obvious questions as she caressed Yasir's cheek. "What are you doing here at such an ungodly hour? And why do you have Yasir?"

The mysterious man's voice cracked as he tried to find the words. "Ms. Johari, something horrible has happened to Bakari and Nasira. Yasir is all that is left of the family line. We need to keep him safe."

Johari opened the door wider to allow him to step through and into the living room to place Yasir onto the sectional. "I just spoke to my son the day before yesterday, what do you mean?" Once she slipped a blanket over him and kissed his forehead, she turned to face the mysterious man, desperate for further explanation, taking him into the dining room to sit. "Bakari cannot be dead. Nasira ... they are not dead. They cannot be. What about—?"

The mysterious man rubbed his forehead, wiping the tears that fell from Johari's eyes, blinking as through willing his own from welling up. "We have not yet been able to find anyone else, but we are still searching. There were bodies everywhere. The ones who could escape found refuge in the mountains and with the Kabila la Maji—the Water tribe."

Johari took a few deep breaths to settle herself, then straightened up in her chair as though she had flipped a switch. With the only surviving member of her bloodline secured, at least, to her knowledge, only one thing mattered. "Are the scrolls safe?"

"Yes, ma'am," he nodded, leaning forward in the chair. "I am so, so sorry. My comfort for your loss. Is there anything I can do?"

A thunderclap startled them, causing an impolite break in their conversation. The rain began its assault on her home as droplets pelted against the windows with such force that they were convinced they were hail stones. More stray bolts precluded the next series of violent crashes as they threatened to shake the house to its foundation.

Johari shook her head, glancing in the other room, feeling the need to check on her grandchild. She rose from her seat, padding over to where she left him, marveling as she heard his light snoring, regardless of the rapid-fire attack going on outside. She chuckled to herself, despite her grief, silently wondering if that little boy could sleep through a hurricane. "There will be time to grieve later. I will commune with my son and daughter once we are done here. Does Ya-Ya remember anything from that night?"

"I had one of the priestesses suppress his memories," the

mysterious man explained. "She warned me that he may have recurring nightmares, but we had to protect him from the trauma of watching his parents die in front of him. That is more than a six-year-old should bear to witness."

"I understand the choice had to be made to protect him. Now, I have a request of the Council ... I will need some assistance in raising my grandson," Johari expressed, allowing a deep sigh to escape her lips. She hadn't expected to raise another baby, but she would not allow anyone else to have a hand in raising him, not as long as she drew breath in this world. "I can handle things for now, but as I get older, he will become more difficult to manage."

"Everything you need to take care of for Yasir will be provided." He stood to take his leave, bowing before her as he trudged to the door. "The Council has already set up the arrangements, but they have made it clear that he cannot know anything until he has reached maturity."

Johari raised an eyebrow, wondering about the vague statements he continued to make. "There are others who know the location of the scrolls. What makes my grandchild special? Why is he being protected above all the others?"

"He is the key to the scrolls, and so much more, Ms. Johari," the mysterious man told her, locking a chestnut brown gaze on her. "What happened to him in Solara may have set off a chain of events that we still are not aware of. Until we know more, we must keep him hidden. The ones who invaded our home may still be out there to finish what they started ... can you ensure his safety?"

"No harm will come to him," Johari proclaimed. "Nyati, our divine mother, will keep watch over him, and the neighborhood will protect him. They have protected me since I arrived here, and he is a part of me. He will be safe."

Ten Years Later

Chapter One – Yasir

Nightmares like the one that's consuming me in its unrelenting grip are the stuff of horror movies, and I'm getting sick of being the leading actor in them.

Tonight's heat has me in my bed, tangled in the sheets, sweating like Olaf on a hot summer day. My breathing is shallow and uneven, my face twisting as I'm going through yet another inexplicable sequence meant to—well, I don't know anymore.

What I do know is that I need them to stop.

I'm standing in the middle of a vast, dark forest. The trees loom over me like ancient guardians, their skeletal-like, gnarled branches reaching out to unsuspecting victims. Shadows dance and shift with the breeze, taking on distorted forms that seem almost alive and breathing. The air is thick with the stench of damp earth and decay, and an unnatural silence hangs heavy around me, broken only by a distant mournful hoot of an African wood owl.

My heart pounds in my chest as I trek deeper into the forest. There's a familiar sense of overwhelming dread that seeps into my skin, like something evil is watching me from the darkness. My footsteps crunch on the leaf-strewn ground, the sound echoing eerily in the stillness.

Suddenly, the figure that has haunted my dreams since I was a small boy emerges from the shadows. The person is cloaked in black, their face obscured by a hood. The only thing that's visible are their eyes, which glint with a cold, predatory red hue. "Yasir Salah," the figure calls out. Their tone feels like a chilling whisper that threatens to ooze into my bones. "You have something that belongs to me."

My mouth dries up, and I take an involuntary step back, crouching into a defensive stance. "I-I don't know what you're talking about,"

I stammer as I struggle to find my voice. "Whatever it is, I don't have it."

The figure glides closer, moving with an unnerving, almost serpentine grace. "Do not play games with me, boy," he hisses. "You know exactly what I seek. Give it to me, and I may spare your life."

I shake my head as confusion and fear battle for dominance at the forefront of my mind. "I don't know what you want, I swear."

The figure raises a hand, and with a flick of their wrist, I'm lifted off the ground and hurled against a tree. The pain explodes in my back from the impact, making it hard to breathe for a few minutes. The figure approaches, their eyes aglow with a sinister lighting.

"Do not test my patience," they say, almost mocking me the entire time. "The artifact, Yasir. Now."

My vision is blurry, as pain mixes in with terror, but my mind races. I have no idea what the figure wants, yet the urgency in their voice makes me think there's something I'm missing. Some clue. Some memory I'm supposed to engage.

"Please," I plea as my voice breaks, "I don't know what you want, and I can't give you what I don't have."

The figure's eyes narrow, and they reach out, placing a cold, gloved hand on my forehead. I cry out as pain shoots through my skull, almost like they're trying to burn my brain from the inside out. Images flash before my eyes—my Nana's house, my friends, my remote-controlled fighter jet…

"Enough!" the figure snaps as they release their grip on me. I slump to the ground, panting and shaking. The figure looms over me, their expression hidden, but I can sense their anger. "You have something within you, something powerful. Find it, or I will find it for you, and you will not like the process."

The figure vanishes into the shadows just as mysteriously as they'd appeared, leaving me alone in the forest, my body aching and mind reeling. I struggle to my feet as my legs feel like gelatin and are unsteady. The forest seems to close around me, as the trees whisper secrets I don't understand.

Whatever the figure wants, it's connected to something I don't know how to access or where to look. Somehow, I better figure it out, and soon.

I awake with a jolt, my body drenched in sweat and my heart still racing. I scan around my room, taking a little comfort in the familiar surroundings. The dream—like the ones before this one—felt as real as ever, and they were becoming more intense as I got older. This isn't a figment of my imagination anymore, despite what my Nana has told me.

I shake off the images and get out of bed, grabbing a t-shirt out of the drawer as I make my way to the basement. I need to take my mind off the fact that something, or someone, is coming for me.

And I need to be ready.

Right. Left. Right cross. Left hook.

I'm up at damn near four in the morning in the basement of my Uncle Xavion's house, waiting for my alarm to tell me it's time to go to school. The sequences run through my head like clockwork, remembering what Unk has been teaching me since I was little. All this negativity I've built up over the past couple of days needs to go somewhere.

Sweat soaks my shirt, but I don't care right now. I just need to get rid of as much of this aggression as possible.

Left hook. Left hook. Right. Right. Left. Right. Uppercut. Just like that.

If I had a choice, I would've gone and done something that, technically, Unk wouldn't approve of. I'm not exactly *old* enough to go by myself to do what I'd prefer to do to blow off some steam. Too many questions to answer. I don't have the connects here that I have in the A, so, I'll have to settle for taping up my hands, pulling on the sparring gloves, and taking out as much frustration on the heavy bag as humanly possible.

Oh, by the way, I'm used to calling my Uncle Xavion, "Unk." It's a thing, and my friends call him that too, so, just so we're clear, cool?

I need this anger to go away, but it only grows with every jab.

My life has been upended. Again.

I mean, my uncle is cool as hell, and I love spending the summers with him, but there's a huge difference between coming down here for a couple of months and living here for the rest of the school year.

No one has told me why I had to move. I've just been given a vague reference to something I have no real memory of, except for the nightmares like the one I had earlier this morning. All I know is I shouldn't be here, and I sure as hell didn't do anything wrong—at least, not this time.

I had a whole life in the A, and my Nana—God bless her—did everything she could to raise me. The SWATs—Southwest Atlanta—can either make or break a person, and I don't break easy. Nana made sure of that.

Hearing the heartbreak in her voice when she said I had to leave her was more than I could bear. She was vague about the why of it all, but she kept saying that it was for my own protection. Still, having my life uprooted against my will should be considered cruel and unusual punishment.

The jabs come faster and harder now, and the impacts echo against the walls. My vision blurs as I blink away sweat and tears.

Right. Uppercut. Left hook. Hook. Keep hooking. Overhand Right. Faster, bro. *Faster*.

The alarm on my phone blares, shaking me from my thoughts. I stand still and clear my vision, and *whoa*, I've left a sizable dent in one spot on the heavy bag, nearly ripping the fabric. I let out a low whistle. A few more punches and that would've torn for sure.

My arms feel like someone tied kettle bells to my wrists. The exhaustion and soreness, though? That's exactly what I need, and I focus on the soothing, burning sensation coursing through my body. I rest my forehead against the bag and take as many breaths as I can to cool down, then stagger toward the stairs to take a shower and get ready for school.

"If you keep that up, I might have to seriously consider getting you into Golden Gloves."

I flinch, mouth, "what the—" and snap my gaze toward the source of my panic before I blow out a breath. It's just Unk. I guess he decided that scaring the hell out of me needed to be checked off his morning to-do list. "Yo, how are you able to move around this house and I can't hear you coming?"

Unk gives me this grin like he knows some ancient secret or something as he leans against the doorframe at the base of the stairs. "Don't worry about all that, I might teach you when you're older."

He makes his way down the stairs, then glances at the bag. "Are you good? Is there anything we need to chop it up about?"

I shrug, unfastening my gloves and pulling them off with my teeth. "I feel like the reset button got pressed on me again, and I'm not cool with that. Sorry about the heavy bag. I'll fix it when I get home later."

He walks toward me, nodding, then finds the scissors and cuts the tape off my hands.

"You've been through a lot," he says, "and I know this feels like another bump in a road full of roadblocks and potholes, but tough times don't last. Tough people do. You're one of the toughest I know, and I am wowed every day by what you can handle."

Bro, does he have to break out the monologue?

"I hear you, and spending summers down here with you was always lit, but on a full-time basis? No disrespect, but this ain't it."

Unk throws away the tape he cut, does a quick check of my hands for bruises, and sighs. "All I ask is to give it a chance. We have to make the best of things for now. Who knows? You might actually like something about Oakwood Grove."

That's debatable, but now isn't the time to argue. I'm gonna be late for school if I don't hurry up.

"Yeah… who knows?" I put the gloves away and then start trudging up the stairs. I take a few steps and realize my legs are dead. It's gonna be a long morning. *Uggghhhh, what was I thinking?*

As I head to my room, I avoid all the mirrors. I know what I'll see. All my emotions are still there, on full display. Raw. Edgy. Volatile.

Once in my room, turning on the shower is the first order of business. As the steam rises, I pray my thoughts are clearer and my body recovers by the time I finish. I step inside to scrub the weird energy off of me, then close my eyes and allow the soothing sandalwood scent from my handmade soaps to transport me anywhere but here.

Despite my uncle's optimism, this town better not be a total snooze fest, or I'll be putting a lot of miles on my Jeep on the weekends.

The anxiety levels already amp up before I arrive on campus.

Different stress-relief techniques I've been counseled to use cycle through my head, taking deep breaths until the 4-7-8 trick becomes the first attempt to calm myself when entering a new environment.

Inhale. Close your mouth and hold. Finally, exhale…

"Yeah. Nope," I say out loud. And trying it a second time doesn't do a thing for me either.

I switch to the 3-3-3 method. First, I have to pick three things I see around me. I scan the immediate area to get a good look at the massive building, noticing the crimson-and-grey dome that accentuates the front entrance to the school, with the words OAKWOOD GROVE HIGH SCHOOL emblazoned across the overhang. The brick surrounding the entrance gives way to long columns that flare out and make the building appear V-shaped. And what's with all the huge windows? I can see right into the classrooms.

Students are making their way into the building, and the sheer number of them pumps up my anxiety again.

I don't even want to get out now, and I'm not rolling down the windows so I can hear three things around me. I just wanna stay in my bubble.

No. Scrap that plan.

I rub the amethyst teardrop pendant laying on my chest—a gift from my Nana meant to center my energy—to ground me for at least a few minutes, as a last resort, but my anxiety levels have shot through the roof.

When I slow-roll into the parking lot in my black Jeep Wrangler Rubicon—I named her Storm, after the baddest and prettiest of the X-Men—I notice all eyes on me, which triggers more anxiety. I know my Storm stands out, and real talk, how can she not? The lift kit and thirty-five-inch oversized tires with glossed black matte twenty-six-inch wheels alone turn heads, not to mention the neon purple lights that glow underneath at night.

The eclectic mix of vehicles spread out over the spaces has my attention, from the sports cars grouped together in one corner, to the pickup trucks that take up most of the spaces, and I even see other Jeeps. At least Storm won't be the only one. They're nowhere as dope as mine, which is why all the attention is so laser focused on me until I get out.

Still, I *really* don't want the spotlight right now. Maybe once I get my bearings, I'll be alright, but today ain't it.

I'm planning to make the best of a bad situation, though. Like Unk said, maybe this town isn't as bad as I think. Still, my plan is simple: Get in. Take the damn classes. Get out. Rinse. Repeat. Pray that graduation day comes faster than a knife fight in a phone booth and get the hell out of this town on the first thing smoking.

When I pass by one of the benches, I notice they're splashed in the crimson and grey school colors, with the words "GHSA AAA State Champions 2019" painted in bold lettering across the back of one of them, and other championship designations on several others.

Yep. Football is religion in the South, and this is undeniable proof.

At the center of the courtyard stands a massive oak tree that takes over the entire area. Okay, so massive doesn't quite cover it, but from the width of the trunk alone, the school had to have been built around it, because that tree was there first. I snap a pic on my phone for later, for inspiration. There's a landscape painting in my mind, and this would fit in perfectly.

When I pull my phone away, I spot a group of girls sitting at the base of the tree. I hadn't noticed they were there.

But… wait a minute… who's *she*?

I don't mean to stare, but even from this distance, her hazel-green eyes capture me, making me want to stay there in the moment. The other girls aren't all that concerned, and they seem to fade into the background, leaving just *her* sitting there, trading glances with me.

She narrows her gaze while we stare for what seems like forever as her honey-bronzed braids frame her heart-shaped face. Her golden-brown skin makes her eyes stand out that much more. I'm already lost in whatever dream I've accidentally slipped into, desperately not wanting to leave any time soon.

She touches her face with her hand for a moment before it moves from her cheek to rest in her lap. Her legs are tucked under her, perched on a blanket she shares with the other girls around her.

What in the world have I gotten myself into already? I haven't been here three seconds and I'm standing here looking like I'm lovestruck.

Settle down, bro. We're not here for all that.

Then she grins, and my defenses almost disappear. I return a smile of my own and consider motioning for her to come and say hello.

Maybe this town won't be so bad after all.

And then reality sets in. I don't know anything about her, regardless of the way she's managed to turn my whole attitude around with a simple glance. I shake out of whatever trance she put me in and head for the front doors.

Inside, I find the front office, and I'm pleasantly surprised at how helpful they are with everything I need to get started. That's a plus. It's definitely the opposite of what I've dealt with at the other high schools I attended. Still, my guard is up.

Ms. Tyler, a petite woman with an oval shaped face and flawless olive skin, gives me my schedule, flashes a smile. "You're all set, Mr. Salah. If you hurry, you can make it to your first class before the late bell rings. Welcome to Oakwood Grove," she says.

"Thank you, ma'am. I'm looking forward to being here." Okay, so I'm lying, but I don't want to be rude, either. I turn into the hallway, look down at the schedule and the location of the first class, and… where's a tour guide when I need one?

I move through the crowd as everyone rushes to their classes, trying to temper my anxiety over the weird glances and all the whispers. I turn around the corner, frustrated over heading down another wrong hallway, and this one's decorated a lot more than the others, with large signs and bold lettering all over the place. One banner sums up the reason why everyone is still in the halls—it's Rivalry Week. I don't have time for this mess. And then I see something about a Bicentennial event or whatever, and I know I'm over it all.

It's bad enough I have to transfer in the middle of the semester, now I gotta deal with school spirit on steroids?

I spin to head back in the other direction and accidentally bump into another kid. I put my hands up to show I'm not there to cause any problems. The last thing I need is to get caught up in something for no reason.

From the irritated look on this guy's face, though?

I better buckle up and prepare for whatever aggression he's gonna bring.

Chapter Two – Yasir

We stand in the middle of the hallway, sizing each other up like we're getting ready to be a part of the undercard for the next UFC pay-per-view event.

I don't know about him, but I'm not in the mood to stir up this type of negative energy during my first day at a new school. I haven't even gotten a chance to observe how things work around here. Can I at least get to my first class so things can be worked out in a controlled environment?

Who am I kidding? This is exactly how today would start off. The only thing I can do now is try to de-escalate the situation, right?

"My bad, I was trying to find my history class," I say, backing up to create more space. "I didn't mean to bump into you like that."

"Yeah, it is your bad, new kid," he spits at me, then grits his teeth. "The history classes are on the second floor. You might need to keep your eyes up instead of whatever you thought you were doing. You're lucky it was me you ran into, not everyone will be willing to let things slide."

What's with the hostility so early in the morning, and why is it directed at me? I barely grazed him. Let's get this over with. "Thanks, I'll remember that. This place is a bit confusing."

I sidestep him, but he steps in my path. "Whoa, not so fast, New Kid. I'm not done with you."

I stare straight through him, doing my best to keep my temper in check. I see he's gonna be that guy.

"My name is Yasir Salah, my boy," I say. "Not New Kid."

"I don't care, and I didn't ask." He cracks his knuckles in front of me like he's trying to make a point, keeping up pressure that doesn't need to be applied.

If he thinks I'm gonna flow with—I don't even know what to call this—he's gonna find out the hard way that I don't follow rules very well, and I don't respond to aggression from wannabe bullies.

"Look, let's keep this simple," I offer. "If you can just slide to your left for me, I'll slide to my left, and we can move on. Sound like a plan?"

I don't even bother waiting for a response. I make my move to my left, brushing against his shoulder since he still wants to block my path. Nah, not feeling this already. I walk down the hallway, and I almost make it to the corner before I hear this dude yell my name.

"I know you can hear me, 'ya-seer say-lah.' Don't ignore me. You won't like how that goes down."

The energy shifts in the hallway, and I feel every bit of the negative energy coming for me. He meant to rile me by saying my name loud and pronouncing it wrong, and now everyone in this hall has stopped to watch, holding their phones out and pointing at me. Like, really… what's with people and their early morning drama?

I already feel the anger making itself present, an avalanche ready to rumble downhill at the slightest disturbance. I dare this dude to go ahead and be the trigger so I can let loose with every bit of icy fury I have. He needs to learn a lesson, and I'm ready to teach and then some.

Just as I start to see nothing but black, my Nana's voice rings in my ears with the force of a clap of thunder. There is more than one way to handle bullies, my child. Promise me you will find another way. If there is no other way, decimate all in your path.

I run a silent count to turn down the rage surging through me, remembering my promise to her. I'm not happy about it, but a promise is a promise.

Fine. I'll have to do this another way.

I turn to face whatever-his-name-is so we can settle this quick, and I come face-to-face with one of the other guys in the group.

He's the runt of the litter, but he's built like a bulldog, with a chihuahua's attitude, and he looks like he spends more time getting groomed than a poodle. Half of his hair is an odd shade of red, and the other half has been dyed dark grey. School colors? This must be a football thing because ain't no way he made this decision for no reason.

I pull back a few feet, but this dude closes the distance on me. "You heard my ace calling you, right? Do I need to shake the wax loose from your ears or something?"

Why is it always the short ones that have all the attitude?

I glare down into his ice-blue eyes, clenching my fists as I consider my options. They don't look good, even with my skills. There's too many of them. "Look, I need a few feet, all right? I don't do well with people in my personal space."

Whatever-his-name-is, the one who started it all, speaks up again. "I can understand why." He sniffs the air. "What is that funky-smelling cologne? Like, damn, bro, you couldn't wear something that wouldn't have everybody running for cover?"

Here we go with the low-hanging insults. Typical.

"Yeah, Ian," Bulldog Boy chimes in. "He smells like someone dipped him in some burnt wood and God knows what else that is… whew." At least I know what the ringleader's name is now. He called him Ian. "If you wanted to make a first impression, you did that. I don't think that's what you wanted to do, but go off, bro."

Okay, shots fired. Nothing I haven't dealt with before, though. "You're worried about my cologne, Ian, but what I'm wondering is where I can buy the crowbar you used to get into them skinny jeans? Did you get it from Home Depot, or did you order through Amazon Prime for same-day delivery because you had to wear them today? Do you need to see a doctor about your blood circulation? I can recommend a few good ones."

Ian frowns as laughter bounces off the walls. I guess he doesn't like it when someone comes for him.

"And for the record," I growl, "my last name is pronounced 'sah-lah.' I know you heard me when I said it the first time. I knew some of y'all football players were slow, but if I have to remind you again, it's gonna be a problem."

To my amusement, Ian retreats to his crew. A few of them stare at me, trying to keep from laughing, and a couple of the others nod at something else being said between them. Ian turns back with this look like he has me checkmated. "So, you got pressure? We can relieve that, for real, but I'm gonna let it ride since you're new and all, but you need a lesson on how things flow around here."

Big bark from a little bitch who has goons backing him up. "And I suppose you're the one who's providing that lesson, huh? Look, can we deal with that, like, next week or something? How about I pencil you in for, let's say, next Tuesday after school?"

Someone walks up from my right side, which surprises me. I usually have a knack for sensing if someone comes close, but I get distracted by the scent of jasmine and honeysuckle. I whip my head in the direction of such sweetness, and what my eyes land on are the most exquisite pair of hazel-green eyes I've ever seen in my life.

The same eyes I'd gotten caught staring at in the courtyard.

"Don't you know it's not polite to harass new kids on their first day?" Her voice is almost as soothing as her gaze. Damn, I'm in trouble. "He hasn't been on campus an hour and you're already starting up. I know you have something better to do."

Ian glares at her, making me feel some type of way. I want to drop a punch to his gut for that level of disrespect.

"Zahra, shouldn't you be off somewhere designing another crappy electric engine or something? Move along, this doesn't concern you."

Someone else pops up behind me, only this time I see him coming. Now, anyone who can make me feel short has my respect off break. This guy towers over everyone, but he stands behind Zahra like he's her bodyguard or something.

"You're funny, Ian," he says. "I'm trying to understand what makes you think you're supposed to be a part of this unwelcoming committee."

Ian rubs his hand over his face, looking all kinds of annoyed. "Kyle, don't think that because we ball together that I won't give you the business, either." He turns his attention back to me. "It's our job to make sure these kids know how things work at Oakwood."

"Nah, you want things to flow a certain way, and I've told you before, the rules have changed," Kyle retorts. He moves to stand in front of Zahra, getting in Ian's face. "You still think you're the dude at the top of the stairs, and I'm telling you that you ain't it no more."

I shake my head. After watching all this go down in front of me, I can't decide whether I want to laugh or take pity on them. I turn toward Zahra, playfully elbowing her as I figure out what I want to say. "Okay, I think I got it now. This was part of the lesson I'm supposed to learn, so let me see if I have it … You're supposed to be the resident 'god on campus.' Is that how this works? I'm supposed to do whatever you say or else, is that right?"

"That's exactly what's up, bro." Ian grits his teeth, glaring at me like he wants to fire off a punch or three. "Either you roll with it, or you get rolled over. I don't know where you're from, but you better head back there before something bad happens to you."

Is this man serious right now? "I see you need to get your life, for real. This ain't no real-life version of whatever teen drama is hot right now, okay? I flow how I want to flow, and I meet people on their level. Whatever energy you give, I'm returning it, with interest. It's up to you to figure out how I treat you, got it? If you bring the smoke, don't be shocked when I bring the hellfire."

Zahra giggles, winking at me before she turns her attention to Ian. "I think he's made himself clear that your 'rules' don't apply to him. Maybe you should take that cue and maybe try something that isn't so, I don't know, stupid?"

Before anyone else can get a word in, a resource officer shows up who could pass for Thor, startling everyone still waiting for more drama.

"Okay everyone, you can head to class," the officer commands. As expected, everyone scatters, including Zahra and Kyle, finding the closest hallway they can find. "Ian Lance, I don't remember whether you and your minions are supposed to be on this side of the building, but I suggest you get to where you're supposed to be before I check for myself."

Ian glares at me, nostrils flaring, despite Thor's stunt double being close enough to rip us both in half. I refuse to back down, feeling so heated I think my skin is burning. He's not ready to eat a punch from me, I promise. We can put the gloves on and keep it clean, and I bet he won't last a round.

Ian backs off, turning on his heel as he walks away from me and the officer. "You're lucky Sarge was here."

I don't care if Sarge is there, I lunge at Ian with every ounce of energy I have. What I'm not prepared for is how strong Sarge is. I know I said he reminds me of the God of Thunder, but I didn't expect him to actually live up to the moniker. He's literally holding me in place with nothing more than his outstretched arm. I give him a glance, and the look in his eyes let me know that if I push my luck, he's gonna have to put me down, and I've been through enough of those to know I don't want that pain.

Message received, good sir. I'm not trying you any time soon.

"I can't wait," I yell at Ian as he turns the corner. I'm trying to save face more than anything now. I've never been held in check like this by an officer before. "I'm sure we'll have lots to discuss."

The faint scent that kept my attention—and calmed me down—has me searching for where Zahra had gone while my bravado was on full display. I can't find her right away, but I finally see her and Kyle making their way down the opposite end of the hall with the other students.

I try to call out to her, but nothing comes out of my mouth. I make another attempt, and still nothing. Wait a damn minute? Why can't I say something? What in the world is going on? I can't be that nervous around her already, can I? I just met her, and I can't even say that we really met, met.

Zahra turns before she disappears around the corner, and she stares long enough to make me uncomfortable, but in the best way. Then she smiles the way she did when I saw her in the courtyard, and… by the gods, her smile shines brighter than the sun and melts me in seconds. Next thing I know, she winks and mouths, "See you later, cutie," before I lose sight of her.

Sarge cuts through the haze quick, grabbing my shoulder to get my attention. "Are you okay? You're new around here, right? What's your name? I'm Sargent Bolton, but the kids call me Sarge."

I still can't speak. Between not really hearing a single word he's said and clearing my head from Zahra's sweet scent being in my space all of five minutes, I need to get my head together quick. "Yasir Salah, sir. I'm good, Sarge, but you might want to see why Ian had problems with me. All I did was bump into him, and I apologized for it."

Sarge nods as he checks me over. "If anything gets to be more than you can handle, let me know. None of the other students want to challenge him because of his father, the mayor. Based on what I've witnessed, you might be an exception."

"I won't let things get out of control," I reply, then make my way to the stairs to head to class. Yeah, I won't let things get too wild—but if he tries me again, things will end differently.

Now, if I can just find my class, that would be great.

CHAPTER THREE – ZAHRA

I close my locker with every intention to make it to study period and help Kendyl with her chemistry project. I enjoy being able to flex my intellectual muscles away from my engineering specialty, and providing an assist to my best friend feeds my primary love language. I can't wait to dig into things, and I admit that it helps keep me distracted from what's really on my mind.

I sprint toward my destination, taking the stairs to the second floor. As usual, I greet the other kids as they head to where they're going, engaging in very little chit-chat because I'm already running late. I don't like being rude, but I don't have a choice in the matter.

I cut around another corner while looking over my shoulder to say goodbye to another classmate, laughing over a bad joke he told. I turn, passing by the library, when I collide with a solid wall of someone's chest. The force knocks my bookbag and purse from my shoulder, throwing me off balance. Both of my bags hit the floor with a loud thud, and thankfully, nothing spilled out on the ground.

I shut my eyes tight, hoping I won't twist an ankle or hit my head, silently praying not to break anything. The way I'm falling, it's all happening in slow motion, and all I can do is count down the seconds until everything fades to black.

Except it doesn't.

A strength I can't explain stops me in mid-air and brings me to my feet. I open my eyes, my gaze following the hand holding me, then up the arm to the face of my rescuer. How the hell he had the ability to keep us both from tumbling over, I'll never know. He has a wiry, athletic frame, but muscles I never noticed earlier in the morning are on full display.

It takes a few more seconds to realize I've crashed into Yasir.

He has such a firm grip, and yet the care he's taking to make sure I'm not hurt—goodness, gracious, this boy is *strong*. The first words out of his mouth sound more like a knee-jerk reaction than an actual question. "Are you okay? I didn't mean to crash into you like that."

I want to say something, anything, but I'm caught inside his stare, and there's no way I can take my eyes off him. He has the most brilliant shade of—I can't figure out if they're amber or honey brown or a combination of the two colors. His irises remind me of the golden sunsets of my home country, so much so that I stayed inside them longer than I planned. Wow, his eyes—they're, just, wow.

I finally find my voice, still scanning around us to figure out how much of a mess we've made. "I think I'm okay. What about you? I mean, did I—?"

"I'm fine, seriously," Yasir replies as he kneels to pick up my bags. "I didn't want you to hit your head or anything. The way you were falling… I couldn't… I mean, it would've been… like, my fault, and—"

I raise my left eyebrow, taking everything in as I stare at him. I stifle a giggle, realizing I'm making him nervous. So, he can be rattled a bit. Why do I find that so adorable?

I snap out of my dreamy haze to get back to reality. "I thought you were… I mean, thank you for keeping me from falling." I can't wipe the silly smile off my face as I study his facial features. They're so familiar to me, but I can't place my finger on it. I have to find out, and soon.

As he places my bookbag on my shoulder, his scent consumes me. In seconds, I subconsciously travel to my homeland, smelling the spices in the market, tasting the meats and vegetables being grilled by different merchants as I walk along the cobblestone paths. The hypnotic beats of the tribal drummers in their circle send my hips swaying through the light breeze of the day. I grin wide as I take comfort in those pleasant memories before his voice sifts through.

"Zahra? Zahra, are you okay?"

I try my best to snap out of my trance, but I don't want to leave the warmth of the fantasy I've conjured. I shake my head a few times, the braids pulled back into my ponytail swaying back and forth as I make my way back to the present. “Yes, I’m fine now, thank you.”

“Good, I’m glad to hear that,” he replies as he turns on his heel to head toward his classroom. “I guess I’ll see you in World Lit later?”

“Yasir, wait.”

He stops, turning to face me. “What's up? Something on your mind?”

I have no idea what to say, but I didn’t expect him to stop when I called out to him, either. I can’t say what I want to say, but when the alarm on my phone chimes in to let me know I’m about to be really late with my session with Kendyl, I have no choice but to cut things short. Dammit, she’s gonna kill me. “Actually, never mind. I’ll see you in World Lit.”

Camping out under my favorite tree, a century-old Southern Live Oak that has been the centerpiece of the Oakwood Grove campus for decades, is a ritual for me. It was originally a part of the Savannah Street oak trees, with their drooping, curved branches and Spanish moss covering their bark.

Depending on the day, I’m either holding court as the younger girls soak up every word I have to say when it comes to app development or the latest tweak to my electric engine, or I simply enjoy the solitude that the tree’s branches provide before jogging to volleyball practice.

Today, I’m dealing with a conversation between Kendyl and Chrisette, her cheerleading teammate and Ian’s current girlfriend.

Kendyl can’t wait to call me out, and it’s not like she’s not wrong. “What in the world happened earlier, Z? We had to rush through my project because you were late,” she shreds through me as she pulls a piece of mango from her lunch bag. “Hell, you could’ve let your ace know something if you weren’t gonna be on time.”

I rub my temples as I create a short version of what happened earlier. “I had a bit of a… I don’t know what to call it, but I was talking to Yasir, and I guess I lost track of time.”

“Oh, so that’s what we’re doing now?” Kendyl huffs. “We’re blowing off besties because the new kid has your attention?”

“I’m sorry I was late, babe, seriously. I promise I’ll make it up to you.”

Kendyl squeezes my forearm, staring at me for a few moments. "You know that's not what we do, babe. I get that no one has really been able to keep your attention since we got here, but that doesn't mean you need to get sucked in so quickly, either."

"Well, I don't know what you see in him, anyway. He doesn't hold a candle to my Ian," Chrisette interjects with a dismissive shrug. "he's not even from around here, and what's up with that scent he's wearing? I could barely handle it when we were in English this morning."

I don't remember asking for an opinion, especially hers. Twit. "Ian's got the whole school fooled, but y'all keep that energy way over there. I don't know how you deal with him. Then again, I'm not you, so I'm never gonna understand anyway."

Chrisette stares at me, shaking her head as she checks her nails like she's unbothered. "He couldn't have been that bad this whole time, you know. I remember when things were friendly between you."

I roll my eyes in disgust. She's writing revisionist history, and I'm about to remind her that history is based in fact, not fiction. "Nah, things weren't friendly at all. *Your* boyfriend was trying to holla at every girl who thought about blinking in his direction when, as you said, we were 'friendly,'" I counter. "Once he realized I wasn't interested in sitting at the cool kids' table, he went on to the next girl who stared him down."

Kendyl frowns, giving me a side eye. "That was before she came to her senses. Everything that glitters… you know what, what we're not gonna do is… on second thought, never mind. At least he isn't infecting the rest of the football team with his drama."

I want to let it go, but my inner petty wins out, and this child needs to be set straight. The glare I give her causes Kendyl to clutch her imaginary pearls. "Look, as much as everyone wants to make him the next 'big thing,' let's keep it a stack. Outside of the fact that his father is the mayor, what's the appeal, because I don't see it."

This girl has the nerve to scowl at me like I personally offended her. It's not my fault she has a flawed taste in boys. "He's *fine*, whether you want to see it or not. He's the star quarterback, and one of the best in the state, which makes him a god on campus. Just say that you're jealous without saying you're jealous."

I hold up my index finger to silence her before she can get on her soapbox. "One, jealousy ain't it, you've got that all the way wrong, and two, I don't worry too much about what other people deal with, especially when I'm not getting anything out of it. It's okay, though, everyone doesn't have to be on the Ian Lance hype train, but we can fake it on game days. You know, school spirit and all that."

"Z, leave it alone, that's ancient history now. We're not changing her mind, and it's not for us to do it, anyway." Kendyl presses her hand on my shoulder, softly rocking me back and forth. "I still wanna know what happened. I mean, since you almost blew me off and everything."

I'm still trying to make sense of it, and she wants me to explain it to her? "So, I was grabbing my things from my locker, and I bumped into Yasir and… I don't know, things sort of took off from there. I fell from the collision and he just… he was so… he kept me from hitting the floor."

"You're killing me, but I get it. If someone had my attention like that, I'd be tripping out too. I guess I can forgive you," Kendyl replies to me. "I'm serious, though, I still need some help tomorrow, babe."

Before I can ask her what she needs, I catch a whiff of the scent that had me spellbound earlier. I close my eyes, allowing its sweetness to fill my lungs. I hummed, low and rhythmic, turning my head on instinct, determined to find its source as soon as possible. I don't think I've smelled anything so good in my life.

Kendyl taps my shoulder, pulling me out of my trance. "Earth to Zahra… chica, where'd you go just now? It must've been something powerful for you to blank out in the middle of our convo. What was it?"

The answer to her question comes in the form of Yasir making his way across campus, toward the parking lot. My gaze follows as he chats away on the phone. For a moment, jealousy creeps up on me. I wrinkle my nose, confused over why I'm unraveling so quickly and so deeply.

I've got to get a grip on myself.

While Kendyl and Chrisette argue between themselves about who knows what, my attention remains focused on him. I shake my head, taking in the whole image, admiring the *Black Panther* hoodie, jeans, and Timberland boots he's wearing. I should be ashamed of the grin on my face, but I don't care. I'm gonna find out more and figure out why everything fades around him the minute he appears.

I jump to my feet, slipping between the girls, and take a few steps toward the parking lot. "I'm gonna leave you two to handle whatever y'all got going on right here. I have something to see about right now."

"More like *someone*," Kendyl quips. "That's alright, I'm gonna press you for the tea when you're done, and don't skip on the honey, either. Now, go and handle that before he slips away from you, okay?"

I press my fingers to my lips, blowing air kisses as I turn to catch up with Yasir.

I hope I don't fumble through my words once he's in front of me.

I guess there's only one way to find out, huh?

Chapter Four – Yasir

After my first week at Oakwood Grove High, I'm seriously not in the mood to deal with people anymore. I'm in classes with Ian and at least one of his crew. The subtle shots and digs at me while the teachers weren't looking took their toll. My promise to Nana to not retaliate is working against me, and it's making me look weak because I'm not fighting back.

I keep my promises, but they're making it extremely hard.

"Hey, Yasir, what's new with you?" Hearing Zahra's voice calling out to me as I make my way to Storm throws me off balance a bit. I don't even know this girl, and the fact that she affects me like this is not a good look.

I drop my bookbag in the backseat, then close the door. "Things are okay, I guess. You good?"

She blushes. "I'm doing okay. How are you adjusting to Oakwood?"

I shrug. "I'm doing the best I can, under the circumstances. I'm trying not to think about it right now. What's on your mind?"

"I'm sorry. I'm a good listener if you need an ear to bend. Maybe we can figure out a way to help you. Word on campus is that you moved here from Atlanta, right?"

I offer up a nod, but I'm still not willing to bare my soul. "I'd rather not dwell on that, either. I just wanna get home and relax this weekend. I haven't had a real moment to myself since I got down here."

"So, does that mean you won't be at the game tonight?" Zahra blurts out before she places her fingers against her lips. She fumbles with her hands, and I wonder for the first time if I make her nervous. "I mean, it's Rivalry Week, and I'm sure everyone will be there."

Oh, for the love of… is she kidding me right now? I rub the back of my head, jumping on the defensive before I realize what's happening. "I have this thing about… I'm not sure… it's probably gonna be packed at the stadium, I assume, and I don't know anyone."

I fight every urge inside me to push her away as she reaches for my hand. She makes me uncomfortable, but I'm craving her touch at the same time. As she slips further inside my space, suddenly I'm as trapped in the moment as she is, and I don't want her to go. I pull away, snapping us out of our shared haze, but she still has this hopeful expression on her face.

She stops for a moment, staring into my eyes with a curiosity that I don't know how to describe. "I would love to see you there. Is there anything I can do to convince you to come through?"

Maybe it's the way she says it, or maybe I just want to switch things up a bit, I don't know, but I nod in response. "I'll try to make it out there tonight, but only because *you* asked me."

Zahra smiles and slips one of her fingers inside her honey-bronzed braids. "Great! I'll be looking for you in the stands. We can even sit together if you'd like."

"You don't have to do that, Zahra."

"Please, my friends call me Z."

In that moment, I freeze. Okay, just like that, and she wants to be friends? Who is she trying to convince, because it can't possibly be me.

I tilt my head toward my left shoulder and try not to frown. I don't mean to sound so irritated, but I can't help myself. "Are we friends, Zahra? Like, deadass."

She gives me a curious glance, biting her lip. "Um, well, would you like to be friends? I guess I shouldn't have assumed."

I'm stuck between giving her a hard time and wanting to apologize for being so edgy. "Okay, let's not pretend here, something's up, but I don't get it. The way you look at me… it's like you feel like you know me, even though we've never laid eyes on each other before. I don't know you."

"Would you like to get to know me? As friends, Yasir?" Zahra's still leaning against Storm, allowing the question to linger between us. I open my mouth to say something else but stop myself the moment she gazes into my eyes again.

I can't afford to let my guard down, but she's not making it easy.

She leans closer, almost like she doesn't want to intrude any more than she has already. "May I?"

I nod as she places her hand against my cheek. She takes a deep breath, slowly exhaling as her gaze never leaves mine. "Tell me what's on your mind, if you feel comfortable, I mean."

What's really on my mind, she asks? How about how I'm vibrating so intensely that I could start an earthquake? Or maybe why I feel so drawn to her, like there's some mystical force that's binding us together?

Or why can't I tell her to remove her hand from my face?

"I'm sorry, I'm just on edge, and I shouldn't have taken it out on you. You've been cool every time I've seen you," I sigh and close my eyes for a moment before opening them. Something still isn't adding up. "Why are you being so nice to me? What makes me so special?"

She grins as she keeps her hand steady. "I can't explain what's happening, either, but I know that there's something about you that makes me feel safe when I'm around you. That usually happens whenever I'm around my friends."

When I pull her hand from my cheek and hold it, her eyes light up. We stand there a few seconds longer than necessary, only this time, I'm willing to be captured by her gaze. It's so warm, welcoming… and all I want is to feel this again. The sooner, the better.

Then I check my watch and realize if I don't get moving, I won't be able to do much of anything later. I pull my key fob out to start the engine. "I hate to cut this short, but I have a few things to take care of at home so I can go to the game."

She jumps as the rumble of the engine startles her, but she moves into my path, cutting me off from the driver's side. "So, you promise you'll be there, right?"

For the first time since we started talking, I give up a genuine smile. I almost forgot what that feels like. Maybe getting to know her might not be such a bad thing.

I hop in the driver's seat, then roll down the window and pull out of the parking space. "I'll see you later tonight."

I try not to focus on the way her nose wrinkles up when she grins, or with the way she keeps playing with her braids, but one thing's for certain, and two things are for sure.

I'm not about to get caught up, I don't care how pretty she is.

I have a plan, and I'm sticking to it.

But that doesn't mean I can't try to have fun while I'm here, either.

Only one thing crosses my mind the moment I step through the door: I need to get everything done quick, fast, and in a hurry.

Where all this energy came from as I speed around the house acting like I want to break the sound barrier or get into the *Guinness Book of World Records*, I'll never know.

Dishes. Done. Trash cleared throughout the house. Done. Bathroom cleaned. Done. Bedroom cleaned. Done.

Wait a damn minute.

This can't be life right now.

If I don't come up with an explanation that Unk will believe, I'll end up in a question-and-answer session that could last hours. Ain't nobody got time for that.

How in the world did I get here?

I work through everything in my head, weighing the good and bad of heading out to the stadium tonight. I don't want to admit that Zahra has some influence over my decisions but, look at me. The whole house is clean, including my room, so I can sit next to her at a football game. Who does that?

I glance down at the clock sitting next to my Black Panther replica helmet, doing my best to keep track of time to make sure I'm not rushing. Just enough time to take a shower, get dressed and freshen up, then make it to the game.

One look in the closet and I want to scream; I didn't realize how much my Nana's paranoia affected my wardrobe. I mean, I know I can't be *flashy*, flashy, but I'm not trying to go out looking all basic.

Maybe giving Storm a bath and wax will make me feel better.

I catch a rhythm, getting into a zone, thanks to the music piping through my air pods, and the next thing I know, I burn through the wash in less than thirty minutes, and I still have time to put on a fresh coat of wax.

I immerse myself, watching Storm shine before my eyes against the waning sunlight. She's gonna turn heads tonight. I can't wait.

"Whoa, based on what I've seen inside, do we need to have a conversation?" Unk asks from the front porch.

I shake my head as I continue working. "Yo, how do you manage to pop up when I least expect it? And how did you get home without me seeing you? Is there a secret entrance I don't know about?"

Unk strokes his goatee, and from the grin on his face, I see the punchline coming. "You probably got so lost in babying your ride and didn't notice me drive right past you. I wonder if I should ask you to wash my truck, since you're being so charitable. You got your Jeep looking *niiiiccceee*."

I've got to do better about zoning out when I'm listening to my music. I give up a shrug, stretching my arm out to keep it loose. "Charitable, Unk? Nah, I just wanted to make sure I got her right before I get dressed and head out tonight."

He tilts his head, a surprised expression on his face. "Oh really? And where are you heading, considering you *never* go out, even when I suggested it?"

I pause for a moment, squeezing the wax on the applicator, scrambling for a reason to give him. "I'm going to the football game tonight. I figure I might as well, since it's Rivalry Week with Baytown High and all. Apparently, it's a big deal around here."

Unk makes his way down the stairs from the porch, giving me a long glance. He raises his left eyebrow, then grins like he knows why I want to go out, but he doesn't say anything. "So, go and enjoy the game. You need to be a teenager for once, instead of being caught up in whatever has been going on in your head."

"Unk, I—"

"Hear me out, kiddo," he interrupts, placing a hand on my shoulder. "For the past decade, we've been trying to play by your Nana's rules, presumably for your protection. In that time, thankfully, no one has come for you, which is a good thing. That means, as much as I bought into her paranoia, I have to admit that maybe we can loosen things up a bit."

I'd be lying if I said I don't want to find out what life looked like with the shackles off. "I'm trying to figure it all out, and some things are easier than others. Just… I don't know."

"Speak on it, Ya-Ya. You know I got you."

I scratch the back of my head. I hate going against my grandmother. She took me in when no one else could. Even the thought of it makes the hairs on my arms stand up. "You're right. I'm not feeling whatever Nana was talking about, either. But maybe we can wait a little longer before I feel comfortable cutting loose?"

He gives my shoulder a squeeze, smiling the entire time. "I can understand that. I'm good with whatever you decide. Now, finish your wax and get moving, I have a few things to do myself."

"Whoa, and what kind of plans do you think you have?" I tease. "Who told you it was okay to get a life?"

Unk laughs, and I laugh along with him. He leans against the front grill, it tickled him so much. "Oh, my God, too funny, I swear. Okay, how about this… you tell me your real reason for heading to the game, and I'll tell you what my real plans are."

I put my hands up in mock surrender. "Nah, I'm not that curious. Have fun tonight, and I promise I'll be home by curfew. Bright and early for the usual ride?"

"As always, kiddo. See you in the morning."

"So, you ain't got time for your Day One no more, bro?'

Hearing Dante's voice and seeing his face on the FaceTime feed while making the drive to the stadium was just what I needed. Dante is my Day One; known him since I first came to the A. He is as close to a brother as I could get, and my Nana treated him as such.

"Hey, what's good, my boy? I've been trying to get my life down here. I feel like I'm in another country with all the madness going on." I settle the phone on the hands-free car mount, rolling along at a steady pace to keep from bouncing the connection around too much.

"If I remember correctly, it wasn't much of a life to get." Dante chuckles. "At least Unk is good with all this. That whole deal with you getting bounced to live with him was foul. Squad been asking about you, though."

Mentioning Squad… he had to know it would trigger me.

I didn't have a chance to really get together with them to at least let them know where I was headed. I left that to Dante to explain it, which I guess wasn't the best thing to do, now that I think about it. Everything happened so fast. All I can do now is move forward and hope they understand.

Most of them would. *She* probably didn't.

"I'm planning to get back up there soon… I have some things I need to talk to Nana about," I reply, avoiding the mention of Squad on purpose. "Once I'm up there, I'll hit you so I can catch you up."

"Where you rolling? And you got the top off, too? You trying to flex a bit, huh?" Dante asks. "Good thing we got that neon kit installed before you left, otherwise you would have been better off just staying at home."

"You got jokes, bro. I'm always on my game, even if I have to play hide and seek," I answer back, trying to watch the road and pay attention to the call at the same time. "I still have a few more tweaks to the engine to make too. I've been scouting the comp, and there's not too many that can keep up with Storm."

"Well, with that hybrid HEMI we put together, what did you think was supposed to happen?" Dante boasts through the connection. "We knew she could decimate everything in her path outside of supercars once we got the proper calculations down. Enough of all that, though… I need to know if the girls are like that, you feel me? And don't say you ain't been peeping game, either."

His focus on girls takes me straight to Zahra. I don't know whether I want to be upset or happy about it, either. Even when I was at Douglass—my last school before I "transferred"—there was only one girl who had a shot at keeping my attention, and she had to work to even get me to look her way.

No wonder I'm so heated about what Zahra is doing to me. She hasn't had to put in half as much energy as the other girls, and I'm already into her. "Yeah, there are some baddies in the mix down here, absolutely. That's why I'm rolling to the game tonight. Oakwood has some rivalry game, and it's supposed to bring out the cream of the crop, according to the boys I heard talking."

"Good, because I have no intentions of bringing sand to the beach, you feel me?" His laughter is so infectious that I can't resist jumping in with him. "I mean, you my boy and all, but you know the drill. It makes no sense to bring girls when there will be girls to holla at while we're down there."

"I got you. I'll holla once I'm done with the game. I know you'll be up, so make sure you got the line clear, alright?"

"Alright, bet." Dante moves with his phone to head out the house. "I gotta head out, too. We heading to the Langston Hughes game. It's gonna be fire!"

I shake my head. When we were rolling deep, Squad never did go to a game at the school we actually attended. I'm surprised they aren't going to one of Douglass' games—they're really good this year, for a change. "Just stay out of trouble, bro. I ain't there to pull you out if things go left."

"You make sure you do the same, little bro," Dante tells me, his face growing serious. "Make sure you find backup down there, alright? We're all a bit tight that you're down there with no one outside of Unk to cover."

"I'm good for now. Ain't like I'm really trying to get into anything down here." I roll my eyes as I think about it. "I'm not built for this small-town life. I'll head down to Jax or something to see what's popping down there if it gets too boring."

"Okay… I'll tell Squad we linked up by FaceTime. I'll get at you later. One."

"One." I close the call, enjoying the breeze. I do my best to calm the rising anxiety, but I have a hard time focusing on the road. With the call from Dante and these reminders of the past, all I can think about is my mom. Today was a lot, and I'm feeling a little overwhelmed by it all. "I miss you so much. I wish you and Dad were here. I need you."

I keep driving down the road, and I don't know whether there's something in the wind, or if I want my wish to come true so badly that my mind's playing tricks on me, but I feel a pair of lips kiss my cheek, and something like a hand touch my shoulder.

We are always here with you, Ya-Ya. Mommy loves you so much.

We are here with you, my son… I promise.

I hit the brakes so hard the tires squeal against the street. My heart races as I swerve to find a parking lot. The minute I cut the engine, I reach for the spot where I felt the kiss, blinking hard and fast as I struggle to make sense of what happened.

"Okay, that was… did that really…?" I shut my eyes tight to bring that feeling, that familiar presence back. But I can't feel it anymore. I bang my hands against the steering wheel, then take a deep breath and wipe away a stray tear, start the engine, and finish my drive to the stadium. I'm already late to the game, and I don't want to disappoint Zahra.

And I'm not sure why, but I won't be right until I see her face.

Chapter Five – Zahra

I pull another torque wrench from the toolbox, sliding back under the hood of my silver Audi RS e-tron GT. My parents bought it for my sixteenth birthday—instead of a Sweet 16 party, because, well, cliché, cliché--as a present to help with my design specifications on my own electric motor. I had the chance to really see what a real one looks like, instead of the fiberglass version at school.

Over the last few months since, I've spent nearly every available hour tweaking the motors on my baby. I've found ways to modify her design, focusing on how to solve the mileage range problem that has plagued engineers for a while. If I can find a way to make her faster an stretch the range between charges, it may be a game changer.

My ultimate goal is simple: get accepted into MIT, get my mechanical engineering degree with an automotive design concentration, and then pick up a professional certification in designing electric motors, generators, and drive systems. The sky isn't my limit, it's the beginning of my powers—a real-life version of RiRi Williams, better known as Iron Heart.

I tune out the world, allowing the subtle hum of the front and rear motors to speak to me as they idle inside the garage, spilling their secrets as I continue to tweak specific parts. I twist the wrench, grinning over the minor change in the cadence, almost like she's telling me exactly where I need to adjust.

"That's it, tell me what I need to do to get you where I want you. A few more adjustments should increase your horsepower." I continue to make the necessary modifications, smiling as she responds to them. "I only beat that kid in the Corvette by a half-car length. I needed more out of you, sweetheart."

I go through the usual steps to get my engines back in order, writing the numbers in my notepad to test out over the weekend. I spent a bit more time on the front engine tonight since the extra torque is needed to keep the front end from lifting at the start line. I rub the sweat from my hands off my "STEM Girls Get Things Done" t-shirt, not realizing the bay had gotten so humid, even though I left the garage door open to keep the air flowing through.

I'm still busy monitoring the diagnostics to get the levels I want when my phone rings. Hearing Rema croon for my bestie to calm down already lets me know who's calling when she knows what I'm doing. "Yes, Kenni, what's up?"

"Chica, where the hell are you? I'm gonna miss the beginning of the game if you don't hurry up." Kendyl's voice amps up an octave, I guess to let me know how pressed she is to get there. "You know I have to be on point if I'm gonna make captain next year."

"And what does that have to do with me, again? I'm on standby tonight on the sidelines anyway, so, we'll get there when we get there." I can't resist stirring her up. It's fun watching her blow a fuse. "If you wanna floss for the cameras, just say that. I know my car is pretty as hell. Maybe I'm feeling a bit showy tonight."

I hear the exaggerated sigh over the phone and burst into laughter. Leave it to my bestie to be her usual dramatic self. The only things missing are the string of groans and other odd noises she makes to keep from cursing me out. I fasten the engine block cover, searching for the clamps to secure it further. I don't mean to ignore her, but the game registers pretty low on my priority list.

"I'm glad you feel like flexing, but that's not the point, Z. You're supposed to be my ace, and if I can't trust you to be there for me, who can I trust?" Kendyl ponders over the speakerphone. "And don't tell me you're tweaking your engine *again*. You smoked that fool in the Vette who tried you, with time to get a smoothie and a pretzel before he crossed the finish line. What more do you need to do with it?"

"Whatever I need to do to make sure she runs even faster, chica," I say as I tighten the last bolt and close the hood. "I'll be there in a minute, okay? I only live a few minutes from you, anyway, so stop with the drama like we're on the other side of the world or something.

I'll get you there in enough time to turn heads like you usually do."

Kendyl makes kissing noises, causing a slight grin to spread across my face. "I love you too, now get over here so we can witness this massacre on the field tonight."

The parking lot near the stadium on campus is a literal car show by the time we arrive. Kendyl scans the area and nearly loses her mind, and I see why. All types of muscle cars and import sports cars from both schools are sectioned off in a large corner of the space. All I notice are hoods raised in the air and neon lighting up the night sky. I shake my head, gazing at all the potential opponents I could tear through after the game.

If I want to cut "Raiden" loose tonight. Of course, that's not happening. I have other, more important things on my mind.

I named my prized machine after the lightning god from the *Mortal Kombat* games and movies. The name fits her—she's lightning quick, and she's lit everything up that's raced next to her—and it stuck. I even have her name splashed on a specialized front plate. It took me a couple months to learn how to race her, but once I got the timing down, there weren't many in the area who could show me their taillights in the quarter mile.

I slow-roll through the crowd, searching for only one person, frowning as I finally find a spot to park. Yasir's Jeep is nowhere to be found, and it's not like it's not easy to spot, that's for sure. The neon kit alone would have eyes drawn to him. I shift between irritation and disappointment, sprinkling in a bit of hope that he'll keep his word. I rarely bother with these games unless I have to be on the sidelines, but it would've been fun to have him around.

I know this much… he better show up or I'll make him pay dearly on Monday, and he's too cute to harm.

Kendyl jumps out of the passenger side, smoothing out her uniform before sprinting toward the end zone to help the rest of her team with the signage for the football team to break through. I barely get a wave from her. "I'll catch you at the half, chica!"

I huff in response, realizing I've been abandoned a lot sooner than I thought. I don't sweat it too much as I make my way around the different people and their cars. I take notice of all the engines on display, turning my nose up at the gas engines, despite the chrome finish on some of them. I shake my head, recognizing that at least half of them need nitrous oxide just to be relevant.

Satisfied I've seen everything, I walk toward the ticket window, figuring that if I find a space somewhere closer to the field, Yasir will have a chance to find me, if I'm not pulled on the field to work, of course. Gotta love community service hours to pad the college resume.

I pass a group of boys who are gathered around a neon orange Dodge Charger Hellcat. I hear the whispers and ignore them as I continue toward the entrance. I guess I could've taken the entrance for players and staff, but I want to enjoy the game from the stands tonight.

One of the boys caught up with me, cutting me off from the entrance to get my attention. I sigh, resigning myself to get this over with as quickly as possible. "So, you're the girl they're talking about, the one with the Audi supercar," he mentions as he stands in front of me. "I heard you've been beating everyone around Savannah and Jax. What you got under the hood? Me and my boys would love to check it out."

I blow air upward, causing my bangs to flow through the breeze. "First, I don't own a supercar, whoever you are. It's an e-tron electric sports car with racing motors enhanced with my modifications. And second, why would I show you what's under the chassis? Do you even know how electric motors work?"

"Oh, so you're one of *those* girls, trying to save the environment. Of, and my name's Evan, by the way," he replies, stepping into my personal space. "You're too pretty to be a nerd. You should be out on the field with your girl getting the squad together."

And here we go again. I cross my arms over my chest, tilting my head toward my left shoulder, gritting my teeth to figure out the quickest way out of this convo. "Is there something specific you need? I really wanna get in the stadium and watch this beatdown y'all Baytown boys are about to catch, so, if you don't have anything else to say to keep my attention, I'm about to go that way."

"I mean, I'm trying to see whether the hype is real, or if you're cheating," Evan says. "And I've got three stacks that says your toy car can't beat what's under my hood."

"Sorry, I'm not interested," I reply, taking steps away from him to create some space. His cologne's overpowering my senses, and I don't need that lingering around me. "If you think you can hang, you can always catch me at the tracks in Savannah most weekends."

I hear a strange, but familiar noise coming from behind him. I don't bother hiding the smirk on my face. He's not too bright, either. "I doubt you'll be able to race straight up, anyway, but if you're up to listening, do you mind a word of advice?"

"There's nothing you can teach me about my car, for real," Evan interrupts me. "You're just a girl, and I doubt you know much about *real* engines."

I raise my left eyebrow, stepping around him to approach his car. He follows me in close pursuit, finally stopping with me in front of his engine. I glance for a moment and notice all the neon surrounding the engine block and giggle to myself. Never mind the weak six-cylinder engine he's running, but he's got worse problems, and he doesn't even realize it.

I stifle my giggles as I walk away from his ride, and he shouts after me, "And what are you laughing at? My engine is top of the line."

"Yeah, if you say so. I can think of better ways to spend ten stacks," I shout back. "And you're probably gonna need to figure out how you successfully drained your battery and blew your alternator because the aftermarket relays you used aren't compatible with your Hellcat. Good luck getting home tonight."

Evan scoffs as he jumps into the driver's seat and pushes the ignition button. Within seconds, the headlamps blink, and then the rest of the lights surrounding the car and the engine go dark. "What the…? Hey, wait a minute! What did you do to my car?"

"I didn't do anything, that's all you, *Evan*." I turn around long enough to acknowledge the laughter behind me. The irritated expression on his face is worth the burn. "I'd call a tow truck if I were you, and make sure you tell your mechanic what you did so he can have a good laugh while charging you the three stacks you wanted to lose racing me to fix everything. Oh, and by the way, never underestimate a STEM girl, okay?"

CHAPTER SIX – YASIR

The roar of the crowd puts me in instant panic mode before I find a parking space. There are too many people in the stands. No space to breathe. What the hell was I thinking, telling Zahra I'd be here?

Twenty minutes pass as I sit in the driver's seat, changing my mind at least a half-dozen times over whether to stay or leave. No matter how hard I try, I can't escape the way my body vibrates every time I have a passing thought about her. Not gonna lie, it's exciting and scary. but I need to find out why she affects me like this, and why I can't shake it off.

I cast my eyes skyward, whispering a prayer for strength before getting out of the car. Each step feels like my feet are encased in cement, but I finally make it to the front entrance. I can't even answer a simple question from the lady I purchased the ticket from, nearly freaking out over the sensory overload.

This would have been easier to deal with if Squad had my back, but they're in the A, probably acting a fool as usual. *Get your life, bro. You can do this.*

My senses heighten at the sounds of the marching band and the cheerleaders. I move through the people standing around in the breezeway leading up to the concrete seating. The crowd is already on their feet as one of the Oakwood receivers catches a long pass and races to the end zone for a touchdown.

"Taylor Ricks for the touchdown!" the announcer booms. "The Grove is now up 28-7!"

The roar of the crowd overwhelms my senses. I clap my hands over my ears to muffle the noise, but that doesn't work *at all*. I stand in place for a few minutes, closing my eyes to calm my heartbeat, which has ramped up like I've been running for miles.

I breathe in through my nose, then breathe out through my mouth. There's a group of kids to my left who are jumping around and vibing with the band, and that throws me off all over again. I squeeze my hands tighter over my ears to silence things for a few fucking seconds so I can calm down.

My heart rate slows, and I exhale a sigh of relief. Now I can get back to the why of it all tonight—if I can get my feet to move.

I have no idea where to begin looking for Zahra, so I head toward an open section near the bottom of the stands, doing my best to duck around the "Cougar Pride" banner that's in my way, close to where the cheerleaders are set up on the track encircling the football field.

I keep searching, losing hope that I can't find her as I hop down each section of seats to get to the open section I found. I almost give up, until I see her sitting near where I'm headed. Zahra's sitting with the cheerleaders, but I get the feeling that she's not a cheerleader. The "Team Manager" emblazoned in dark grey lettering across the back of her crimson zip-up hoodie is a dead giveaway, now that I've paid enough attention to notice.

I stop for a few seconds, completely focused on her, unable to move. She's so pretty, no wonder I have so much trouble talking to her. I mean, *look* at her.

The torture I'm putting myself through for someone who hasn't yet proven whether their connection was a figment of my imagination or not… I'm better than this nonsense. The more I try to free myself from the negative thoughts in my head, the more a pronounced rage makes itself clear and present from somewhere deep within my core.

I don't know how to explain what's going on with me, but whatever this is, it's rumbling deep, confusing, and I'm low-key irritated. It's like something's crackling beneath the surface, influencing my mood. It's weird, and I don't like it one bit.

I'm irritated that I put myself in this position. The loner routine was a vibe, but then I had to go and get caught up in a pretty girl who has me twisted. I don't wanna be here, but I wanna be here. This constant back and forth is wearing me out, and I wanna yell just to ease the pressure building inside me.

I look to my right, noticing a few of the kids from school staring at me. I pay too much attention to their hand motions and body language, making it plain that being in their space is not wanted. I ignore as much of it as I can, choosing to focus on suppressing my fight-or-flight instincts. Lashing out, even in self-defense mode, would be worse… way worse.

My senses are on tilt now, and it's only a matter of time before I would need to figure out how to get out of here. What throws me off even more is this constant vibrating and rumbling from deep inside my body. It's growing more and more this time, as though it were preparing for something, like an eruption.

My skin suddenly feels hot, and I swear there's a deep crimson glow surrounding my body, brightest on my hands and arms. Even when I close my eyes to will it away, the moment I open them, it looks like it's only intensified its brilliance. And—wait—are those sparks shooting from my fingertips?

I gotta get my emotions under control, but all my senses become more heightened by the minute. I'm close to panicking. I try to force the vibrations to stop, convince myself that no one around me means any harm. I take deeper breaths, relying on my Nana's voice, encouraging me to calm down and focus. The last thing I need is to let my anxiety turn to anger.

The conversations around me grow louder, but I don't see anyone moving closer to me to be able to hear things so clearly. The negative comments come more frequently, aggravating me to the point where things almost overwhelm me. I want to get away from it, to silence the noise for a few moments, long enough to settle down.

Okay, enough of this madness.

When I search the last area that I remember finding Zahra, I don't see her there anymore. I scold myself for simply not moving closer to her, so she can see I was here. Now, I have no clue where she could've gone, and I'm stuck dealing with these jackasses who haven't moved and whose voices I can hear as though they were sitting next to me.

"Hi, Yasir, I'm glad you didn't abandon me after all. I almost gave up on you."

I jump out of my skin, annoyed over how I didn't feel her walking over and sitting down next to me. All the other distractions must have caused me to lose focus, and I make a mental note to do something about it. The jeggings and a graphic t-shirt peeking from inside her hoodie that depicts RiRi Williams catches my attention first. She has her braids swept up in a messy ponytail, and she's wearing a peach lip gloss that brings out her bronzed skin tone, but the stadium lights play tricks on me. I'm convinced it's an intoxicating mix between bronze and amber, almost matching my eye color. She's been kissed by Ra, the Egyptian sun god, and I'm willing to go blind staring at the glow surrounding her.

I blink a few times, praying I'm not dreaming, checking around us to notice that the crowd in the immediate area around us has suddenly disappeared. It must be halftime. "Um, hi, Zahra."

"Are you okay? You looked like you needed a friend." She moves closer to me, and my heart races faster than it takes The Flash to go from zero to Mach 1. *Keep it together, bro.* "I should've come and found you. This stadium can be a bit much for people who haven't been here before."

I turn to meet her concerned gaze, and I swear everything melts away in seconds. I'm lost inside her eyes, and I have a harder time forming words than usual. "Yeah, I don't do well in large crowds, but I try to manage. Having you here helps, thank you for finding me. It means a lot."

We keep shifting around each other like we're trying to figure out if we want to be close to each other or if we want to act like we don't. I catch her blushing as our eyes meet for a few seconds, and I sweep a stray braid out of her face, grateful for the excuse to touch her. I don't even care that the crowd is as large as it is, as long as she's sitting next to me, none of that even matters.

"I don't know if I'm actually helping or not, but I'm really glad you didn't ghost me," Zahra replies, putting her hand on top of my arm. There's an instant spark the moment she touches me. "I'd really like to finish our convo from earlier, if that's okay?"

All of this is happening too fast, there's no way she can be this into me in such a short amount of time. As much as I don't want my insecurities to rise to the surface, I can't help myself. I stare at her, ignoring her surprised expression. "Can I ask a question?"

"Sure, ask me anything."

"Um, so about you saying you felt safe around me. How are you able to figure that out in one day?" I avert her gaze, choosing to focus on the field and the game. I'm a bit scared that I ask the question, but I fear the answer even more. "I realize actions speak louder, but I guess I want to know… I *need* to know…"

When she leans in and wraps her arm through mine, my whole body ignites against my will. She blushes as she says, "Let's just say I can read people pretty well, but I still want to get to know you better to make sure you are who I think you are."

"And when will we have time to get to know each other better so you can be sure you're right or wrong?"

Her eyes never leave mine. I can't take my eyes off her, either. I just don't want her to leave. "Soon, I promise. I don't want to keep you waiting too long, but I said what I said. I need to see you, and I plan to do just that."

Zahra leans in closer. Her smile takes down any walls I've built up to keep her from getting in deeper. I don't press my luck, though; I've been down this road one other time, and that ended badly.

Considering I don't know anyone in Oakwood Grove, I'm better off having Zahra as a friend more than anything else.

Even if the butterflies in the pit of my stomach threaten to have their say.

The minute I sink into Storm's leather seats and push the ignition button to hear the engine roar to life, I let out a long, relieved sigh. I made it through the game without any other issues. That alone is a victory I have no problems claiming.

Recharge. Needed. Badly.

I burned way too much energy, and I have no problems going home, pulling the covers over my head, and crashing out until early morning when it's time to head out with Unk.

I take a moment to reminisce over what turned out to be a wonderful night. The highlight came when I escorted Zahra and her best friend, Kendyl, to Zahra's car. Kendyl is on the cheerleading squad, and while Zahra isn't squad, she does function as a team equipment manager—thank goodness I was right—which gives her access to the field, which makes her cheer-adjacent in my book.

Kendyl's a little taller than Zahra, and she struck me as Afro-

Latina from the hint of a sing-song cadence in her voice, and her saddle-brown skin shined under the lighting in the parking lot. Her hair was pulled back into a naturally wavy ponytail, and her striking hazel eyes and pouty lips attracted attention from the boys all the way to the car. Still, she kept a close eye on me the entire time, something I expected a best friend to do, so it didn't bother me all that much. Sooner or later I'm gonna have to handle the third degree questioning from her, I'll just have to be ready.

I tried to hide how impressed I was that she drove an Audi RS e-tron GT electric sports car. It was silver and gleamed against the moonlight, and Raiden—Zahra's nickname for this pretty piece of machinery—was part of her master plan to eventually design electric motors and jet engines. I made a mental note to have a longer convo about what she knows about engines in general and a few other things that have my imagination in overdrive.

There's something about a STEM girl. If you know, you know.

I watched as she gushed about her prized machine, and she even races, which made me wonder if she really had skills like that. I'm not gonna lie, though: I honestly thought it belonged to one of the group of boys who were bragging about their cars when I first got to the stadium. That's what I get for assuming too much, huh?

While I want to settle down a little bit, the truth is I'm amped up. I'm not feeling HipHop tonight, so I connect my phone and scroll through my playlist. I smile when Burna Boy pops up; this is what I need for real! The bass in the speakers sync with my heartbeat, influencing the aggression in my driving as I cruise down the road. I make it a few miles into my drive when I notice a group of boys off to my right.

I check in that direction, focusing on the one in the middle of the group. As I get closer, I see Ian getting punched by one of the other boys, while another holds him down to keep him from protecting himself. They're all wearing Baytown colors, and it doesn't take long to figure out that Ian is in a world of trouble.

My instinct takes over as I slam the brakes, then hop out of my Jeep to confront the group. Things might be complicated between us, but he doesn't deserve to go out bad like this.

"Let him go, right now, and you can walk away without a

noticeable limp."

All eyes are on me as they snap their glances in my direction, as the one throwing the punches steps away from Ian and heads toward me. "Who the hell is this? Do you know this man, Ian?" he barks, balling his fists. "Maybe you need to help him catch these bows for costing us the game, huh? You Oakwood too, my guy?"

"I don't know him, Jordin," Ian replies. He glares at me, tilting his head toward my car. I know what he wants me to do, but that's not an option. "Just some rando who has a savior complex. He needs to learn not to stick his nose in business that doesn't pay him."

"It's obvious that I don't learn lessons, but I'm not about to stand by and watch while you beat someone down without making it a fair fight." The other two boys close a circle around me, each with a problem that they feel needs to be handled. I keep my cool, still talking big, whether we are outnumbered or not. "Step away now, and no one will get hurt. Last warning. You won't like how this is gonna end, trust."

My nerves are on edge all over again, and I'm scared that I've broken off more than I can handle. One on three, with Ian held down and unable to help? The odds are definitely not in my favor.

"Are you kidding me?" Jordin scoffs, looking at the boy standing next to him before he turns his attention to me. "You're out of your depth on this one. Just take the L and go home."

I grit my teeth as I try to keep a line of sight on the other three boys who are circling me. He might have a point, but I'm not about to let him know that. "Can't do that, bro. If I have to catch a fade, then bring it. Let Ian go so it can be a fair fight. I thought you South Georgia boys were supposed to be nice with your hands."

Jordin looks at the other boys, then shakes his head as he stares at me. "Reggie, Mark, drop this fool, please. Larry, keep Ian steady, this won't take long at all. This one needs his mouth shut."

"Why don't you come and shut it, huh? Big talk when you got back up, yo." Yeah, fear is controlling my mouth, and it's wrapping itself in a swagger that I don't have the greatest confidence in right now. To put it in my Unk's terms, I'm writing checks that I'm not sure my fists can cash. "Or maybe you ain't got it in you to do it?"

Mark and Reggie rush me from behind, trying to grab at me and pull me down. I turn to confront them, ducking one wild swing from Mark at my head and dropping him to the ground with a swift left hook to his jaw. I'm already in motion, staying on my toes to keep my movements as random as possible. I stay in the view of my headlights, keeping the fight from shifting into the darkness. Mark's completely out of commission, which makes it easier for me to concentrate on the other one.

Reggie steps in, getting a punch into my ribs, causing me to yell out in pain. He gets me good, and the power behind that punch worries me. I sidestep a couple more swings from him, landing a left hook to his rib cage that causes him to wince, holding his side for a moment before he comes at me again. He manages to get another punch across my jaw as I try to get in to crack a few bones, drawing blood with the strike, sending me crashing against the front of my car.

"Okay, you got some pop, I'll give you that. I'm gonna need to put you down quick," Reggie yells as he continues to swing at me, going for the knockout punch. "Hold still, you're making this hard on yourself."

I keep weaving and ducking, but the adrenaline has me on edge and unable to focus. I feel like I'm gonna pass out if I don't end this fast.

And then, in the middle of the fight, this strange sensation comes over me, and it adds to my confusion. I'm faster, stronger, and it seems like I can't run out of energy, no matter how much I burn. Everything moves in slow motion, like I'm a part of an anime battle sequence and I see every move as it happens and avoid getting hit while landing bone-crunching hits to my adversary. I've never moved like this before, and it's a bit scary, but not to where I can't make short work of Reggie.

He stares at me with this bizarre expression on his face, and he starts pointing at my hands. "Yo, what is going on with you? You… your hands, they look like they're… what in the hell are you?"

I quickly glance at my hands, and Reggie's not bluffing. My hands look like they're on fire, as the smoke intensifies a bit. And are those… *claws?* They look like they're extended from my hands, but they're not my hands. There's this calming energy that sets in, even though I should be shifting from fear to abject terror.

I'll be scared later. I gotta rock this fool to sleep first.

I land another punch to his jaw, but the way he screams in pain almost takes me out of my zone. I can't make out what he's trying to say, and from the way he's flinching as he tries to move his mouth, it's easy to figure out that I broke it—and I must have scratched him in the process, because he's bleeding badly from three open wounds on his face and neck. He yells out as he rushes at me in anger, ready to do whatever it takes to end me, regardless of how much I hurt him.

I finally find the opening I'm looking for, landing three or four hits to his ribs and chest, hitting him hard enough to make him drop his right hand to protect his body. From there, it's easy. A right-handed uppercut to his chin, and a couple more to finish him off as Reggie falls unconscious to the pavement.

Two down, two to go.

I'm still a bit disoriented by whatever is happening to me. It's almost like I'm coming down from the most intense adrenaline rush ever. I stare at my hands and arms, and I swear they look like they're… glowing? Not again. I blink a few times to figure out if I'm hallucinating, and while the glow is still there, it's switched from deep crimson to a darker purple, almost a radiant indigo, causing me to panic. Am I on fire? What's happening to me?

The next thing I know, the aura flows from my fingers, and I see symbols inside of what looks like smoke, and suddenly my hands move in these intricate patterns. I have no idea what these movements mean, and I'm seriously wondering if I've entered a real-life version of *The Magicians* and I'm two steps away from opening a portal to Brakebills University. I quickly narrow my eyes to concentrate on suppressing the smoke and slow down the glow around my skin, praying it calms down soon.

It finally disappears, and I switch my focus to the immediate threat before I get caught slipping—the other two boys who are still upright and probably coming for me. I close my eyes to try to focus for a few seconds. I need to not get damaged too badly, or worse. That's not part of my plans, either, dammit.

Before I can turn around to deal with Jordin, I feel a blow to my lower back, dropping me to the pavement. I stare into Jordin's eyes before noticing the metal bat in his hand, and in that moment, I know I'm in real trouble. I have no way of protecting myself if he decides to start swinging, and I'm trying my best to scramble to my feet. I can't get my footing, and fear quickly turns to panic now.

"That's it, that's the look I was waiting for. Sooner or later, you were gonna get got," Jordin spits on the ground as he crouches over me. "You got heart, my guy, but that's over with now, time to put you to sleep."

"Nah, bro, it's time to sing *you* a lullaby," Ian interjects as he throws a punch to the side of Jordin's face, watching him drop to the concrete like a sack of potatoes. "Rock-a-bye, playa."

He comes face-to-face with me in the next instant, both of us checking the unconscious bodies around us. I study Ian's irritated expression. "Why are you looking like I stole your favorite chain?"

"I told you to stay out of it," Ian shouts. "I had it under control. What do you want, a 'thank you' or something?"

"Oh yeah, you had it all under control, my boy," I point out, stepping further into his personal space. Fear is still driving the adrenaline rushing through me, and I don't care that I'm on the verge of talking reckless. I just covered him, and he wants to sound ungrateful? "And nah, you don't need to say thank you, but you're welcome, anyway."

As the sirens blare in the distance, Ian pushes me toward my car. I don't know how they knew to come, maybe someone must have seen us fighting and called 911. I keep resisting, confused over what he's doing. "What the hell is going on? You need a witness to deal with this mess. These boys are bleeding, they may need medical attention."

"You don't know how Oakwood Grove works yet. Just get out of here and let me deal with this," Ian roars before opening my door and pushing me inside. "I'll make sure the paramedics are called, but you need to go."

"Do you hear what I'm saying? They'll never believe you did all this damage by yourself," I protest as the sirens get louder. "I'm not letting you take this weight."

Ian glares at me, pointing at Storm. "I won't repeat myself, get the hell out of here. Right now! Go!"

Chapter Seven – Yasir

It takes a lot for me to get out of Storm and drag myself through the garage door. I can't remember the last time I hurt this badly. I gave as much as I got, but I'm gonna feel every bit of that blow to my back for at least the next couple of days.

I hope Unk doesn't stick to his usual routine whenever I go out. He doesn't go to sleep until he knows I've made it through the door safely, regardless of the time of night. It's always been a comfort, but I need him to be asleep tonight. I really don't feel like explaining why I'm moving so slow, and I know he's gonna notice and ask questions I don't want to answer.

I'm dragging so badly that I don't realize that I've bumped the end table by the door, which disturbed the statue of Nyati, the Divine Mother of Kindara. Unk keeps a lot of them around each of the entrances into the house as an otherworldly layer of protection. I'm groaning as I stretch out to keep the figurine from falling to the floor. I secure her back in her space and breathe a sigh of relief, leaning against the wall to steady myself before I move again.

I don't want that smoke. Nope. If he doesn't kill me, Nana will have a whole meltdown if she were to find out I broke one.

My phone vibrates in my pocket on a rapid-fire kick, and I ignore it for the time being. It's probably Dante and Squad rubbing it in about the Langston Hughes score. They've been lighting everybody up this year. I'm not trying to hear any of that right now, I have my own issues to sort out.

The great room is dark, which is a good sign that I might get to my room without too much fuss. I stop through the kitchen to grab a bottle of water so I can trudge up the stairs as quietly as possible.

My phone is going off for real now, which irritates me big time.

I'm already kicking myself for not getting Zahra's phone number while we were vibing, so I know it's not her.

I fumble with my phone to turn it off or something, so I don't make myself so freaking obvious that I'm home. The house is already quiet, so any noise is liable to alert Unk that something's going on and he needs to see about it. He's already gonna be awake in a few hours to get ready to head out to the boat so we can work on the day's catch—he owns a seafood shop in downtown Oakwood Grove—so interrupting his sleep is a sitch I don't want.

Hearing the light switch flip is a dead giveaway that Unk stuck to his normal routine after all. Dammit. "How was the game, kiddo?"

Okay, two options.

First option: come clean and drop everything on the table and be up all night fleshing out the good and the bad of it all.

Second option: hold some cards close to the chest until I can figure out what else I need to tell him later, which will be a shorter convo and I can get some sleep.

Considering everything I've gone through in the past few days, and I went to a whole football game after being at school, wanna guess which option I'm about to take?

"The game was lit, no cap." Well, I'm not lying about that. The football team is pretty nice, for real. "I guess Oakwood might not be so bad, but I'm still not sure yet."

"Well, it's a start." Unk leans against the wall, and I can feel him studying me further, like he's looking for something. He pauses for what feels like forever before he says, "Are you gonna be good to roll in the morning? You look like you got into the game a bit more than what you're letting on."

I grip my ribcage as I flinch over his question about going out on the boat. Playing this chess game in my head is wearing me out more than trying to hide legit injuries I took earlier dealing with Ian and his drama. I can only hope to be sore in the morning so I can roll out and avoid more questions I'm not ready to answer.

So, instead of taking the out my uncle is giving me, I tell him, "Yeah, I'll be ready to go in the morning. You know I can't leave you out bad like that."

Unk furrows his brow, and I know he's not buying it, but I gotta sell it so he can rock with it. I'll make it up to him another time, but for now, I'm putting on as good of a performance as I can pull off. I breathe a sigh of relief when I see him nod. "All right, Ya-Ya, get some sleep. Wheels spin at four in the morning."

As he walks back to his bedroom and closes the door, I shake my head and wonder how in the world did I get myself into another fine mess. I get to my room, drop my keys on the desk and groan as I pull my hoodie over my head, leaving a trail of discarded clothing on the way to the bathroom so I can get a nice, hot shower going. It's been a hell of a first day, and I pray I'll have as much of a dreamless sleep as humanly possible.

I play out the whole night from start to finish, and I'm already criticizing what I should've done and the moves I was better off not making. I don't like doing this to myself, but I can't help it sometimes. Nana's always said I should never be my own worst enemy, but I don't see it that way. Still, I try to find the silver lining through all of the doom and gloom I insist on bringing to the surface all over again.

That silver lining stands about 5-foot-6, and I swear is made of brown sugar, cocoa, honey and gold.

I just wish I'd at least swapped numbers with her or something.

Okay, Yasir, chill, focus on the positive. She rocked with you the whole game, the vibe was fire. That's gotta count for something, you know?

I let the water cascade over me, pretending that it's washing all the negativity off me and circling down the drain. The heat feels good against my bruises, and I stand in place for a few more minutes until I don't wince every time I move.

I still try to make sense of what happened with Ian and that whole incident. More to the point, where in the world did that crimson-slash-indigo glow come from? I know I was running a little hot, but for it to manifest itself like I was about to catch fire doesn't make any sense. I felt like I could've broken more than Reggie's jaw. As angry as I was, his jaw would've been the least of his problems.

Paralysis was on my mind.

It shouldn't have been, but he pissed me off.

Since I have a moment to myself to think about it, where did all that seemingly endless supply of energy and strength come from?

And where did it all go like it never happened in the first place?

So many questions to answer, but I'm not about to lose sleep over it tonight. I have to shut things down and be ready to go in a few hours.

I turn off the shower, grabbing the towel off the bathroom counter, stretching across my bed to scroll through the messages I ignored when I was trying to keep Unk from ripping off the third-degree questioning. Sure enough, it's Dante giving me the updates on the Langston Hughes blowout. I do my best not to get upset, knowing I'm supposed to be up there with my people instead of down here hitting the reset button, but with each picture I see, it gets more difficult to keep from raging.

I decide it's better to head up to the studio and get some painting done or do some sketching. I'm not in a violent mood, well, not anymore, so going downstairs to work that off isn't necessarily what's needed right now. I want to feed into the vibe I felt with Zahra earlier. I think that'll help ease me into a better headspace so I can sleep.

The top level of Unk's house is split into two large spaces, one for him and his hobbies, and the other one is for me and my creative energy. He had my space designed and crafted in such a way that I can see the stars at night or bask in the warmth of the sun during the day. It's airy, and has a lot of windows, including the skylight.

I keep all my paints, pencils, chalks, everything is in separate bins against the wall opposite the large window on the other side of the studio. The skylight shows the clear and starry night sky, and I admire the beauty and darkness being shown before me. An inspiration with a pretty girl at its center takes hold of me.

All the easels are covered except for one, since I have a thing about not wanting to see the pieces as I'm creating them. I move to the bins, take out the pencils, then slide over to the chair in front of the easel with the blank canvas and get to work.

I focus on her face first, capturing the contours of her cheeks, the oval-shapes of her eyes, and before I know it, my fingers act on their own. It's like they have as much of a memory of what she looks like as my subconscious, and I don't question how my hands move. I simply sit back and let the magic happen.

I capture the intricacies of her face and hair with a precision that scares me at first. I feel like I'm invading her privacy with the way I pay attention to the perfect shape of her eyebrows, or the way she bites her bottom lip when she wants to keep from grinning. Before long, I've added a headdress that wraps through her hair, and I imagine her on a beach, wearing a maxi dress, walking barefoot along the edge of the surf.

I'm sketching so fast I feel like the lead is going to break from the pressure and speed, but I don't want to lose the image that's forming in my mind's eye before I'm finished with the capture.

As I put the finishing touches on the piece, I hear my phone vibrating against the table next to me. I pick up the phone to see what the notification is about and almost stop breathing the minute I see the message coming from my IG.

Hi Yasir, I hope you're awake. I just wanted to say I had fun tonight.

Chapter Eight – Zahra

If looks could kill, I'd be a dead girl right now.

The constant glare from my bestie while I move through traffic as we leave the stadium is enough to drive me absolutely bananas.

She literally stares a hole through the side of my head as we wait in line to leave campus. "So, are we gonna talk about what happened with Yasir earlier or nah?"

"I don't know what you're talking about."

"Oh, we're suffering from selective amnesia now, huh? Okay, let's play that game."

Kendyl has a knack for working my last nerve when she wants answers to questions she's not prepared to hear. The last thing I need is to play out everything that happened while we were in the stands. I'm glad I didn't have to be on the sidelines the entire game to help as a team manager. It gave me a chance to flirt and enjoy being around him.

She had a bird's eye view of it all from the cheerleading area, and the concern on her face cracked me up. To let her tell it, Yasir might as well have been an apex predator, and I was prey waiting to be taken. I mean, she saw what she saw, and I couldn't deny it, right?

What can I say? The connection between us stayed with me even after Yasir walked us to my car. Now, why'd he have to go and do that? Talk about smooth? I got lost in his eyes—by Nyati, *those eyes*—and his gaze seemed to peer deep inside me, taking up residence in spaces he shouldn't have been able to get to. What shocked me more than anything was that I allowed him to go that deep. I like it, and I want more.

I keep my focus on the road, more to avoid facing the disapproving glances from my shotgun partner. "Okay, fine, so maybe I had a moment with him earlier tonight. The last time I checked, I could talk to whoever I wanted."

"Oh, you had a moment with him, alright," Kendyl points out as she keeps typing away on her phone. "Face it, girlie, you're into him, and the whole school saw that on full display at the game. He has your undivided attention."

I pull into Kendyl's driveway, turning off the battery power to the motors. I rub my hands over my face, trying to make sense of it all. "I wish I knew what was going on. I mean, he's not like any boy I've been around, and there's this draw between us whenever we're around each other. But he's new to Oakwood, and I meant what I said when I told him I wanted to get to know him as a friend."

"Okay, let's take a look at the whole picture," Kendyl explains to me. "I mean, you've been into nothing but your electric motors and volleyball for the past couple of years. The boys who were interested in either of those things weren't worth your time or attention, in my opinion. Maybe, just maybe, there's something to Yasir that we don't know about yet."

I don't even bother hiding a nervous smile and silently wonder if my bestie is on to something. "I'm telling you, there's something about him I can't explain. This is just… it hits different. I don't know how to explain it to you."

"Well, don't try until you know what it is," Kendyl says. We get out of my car and sprint into the house, making a beeline for her bedroom before her parents can ask about the game. "I'm not about to pretend I know how it all goes down in Kindaran culture when it comes to attraction, but we're still in the States, babe. Certain things have to be explained."

Once we settle into her bedroom, she gives me a knowing wink. "Find out more, maybe go out on a date or something. See if there's something there. You're gonna obsess over it until you get it out of your system, and you're not about to worry me to death over it."

"I do not worry you, and you know it." I playfully slap her thigh. "We wouldn't have been friends this long if I did."

"Yes, you do, but that's not the point. Hit him up. See what's real and then make up your mind."

I'm up most of the night going through the limited social media platforms I can find connected to Yasir. Talk about finding a needle in a haystack. I tend to have a limited presence for my own reasons, but this is next-level restrictive. The things I do find center around his artistry and his Jeep, which doesn't help me at all when I need to deep dive.

Every platform has more privacy restrictions, which really frustrates me more than I want to admit. Why doesn't he want to be seen? What is he hiding?

The more I search, the more I want to discover. Everything leads back to his imagery and artistry—and the things I see are so strangely soothing and comforting that it defies logic. The mountain ranges, the houses that litter the hillsides, the village clusters that are such a part of Kindara's beauty. He may as well have ripped the images from my mind.

One question keeps gnawing at me, taunting me until I know the answer: how is he able to capture so much of my home country's beauty in such vivid detail? And why is Kindara the focus of his art?

I don't know if I hate him for making me miss home as badly as I do or not. I feel more connected to him with each image I scroll through on his feed. I swear, we need to have a conversation as soon as possible.

I act on impulse, sending a direct message to him on his IG. I close the app the minute I do, covering my mouth with my hand to stifle a gasp. I don't want to alert Kendyl to what I'm doing—at least, not yet anyway. When I look up to see what she's up to, I notice her grinning while texting with Kyle. He's my other bestie and all, and while I still don't know how to feel about them hooking up, I can't worry about them right now.

A notification lights up my phone, and I grin when I see the message from Yasir. I keep breathing as I open the message, not sure what I'll see.

The message is innocent enough, but I can't avoid how warm I feel over getting a response from him. The butterflies follow, and a wide smile spreads across my lips. I switch my gaze from Kendyl to my phone and back, glad she's too into her own conversation to worry about me.

I wait a few more moments before I type a response. almost regretting the message the minute I send it. The pause in the conversation causes me to wonder if I said the wrong thing. The message hasn't been read yet, and I tap my fingers against the side of my phone, almost willing a response. I don't want to come off thirsty, so I do my best to not send another reply to keep his attention.

A few minutes later, the familiar three buttons start bouncing, but they move a bit too long for my taste. I catch myself quick, giggling to myself over my impatience.

Finally, his reply comes through, and I wrinkle my nose as I lean into the banter between us. I slide under the covers, getting more comfortable in bed and with him.

"Z, really?" Kendyl shatters my whole vibe, jumping on the bed to be nosey. By the gods, she can hover better than my mom sometimes. "So, he does have your attention after all. Go ahead, sis, finish what you were doing. I'm gonna need to know what's up since you're flirting in my room."

I clutch my phone to my chest, placing my index finger to my lips like I'm shielding him from a video call or something. "Girl, hush, I'm handling my business, I thought you were doing the same. Let a playa work her magic and get back to your convo with Kyle, we'll dish later."

"And how did you know I was on the phone with him?"

"Don't worry about all that, just do what you do and let me work."

I'm so busy arguing with her that I don't notice that he's sent another message. The minute I read it, I almost drop my phone. My breath catches in my throat, which grabs my bestie's attention. I close my eyes for a moment, realizing the gravity of the question he asks. I haven't *really* messed around with anyone at Oakwood, and most of the ones who had my attention happened during summer camps away from school, but they were flings, nothing more.

This thing with Yasir, no matter how much I want to fight it, it hits different.

So, why am I doubting myself?

I drop my phone on top of the comforter after saying goodnight, unwilling and unable to wipe the grin off my face. I look up for a few seconds to get my head together, only to see Kendyl still in front of me, propped on the pillows, a captive audience of one in need of answers. We stare at each other for a few minutes while I try to figure out how to keep her from saying, "I told you so."

I can't find anything that won't lead to those dreaded words, so I bury my face in the pillow to let out an excited scream. I lift my face, glare at my best friend, and accept the inevitable. "Okay, okay, so there might be something more going on, but it doesn't mean anything."

Yeah, who am I kidding?

He has my attention.

It's the why of it all that has me confused.

Chapter Nine – Yasir

My anxiety shot through the roof the minute I responded to her message. After I ask for her number so we can move this out of DMs, I end up playing the "what if" game the rest of the night and into the morning. My head swirls when I try to sleep, bordering on a full-on headache, and the walls close in on me at home.

Never mind the *other* incident that happened, and the unanswered questions that came with it.

The *inhuman* strength. All the bodies lying on the ground.

The glowing around my arms and hands, like my name is Bruce Leroy in *The Last Dragon.*

The magic-*ish* sparks, the symbols I saw, and the ghost-like claws that I used to badly hurt one of the boys in the fight. I mean, I can cause a lot of damage on my own, but that was some next-level *holy shhh.*

And of course, the bruises all over my body, with no way to explain it to Unk, which was especially awkward when I pulled up the nets from our fishing trip. He pretty much kept quiet about what he saw, but that lasted about two-point-five seconds, and I ended up spinning a tale about how I helped someone change out a tire to try and gloss over the fact that I was in a full-tilt melee and barely escaped with more serious injuries.

At least we were able to pull a large catch for him to pick through, which would keep his attention off me for the rest of the day. It was a better day than normal, which had me questioning whether what happened to me last night had anything to do with it. It's like I knew exactly where to find the premium seafood and stopped right on top of that spot. Normally, it takes a couple of tries to figure it out.

Alright, focus, Yasir. One sitch at a time. That can wait.

I've never been in a situation where I had to fight more than one person at once. If I didn't know any better, I'd swear it felt like I'd blacked out and my body took over for a few seconds. Except, I was there, in the fight, the whole time.

And the thing that puzzled me the most… why did Ian make me leave the scene before the police arrived?

I could've used a self-defense argument, but since I'm new in town, maybe Ian was right to get me out of there. I still had no clue whether the other boys would say something to the cops, nor could I really trust Ian, but sticking around to find out wasn't the best option, either. Perfect definition of a no-win situation.

I recall being in the fight with Reggie and Mark, two of the boys in the situation, and I remember one of the other boys holding Ian down when I first got there. I was so involved in the fight that I have no clue how Ian even got loose to be able to save me from having my bones broken. What's most confusing is the severe state that all the boys were in once it was only me and Ian left standing. It looked bad, seriously speaking, and I'm wondering if he called the police himself to try to cover for me.

None of this adds up.

Not knowing any of the answers kept me awake, which is why I took Storm out, and am now rolling down the highway, my speed nearly matching the I-95 South signs. I'm on the verge of erupting—a desperate urge to release the tension is the only solution I could see—but it had to happen somewhere other than at home.

That's simply not an option.

Thankfully, I already have a place in mind where I can cut loose a bit without anyone being too nosey. I found it while scouting other locations for me and Unk to find more seafood for the shop. Considering tonight is a full moon and the tides would rise, seclusion would be both expected and welcomed. The change of location would do wonders for my psyche, that's for sure.

That location is called Driftwood Beach.

An iconic location known for its driftwood speckled throughout the beachfront, a result of decades of erosion, according to historians. What used to be a maritime forest is now a sandy shore lined with weathered tree trunks and branches, creating an enchanting, or spooky—depending on the perspective—sight unlike any in the country. It's a haunting and mystical locale I need to sort things out in my head, and it would also give me the much-needed inspiration for, well, who knew what may come from it.

I already have a spot picked out, ready to see the night sky. I have to sort out so much in such a short amount of time, it's overwhelming me. I should talk with Nana or Unk, but my head isn't there yet. The clarity I need, I want to find it from within first, and then I can find the courage to speak my heart as clearly as possible.

I put the doubts out of my mind while parking Storm as close to my favorite spot as possible. It's not where I'm supposed to park, but no one came looking after the operating hours, and her off-road capabilities make it easier to slip away in the unlikely event that someone does happen to stop by.

I step out of the driver's seat, sauntering toward the shore while witnessing the shades of purple and orange framing the evening sky as the sun makes its descent toward the horizon. It's a stunning display I capture on my smartphone as inspiration for something I may want to create later.

I close my eyes to bask in the warmth of the waning heat of the sinking sun. Nothing else matters. Not the insanity of being in yet another new high school, not the anger of being away from the A, not even my rising angst over whether Zahra would hit me up to talk. The sunset provides a simple lesson: don't rush. Stressing won't change the outcome. Things have a way of working themselves out.

The moment I find the set of driftwood that forms an oval on the far side of the beach where no one would dare travel, I plant my feet into the sand in the center of it and stare into the darkness. I savor the brief period of isolation, both inside my mind and within my temporary surroundings. These times are rare, and I want to indulge in them for as long as possible.

I search for some kindling and rocks to build a fire, digging a small circle in the sand to start the burn. After the flames roar to life, I drop to my knees to enjoy the flickering light, delighting in the brilliance and the various colors, watching as it dances against the breeze. The oranges and yellows provide a lovely contrast against the blackness of the night, except for the stars speckled throughout the sky.

I purposely lose myself in the fire, asking for guidance as I continue playing out the incident with Jordin and the group of boys who tried to take me and Ian out. I go through every minute, frame by frame in my mind, trying to figure out if I missed anything, any detail that would answer at least one of the questions I had.

My phone rings, breaking through my thoughts. I don't mean to react like someone shocked me with a taser, but I'm so far inside my head that the disturbance jolts me. I reach to grab it before the ringing stops, not bothering to check the caller ID. Then it hits me… what if it's Zahra? I'm not ready.

"Hello?"

"Hi, baby, how is your weekend going?" Nana's voice pops through my earpiece, sounding like sweet syrup over a hot stack of pancakes. "I wanted to check in on you to see if you are doing okay. I had not had a chance to talk to you since you moved."

"Yeah, I'm a bit better. I'm glad to hear your voice," I tell her, hoping my tone sounds upbeat enough that she won't ask any questions. "I just headed out of town to unwind a bit. I needed the exercise and the isolation to clear my head."

I think I hear her say something, but the words come out choppy. "Where are you now? The connection is spotty, and I couldn't hear what you just said. I got something I wanna ask you."

"I am at home, as usual, but I am in the backyard. You know how bad reception gets out here. Let me see if I can move to a better spot." The sound was muted for a few moments before she pops back on the line again. "Okay, hopefully, that is better. What is on your mind, my child?"

"Well, Nana… there's this girl, and…"

"Whoa, whoa, and whoa," she interrupts. "Nana needs to make sure she heard that right. You know my hearing is not what it used to be. There is… a… *girl*?"

And the headache's coming on again just that quickly. *Oh my God, bro. Don't go overboard, please?* "Yeah, there's this girl, and she wants to link up, and I was hoping to get some quick shopping done for a new outfit or two. Like, I wanna impress her."

"Yes, sure, I will send some money over, and you get whatever you need," she says. I hear the excitement in her voice, but I don't want her to get her hopes up yet. "And while you are at it, you should do something special for her."

"Pause… I didn't say it was a *date*, date, Nana," I caution as I try to calm the excitement. That failed as soon as I see the large deposit notification come through on my phone. "Whoa, I thought you said some money, not two stacks? I still can't do a lot on the wardrobe. I have to keep a low profile, remember? Isn't that what you told me and Unk?"

"You have one shot at this, and I do not want you to blow it," she warns. Her whole tone worries me. Why the change of heart now? "Besides, it will give you a reason to come see me. You can bring her up here so I can get a good look at her."

I glance up at the sky, trying to gather what little patience I have left to keep my emotions in check. Sure, I want things to go well with Zahra, but not at the risk of my mental health. "We're just spending time talking… I think there's something there, but I don't know where things will go from here."

"Trust your gut, Ya-Ya. That is all I am trying to tell you. Now, is there anything else I need to know about?"

An incoming call saves me from having to answer that question. I pull the phone up so I can see the number. I nearly panic when Zahra's name pops up on the screen. "Nana, I'll call you back, I need to take this."

I switch calls with the quickness. "Hello?"

"Hi, Yasir? Um, it's Z. I'm sorry I didn't call earlier. I was working on some songs and lost track of time. Is it too late to talk?"

Hearing her voice stops my world in moments. I keep my composure as best I can, grabbing some water to help clear my throat so I sound like I have some sense. "Hi, Zahra. No, it's cool to talk, I'm just relaxing down near Jekyll Island. I wanted to get some inspiration for a few new art pieces."

"That's dope. Maybe you can take me down there one day," she replies, throwing me off balance. Did she just suggest…? "Can we link tomorrow so we can talk?"

I check around the beach real quick, battling with the negative thoughts in my head. *You're not being punked, bro. Just be cool.*

“Um, can we meet up after school on Monday? There are some things my uncle wants me to do, and I can’t get out of it.” Yeah, that’s it, throw Unk under the bus to buy some time. He’ll be alright. “I mean if it’s okay with you.”

“It’s fine, I’m good with Monday after school.” I hear a giggle come across the earpiece that makes my heart thump through my chest. “It will give me some time to get myself together for you, especially since I won’t have anything going on.”

“I don’t know why, you’re perfect. You’ve always looked pretty every time I’ve seen you,” I blurt it out before I have a chance to stop myself. “Um, I mean… cool, it’s a date. Maybe you can show me some of the motor designs you’ve been working on. Who knows, maybe you might convince me that EVs are the way to go. I doubt it, of course. My engine might not be fully electric, but she burns clean and fast… probably faster than yours.”

“And what makes you think you can beat me?” she scoffs. “Wait a minute… how did you know I worked on electric motors?”

“You’re not the only one with sources.” I can’t contain my smirk. Thank the gods we aren’t on a video call. “I may be new, but I’m not without my methods. Besides, *maybe* I signed up for the engineering club when I first got to Oakwood. I mean, you probably know I’m into IT and information systems. Maybe we can teach each other a few things.”

“Hmmm, maybe, if you show me some of your designs, then I might be willing to show you mine. It’s only fair, right?” she coos. “See you at school on Monday. I’m looking forward to our chat in person.”

I disconnect the call, grinning so hard my cheeks hurt. For the first time since I could remember, I can’t wait to get to school.

Chapter Ten – Zahra

Dragging Kendyl to Oglethorpe Mall in Savannah against her will to help me make a boy I barely know pay more attention than he already does is gonna get me cursed out in three different languages.

But it's worth every bit of the stress she's gonna put me through, considering we live in more than a few designer stores almost every other weekend anyway.

"Kenni, what do you think of this one? Too much? Not enough?"

"Chica, what in the world are you doing? All the clothes you tried on before this one were just as gorgeous on you. Keep this up, and I'm gonna put you in timeout."

As much as I want to argue, she has a point. The problem? Nothing seems to satisfy what I have in mind for Monday. The frustration comes close to a boiling point as we keep putting different combinations together.

"I'm trying to find something boss level," I explain to her as I try another top and skirt combination. I love the way neutral colors pop against my golden-bronzed skin. "I don't remember it being this hard to put a simple fit together."

"When you're trying to impress a boy who has captured your imagination, things aren't so simple," Kendyl quips, taking yet another skirt off my hands. "I'm still trying to figure out why you're going through all these changes. I get it if this was a date, but this ain't that, so, why are you tripping?"

I take a deep breath, closing my eyes before I focus my gaze on her. "Now, if we were talking about doing this for *Kyyyllllleeee*, tell me you wouldn't be losing every piece of your mind, okay? Don't worry, I'll wait."

Kendyl blushes at the sound of his name, just like I thought she would. She glares at my smirk, shaking her head. "I wanna shake the shit out of you, Z. Fine, I get you, but I hadn't planned on spending my whole Sunday trying to help you find the 'perfect fit' for a boy I haven't approved of yet."

"And I haven't approved of yours either, so we're even. I don't care if he is my best friend." I take another look in the mirror, a smile finally spreading across my lips. "Yasss, this will work! And it's still warm enough to get away with it."

Kendyl slips behind me to get a better look. She nods excitedly, kissing my cheek. "Sold! Now, can we go, please? Some of these wannabe ballers are staring at us like we need to be the next items to be picked up."

I peek around her, getting an idea of who wants our attention so badly, avoiding the approving glare of a boy I've never seen before. Actually, that's a lie. I remember him from the Baytown game, when he was around Evan's Charger when I gave dude the business about his ride breaking down. He's wearing a Beach Creek High football hoodie—another one of Oakwood Grove's rivals.

Great, just what we need, a Beach bum trying to holla. I shouldn't have taken so long. Ugh!

I pick up the outfit I want and grab Kendyl's hand, leading her to the counter. Out of the corner of my eye, I spotted the hoodie heading toward us too. I squeeze her hand to get her attention, letting her know we may have to come up with a decent blowoff.

The moment we place our clothing on the countertop, the hoodie shows up, clearing his throat. "Did you need someone to handle that for you? It'd be my pleasure, cuteness."

I ignore the offer, focusing on the cashier instead. His cologne shows up before he does, causing me to find an expression that doesn't say that he needs to go rinse off in the Atlantic. I shoot a glance at Kendyl, who has a similar facial expression. I guess Mr. "Deep Pockets" wants to try to buy his way into a convo, huh? The last thing I want is another pretentious jerk in my face.

I spot the other cashier having trouble with another customer's transaction. The familiar buzzing sound of a declined credit card is a bit distracting, but I manage to keep my wits at close distance. "That's alright, I can handle my own, but you're more than welcome to help that girl over there. I'm sure she'd be grateful for the assist."

Hoodie slips a couple of hundred-dollar bills to the cashier, nodding toward her frustrated co-worker to settle the bill. "So, now that I've done my good deed, can I at least get your name?"

"And you think your act of charity entitles you to know my name?" I narrow my gaze, picking up my bags as we walk out of the store. "I'm confused. Is this how you get attention or something? If I was feeling it, I would've said something."

"Well, my name is Vonte, and I'd love to see if I can change your mind," he says. "Maybe dinner on me so I can get a second chance to make a first impression?"

I force a smile as Kendyl and I glance at each other. I give her a *look* that makes her blush, a subtle tell to jump into our normal routine whenever unwanted attention finds us. "Okay, I see you're gonna be one of those who can't take a hint, so let me be blunt. One, I'm taken, and two, since I remember you from when you were trying to floss at the Baytown game, how about we have a conversation on the blacktop, if you think you can keep up."

Vonte gives up a puzzled shrug, then switches his gaze between us, noticing that we're still holding hands. "Oh, so it's like that? Okay, we can have that other chat, but I doubt you want that smoke. You saw my ride, and I know your rep too. You're not ready."

"I said what I said, and the last time I checked, my English is pretty stellar." I scowl at him, wondering if this is a bad idea, but he's already pissed me off. "Two stacks says you can't take me in a quarter mile, and I know you got it, since you were so willing to drop a couple of C-notes at the drop of a hate to try to impress me."

Vonte stares us down, a slick smile all over his face. "Bet. Let's see what you got. There's a strip my boys and I use to keep Twelve off our backs. Follow me."

Kendyl's panicked the minute we're out in the parking lot, watching Vonte as he strolls toward his Nissan Z. Is he serious? "Are you out of your mind? It's one thing to handle things on our turf, but we're not, and there's no backup."

I giggle for a moment and then lean over to kiss her lips to keep up pretenses, offering up my highest wattage smile. "Relax, babe. Look at his car. All noise, no muscle. He'll blow a piston ring or two trying to keep up, and that'll be that. Besides, you have more important things to worry about, like helping me put my fit together so I can make a certain someone's eyes pop out of his head."

Okay, so, hear me out.

A high-speed chase is the last thing I expected after I smoked Vonte on the track, but here we are. I'm doing everything I can to keep Raiden on the road, pushing her to the limits of her handling ability. All that matters is getting to the safety of Oakwood Grove and the officers we know.

Thankfully, we aren't far from the city limits. One of the sheriffs usually sits at the line, on deck to watch for anything suspicious. Coming through at nearly ninety with an irate driver on our tail more than qualifies.

Kendyl's holding on to anything that'll keep her from panicking while I avoid crashing my pride and joy. "I told you to let it go. You knew they weren't gonna stand on business."

"Let's get back to Oakwood and you can yell at me then, okay?" I shout as I slip through a couple of cars that are in the way. "How was I supposed to know that idiot would be butthurt over getting beat by a girl?"

"Not the point, Z. I'm calling the sheriff's office. We're not okay."

"Okay, let them know the vehicle is chasing us, we're not racing. Give them the description, alright?"

"I got it, I got it. Just drive, he's getting closer."

In hindsight, maybe I shouldn't have embarrassed Vonte as badly as I did. He didn't get off the starting line too well, and by the time he even came close to catching up, I'd already crossed the finish line.

It probably didn't help matters that he got ripped by his friends who witnessed the race. I guess he thought he had a girl who looked pretty in a sports car or something. When it came time to pay up, he balked at first, trying to make excuses that I used my nitrous tanks when we agreed to race straight up. His excuses went up in smoke when one of his friends checked where he thought I kept my nitrous oxide tanks and confirmed that they were disconnected.

Someone should've told them that electric engines don't need nitrous oxide injection systems, but it's not gonna be me.

Still, in his mind, I beat him with an inferior engine.

Now, I'm dealing with a sore loser.

I never thought I'd be so relieved to see an Oakwood Grove Sheriff's cruiser waiting at the usual speed trap. I don't bother to slow down, either. I want the officer to turn on the sirens and scare Vonte off from pursuing us.

Right on cue, the sheriff turns on the lights and pulls out on the road just as Vonte follows us into Oakwood Grove. Kendyl's still on the phone with the dispatcher, informing them that the officer is behind us. I pray things will end soon, because despite it all, I don't want anyone to get hurt.

Finally, Vonte veers off as the officer follows him, shouting over the loudspeaker for him to pull over. Once I find a spot to pull over, I keep my hands on the steering wheel, pressing my forehead against the top of the wheel. I say a few silent prayers that nothing bad happens to anyone. I take a few deep breaths to settle my nerves, thanking Nyati my father taught me how to drive and race, although he'll likely kill me for getting myself into this mess.

I glance at Kendyl, noticing her trembling from the adrenaline rush and shock of what we've just gone through. She frowns at me, shaking her head several times. "I love you, but that was some drama we didn't need to go through. I can't feel my fingers right now from grabbing the door so tight."

I shrug, choosing to listen to her than say anything. I feel like I'm about to hyperventilate, so I can only imagine what she's going through. I slow my breathing so I can put the car back in gear and head toward the sheriff's office to file a formal report. "I hear you, babe."

"I mean, don't get me wrong, you obliterated him, but was it really worth it?" Kendyl muses. "It's like you have this chip on your shoulder to prove something when there's nothing to prove. You're a badass, period. My dad always tells me, 'Those that mind, don't matter, and those that matter, don't mind."

"Okay, okay, you're right, babe. I shouldn't be looking for a fight when there's nothing there," I confess. "I won't put either of us in that situation again. Promise."

"You better not, or I'm telling Daddy, and I don't mean mine."

Chapter Eleven – Yasir

I sketch away on my notepad, chilling in my studio after suffering through yet another nightmare. The piece I immerse myself in serves as a distraction from whatever's going on in my head, but I'm not sure if I really want to create it, either. This newest sketch centers around a subject I'm hoping to avoid, but with tomorrow on lock, there's no way I can keep my mind off her.

Ever since our brief conversation yesterday, I've been shaking over the implications. The meaning of our potential chat hits with the force of a bullet train, and I have no way of slowing it down or changing its direction. I'm not gonna lie, she has the ability to derail everything I've planned, and I don't know if I want her to or not. I'll choose to face a firing squad instead of laying my feelings out in front of her.

What has me curious—and baffled—is this focus, this clarity that I don't remember having before. It doesn't freak me out, but now I'm noticing things that I haven't paid attention to before. I can't explain it, but the connection between us seems to be intense, despite it only being a few days.

Still, I can't stop the voices from suggesting it might all be a dream. Is there more between us? Do I even affect her the same way?

I put the questions out of my mind, heading downstairs to my bedroom to get dressed and ready for the daily drive out to the harbor. Unk's already waiting on me—he's consistent like that—so we can take the boat out to the prime spots to capture as many crabs and shrimp as possible. The better the catch in the morning, the better the sales at Unk's shop in the afternoon.

Unk already has the engine running when I come out through the garage, so I open the passenger door, stretching before I settle into the seat. I glance at him, trying to make sense of the concerned expression on his face. “Morning, kiddo. You were up earlier than usual. Sketching and painting again? Did you get some speed bag work in too?”

“Yeah, but how did you know I was awake?” I ask, snapping the seatbelt in place as he turns up the heat in the cabin. “I needed to give my hands a break on the bags for another week. My wrists were getting a bit sore.”

“Well, I heard the humming while you were sketching. Hard to ignore it, your Nana used to hum that song to you when you were little,” Unk tells me as he puts the truck in gear and pulls out of the driveway.

“Dang, you heard that? I thought I was insulated up there.”

Unk chuckles as we roll through the neighborhood. “You’re insulated, yes, but the rooms aren’t soundproof… you know, in case you get any bright ideas this year.”

I recoil, embarrassed that he’s bringing *that* subject up for a possible discussion. Just the idea of him hearing me getting physical with a girl… yeah, nah. “Okay, that’s a visual I didn’t need this early in the morning, for real. Consider it noted, and do we need to have a code or something, in case one of us has company?”

“Hmmm, I think we do need to have a conversation, and it starts with the question, ‘Who is she?’ Oh, and don’t say there isn’t anyone, either. Nana called me asking about it.”

I want to hide my face to shield the grin creeping up on me, but I change my mind. No need to hide it now, but I can’t jinx it, either. “Well, there’s someone… I mean, I’m linking with her tomorrow to talk, but I’m not sure how that will turn out.”

“And why won’t it?”

I shake my head, wondering if Unk has been hiding in a cave for the last few years. “Are you kidding me right now? Have you forgotten the things I’ve had to do to ‘hide’ from people who are still *supposedly* trying to kill me, according to Nana? You know, the same warning she’d been drilling in my head since I was seven? If I have to hide from whoever ‘they’ are, then how am I supposed to be real with her?”

To let my Nana tell it, when I was seven years old, I was brought to her to raise because my parents were involved in a tragic event that took their lives. She was vague on the details, but there was one thing that was repeated over and over and over again—those same people wouldn't stop until my entire family was erased.

The problem? I can't remember a single thing about what happened that night.

Unk exhales slow and easy while he waits for the traffic light to turn green. "I get it, this wasn't the best of circumstances for either of us. You lost your parents. We lost the safety and warmth of family. Outside of your Nana, there's no one connected to your past… at least no one we've been able to find yet."

I remain silent for a few minutes, letting his statement sink in, realizing how true his words are. I blink away the dread that threatens to overtake me, intent on changing the subject to something more pleasant. "You are my family, Unk, and that's all that matters at this point. I mean, outside of Nana, but… you know what, I don't want to talk about that right now."

"Okay, what do you want to discuss?"

"How about the woman who's been trying to holla at you in the shop in the afternoons?" I raise my left eyebrow. "Yeah, let's chop it up about that."

He smirks. But a few seconds later, he flashes a smile, then slides out of the truck to head toward the boat. "Boy, get the gear so we can get this catch for the day."

"Hey, Yasir, how was your weekend?" Zahra asks at school on Monday.

"Hi, yourself." I flash her a smile. "Crazy weekend, but nothing I couldn't handle. I like your outfit. And you changed your hair, too. It's a good look."

I bet she wasn't expecting me to notice, from the way she's blushing. She changed from the honey-bronze braids to dark-brown faux locs with a hint of purple, and she has the nerve to show off with the same peach makeup combo that had me under her spell Friday night. The denim skirt is a nice touch too, and the collared shirt she's wearing over the top of a t-shirt that says "STEM Girls Get Things Done" really catches my attention.

I put my own fit game together too. I decided on one of my navy-blue hoodies that has "Don't Sweat the Technique" emblazoned on the front in gold lettering pretty much says what I'm thinking today. The khaki cargos and the matching Timbs are working their magic, too. Oh, and I may have changed my oils to give off a different scent that, from what I can tell, hasn't had anyone reacting like there's a skunk in the building like normal.

Zahra leans against the locker, glancing at me like she's trying to figure out what to make of my new look, then she winks at me. "I have a feeling you can handle a lot more than you let on." She pauses. "Are we still good for later?"

I place the books in my locker, then close it and reset the combination lock. "Yeah, we're still good, but I'm not gonna lie and say I'm not nervous. You make me nervous, Z. It's a good nervous, but damn… I can't even figure out the words to say to you right now."

She grins like I just let her in on a whole cheat code or something. She slides her hand against my shoulder and gazes into my eyes. "Oh, and you don't make me nervous?"

"I would have never guessed that I did, for real." I lean against the lockers, matching her body language. I can't stop staring at her. "I mean, who am I to make anyone nervous or anything? I'm not that dude, I just do what I do, you know?"

"You have more power than you realize," she points out, closing the distance between us and then lowering her voice. "I know things have been a bit new and weird for you, but I sense a shift in the winds. Don't ask me how, I just have a really good feeling about it."

"I'm sure Nyati will have the final say, but I'll trust your 'feeling' on things, too." I don't know what made me evoke the Divine Mother, but should I let it go or try to explain? No way she knows who I'm referring to, right? Or maybe she doesn't care and I'm making more out of this than I should be.

Zahra doesn't say anything, though. She just… I don't know, she sort of looks through me like I'm not there. After a few more seconds of silence, I've lost my nerve. "Z, are you alright? Hey, talk to me, you're spacing out."

The bell rings, alerting everyone to get to their classes, but I can't leave her completely off balance. She finally snaps out of it and looks at me like it's the first time she's ever seen me. "I'll explain when I see you later today," she says. "We have a lot to talk about."

She places her hand against the left side of my face. I'm caught off guard, but it feels natural too. For the next several moments, no one and nothing else exists, and I notice a curious expression on her face, like she sees something weird.

"Is there something wrong with my face?" I say, half teasing but also wondering what exactly is going through her mind.

She smirks. "We both need to get to class now. I'll see you later."

For the most part, I manage to get through and make it to Storm in one piece at the end of the day. I place my bookbag on the backseat so I can get home, when I get a quick reminder that the more things change, the more they stay the same.

"I see someone just upped their profile a bit today. You must be riding high after the campus caught your buzz, huh?" Ian approaches me, with Eric—Bulldog Boy—in tow, flanking him. "Well, enjoy it while it lasts, buster, because I'm gonna dim that shine the best way I know how."

I look skyward, sending a silent prayer to Nyati for strength and patience. The last thing I want is to get suspended over nonsense. "By the gods, bro, I need you to get a hobby or something. This is getting to be a bit more than I'm willing to deal with right now. Say what you need to say so we can get on about our days, please? I got things to do that don't include you and your minion."

Ian looks back at Eric and shrugs before he turns to face me. The smile on his face confuses me. What's his angle? "My bad, folk, I'm just messing with you. I actually wanted to say thanks for bailing me out of that sitch with those Baytown boys. Good looking out, even if I said I didn't want you there."

I flinch for a moment, trying to understand where this is coming from, and why he decides to say something now. "Okay, pause, what's your angle, on the real? One minute you're applying pressure, and the next minute you're trying to squash it. Tell me what's really good because I don't know if this is it."

Ian shakes his head, and I lean against my car, waiting for him to figure out how he's gonna spin this one. "Okay, look, maybe I gave you a hard time to see if you could handle it, you feel me? The truth of the matter is, I did some digging, and it turns out you had quite the following in the A. I should have respected that when you didn't try to come through acting like you were all that."

Is this man serious right now? And who the hell did he run through to check up on me? I make a mental to get at Dante, ASAP. In the meantime, I'm keeping this guy within arm's reach, because he's not telling it all. "I'm glad that you saw what you saw. All I'm trying to do is deal with my madness and do what I do. Whatever happens, happens, but I'm not here for whatever you think I'm here for."

"And that's my point, Yasir… there's no reason why we have to have any beef, right? So, I want to put you on and invite you to a party I'm hosting on my dad's yacht in a couple of weeks." Ian holds out his fist, waiting for me to tap up. "Consider it my effort to bury the hatchet between us, let you see how the other half of Oakwood rocks."

I consider the tense cease-fire for a few minutes, keeping my eyes trained on him and Eric the entire time. I wait for either of them to blink, twitch, anything that gives me the go-ahead to light them both up for trying to okie-doke me. A few more moments pass, and they're still acting like the invite is legit.

I raise my fist to tap Ian's, nodding at Eric as I slip into the driver's seat. I still feel like I'm being set up for something, but I can't see all the pieces on the board to be certain. "Bet. I'll catch up when we get closer to when you're hosting and get the details from you."

I'm willing to play the long game if it gives me a few moments of peace, but at the same time, I still can't trust him farther than I can throw him.

So, I'm good with being civil.

Until he does something to disrupt that peace.

And when that happens?

All bets are off.

Chapter Twelve – Zahra

I rush to get out of the building so I can meet up with Yasir, unable to wipe the grin off my face on how things could go later. I'm so immersed in my thoughts that I don't hear someone trying to get my attention.

"So, I guess the rumors are legit. You're rocking with the new kid," Eric snaps, throwing me off balance. "And here I thought you were cool, Z."

I tilt my head, wondering what in the world he's talking about, and why he's even in my space. "Okay, I don't know what you're talking about. Who's spreading these rumors?"

"Look, I'm trying to understand why you're so into him, when all these dudes been trying to get at you since freshman year," he says. "Is he magical or something? Did he put a spell on you?"

"Okay, wait, I'm confused. You and the rest of the boys on campus have some sort of revisionist history going on," I counter. "You and the rest of these wannabes decided I wasn't worth the trouble once your 'god' decided I wasn't worth the trouble because I didn't fawn all over him. Y'all fell right in line, and you were the first one out the group."

"Yeah, whatever, I didn't do that, and you know it," he points out. "But it doesn't matter now, anyway, right? The new kid has your attention, and the whole school knows it."

I cross my arms over my chest, realizing that this is gonna take longer than I planned. I just hope I can get through this as soon as possible. "Since you've got your mind made up, why are you in my face? Just get whatever off your chest so this can be over and done. I don't have time for simp behavior."

"Damn, you're really tripping right now, huh? Okay, fine… I've been feeling you for a minute, alright?" Eric slips into my personal space, causing me to step back a couple of feet. "We could've been a vibe."

What the what? I need to get on the road, and this fool wants to holla. "I'm not having this conversation right now. I don't care if you've been in love with me since freshman year, it's a no for me. You're on one because it looks like I'm about to be someone else's girl, when there are no signs pointing to that at all. Yeah, that's not how any of this works."

I push past him to make my way out of the building, and he steps in front of me with this dumb ass smirk on his face. I shift to my left, only to get blocked again. "Do you all read from the same book of stupid or something? Do any of you write your own material or do you just follow Ian off a cliff? Get out of my way."

"I'm not done talking," Eric insists. "Not until I've said my peace."

"Oh, my God, dude, you're killing me. Move!"

Before Eric can move in front of me again, someone grips his shoulder, stopping him cold. It doesn't take long to figure out who has him by the nape of his neck, and I don't bother to contain the grin on my face. I swear, I love my bestie.

"I believe she told you to move out of her way," Kyle barks as he keeps a vice-like grip on him. "And for the record, whatever you were thinking, I'm gonna need you to think again."

"Bro, what the hell are you doing? We're supposed to sit around and let Z get at someone who ain't from the Grove?" Eric pleads his case as he struggles to get free. "That's not how it's supposed to go down, and if you're good with it, then maybe you're not who we thought you were, either."

"You're about to find out who I really am if you keep running your mouth," Kyle scoffs. He releases his grip, glaring at him, asserting his massive size advantage. "Run along, little boy, I don't have time to entertain your madness. If you touch Z like that again, you won't have use of your hands any time soon. Are we clear?"

The shock on my face when Eric turns around and disappears before I can blink twice must be funny because my bestie covers his mouth to muffle his laughter. I cut my eyes at him, flashing a quick grin to let him know how glad I am that he's always around when I need him. "Thanks Ky, I don't know what that was about. What in the world is going on around here?"

Kyle leans against the wall and shrugs. "I don't know, but I'm over it. It's time to do something about it."

I pull him into one of the open classrooms, hoping no one will find us in there while we talk. "I hear you, but what about your status on the football team? I don't want you getting caught up."

"I'm not worried about them. They need me more than I need them, and that includes Ian." He leans forward in the chair for a moment. "Their antics are messing with my game plan. All I care about is winning a state title. That will bring the scouts, and my D-1 offers."

I chuckle at the deadpan tone of his response. "Okay, it took you long enough, damn. If you've been sick of their nonsense, why stick around him and the crew? Like you said, you're the highlight reel, not him."

"Look, Z, you know how things flow around here. Everything revolves around Ian because of his pops," Kyle says. "I don't have to like what he does to stay in his orbit, but I don't like seeing anyone who clearly wants nothing to do with him be forced into a problematic situation."

"So, you're looking out for me, but you're allowing other people to get bullied by him? Okay, I've been meaning to get at you about that, anyway." I take advantage of having his undivided attention to voice my issues. "Ian's been terrorizing kids like Yasir for the past couple of years, and you acted like a parti-time goon before you switched up at the end of last school year. Make it make sense."

Kyle stays quiet for a few moments while I wait for an answer. "And while he was terrorizing kids like Yasir for the past couple of years, you didn't say a word because as long as he didn't focus on you, it wasn't your problem. Now you wanna act like you're enlightened because you're feeling Yasir? Make *that* make sense."

I blink a few times while trying to avoid the truth in his rebuttal. I hate it when he does that. "I don't know what you're talking about."

Kyle tilts his head toward his right shoulder, giving me a curious look. "So, you're gonna act like you weren't swooning over this man like the rest of these girls last week because he was giving y'all the 'Stefan Salvatore' vibes, huh? Okay, keep playing with me, you forget who you're talking to."

I fake ignorance, but for real, who *didn't* watch that epic show? "I'm sorry, Stefan, who?"

"Okay, that's cap, and you and I both know it. You've never watched *The Vampire Diaries*, Z? That man had the whole loner vibe down, and the girls on the show all tried to get his attention before he ended up with Elena." Kyle chuckles as he shakes his head. "I thought you and Kenni hinge watched it together last summer. She doesn't finish a conversation without at least one reference to that show."

I can't stop giggling now. Kendyl swears she and Bonnie Bennett would've been sisters in that world. "Okay, so I remember what you're talking about, and for the record, I had the bigger crush on Damon. Is there a point you're trying to make?"

"My point, *best friend*, is that I think you're feeling Yasir because he's not like Ian or any other boy at Oakwood," he says to me. "I'm gonna need you to figure out whether I'm right or not, but I'd rather you be wrong, for real. I haven't had a chance to have a convo yet, but from what I heard, he's got a lot rocking behind the scenes."

"Like what? I'm gonna need you to dish, please and thank you."

"I heard he's got mad IT guru skills, and he's got hands too, like he's on some young Ali type level," Kyle recalls as we keep chatting. "Word on campus is he was the one who bailed Ian out when those Baytown boys that jumped him after the game."

Well, that's interesting and confusing at the same time. Why did he save Ian from his fate? And why is he walking around like nothing ever happened? "So, what do we do now that we're trying to figure out if I'm into Yasir for Yasir or not? Not saying I am, but I'm saying."

"I'm gonna step to him and see what he's about," Kyle announces. "He's gotta be freaking out. He's dealing with a new school, and folks got hostile within the first week through no fault of his own. That's gotta rattle anyone, even though he comes off like he's cooler than a polar bear's toenails. Oh, and since we're talking about people we're feeling, I need to purge."

"What we're not gonna do is bypass that OutKast reference, nope." I try to keep the mood light, but I have a feeling he'd eventually say something, but I don't want to assume. "Okay, what's on your mind?"

Kyle leans forward in the chair, staring into my eyes. "You and I have always been cool, and I hope we still can be after I say this. I'm feeling your best friend. Like, for real, for real."

"Ewww, isn't there a law against best friends hooking up or something?" I laugh as I tap fists with him before we got up from our chairs. "Nah, it's cool, Ky, I saw this coming a while back. You two have been pretty obvious, at least you have been to me. I care about you both, but I'm not gonna lie… if you hurt her, I'm gonna hurt you."

"Damn, like that? Okay, okay, I can't blame you for saying the quiet part out loud. Good thing I'm a good dude," Kyle mentions as we stroll out of the room. "First things first, I might need to get at Yasir and see if he's open to dialog or something. I can only imagine what he may think if I approach."

As we go our separate ways, I shake my head at the interesting turn of events. It's the best way I can explain it. If anything, it added yet another intriguing layer to a potentially deep conversation. I just hope he's ready for whatever happens. If I'm honest with myself, I'm not even close to ready, but I have a feeling it's gonna be a fun ride anyway.

Chapter Thirteen – Yasir

I lounge around the park for a few minutes, grateful for the time I have to myself before Zahra arrives. I wrack my brain, trying to understand how things have gotten to this point in such a short amount of time. I need to get my life together with the quickness. Once we're in each other's space, anything can happen.

My stomach knots up in every way imaginable as my thoughts race through my head at speeds that would have made Usain Bolt jealous. Weeks ago, I was still at my Nana's, settling into a rhythm and figuring out what to do about my junior year. Now, I'm in a new town, new high school, and might be barreling headfirst into a full-blown… I don't know what to call this thing between me and Zahra.

No matter how much I try to rationalize it, I'm at a complete loss over how I managed to capture her attention. Hell, I'm not anyone special, I'm simply doing me.

I scan around the spot I've chosen, Palmetto Square Park. I don't know Oakwood Grove all that well. I literally Googled somewhere to meet up. She lit up when I suggested it, so I guess I got something right.

I stroll around the park until I find an empty bench in a row of them, surrounded by the ever-present Southern Live Oaks that lead to the iconic fountain in the center of the park. At least, that's what the article I found said. Did I go too far in choosing a location to have a conversation? What if she takes this the wrong way? Ugh, I have half a mind to text her and suggest somewhere else.

The way the trees almost perfectly frame the fountain calms me a little bit. The pattern of the water spraying from the statues adorning the fountain provides a quick inspiration to sketch. The branches offer an eerie, yet beautiful and mysterious intimacy that lends a glimpse into what's on my mind and heart.

The fading sunlight gives way to the ambiance of the evening. By Nyati, I'm starting to sound like a whole sappy romance movie. I mean, who says words like "ambiance?" Am I overthinking all of this? I mean, it's only a conversation, right? But, like, what if I read this the wrong way? What if I'm making this more than it is?

I almost decide to text her to meet me somewhere else… anywhere that doesn't feel so over the top. The last thing I need is for her to give me a glance like this isn't supposed to be what I think it is. That would kill me on the spot. Now, do I want to do something like this for her that includes a location like this? Absolutely. But right now? The more I think about it, the more anxious I become.

Then, something strange happens.

A warmth I haven't felt since I heard my mother's voice radiates through my body, calming things down within minutes. It doesn't last too long, since my emotions insist on ruling instead of logic, but I sense everything at this point. I need to get it under control.

I check my watch, realizing that Zahra's at least twenty minutes late. I shake my head, willing every negative thought out. I have to keep it together. There's too many people in the area for me to lose it.

I want to text her, but I don't want to look clingy, either. I should have known she wouldn't show. Maybe it's all an act in the first place. Why does she want to bother with me, anyway? I figure I'll chill here for a few more minutes before I head home.

Before I can make a move to stand, I hear something rumbling. It sounds… I don't know, like a growl, to the point where I check around me, thinking there's a wild animal in the area. The growling continues, low and rumbling, and before long, I hear a voice.

"Relax, be patient, kiddo. She will arrive soon."

I panic, my eyes widening as I scan the area around me. Why am I hearing a voice that doesn't belong to me, and why is it telling me to stay and wait for Zahra?

"Trust me, Ya-Ya," the voice continues, sending the familiar warmth to calm me. *"I promise, you won't regret it."*

"Dad, is that you?" I whisper into the air, wanting desperately for it to be him.

“Hi, Yasir, sorry I’m late, there was an engineer’s club meeting that got called at the last minute—” Zahra stops in front of me, a worried expression splashed across her face. “Are you okay?”

I close my eyes, cursing under my breath. “Sorry, I was trying to settle my nerves. I wasn’t ignoring you, promise. I’ve been looking forward to this all day, but I wasn’t sure if you would show or not.”

Zahra scratches her head. “Um, did you check your phone? I sent you a text, like, twenty minutes ago.”

Nah, I can’t be that clueless, right? I pull my phone from my pocket, and to my shock, the message she mentioned pops onto the screen. I don’t have the guts to meet her gaze. I feel like an idiot for not doing something so damned simple. “I’m sorry, I guess I zoned out a little too deep.”

Zahra sits on the bench, turning her body toward me. “It’s okay, you can make it up to me in the future.”

I grin, thankful she’s letting me off the hook. I take a deep breath, running my hands through my twists before I think about what I want to say. I come up with absolutely… nothing. “I feel like I have all these questions, and now that you’re here in front of me… I don’t know where to start.”

“I think we’re in the same boat,” she admits. “I’m still trying to figure out how we got here too. It feels so wild, but it’s been that kind of a week.”

You have no idea, girl. I brace myself before I gaze into her eyes, hoping I won’t fall victim to the way she looks at me. Nope, that doesn’t work at all. Her eyes leave me so enchanted, it should be illegal. I can’t stop staring, no matter how badly I want to stop.

I focus on her, watching as her eyes widen, feeling my heart skip a beat, wanting desperately to know what’s on her mind, and petrified over the answers. Her eyes are so clear, the most brilliant shade of jade I’ve ever seen in my life.

Wait… weren’t her eyes hazel-green? How are they so much greener right now?

I place my hand on top of her thigh, feeling her tremble beneath my touch. I sigh, relieved that I finally have a real idea that I’m not in this alone. Maybe she’s as nervous as I am.

“How… how did we get here, Z? I can’t come up with any

realistic reason. I haven't been in school long, and the next thing I know, we're… well, *here*."

Zahra averts her gaze for a few moments before facing me again. She slides closer into my space, staring into my eyes. "I can't explain why you're on my mind so much, and to be honest, I don't know if I like it or not. All I know right now is I want to be your friend."

I inch away from her when she says that and flinch when she tries to reach for my hand. I don't want to react that way—every fiber in my being rebels against it—but after what she just admitted, I don't know what to think. "So, what exactly am I supposed to do with that, huh?"

I pull away, but she grabs my hands, and I freeze up. Her hands are sweaty, or maybe I imagine they are to keep from thinking about how wet my palms are to the touch. I don't have the heart to face her after what I'd said seconds ago, not when I'm acting like a spoiled child who didn't get his way.

Instead, I feel her fingers caressing my cheek. I close my eyes and lean into the sensation, surrendering to my selfish desires to not have her hand leave my skin. I hold on to those thoughts, hoping her small gesture leads to something more.

But I don't know what *more* I want, much less what I can handle.

And I wish I could ignore this desperate urge to kiss her. Dammit. Not good. At all.

Whatever this is, I don't like it. My mind and heart are at war with each other, and it's the last thing I want right now.

"Yasir, I know it might not mean a lot right now, but I hope that things are getting easier," she says to me, ignoring my last question. "I've lived in Oakwood Grove since I was a little girl, so I can't imagine what it must be like for you. Can you forgive me for not understanding?"

I clasp my hand over hers, even as it still lays on my face. I hear the mysterious voice in my head, urging me to get my genuine feelings out. "I'd be lying if I said that I want to live here… but I do know one thing. You're the first friend I've made, and I don't want to screw that up. It's made being here a little easier."

Zahra stares into my eyes, making me melt instantly. "So, does that mean you forgive me?"

I study her face, taking special notice of the way her lip quivers. Her hand hasn't left my face the entire time. If anything, she presses it deeper into my skin, playing with the area where my dimple normally shows. I take my hand and caress her cheek, lighting up the minute I see a smile spread across her lips. I can forgive anything if I get to see that smile every chance I get.

I break the silence between us, giving a subtle nod I hope she doesn't see. "I forgive you, Z."

Her smile widens, her face glowing under the waning light giving way to the sunset. "Thank you, I was worried there for a minute."

"So, now that we've gotten that out of the way, what's on your mind?" I ask as my gaze lingers over her face. "I mean, we were supposed to be getting to know each other, right?"

"Now that you mention it…" she ponders. "Where are you from? I know you came here from Atlanta, but where were you born?"

I scratch my head, trying to pull the answer out of my head to respond to her question. The more I think about it, the more frustrated I become. "I wish I knew. My Nana said that I was brought to her when I was little, after my parents died, and my birth records had to be manufactured so I could live with her in Atlanta."

"I'm really sorry. If you don't want to talk about it…"

"No, I mean… they've been gone a long time, and as much as I miss them, all I can do is keep them in my thoughts and my heart as best I can," I try to explain. "All I've known… all I can remember… is growing up in the A."

"So, tell me about your Nana."

The mere mention of her warms me up and sparks a curious grin from Zahra. "My Nana is the strongest woman I know. The neighborhood I grew up in, they protected her like she was some sort of sacred treasure. The kids I grew up with swore she was a witch, but like a good witch."

She leans in closer, genuine interest lighting up her eyes. "Do you know where your Nana is from? Did she ever tell you? Maybe that might help you understand where you're from?"

She has a point there.

I shrug, unsure of what I want to say. "It never really came up in conversation, to be real. I had questions about my parents while growing up, but she always said that we would have a conversation about it when I was old enough to understand."

"Well, you're almost seventeen. I would say that kinda qualifies, right?" she points out. "My daddy always told me that if a person can't embrace their past, they can't possibly have a future. Maybe we can talk to your grandmother, see if she might be willing to have that talk, now that you're 'old enough'?"

"You… you would do that for me?" I arch my right eyebrow, studying her face. "I don't know what to say. No one has really ever wanted to… I don't know where to start. Should I get, like, one of those DNA testing sites or something? I heard they're really vague."

She giggles, shaking her head. "We can find another way, starting with your grandmother."

"Okay and thank you for wanting to help… it means a lot to me."

I rise from the bench, pulling her up with me, and escort her back to our cars. I open the door to her car, leaning inside once she settles into the driver's seat. My gaze widens as I take note of all the tech she has inside her car. From the dashboard to the middle console, I wonder how deeply connected everything is inside. "Um, we need to talk about the IT security upgrades you're gonna need in your car. I wouldn't want something this pretty to get hacked."

"Oh, I don't think I have to worry about that." She winks as she presses the ignition button. "I made sure to take all the precautions to keep that from happening."

I smirk as I pull out my smartphone, open an app, and click a few buttons as Zahra looks on. A few minutes later, I press and hold a button down, and the accelerator pushes down about halfway to the floor.

"What are you…? How are you—?" She stutters in shock.

I keep clicking on the button, revving the engine without Zahra applying any pressure to it. I continue pressing the button, mimicking her shocked expression before giving a satisfied nod that I've proven my point.

"Like I said, we might need to talk. I'm kinda good at what I do," I tell her as I disengage the app and place my phone back in my pocket. "I enjoyed our talk, and I look forward to the next one. I'll see you at school tomorrow."

She gives me a little wave, and I close the door, waiting for her to pull out of her parking space. Once she leaves, I hop in the driver's seat of my Jeep before I burst into laughter. It's the first time I've felt comfortable around anyone since I've moved here. The last thing I need are complications, but I've gotta figure out how to deal with the rising romantic tension between us whenever she's around me.

For now, it's best for me to focus on being her friend. I need that more than anything else.

I can only hope that's enough.

Chapter Fourteen – Zahra

After everything that happened earlier at the park, I don't know whether I'm coming or going. I don't know what to do, but I need to tell someone what's going through my mind.

The first call was easily Kendyl, and she guessed from the sound of my voice that she needed me to come get her while on my way home. Thankfully, she has another day off from cheer practice, and it gives us the chance to really dish without any prying ears. Lately, it feels like we're under constant scrutiny, especially now that the halls have been buzzing about her and Kyle.

Truth be told, I'm glad I won't have the spotlight on me for a little while, but it'll find its way back to focusing on whatever Yasir and I have, or don't have, going on.

Kendyl grabs her spot at the foot of my bed the minute we crash through the door. "Chica, you look like you're on a whole other planet. Now I know there's something to talk about."

I can't argue with her, and I don't even hide the conflicting emotions racing through me. "Kenni… oh em gee… I don't know where to start."

She notices me trembling, and she presses her palm against my forehead. "I hate you, girl. You love dragging out the good stuff. Spill it."

"Listen, babe, I have every reason to do it this time. Like, I'm legit trying to wrap my head around what actually happened." I pull a pillow from behind my back to muffle a frustrated scream. The last thing I want is for my mom to come in. "And all it was… I mean, there was this thing that happened, but then the moment passed, and… I don't know how to describe it."

Kendyl takes my ramblings in stride, since she's used to me doing it when I'm nervous or excited about something. "Whoa… and you look like… and why are you acting like you need a do over or something? I'm so confused right now. I thought you were feeling him."

"I-I mean… it's like you said, we really don't know a lot about him. I feel like I curved him when I said I wanted to be friends, and I wasn't sure if I wanted to, but here we are." I ball my fists and press them against my temples, tapping them repeatedly. "Did I blow it? I think I completely blew it."

She pauses for a moment, which throws me off a bit. "Okay, to answer your question, not really. I mean, you were already hyper before you left to go see about him, although I'm still trying to figure out why you're so…"

"Why I'm so, what, Kenni?" I furrow my brow, reading the change in her body language. "I know he's the new kid and everything, but seriously? There was a time when Kyle was out there on the fringes with me, and not at the cool kids' table, remember?"

Kendyl stops the moment he's mentioned. "I get it, babe, but let's keep it real. He's cute as hell, but he's an unknown. Can we at least find out more first? I'm just looking out for my bestie."

"I have everything I need right now," I shoot back, causing her to jump a little. "In fact, I'm helping with a fact-finding project with him soon."

"Okay, wait, this isn't like you," Kendyl points out. "If it was anyone else, you'd be even more cautious than me. This boy is more mysterious than the Phantom of the Opera."

"Yes, he's mysterious, among other things," I blush as I censor myself. "Look, I'm not sure how this is all supposed to work right now. There's something there, just below the surface, and it's intense as hell, but I told him it's best for us to be friends for now."

"Okay, but if that's not how you really feel, how long will it be before your true feelings rise to the surface?" she poses the question. "And they won't show themselves when it's convenient, either. Remember what happened last school year when we saw a whole situation play itself out in the middle of a pep rally? That was an epic fail, and I don't want that for you."

I close my eyes to shake the images of that day from my mind.

"Ugh, I mean, I really like him, I won't be able to hide that. That whole thing in the park was everything, even if we didn't—"

Kendyl gently cuts me off while wrapping her arm around my shoulder. "It's okay, babe, for real. You're glowing every time you talk about him, so whatever effect he has on you, it's showing in ways you didn't intend. I like it on you, and if your ace can't have your back, then who can?"

I exhale, closing my eyes again as I consider how in the world I've gotten myself into this mess. "I don't think we're there yet, but you'll be the first to know. Now, we need to figure you and Ky out, right?"

"I mean, it's obvious we have our own situation to deal with, especially when things are starting to click," Kendyl shrugs with every bit of confusion as I have. "There's something between you two, and the other kids on campus will pick up on it soon. Do we even have a clue what might happen if the boys are around each other and you and Yasir aren't boo'd up yet?"

I snap my fingers as I remember the earlier convo with Kyle. "Well, he mentioned he and Yasir were gonna sit down and chat, so, I guess we'll see what happens."

She narrows her gaze and sighs heavily. "Not sure how some of his teammates will feel about that. Ian's liable to be heated about my baby's change of heart."

"You know Ky, when has he really been so easily influenced? He's always managed to stand on his own and make other people move," I tell her. I chuckle over how he tends to have everyone guessing, including me. "I don't think anymore can really sway him once he's made up his mind. Believe me, I've tried and failed."

Kendyl gives up a mischievous grin. "It depends on who's influencing him, chica. Believe me, there's no doubt who has his ear now—among other things."

"Ewww, I'm not ready to have the talk with you yet, girl, damn," I offer, trying to erase the images from my mind. "I mean, we can talk in another month and all, but too soon, babe. You're both my besties, for Nyati's sake."

"Like I'll be ready when things go down between you and Yasir?" Kendyl huffs. "Girl, if you don't stop acting so extra virgin, I swear

I'm gonna choke you."

"I *am* a virgin, and you can't prove otherwise."

"Whatever. Don't make me pull receipts." Kendyl blows air as she changes the subject. "I guess we'll have to prepare for the new wave of madness coming your way once you two finally figure it out, huh?"

"Yeah, I know Chris is gonna come with her usual salt disguised in wannabe pragmatism." I shake my head, tempering whatever anger that wants to rise. "She's starting to wear me out. I know she's your teammate, but sooner or later—"

"I've always wondered what's her deal," Kendyl says. "She's always hanging around like she wants to be in the clique but then throws subtle shots whenever either of us gets any shine."

"She's been lusting over Ian forever. I remember how she was when we were younger, and she was hopeless even back then," I sigh. "You would think she'd calm down now that they're together. He comes with a lot of drama, and if she wants to deal with that, let her."

"She has enough of her own drama to balance that out. I mean, okay, her ancestors helped settle Oakwood Grove, but they were known as the town eccentrics too," Kendyl replied. "I think she's salty because no one cares about that anymore."

"Maybe if they did more than host the debutante ball that no one wants to do because it's too pretentious and high society, then maybe things might be different."

"Enough about her, we still have to deal with more important matters," I say to her while trying to hide the grin spreading across my face.

"Like what, exactly?"

"Umm, like figuring out whether this thing with Yasir is a waste of my time. Are you in or nah?"

Chapter Fifteen – Yasir

The next morning isn't total chaos, but it hasn't been a walk in the park, either.

I finally reached my limit dealing with Ian's crew and their constant focus on making my life at "The Grove" miserable. I'd hoped that Ian had gotten the word out about how I bailed him out with that Baytown crew, but I guess they either didn't get the memo, or decided to ignore it.

After the confusion with Zahra last night, I have some extra aggression I need to get rid of, and I want all the smoke so I can apply as much pressure on them as possible.

And I promise, *pressure* got applied.

By the time I finished with them, there's nothing but crickets and whispers in class over how I'm not the one to play with anymore. Not gonna lie, it feels good to give what I've been getting, and the only way to handle bullies is to match their energy. I'm SWATS-certified, which means it's gonna take a lot more than what they've been bringing to break me.

Now that that's done, my hope is that they run back to the fort and tell their leader to clear up all this confusion so we can finish up the semester in one piece. The whole point of being down here is to keep a low profile, and they're making sure that doesn't happen.

The downside of expending all that energy is that it leaves me in a weird headspace, and I'm not always strategic in my attacks. That's where having my Squad helps the most. One of them would've been able to at least get me to calm down before things got out of hand.

It's why I don't pull punches when I see Kyle approaching. I'm not in the mood to deal with whatever he wants to discuss, and as much as I don't want to admit it, I'm feeling isolated and attacked from damn near every angle. "I don't have the energy to put up a fight today, so, say what you came to say and let's get it over with. Sounds good to you?"

"Bro, this ain't what you think. I didn't come here to fight." He keeps his palms open, which really doesn't faze me. It's giving Trojan horse vibes and I'm not going for it.

"So, what do you want? Make it quick, I ain't got all day," I say. "I'm late for work with my uncle."

The weird part about all of this after seeing Kyle at my locker this morning boils down to one thing… he's the textbook definition of an enigma. One minute he acts like a barrier between me and Ian and the rest of his crew, and the next minute, he looks completely unbothered by it all. It keeps me on edge, second-guessing whether I should be on guard whenever we're around each other.

I should've seen him coming. He and Zahra are tight, so it was only a matter of time before I got a visit. I expect Kendyl to start up sometime soon too. It's just a matter of time before she comes for me once she's done her investigative work. Best friends are funny that way.

Kyle breathes deep, closing his eyes for a few moments before he focuses on me again. "Look, yo, I get it, trauma response and all that from them coming at you all the time. Whether you believe me or not, I'm not your enemy. I don't rock with Ian like that."

"Could've fooled me," I reply, trying to figure out his angle. I flex my fingers, anticipating an ambush.

"Okay, look, let's keep it a buck." Kyle steps to me, his palms still open and hands held up. "You have every right to feel how you feel, but I promised your girl and my girl that I would make sure there's no pressure between us."

Hearing Zahra and Kendyl mentioned in the same breath causes me to narrow my gaze at him. "Z isn't my girl, we're just friends, and… wait a minute, you and Kenni are a thing? If that's true, then that means…"

"Yeah, bro, it means sooner or later, we're gonna have to deal with being in each other's space. And you two can play games all you want about being 'friends,' but I know my bestie," Kyle says. "For what it's worth, I'm sorry about my part in not helping to block what you've gone through and not doing more to make you feel more comfortable. It's not right, but for some reason, Ian's zoned in on you now. He only does that with people he sees as a threat."

Dealing with the noise is nothing I haven't handled before, but I'm getting tired of proving that I can rise above it all, especially when I haven't done anything to deserve all this unwanted attention. "I'm not a threat to anything or anyone, I just got here. All I wanted to do was get through high school in one piece so I could do what I wanted when I graduated," I shrug, at a loss over what I could've done. "I mean, what the hell could possibly be on his mind?"

"I don't know, but the one thing I do know is that we all try to figure out how to fit in." Kyle points out, shaking his head over where his conclusions lead him. "That amps up a few levels when you're playing for Oakwood."

"I can't relate. I'm not an athlete, and I don't have any designs to ball here."

"Could've fooled me. Rumor has it you're real nice with your hands."

I scoff at that take. "I only took up boxing to keep from really getting my ass kicked. I figure if I can get a few good shots in, that it might take the heat off me."

Kyle stares at me, tilting his head to his right shoulder. "Yeah, but rumor has it you put two of those Baytown boys to sleep… if that's not nice with your hands, I don't know what to tell you."

I'm a little disturbed by what Kyle just said. If Ian's telling people that I helped him, it could get to ears that don't need to hear about, or know, where I am. I've got to find a way to shut down that noise before it causes more trouble than its worth.

"Good, maybe I can enjoy my school year a little more if that word keeps going around." I feel that familiar twitch that throws me off, and I close my eyes to calm down. I return my attention to my new… acquaintance? Calling him a friend feels way premature. "I appreciate you wanting to ease the pressure. It's a start, but we're not cool, at least not yet. It's gonna take time to build trust. I get that you and Z are close, but that means nothing to me."

Kyle extends his fist, tapping mine as a sign of good faith. "That's fair. How about this… I'm hosting a party this weekend. My birthday is Saturday. Come through with Z, we can hang some more, build up some more good will."

I hesitate, unsure of how best to explain myself without sounding ridiculous. "I don't handle large crowds well for long periods of time. It's kind of a thing for me. And I don't know if Z and I are even a thing to be coming to a party looking like a couple when we're not."

"Look, you gotta start somewhere, and whether you want to believe it or not, my best friend is feeling you. She may not show it, but trust me, I know her," Kyle advises. "And as far as my party is concerned, I got your back if any outside pressure comes through. You have my word."

"I'm still not sure…" Okay, this is going in a direction I'm not comfortable with, and I need to put a stop to it quick.

Kyle puts his hand up to cut me off. "I'm not trying to hear it. If you like her, and it's obvious you do, then I'll see you this weekend."

I rub my hand over my face. He's right. I can't sit on the sidelines anymore. "Fine, I'll ask Z and let you know if we'll be there."

"Bet. And tomorrow, I'll introduce you to some of the others who don't roll with Ian if you're up to it. Meet us in the courtyard after school."

"What's good, kiddo? How was school?" Unk asks.

I have so many ways to respond to that question, and for the first time that I can remember in the past three weeks or so, there are some positives. I nailed my English paper. I didn't have to deal with too much drama… even the convo with Kyle turned into something good.

So, why am I still so anxious? "I feel like I'm trapped in a new alternate universe, Unk, for real. I know yesterday was Monday, but it feels like somebody's trying to play games and forgot to tell me."

I catch him in the living room, in the middle of a binge watch on Netflix when I come in and stretch out on the microfiber sectional. We only have about five minutes before the current episode ends, so I'm content to relax until it's over before he picks up the convo.

Unk sits up, lowering the recliner back to a seated position and pauses the stream before he turns to face me. "Lay it on me, Ya-Ya, it sounds serious."

I manage my nerves as best as possible. The answer to his initial question probably turns into a whole other game changer. "I have a... well, I think, I don't know. The one I was talking about before? Anyway, her name is Zahra."

"And Zahra is?"

"A friend."

He strokes his beard, processing my answer. "Hmmm, sounds complicated."

"Yeah, at least... it's kinda is complicated." I shrug, interlacing my fingers and tapping my thumbs together. "Or maybe it isn't and I'm just making more of it than I should."

He narrows his gaze. Yep, here comes the investigative session. "Why do I feel like you're dreading this more than you need to? This is an exciting time."

"Okay, maybe it should be, but I don't know what to think right now."

He points toward the recliner in the other corner of the room. I feel like the only things missing are cigars and his single malt bourbon. I get up from the sectional and move to sit in the recliner. He leans forward, making sure I have his full attention. "So, enlighten me, youngster. What have you been dealing with?"

After settling into the plush leather cushioning, I take a deep breath to get my thoughts together. I realize I have been keeping a lot of things close to the vest, so to finally unleash some of it feels like a weight is lifting from my shoulders. "So, I was kinda rocking with this girl when I was in the A. When I left, I didn't really close things out with her."

"Okay, and what does that have to do with this new... friend?"

"Yeah, I don't know, it probably doesn't, but I'm not sure," I say. "I told Nana about her, and she's kinda expecting me to bring Z to see her."

"Now I see why you're hesitant. Things might get messy if you take her," he advises. "So, tell me about Zahra. She must be something if you're going through all these mental chess moves."

I light up the minute he asks the question. "She's... there's something about her that's enchanting, and the things she brings out of me, I can't explain it. She has me under her spell without even trying. And she's smart… like, *smart*, smart. She can teach me a thing or two."

"That's the way it's supposed to be, kiddo." He's grinning, but I don't see why. "So… when am *I* gonna meet her?"

Um, wait… what?

I don't know how to answer that question. I mean, she's not my girl or anything like that, but who knows? "If she's game, I can ask her to come over tomorrow night," I offer. It sounds good, but now I want to backtrack. "I know she's not the first girl I've felt *this* way about, but there's something special about her. I mean, it's like… I don't know how to explain it."

"Don't try to, just enjoy the ride," Unk replies. "Now, since we're dropping bombs and such, I guess I should tell you about Lennox, the woman I'm seeing."

Whoa, and whoa… now this I gotta hear. I sit up in the recliner with this silly, surprised expression on my face. "Pause… you mean, it's getting serious? And her name is Lennox?"

"Yep, we've been out on a couple of dates since you and I last talked. I like her a lot, and I think the feeling is mutual." He tilts his head toward his left shoulder, studying my reaction. "It's a vibe, that's for sure."

"Then we need to have them both over for lunch or something, right?" I inquire. "I mean, if it's a vibe, then I need to see what's up with her too."

"Do you think it's a good idea? I don't want to move too fast."

Is he kidding? What is it that he loves to say? "It's nothing until it's something." Well, it's something. "Man, yes, why not?"

"Okay, we can keep it light, no expectations. Just enjoy things out in the backyard until you and…?"

"Zahra."

"You and Zahra have somewhere else you need to be."

I smile as I get up from the recliner. Today's turned out to be a good day after all. "Good talk, Unk. Thanks for not making this weird, I was kinda stressing about it. It's gonna be an interesting time, for sure."

"Yeah, but I'm sure we'll figure it out," he says. "This is new territory for both of us."

Yeah, he can be casual about it all he wants.

Having her at the house could cause some issues I'm not ready to handle yet.

It's too late to back out of it now, though.

I mean, what's the worst that can happen?

Chapter Sixteen – Yasir

I finally have a chance to crash in my room for a few minutes, taking a moment to close my eyes and breathe. I'm doing everything I can to keep my mind off the convo with Kyle earlier, and, let's face it, there's someone who's probably waiting for one of us to give up the details over what happened.

I mean, it's not like we were gonna scrap or anything like that, but even if we did, I'd hold my own. Kyle's tall and built solid as hell, which is saying a lot for a seventeen-year-old boy. He doesn't strike me as the type to fire off just for the hell of it, and I didn't ignore his attempts to stay civil, despite giving him every chance not to do it.

I lay on my bed to get my head together before I FaceTime Zahra, doing a silent count before her face pops up on my screen. I'm still wondering why I get so nervous and so calm at the same time, but I don't think about it anymore. She makes me smile, and that's all I care about right now.

"Hi, Yasir, how did it go with Kyle?"

"Well, damn, Z, hello to you too. It went… well. I mean, we both have our limbs, so I guess that counts as progress." I chuckle for a minute as I think about how things eventually smoothed out. "I'm still trying to trust people, but it's not a walk in the park."

"Okay, so, I was low-key trying not to let this be the first thing I wanted to talk about, but when I didn't hear from either of you, I started freaking out," Zahra confesses as she bites her bottom lip. "I'm glad things didn't go left, but part of me kinda wanted something to happen. It would've given me a reason to see about you."

The convo feels like we're out of sync. This version of her? This ain't it. She's unsure of herself, and that worries me. Any plans I had to get any homework done are gonna have to wait until later tonight. Once I know she's okay, I'll be able to focus.

"Yeah, he said something about hitting me up about his birthday party this weekend, so it's a start," I tell her. "Your bestie seems to be cool people, and I'm hoping I'm right about that."

Zahra sits there, bouncing on her bed, and it's not hard to see she's excited but she's trying to keep it in check. Now, that's the girl I'm used to vibing with. "Yay, at least neither of you is in the hospital. I was checking TikTok to make sure you weren't on the feed. I'm relieved, for real."

I hesitate for a moment, unsure if I want to say anything, but I change my mind at the last minute. "So, quick subject change… I kinda told my uncle about you earlier."

She blushes so hard she turns the camera away. I hear her say something under her breath, but I can't make it out. She finally turns the camera back to continue the chat. "Oh, wow, I really must be special now. So, when's dinner, and should I wear something subtle or just be me?"

"Actually, it's lunch, and how the hell did you know?" I raise my right eyebrow, wondering how she managed to guess almost right. "Are you psychic or something? Do we need to have a different conversation right now?"

She shakes her head, placing her index finger to her lips. "Hmm, just a wild guess, pretty boy. Now that I think about it, I can't wait to tell my mom about you. She's been curious about my good mood lately."

I don't know how I get triggered, or even why her mention of her mother causes it, but my mood changes in seconds. I ignore her confused expression so I can turn the focus away from me. "Tell me about her, if you don't mind? Where are your parents from?"

She gives me a curious look, and I know I sort of changed the tone of the convo, but I just don't want to think about my parents right now. "My parents are from the Island Republic of Kindara. What about your parents?"

Yeah, this isn't going all that well. I don't want to talk about them. "I don't remember a lot about my parents. They died when I was really young, but…" A sudden wave of grief flows through me when

I least expect it, shutting me down. Nah, I can't talk about this right now, so I find a way to change the subject. "You know what, tell me more about your parents and Kindara. Where is it? I'd love to know more about it. Sounds like an amazing place."

Zahra's eyes light up, and I'm equal parts jealous and relieved. I can't help but wonder where I come from myself, and the fact that she revels in her homeland is something I would love to do. "Kindara is so many different things to me, but even the word paradise doesn't cover it." She taps her index finger against her left temple as she continued to think about what she wants to say. "As far as where Kindara is, it's not far from the West African coastline, and we can get to anywhere from Senegal to Ghana."

I lean back against the wall to get comfortable as she grins while thinking about the other things she wants to tell me about her home country. "Now, what Kindara is? Oh em gee, we might be here all night if I start up."

"Well, I don't have anything going on right now," I reply, matching her excitement to keep her talking. "What is Kindara to you?"

"Paradise." Zahra beams as she considers her words. "Everything that makes me fall in love with the island is there: the white sand beaches, the crystal-clear blue water that makes you feel like you can see almost to the bottom of the ocean, the lush tree line that surrounds the inside of the island. It's the food. Her people. The animals that live in harmony with us. The twin volcanoes that are named for the Vodaran fire goddess, Nahara, the River Ko, where you can float on a boat from the north side of the island to the south. Mount Kindara with its mysticism and legends that are said to be housed inside. Kindara is probably the most magical place on earth for me."

"And what about your parents?" I continue to keep the focus off me for as long as I can, trying to find anything that will keep her talking and not asking questions. "Did they grow up on the island? I remember you said you've been here in Oakwood Grove since you were little."

"Yes, but we spend the summers out there, and just about every spare moment we can. My parents are from the Kua village, on the southwest corner of the island. There are several different villages that make up Kindara, too. Kua is where the farmers grow the food and distribute it throughout the island. Then there's the Mipaku, they protect the island's perimeter and shoreline." Zahra gets comfortable in her bed, and I breathe a sigh of relief, at least for a few moments. "The Wahunza, they forge the metals that are needed for construction in Drana Trini, the capital city, and all the larger cities on the island. The Sayansi village is the science and technology area of the island, where I hope to settle once I'm done with school. Then there's Solara, which is the academics and scribes and the educators, and finally the Serykala, which is the government and politicians, and the Kabula la Maji, the Water village tribe."

She tilts her head toward her left shoulder, and I immediately feel a shift in the focus in the convo. "Do you know anything about Kindara?"

I shrug. That's a nope from me. "Nana's mentioned it, and she didn't give up much information—at least, not enough for me to be curious. I've never really been outside of the States. Boring, huh? I mean, I'm sure you've been back to Kindara a few times, right?"

"Yes, I have. Maybe I can find a way to show you one day. It's a beautiful island, but I know I'm biased," she says, but all I can give up is a not-too-convincing nod. "Don't worry. If you're willing to learn, I would love to tell you everything I know."

"I'd like that, I really would," I reply. I'm serious too. I love the way her eyes light up when we talk about her home country. "Maybe it might be somewhere I can put on my bucket list after we graduate."

"If you don't mind me saying it, but I'm just loving the way things are flowing between us right now," she reassures me. "I'm glad things don't feel weird or anything. You're the first boy outside of Kyle who knows how to act right."

"Okay, I don't know what to say to that, but I'm gonna go with it being a good thing. Not gonna lie, I like the way things are with us too. It feels good." I smile, like really smiling as my dimples sink deeper into my cheeks. "I guess I need to go. I have to create my oils for the next few weeks."

"About those oils, though." She closes her eyes for a moment, and I wish I could see inside her head to know what she's thinking right now. "Why do you need to wear them? I mean, I love the way they smell on you, but I can sense something beneath the oils. It's hypnotic, if that makes sense."

"I guess that's something else we can find out." I get up and walk into the bathroom, carrying my phone with me so we can keep talking. "All I have been told is that I need to use them because there are people who would be able to track me down and take me out."

She covers her mouth to stifle a gasp, and I instantly regret letting that information slip out. "Why would anyone want to kill you? Did your parents do something to someone?"

"Yeah, I'm starting to wonder if it's all a shell game, to be honest. Whatever happened, it has nothing to do with me, but my Nana is convinced that I need to be careful. Anyway, I made a few changes, so, we'll see how that goes." I glance at the time and realize there's some things that need to get done or I'll be up way later than I want to be. "Enough of all that, I need to get busy and get some homework done too. Can I check on you before bed? I still have to tell you about Kyle's birthday party invite."

"Sure, I should be awake," she counters. "I can't wait to hear about it. Sounds like it will be fun."

I don't know about that just yet, but anything's possible, right?

Chapter Seventeen – Yasir

Okay, so it may not be best to ask why I have the urge to roll out in the early morning when I'm supposed to be at school and drive down to Jacksonville. But here I am, taking Storm down I-95 for the two-hour trip down, with only one goal in mind: upgrades. I'm due for a makeover on a lot of levels, and as much as I would've liked to do it in Atlanta, the streets would get back to Nana and the Squad the minute I got there, and I don't want those problems yet.

The main thing on the to-do list is to get my hair cut. I haven't had a decent cut since I got to Oakwood Grove and going to Savannah hasn't worked out all that well. Since Unk keeps a bald head and beard, he wouldn't have been much help finding a good barber. I probably won't find one in Jax, either, but I have to fare a bit better.

A quick Google search landed me at a spot called Man Kave Barbershop. I might have been taking a chance that they won't be full, especially on a Thursday morning, but I figure it's worth the try. Once I got close, I set up an appointment with a dude named P, and I set the GPS for the south side of the city.

When I step into the building, it feels like home in seconds. How can I explain it so it makes sense? Old men arguing in the front about whatever hot topic that's happening today, music flowing through the surround sound speakers in the space, and intermingling conversations between barber and customer, with the occasional opinion asked among everyone in the spot over whether Kobe deserves GOAT status or something crazy like that.

It's not the SWATs, but it works for me and then some.

I dap P as soon as he waves me over to where his chair is located, dropping the apron over my shoulders and prepping me for the cut. He has a whole smoove vibe to him—yep, not smooth, *smoooooove*, there's a difference—and when he finally locks me in and gives me a quick scan of the mop on my head, he doesn't even ask what I need. "High Temp fade, so you can twist your hair out when you get back home, right?"

"Yo, how'd you know?"

"It's my job to know, my boy," P nods as he continues to comb out the top of my hair. "I have a feeling you're needing a different look, since you've been rocking this for a good minute, am I right?"

"Yeah, since freshman year." The convo flows like honey between us, and I don't even worry about the time too much. I mean, I need to, if I'm gonna get everything I need and get home in enough time to put the look together and get to school. "I'm in a new city now, and I feel like I need to switch it up, you feel me?"

"Yeah, young buck, I feel you," he replies as he takes the clippers to the left side of my head, working with the usual precision I expect from a seasoned barber. "And I think there are a few baddies you're trying to impress, too. I got something that will fit you and have them coming to see about you, no cap."

"No cap? Oh, you got the touch like that, then, huh?" Man, he has me rocking with this convo, and he doesn't even miss a beat with the cut. I sneak looks in the mirror as we're vibing, and he's not playing. The lines and the blend on the fade look a whole lot different than what I've done before. "Man, P, I'm digging this so far, keep it coming."

"I thought you might be feeling this, Yasir." P keeps vibing with the music piping through the speakers, and I'm right there with him. "So, where you from? You don't give me Florida vibes, and you ain't from Duval, so give me the real."

"I'm from the A," I tell him. "SWATs raised, but I had to move down to Oakwood Grove, right outside of Savannah."

"Yeah, I know that area, my wife's from the Grove," P drops that nugget on me. "That place is some kinda special, but Savannah and all those towns have that mystical type of vibe. You'll find out soon enough."

"Nah, I'm not trying to find that out if I can help it," I confess. "I got other things to do than get caught up like that. It wasn't like I had a choice to move from the A, anyway."

"Aye, life's its own journey, and sometimes the side trips are more valuable than you originally thought," P says as he starts to tighten up my hairline. "You'd be amazed at what this unexpected stop through the Grove was meant to teach you. Look for the lesson, it might serve you well."

I never thought about it like that. I was so irritated to be ripped away again that I didn't stop long enough to think that maybe this part of my journey was meant to be with Unk. Maybe he's supposed to be the one to take me from a boy to a man.

"I'll keep that in mind, for real," I reply as P applies the alcohol over my skin before hitting my new cut with the sheen. "I needed this convo more than I realized, thank you for the insight."

"Never a problem, A-Town. I appreciate the time and patronage, too. If you're ever down this way again, come through, we can do this again."

As I get back to Storm, I check the time and realize I have enough time to get to school without it being considered an absence. I figure, why not, I can turn a few heads, since I'm feeling a little GQ. Nothing like a new cut to boost your confidence.

So, let's see what develops once I get to school, shall we?

"Whoa, is that Yasir? He looks like a whole different person."

"And he's not wearing that God-awful cologne anymore. It's a good look on him."

"And he's changed his hair too. He trying to get *fine*, fine."

I can't stop chuckling as I make my way through the halls this morning. Everywhere I go, all eyes are on me, with a few of the girls turning into insta-groupies when I swear to the gods, they didn't know I existed. Last night while I was FaceTiming with Z, some clothes and oils I ordered finally arrived. No disrespect to my Nana, but the things she cosigned on were not it. My fit game was in desperate need of an upgrade, and I'm low-key grateful that all it took was an interest in a girl to get her to loosen up.

By the time I stop at my locker, the halls are buzzing. Whether I want the attention or not, the spotlight is focused on me and bright as hell.

While the attention is both appreciated and anxiety-inducing at the same time, I don't care about the newfound crowds who did what they could to find out what the fuss is about. Only one mattered, and as long as *she* approves of the new look and the subtle changes I made to my "signature" scent, it's worth all the trouble.

I soon find out what the price of instant fame after being shunned looks like, as Amber Waters, one of the girls on the cheerleading squad with Kendyl, and a couple of her friends, Tori and Jenna, all descend on my locker. I don't see them while I pull my books to prepare for my first classes of the day, but the moment I turn around, they enclose in a circle around me.

"Well, damn, Yasir, we'd heard that you'd leveled up a bit, but I didn't know it was like *this*, though?" Amber licks her lips as she does the head-to-toe check. With the way she's eyeing me, I better get out of there before she gets the wrong idea. "If this is how you're gonna rock your fits from now on, a girl might have to see about you."

I search for anyone or any opening that can get me out of this situation. She's been checking for me since I got on campus, according to Kyle, but never said two words to me until today. Like my Nana loves to say, "Something in the milk ain't clean."

"Um, Amber, I appreciate the compliment, but I need to get to class."

"Oh, I'm sure you can spare a few minutes for me, cutie," Amber retorts as she moves into my personal space. "I mean, you can't be smelling all delicious like this and not expect someone to want a taste, right?"

"Okay, Amber, I get that you appreciate the fit and the new look and all but..." I lean against the lockers, resigning myself to the fact that the only way I'm gonna get out of this mess would be to ask the question I don't want the answer to. "Why are you applying pressure now? I'm not understanding how you and your girls are all up on me when I wasn't the flavor of the week last week, anyway."

Amber looks at her girls, getting the nod from Tori and a smirk from Jenna, before she moves even closer, placing a palm on the locker above my shoulder. "Okay, so, I know the buzz is that you're trying to get with Zahra, and I'm feeling that, so do you. But that doesn't mean we can't have a situation of our own, though. Y'all ain't together yet."

I shake my head, sliding away from Amber to create some distance between us. "All right, ease back a bit, I'm not feeling this sudden change of heart, deadass. The only reason you're getting this bold is simple: the buzz is hot on campus, and you're chasing the heat."

"What's past is past, pretty boy, and the only thing that's important right now is that I see you, and I like what I see."

"That's cap. Look elsewhere, shawty. I ain't going for it."

I can't decide whether I'm relieved or worried as I notice Zahra and Kendyl standing behind Tori and Jenna, grabbing everyone's attention in the hallway. I play it cool for a few moments, but inside I want to freak out over what happens next. Girls are wildcards in situations like this, and while Z and I aren't *together*, together, this ain't the type of drama I wanted to deal with first thing in the morning.

And then Zahra winks at me. When I say the relief that comes over me when she does that? I need the bailout, please and thank you.

I smirk as Amber turns around, caught off guard by Zahra being in her personal space. I stifle a chuckle, surprised over being involved in something out of *Riverdale*. The only thing missing… well, I don't want to think about that.

"Z, hey girl… I was just having a conversation with Yasir. What are you doing here?"

Zahra's answer to Amber's question shocks me to the point of wondering if I'm hallucinating. Things happen in slow motion, and I'm powerless to stop it. Zahra slides Amber out of the way, then steps in front of me, wrapping her arms around my neck and pulls me down for a kiss that makes me forget anyone is in the immediate area.

What. The. Hell. Is. Happening?

Instinct takes over from there, and I straighten up to my full six-foot-three-inch height, taking Zahra a few inches off the ground as we create a spectacle with the unexpected PDA. While we kiss, my senses heighten, and I hear Kendyl being, well, not so polite in her "request" that Amber, Tori and Jenna leave the area before something bad happens to them.

Well, damn, if I'd known it would be that easy, I'd have said something sooner.

I finally feel her break from our embrace, then gently set her down to the ground. I don't want to be rude to her bestie, so I make sure to acknowledge her first. "Hi, Kenni. At the risk of sounding cliché as hell, that wasn't what it looked like."

Zahra keeps her hands around my face, placing small kisses across my lips. "Don't worry, Kenni sort of saw this coming once word got out. I guess I need to worry about your expanding fan club now, huh?"

I blush, causing both girls to giggle. I shrug, truly at a loss over all the fuss, but I have a twinge of anxiety creeping up my spine too. "I didn't do much of anything to get all this attention, Z. I mean, the outfit is a bit outside of what I normally wear, but I felt like it was time for a change."

Kendyl scoffs, tapping me on my shoulder. "Yeah, about that… whatever you decided to do, I'm gonna need you to keep that same energy. People were legit trying to find out who was wearing the new scent, and when they found out it was you—"

Zahra chimes in, almost finishing Kendyl's sentence. "Let's just say, we had to get to ground zero quick, because it was only a matter of time before someone would act on it." She leans in, then closes her eyes and lays her forehead against my chest. "I sense the change in your oils and lotions too. You increased the sandalwood, didn't you?"

I grin like I won the lottery, impressed that she noticed the difference. "Actually, I increased the sandalwood and the coriander, and it seemed to do the trick."

"Yeah, I'm gonna need you to keep that mixture from now on, okay?" Zahra bats her eyes, tapping her index finger against my lips. "And as for this fit… what are you doing after school, sir?"

Kendyl laughs out loud, checking the clock. "Chica, we need to get to it, and so does he. Love you, mean it."

I steal one last kiss and wave at Zahra as Kendyl pulls her around the corner. "We're gonna need to talk about what just happened, Z. I thought we were, you know?"

"Um, friends can kiss, right?" She teases before she disappears.

I smile, wondering if things are starting to shift the way she mentioned the other day. I recover and make my way to class before the resource officers start making their sweeps of the halls.

I slip into English class and get to my seat, but I'm already causing a distraction the moment I sit down. By the time I figure out what's happening, the girls in the class, who had taken great pains to be in other areas of the room, all but encircle my seat, much to the chagrin of the other boys observing the situation.

Oh, boy, today's gonna be tough sledding.

I resolve to just get through the day, including the classes I have with Zahra, and figure out a way to, as my uncle loves to say, "govern myself accordingly."

Chapter Eighteen – Zahra

I manage to get through the rest of the day as best as I can, but I'm really not in the mood to be in class. Not even my favorite subjects are able to keep my attention all that much. Kendyl's giving me the side eye the entire time in our last class together, and I know she's trying to figure out why I'm so off balance.

Solitude at the base of the Live Oak usually does the trick when I'm like this, but the overcast skies and the hint of a misty rain linger in the air. It reflects my mood right now, considering what I want to do, but that's not an option. If I had half a mind, I'd jump in Raiden and head home so I can press the reset button and hope the next day turns out better.

I scold myself over my behavior, but I want what I want, and I'm spoiled. Still, he's not my boyfriend, even though he's doing boyfriend things, and I'm reacting like a girlfriend when we're supposed to be friends.

I'm not the only one who's noticed, either. "Traquan Preston asked me about you in Chemistry class earlier. Wanted to know if you had anything popping this weekend."

I dismiss Kendyl's attempt to break through the haze, but I put my phone down anyway. "Traquan has the IQ of a raisin, and him being cute doesn't make up for it. He'd bore me in twenty minutes. Are you trying to torture me or something?"

"Nah, you're doing a good job of that on your own, but I'm trying to figure out why some of the cutest boys in school are trying you and you're unbothered." Kendyl offers me a pineapple chunk from her container, taking a bite of the one in her hand. "At the risk of sounding like I might be 'mothering' you, what's going on, babe?"

"I guess I'm low-key irritated with people today," I shrug as the resting bitch face shows all across my facial expression. "I shouldn't be feeling this way, but I am, so, there it is."

She presses her palm against her forehead, shaking her head several times before she grabs me and pulls me to my feet. I don't understand why she's doing it, but one thing I've learned about her is when she wants to assert herself, very few people stand in her way. "We need to head home anyway, so, let's go. Now."

I pout because she's making me move, but once we get everything together and head for Raiden, I feel my mood lifting. I no longer sense the negative energy I now realize Kendyl wants to get us away from, and I wait until we're settled in the car before I reach over and kiss her cheek. "What would I do without you, bestie?"

"Yeah, yeah, I love you too, now drive, please?" She insists as I hit the ignition button and wait a few seconds before pulling off. "The sooner we're away from here, the better. Something didn't feel right."

"And when did you decide to be so bossy today, mommy?" I tease as I ease out of the parking lot. I wait until we're far enough away from campus before I pick up the convo. "So, now that we're away from whatever was swirling around us, what's on your mind?"

"What's really going on between you and Yasir, seriously?" Leave it to Kendyl to cut to the point. "I'm feeling every bit of the push and pull between you, and I don't know about you, but it's wearing me out for you."

"I wish I knew, chica." I turn on the wipers to deal with the increasing rain coming down. "It's like there's this way about him that speaks to something deep in my core. It's been a whole mystery that I can't figure out."

"How about you try, and we'll figure it out as you talk?" She turns her body toward me to give me her undivided attention. "Tell me what it is about him that has made you bypass every other boy at Oakwood who has tried to get your attention?"

I think about her questions and her observations about the other boys at school. I didn't freeze all of them out before Yasir showed up, did I? Like, let's flesh that out, okay? Since freshman year, there were at least three different boys to tried to holla, and that included Ian and his messiness. Last year, I tried to step out a little bit, but no one did anything for me because they were too busy flossing for social media and that's not my vibe. Throw in the minor fling over the summer before the school year started and—okay, so maybe my best friend has a point.

"Have you ever met someone who, almost from the moment you see them, something just 'clicked' inside you?" I sigh over the romanticism of what I've just suggested. The mere thought of him not even being in school for half a day affected my mood on such a deep level, it scares me a little bit. "There's something about Yasir, and he has my attention—by Nyati, does he have my attention."

"Real talk, I feel that way about Kyle, but I've been around him, through you, since we were younger," Kendyl stresses to me as I turn into our subdivision. "Yasir hasn't even been at school a solid month, and he's managed to have you as mesmerized as Kyle has me completely swooning. I don't get it."

I try to find some way to help her understand what makes things so intense for me. Then it hits me. "Did I ever tell you how my parents met?"

"That would be a no from me, Z." She crosses her arms over her chest as I turn onto her street. "What does that have to do with anything?"

"Okay, so according to my parents, their union was blessed by the goddess Ashanti. She's the goddess of love in my country." I take a breath as we finally pull into her driveway. "They met as teenagers through their parents, and while it might sound like it was an arranged marriage to anyone on the outside, they told me that it was love at first sight for them."

"Yeah, you're right, it sounds like an arranged marriage, but I've seen your parents together," Kendyl points out as we take our bookbags out of the car and head into the house. "They're all over each other on levels that make me wonder sometimes if what you're saying right now is actually the case."

"There's a magic in Kindara that's so hard to explain sometimes," I tell her. We slide inside, saying hi to Kendyl's mom and raiding the fridge before heading upstairs to her room. "I don't quite understand it all myself because we only get a chance to go back during summer break. The mysticism that surrounds Mount Kindara itself is the stuff of legend."

"So, let me understand this the best way I know how. One of the gods that your country's religion is based on can see and pair everyone up before they're even born?" Kendyl drops her bookbag on the desk, giving me a skeptical stare. "I don't know, chica, it's sounding a bit wild, to be honest."

"Is it any wilder than people who actually believe in love at first sight?" I lie down on the daybed, rubbing my hands over my face. Frustration creeps up into my shoulders, and I take a few deeper breaths, exhaling as I turn my attention back to my girl, willing the tears away. "I wish there were something I could say to help you understand what I already feel deep down, but I guess you can't."

Kendyl rushes over to sit with me on the daybed, wiping the tears that fall, hugging me tight. "I'm sorry, sis, I'm not making a joke or taking what you're feeling lightly at all. I've read about these types of loves," she points to the stacks of books on her bookshelf, "but to witness it in person? I'm low-key jealous of the potential epicness that you're about to go through. I'm getting a contact high just being beside you. This is some Stefan Salvatore/Elena Gilbert type of intense."

"By Nyati, I hope not. Yasir reminds me too much of Damon," I admit as I lean on her shoulder. "I just hope he doesn't put me through the drama he put Elena through before they could finally be together."

"Girl, not gonna lie, I had a slight crush on Damon too."

I snap my head around, glaring as she blushes and tries to hide her face. "What? He's hot, dammit. Who wouldn't have wanted to be with him?"

"I swear I wanna choke you. You gave me grief for wanting the bad boy of the Salvatore brothers." I wink my nose and land a playful slap against her thigh. "So, what, you decided you had to pull for Stefan throughout the binge watch? Now I gotta give you the side eye. For all I know, you were falling for Klaus Michaelson as much as I did."

Kendyl buries her face in a pillow and screams, and I almost rip it from her hands. "Really, Kenni? I'm gonna kill you!"

We both crack up over the new post-show revelations, and it

makes me feel a little better not having to think about the "in-between" I find myself in. "I wish my cousin, Imara, were here. She would've been able to help us through whatever this is that's happening to me."

"Where is she? Can we call her?"

I shake my head, taking her hand and giving it a squeeze. "She died when I was younger, in an invasion that almost destroyed the island and scattered a lot of us all over the planet to escape the horrors. That's how we ended up in the States to begin with."

"Okay, so let's try to work through things as we go along." She offers her usual bright smile that always manages to improve my mood in minutes. "I might not be a 'Vodaran priestess' or anything like that, but I can still use this black girl magic of mine to make sure my bestie is good with the boy who seems to have captured her heart."

"I didn't say he had my heart—"

"Not yet, chica, but it's written all over you," Kendyl levels with me, grabbing a pocket mirror from her desk and holding it up to show our faces, side by side. "Watch, I'll prove it. *Yasssssiiiiiiirrrr.*"

And like clockwork, my smile widens, and I can't stop blushing. "I hate you but thank you for wanting to help me get through this. I know you're not his biggest fan."

Kendyl shakes her head, placing an index finger in the air to shut me down. "As long as he's good to you, then he's good with me. I'll put the same ultimatum on him that you put on Kyle: if he hurts you, I'll hurt him."

Chapter Nineteen – Yasir

Okay, Kyle's true to his word, and the way he's coming through in the clutch is impressive. That's all I can say about that right now.

Before I have a chance to even get out of the school parking lot, he literally pulls me into this crowd of kids and starts making the introductions before he turns them loose on me. For real, I feel like I'm in an impromptu initiation into a secret society with the way they're coming at me with all these questions. I don't remember the last time I went through something like this, but I'm not about to let them smell any type of weakness on me, either.

It's a rare extrovert energy burn for me. Normally, I'd have shied away from the rush of personalities, but after the quick convo Kyle and I had after I thought he was betraying the precarious trust between us, I feel like it's time to show them who I am.

Once I realize who they are, the walls disappear, and the flood gates are wide open.

And I'm not the only one who notices, either. "You're cooler than I thought you were, Yasir. It was fun chopping it up with you," Taylor Ricks, one of the boys Kyle told me about yesterday, mentions as I keep managing all the different chats happening around me. He's not as physically imposing as Kyle, but not many boys our age are, either. Taylor's maybe a couple of inches shorter than I am at six-foot-one, and considering he's the starting running back, he's built like a brick wall. I couldn't help noticing the girls gawking at him, but it's hard for them not to. His tawny skin, arresting light brown eyes and wavy brown hair—I mean, he's giving runway model looks, for real. "It's too bad you're not on the squad. I think you'd be nice on the field."

Marco Grant, one of the basketball players in the group who looks like he's Kevin Durant's younger cousin, height and all, jumps into the chat. "Nah, yo, he'd be nice on the court. We might need to run a pickup game, see if you got something."

Man, listen, the way the conversation is flowing while I'm chatting with most of the members of the football and basketball teams… well, the football players who aren't in Ian's circles, anyway. While I realize that there might be some on campus who associate with him on a limited basis, I'm not convinced that they'd be a part of the same circles.

Maybe I've been going about this the wrong way all this time.

Everyone in the group isn't athletes, though. A few of the boys, and all the girls, were STEM kids who are very familiar with Zahra. The girls consider her the queen bee when it comes to that world, which shouldn't have surprised me. I got that vibe after a couple of the engineering club meetings I attended. It's cool to know that the larger world inside the school doesn't revolve around one group of kids, and it puts me at ease, for the moment.

It's also wild that the weather is as warm as it is for early October. The sun beaming down on us while we're vibing feels like this is supposed to happen. Even the breeze came through easy and low-key, adding to my good mood.

I can't resist peeking over at the girls as they observe the situation for themselves. I smirk as I zero in on Zahra, her grin boosting my confidence to stay in the thick of the chatter happening around me. I ignore the anxiety—at least, I try to—of being in larger groups where possible, but it doesn't take away from the fact that I'm not being shunned, and things are working out well.

I shoot a text, asking Zahra to meet me at Storm. While I had seen her in class earlier in the day, I hadn't *seen* her, seen her.

I jog toward the parking lot with Kyle, beaming as I notice the girls making their way in our direction. I elbow Kyle to give the heads up, watching him light up the minute Kendyl gets close enough for him to reach out and embrace her. Zahra hesitates when we get close to each other, and I don't know about her, but I have no idea what to do, either.

I mean, can you blame us?

"You're in a good mood," Zahra remarks as she stands in my personal space with this slick grin on her face like she conspired with

Kyle. "You looked comfortable hanging with the boys. If I didn't know any better, I'd swear you were starting to get acclimated to your new element."

"Don't get it twisted, I'm still feeling them out, but so far so good. I guess the real test is this weekend."

"Well, you know I have no issues figuring out how to calm things down," she coos in my ear. "Besides, it shouldn't be too busy in certain areas at the house. Kyle's parents have a pretty expansive estate, so, it should keep drama to a minimum."

"And what makes you think I want you to calm things down?" I tease, leaning away when she tries to touch me. "Maybe there might be some other girls at the party who might wanna see about your boy."

The look she gives me could've pierced through steel, and I burst out laughing. She slaps my shoulder *hard*, crossing her arms over her chest. "And maybe a few of the fellas that will be coming with Kyle's cousin might wanna holla too. I mean, they all play with him, you know."

I react like I've been shot with an arrow, which makes her giggle. "You ain't have to do me like that, though. I was just kidding."

"I don't know, pretty boy. We're just friends. Why would I want to keep another girl from seeing about you?" She winks at me, biting her bottom lip. "Maybe it might make me want you more."

Kyle cracks up laughing as he wraps his hands around Kendyl's waist. "You two are funny as hell, for real. I'll bring the popcorn to see how this plays out, if you two are serious about this, of course."

"I guess we'll see." I brush off the gauntlet she's laid down, determined to not let her get to me. "So, according to the fellas, this party is gonna be huge. Is everyone expected to show up?"

Kyle rubs the back of his neck, staring off in the distance for a few seconds before he lets out an annoyed sigh. "Yeah, and that's what worries me. Despite what we might be able to do to keep it exclusive, you know Ian and that bunch may come through. They take the air out of any room they're in, and that's not gonna happen, not when I'm supposed to be front and center. I tried to tap dance around the subject all day today, but one of the other kids opened her mouth about seeing me at the birthday party, and the flood gates took over from there."

"So, what's the backup plan, in case they do show up?" Zahra leans against me as they all continue to muse about what to expect. The traces of her perfume make me weak, despite my attempts to suppress my reaction. "I mean, your parents usually contract security with these big parties, I'm sure this one will be no different, right?"

Kyle snaps his fingers, pointing his index finger against his temple. "Yeah, and that might calm some of it down, but Ian's pops and mine are… well, they're cordial. My dad is on the city council, and there's some tension. There's a lot of other moving parts that complicate things. They might not have a choice but to let him in."

"So, we deal with him by icing him out," I say. I've dealt with wannabe bullies like him before, and some solutions are universal. "Look, you said it yourself: he loves the spotlight. The more we take it away from him, the more he will loathe it. Once he realizes it's all about the birthday boy, then they'll roll out on their own."

"Yo, that's not a bad plan." Kyle takes Kendyl by her hand to head toward his car, tapping fists with me as they walk. "Let's do that. I'll check up with y'all later, Kenni and I have some shopping to do, or so she keeps telling me."

I nod, tapping fists with him again before opening the passenger door for Zahra to hop inside. Once I ease into the driver's seat, I turn to Zahra… wait a minute, what's this look on her face? "What is it? Was it something I said?"

"I'm literally trying to figure out where this version of Yasir Salah has been this entire time," she muses, caressing my face like she hadn't every seen me before in her life. "It's a good look on you."

"Well, you're the one who's helped create this version, I guess you kinda have a say in how long I can stick around, huh?" I flash a grin that makes her blush. I'm not exactly being subtle, though. Blame it on the good mood I'm in. "But how are you gonna be all flirty and everything, and then act like we're supposed to be… you know… friends?"

Zahra pauses for a few moments as she ponders her response. "I can do what I want, *best friend*. That's how it works. Haven't you read the best friend code before?"

"So, I think the others had a pretty good idea. We might need to get the outfits together for the weekend. We can at least do that, so you can make me look good for all the other girls that will be at the party."

"Yeah, yeah, here you go, tempting fate again. Pick me up in a couple of hours?" Zahra asks as she slides out of Storm and skips to her car. "I have a few spots we can go to get what we need, and there are a few things I wouldn't mind showing off just for you. You know, since we're figuring things out and all that?"

"Say less, bestie. I'll see you in a couple of hours."

"Yo, Unk, can I holla at you for a minute? It's kinda important."

The minute I get home, finding Unk tops the to-do list for the afternoon. I need to have "that" talk about girls, and he's the nearest source to use as a sounding board. I have questions… man, do I have questions… and this happens to be one of those times where I need the uncut version.

We head out to the back deck and sit in the wicker chairs, enjoying the cooler weather. He pops open a Modelo, his usual wind down beverage of choice while I sip on a ginger ale. He leans back in his chair. "Okay, kiddo, what's on your mind?"

I rub my hands together while I figure out how to start things off. My nerves are on edge, which only seems to happen whenever Zahra is the topic. "How do you know when you're treating a girl right?"

Unk turns up the bottle, taking a gulp and drumming his fingers against his thigh. "Let's see. It might be as simple as seeing a smile on her face after you've done something for her. Sometimes, it's a matter of being consistent in your words and actions. Women are hard to figure out like that."

"Well, that's not much help at all." I laugh as he cuts his eyes at me, taking another sip of my drink. "Like, is there a way to not feel like you're messing up at every turn?"

"You know, if I had that figured out, I'd be on a Ted Talk tour right now, making millions." He chuckles at his joke before he glances over and realizes I'm serious about my follow up question. "Alright, here's the real, young'un… if you're comfortable with yourself, and you do the things that make her grin, keep that in your memory and repeat when necessary. Do you know what she likes?"

"Kinda."

"Then you're gonna need to find those things out through the times you just sit and talk."

I think about that for a minute, and I'm still drawing blanks. "I guess I really don't know, for real. All I know is I like seeing her smile when we're together."

"That's the new energy swirling around you. When that calms down, that's when the things you've found out become more important." He nods a few times, rubbing his goatee a few times. "Case in point: I know that Lennox likes it when I cook for her at the shop after hours sometimes. When her birthday comes around, and that's soon, I'll put something together and we can lounge around in the back of the truck while she enjoys what I've created."

"But isn't that boring, though?" I'm starting to regret asking these questions, they aren't getting me anywhere. "I mean, I'm trying to impress her when… well, if we ever go on a date."

"I can dig it, but it doesn't always have to be something big for a first date," he tells me as he studies my reaction. "If you really want to impress her, you can find somewhere that she hasn't been before, show her something new… you know, if and when you ever go on a date."

I sigh heavily, remembering some of the #couplegoals I'd been noticing on social media, both around Oakwood and back in the A… including one I shouldn't have checked up on. "But I can't get caught up doing something weak. The pressure is real, and if it don't give what it's supposed to give, I'm already starting out digging myself out of a hole."

Unk can't stop laughing, and I'm sitting there trying to figure out what the hell is so funny. "Man, where do y'all come up with these sayings? Look, nephew, if and when you and Zahra get together, just stick to the four simple words that have helped me."

"And what words are those?"

"Listen to your woman."

"Come on, Unk? For real?"

"It kept your parents together, and so far, it's keeping Lennox smiling, so, yeah, I'm serious."

The thing I always love about my uncle is that, despite his

methods sounding completely foreign to me, he's been spot on almost my whole life. He was right about boxing. He was right about learning about computers. Why would he be off the mark when it comes to dealing with girls?

Never mind all of that, though. He gave me the perfect chance to switch subjects. "Speaking of keeping Ms. Lennox smiling, I think you need to keep doing what you're doing. I like her a lot, she fits you."

"And you'd be better off making sure you learn what makes Zahra smile, I'm just saying," Unk says. "I know you're still frustrated because you're kinda in the friend zone but you're kinda not, but that doesn't mean you can't learn things as a friend."

"Nope, not putting this back on me, that's not how this works."

He takes another sip of his beer, furrowing his brow. Yep, that's my cue to stay in my place. "I'm glad you like her, because I'm trying to see where that goes. She puts a smile on my face too."

"Yeah, I've noticed. You've had a lot more energy around the house and at the shop." I finish my ginger ale, getting up from the chair to grab another one. I come back with another beer while I'm up, sitting down to finish my thoughts. "Not gonna lie, she's a baddie. I didn't know you had that kinda game."

"Yeah, I see I'm gonna have to learn you a few things, kiddo." He waves me off, giving up a slick grin that makes me crack up all over again. "Alright, I think we've had enough for one night, you've still got homework to finish, and I have to work through my reports to make sure we're still able to live in comfort."

I give a thumbs up, letting him know that, for once, he didn't have me dead to rights. "Actually, I handled homework before I got home. I'm meeting up with the fellas to get some shopping done. I'll be home before curfew, of course."

"That works for me. We can relax tomorrow morning too. I'm good for the rest of the week."

Man, that's music to my ears! I tap fists with him as I move toward the front door. "Good talk as always, Unk. I'm sure it won't be the last one."

"Nah, I know it won't be," he says. "Whatever goes down, just be yourself."

Umm, just be myself, he says.

The problem with that advice is that I really don't know who that is right now.

What I haven't told him, or anyone for that matter, is that I have this nagging feeling in the back of my mind that there's a part of me that's missing, or it's been hidden from me.

I hope that feeling goes away, but something tells me I'll have to deal with it sooner or later.

I vote for later.

Chapter Twenty – Yasir

How did Kyle and I get caught up in the girls' mini shopping spree like we don't have our own outfits to figure out? I mean, some of the stores aren't a bad look—because reasons—but they're taking way too long to get things worked out.

I try, and fail, to stop laughing at the outfits they keep trying on while inside one of the boutiques. While it's fun for the moment, my patience is running thin. I know what Unk said, but this is torture, for real.

Zahra's doubles over in laughter over the ridiculous combo Kendyl comes up with. "Oh my God, where in the world did you come up with that? Did you just cover your eyes and pick or something?"

Kendyl can't keep a straight face as she holds up the outfit in the mirror. "I really tried to find something off color, I promise, but this is hideous. What do you think, baby?"

Kyle has this expression on his face that says, "I'm over it all." "I know you can rock an outfit that's off the beaten path," he says, "but this ain't it, seriously speaking."

"Do I need to check your closet again to make sure you're still the fashionista I know and love?" Zahra asks as they continue putting wild combinations against their bodies. "I get you wanna be edgy since Halloween is coming up, but that look is a nah from me, sis."

Kendyl's still a bit nervous as we continue to pick through pieces. "Love you, chica, but as much as I enjoy torturing the boys, I don't want to linger around in Beach Creek territory. We play them tomorrow, and the last thing we need is to be caught out here."

Zahra dismisses her confused expression, and I'm a bit in the dark too, real talk. "It wasn't all bad. There weren't any issues that couldn't be handled. I smoked that boy straight up… well, not entirely straight up. He had to use NOS to try and keep up, but he asked for it."

Wait. Pause. "You were racing?"

Kendyl rubs her temples, reaching out to mock strangle Zahra's neck. "You have a damn gift for understatement. Things could've gone way left that day, sis. Come on, now?"

I jump into the convo quick, almost demanding an answer to my question. "What happened, Zahra? What did you get caught up in?"

Zahra holds her index finger up to silence Kendyl quick before she turns to face me. "Nothing happened, I promise. We got out of there without too much trouble, okay? Kenni's making a bigger deal out of this than it is, so I don't need you getting amped up about it, either."

Kendyl scoffs, frowning so much that I'm willing to believe her version of how things went down. "Right now, all I care about is getting out of here in one piece. It's bad enough we have to be in their place tomorrow night. If you thought the rivalry game with Baytown was bananas, Yasir, the game with Beach Creek will feel like a blood feud."

Kyle chimes in to add to her comments. "She's not wrong. Things got out of hand last year, and it almost took the game off the schedule for this year and beyond. Some things just aren't worth the trouble."

"So, why did we come out this way if things are tense like that?" I ask. I don't know how the lines are drawn down here. "We could've jumped down to Jax if it was gonna be all this drama."

Zahra takes her index finger and turns my head to face her. "Don't worry about them, they're overreacting."

"Nah, we're doing what has to be done to keep out of the line of fire," Kyle objects. "Let's get up outta here now while we're ahead. I gotta get back home and get things together for the party, too."

I don't like the warning bells sounding off in my head. Zahra's being a little too casual about whatever happened that has Kendyl spooked, and I'm not in a place to ask. Being in this in-between with her has my anxiety levels on tilt. I want to protect her—and there's something from deep within that almost compels me—but that's doing boyfriend things when I'm not her boyfriend.

As the girls head to the register to check out, I step out into the mall to try and get my head together. I feel a serious headache coming on, but I can't figure out why it's shooting through me so quickly.

Kyle presses his hand against my back, snapping me out of my discomfort. "Yo, you good? You look like things are a bit off."

Before I can answer him, we hear someone yelling at us. Next thing we know, we're surrounded by boys wearing Beach Creek lettermen jackets. By my count, it's at least six of them, and they have cut off every possible way to get out. In an instant, my headache goes away, and in its place, I feel a heat that I can't explain. I want to say it's a fight-or-flight response, but I know when I'm in a fight, and I don't run.

"Well, well, well, I didn't think anyone from Oakwood would show this close to the game, much less one of the superstars on squad," one of the Beach Creek players spits out. "Any other week, and it wouldn't be a problem, but you just had to pick this week, huh?"

Kyle keeps his cool, cutting his eyes in my direction, placing his palms down in a silent cue to stay as calm as possible. *Easier said than done, my boy.* "Look, this ain't gotta get messy, alright? We were just rolling out, so just break up this circle and let us and our girls roll. Nobody has to get put on ice before the game tomorrow, we can settle that on the field."

I stare down one of the other boys who seems to be focused on me for some reason. "You got pressure, yo? You looking at me like I took your favorite toy or something."

"Yo, we got a problem, Vonte?" Ian cuts through the circle with force, facing the boy who started yelling at us. Where the hell did he come from? And I'm even more confused as Eric follows him into the mix. "You boys know better than to roll up on Oakwood players like this. I know y'all don't like to play fair, but this is just stupid."

I don't know what to make of this situation at all. Ian's acting like we're crew, but when we're on campus, we got issues. Make it make sense.

"Yeah, we got big problems, and we have no problems solving them, Ian." Vonte steps closer to me, tripping my protective instincts. "This dude is new, though, but he doesn't look like he's squad."

"Yeah, but he's one of us, and the Grove takes care of its own," Ian bites back, throwing me and Kyle completely off balance. This solidarity nonsense has got to be an act. "Now, run along now, before something bad happens to you."

I stare Vonte down as he continues to move closer inside my personal space. I don't have time to explain any of this to Unk, so I step back to create some space between us. "Bro, I don't know you, and you don't know me. Let's not do this tonight, alright? I'm not even from around here, so I don't know what this is all about."

"Doesn't matter to me. You rock with the Grove, then you have to be dealt with," Vonte sneers at me, balling his fists like he's ready to shoot a fade. "I don't know why I'm even bothering with you, you're not even in my weight class."

Shots fired. "That's alright, it just means it's gonna be more embarrassing for you when this is all over."

Vonte wastes no time, throwing a right hand that misses badly, followed by a left hand that I duck just as easily. He tries to throw another right hand, and I catch his fist in mid motion.

And then, *something* takes over. The next thing I know, I'm squeezing his fist with every ounce of energy I have in my body, dropping him to his knees as he shouts in excruciating pain. I start to twist his arm as I keep his fist in my grip, gritting my teeth and applying more pressure.

The crimson glow shines over me, taking me out of my headspace for a few moments while I'm still focusing on doing as much damage as I can. I want him to suffer, and for a few seconds, I don't care if I do permanent harm.

The sparks start up again, this time they're more intense than the incident where I saved Ian from a severe beatdown. A few seconds later, my whole body radiates, and it feels like I'm beyond feverish. I can't cool off—or maybe I don't *want* to cool off.

"Yo, let me go, you're gonna break my arm," he yells out. "My bad, bro, for real."

"I thought I wasn't in your weight class, my boy?" I hear the words come out of my mouth, but the accent that comes with them shocks me to my core. "I'm not that strong, right?"

Where did that come from, and when did I have the ability to speak like that? It sounds like I've picked up a sing-song cadence and something that sounds like a combination of a Jamaican Patois and Ghanaian Pidgin English dialect, and where the hell did the bass in my voice come from? "If you want your arm back, all you have to do is ask. Not sure if I'll grant your request, but you can always ask and find out."

"Yasir, let him go! It's not worth it!" Zahra's voice cuts through the crowd. "Please, Yasir, let him go so we can go home."

I drop Vonte like a switch flipped inside me. I turn to face her, but I see her reacting to something happening behind me. I guess that Vonte is trying to get the drop on me while my back is turned, so I immediately turn on my heel to size him up for another fight.

Ian yells at the rest of the Beach Creek players, waving his index finger at them like they've broken some sort of code. "I should've known y'all were soft, coming at someone who can't be on the field to get some get-back. That's okay, we'll settle it for him tomorrow night."

Vonte continues to flex his fingers, glaring at me the whole time. "You won't be settling anything at all, bro. You're the ones who came through with all the noise, we're just making sure you get silenced. Tomorrow will take care of itself, I promise."

I hear Kendyl say something that trips my anger into another gear. "What are we supposed to do, Z? We can't just let them roll through like they own the building. I even recognize two of them. They were the ones you raced and got salty because you beat them and then tried to run us off the road."

Kyle reacts before I do. "They did *what*? Point these fools out, baby. Now."

I turn to Zahra again, and she buries her head in Kendyl's shoulder like she didn't want that part of things to get out. "Kyle, for real, let it go. This isn't worth it."

Nope. It absolutely is worth it now.

I close the distance on Vonte before he has a chance to react. "You tried to harm her," I say, my newfound accent is coming in full force now. "I can't let you see your next sunrise. You will feel pain tonight."

My hearing dials up to a thousand, causing me to pick up all sorts of conversations happening, even with all the shouting happening around me.

That accent... he can talk like that to me anytime.

I wonder if that's his actual speaking voice because... goodness, it sounds like a soothing lullaby.

Yo, that Oakwood kid ain't playing around. He's got Vonte scrambling. I've never seen him look so shook.

Despite the distractions, I'm focused on Vonte, and I have no plans to stop until he submits to my will. The familiar otherworldly strength returns, and the surge feels so good that I don't want it to stop. Ever.

Zahra tries to get my attention again, but I'm not hearing her. All I can see is black. "Yasir, let it go, I'm begging you. We can deal with that later, okay? Let's not do this here."

Ian begs to differ, which is funny to me. I want him to amp things up. "Nah, Z, let him handle that. Show these Beach bums how the Grove handles business. Let the champ do his thing, those hands are lethal."

"Ian, you don't know what will happen if Yasir cuts loose," she cautions. "He needs to calm down. I'm serious, this isn't the time."

I'm too far gone to worry about consequences anymore. He needs to bleed.

I throw a left hand, hitting Vonte's ribs, causing him to bend over. I grab his forearm, making him repeat his plea for me to let him go as I apply more pressure. I don't know why he's screaming, it's not like I've broken a bone—at least, not yet.

On second thought, he hasn't suffered enough.

I continue my assault, holding Vonte's arm in place while I alternate between body punches to his ribs and stomach and tagging him a few times across his jaw. I'm not gonna lie, it feels good to really cut loose, and I'm oblivious to the spectacle I've made of myself. All I care about is making him pay for even considering harming Zahra.

Vonte holds his free hand up in surrender, but I ignore his gestures to inflict more pain. He's gonna feel it well after I'm finished with him. The fear in his eyes doesn't even move me to ease up on him, despite his desperate screams for me to stop. I cut my eyes in the direction of the other boys, grinning as they've stopped fighting to focus on my dismantling of one of their own. I shoot a quick glance, silently daring them to try to rescue him so I can give them a taste of the fury in my heart.

"Yo, he's had enough, Yasir!" Kyle's shouting at me, but he can forget about getting through to me. I don't want to stop, and I'm not gonna stop. "He's giving up, bro, come on, let him go!"

I hear someone humming through the noise. It starts out low and soothing, and then the pitch changes, coercing me, trying to get me to stop what I'm doing. I ignore the sounds, waving them off as an unwanted invasion of my mind, turning my attention back to the task at hand.

A few seconds later, Zahra's voice cuts through the crowd, and it's as clear as though she's standing next to me, whispering in my ear. "Listen to me, Yasir, please. This isn't the time, there will be another opportunity. Just step away and come with me."

By Nyati, how is she able to bring me back from the edge? I close my eyes to tune her out, but I can still hear her humming, cutting through the darkness, almost willing me to snap out of it. Can't she see I'm making this dude pay for what he tried to do to her?

"Just come with me, Yasir. Let him go and come with me," she repeats until the fog lifts and the heat dissipates. "I promise, I've got you."

I know the cliché, "resistance is futile," can be a bit overblown, but I swear I can't say no to her. Fine! I'll delay the inevitable and deal with him later.

I release the grip on Vonte, but I never take my eyes off him as I back away, but not before I get one last warning out. "If I even hear that you've breathed in her direction, I will end you."

Zahra's hand grasps mine, pulling me to her. I lean down as she continues to hum in my ear to settle me down. "Z, I—" The words don't come out immediately as I try to come down from an adrenaline rush that leaves me trembling in her arms. "I'm sorry, I just—"

"Shh, it's okay, I promise. We weren't harmed, just a little rattled." She keeps her hand against the back of my head, and it's the most soothing feeling as she caresses my neck. "I know you wanted to handle that, but it will get handled, just not here, and not now. Do you hear me?"

"I hear you, but I wanted to bury him so deep in the ground I saw nothing but darkness," I explain as I lean into our embrace, burying my face in her neck. "I can't let that ride, baby. He's gonna pay sooner rather than later."

By the time she lifts my head to get a better look, Savannah PD and mall security swarm into the area to handle the crowd. Kyle and Kendyl are heading for us, and I notice Ian and Eric walking off in a different direction now that the almost-fight has been broken up. I scowl at the smirk on Ian's face before he disappears into the crowd.

Once we have a chance to get to the parking lot to breathe a little, Kendyl and Zahra both are giving us the side eye. Zahra glances up at me, a worried expression splashed all over her face. "What in the world just happened? We left y'all for two minutes and all hell nearly broke loose. I thought y'all were supposed to be the cooler heads."

"We were minding our own business, when those Beach bums showed up and closed in around us," Kyle recounts. "One of them said something about trying to cancel our season before we even stepped on the field, and I wasn't about to step away from a threat like that. So, we stood and made it clear that everybody's season was gonna get cancelled, since they wanted to play mind games like they wannabe gangsters."

"But we watched Yasir ducking punches when we got there," Zahra says. "How did they focus on him? He's not on the team."

Kyle grumbles, still flexing his hands to calm down. "They came for Yasir first, I guess they assumed he was a part of the team, and when dude tried to rush him, Ian and Eric popped up out of the blue. Next thing we know, things amped up a few notches. You know Ian, always down for the brawl if he can get away with it. Yasir dropped dude to his knees before we could react to the situation, and I was convinced he was gonna put him to sleep." Kyle looks over at me, shaking his head in disbelief. "If I hadn't seen it for myself, I wouldn't have believed it. That kid had you by at least fifty pounds, and you had him ready to tap out."

Kendyl slides into the convo, asking the question I think is on all our minds. "Why was Ian egging things on like he wanted things to escalate?"

Kyle shrugs as he continues to pace back and forth. "Who knows what's going through that boy's mind when things are happening around us. I knew we could handle things if they did crank up, but it didn't need to get to that point."

"Well, I'm just glad things didn't go too far," Kendyl announces as she slips her arm inside Kyle's. "I think it's time to head back to The Grove before something else happens."

Zahra grasps my hand to pull me toward the parking lot. "Let's get these boys home before something else goes left. We'll catch up with y'all later."

"Sounds good to me," Kendyl replies as she walks off with Kyle. "Later."

Once we're outside, Zahra slows the pace. I already have a clue of what's coming, but it doesn't mean I need to talk. "What really happened? It's not that I don't trust Kyle, but something's not adding up."

I gaze into her eyes, and I come up with the easiest answer I can say. "Ian saw us getting surrounded and he and Eric jumped in, looking to get someone to fire off. He came in jawing, and no matter what we tried to settle things down, he kept the pressure coming."

She shakes her head and sort of huffs. "I saw you avoiding wild swings from that kid from Beach Creek before you took him down. Did Ian amp that up too?"

"Can we talk about this later? I'm dealing with a ton of adrenaline that's still racing through me," I say. "I need to get you home before I crash, or you'll be the one driving. I promise, we can talk about the fine mess Ian almost got us into once I've had a chance to calm down."

I can tell she wants to push the issue, but the moment she places her hand against my chest, her expression changes. She can feel my heart racing, I know it. "Okay, but we have to figure this out. Something happened to you that I'm gonna have a hard time explaining to my bestie later. For now, just take me home. Tomorrow will be better."

"I know. It's been a bit wild, but maybe you're right. Tomorrow might be better… at least, I hope so."

She slips a kiss across my cheek, but she keeps staring. "Yasir, I need you to know, whatever it is that's going on with you. You can tell me. I'll understand. We'll get through it."

I rub the back of my head, avoiding eye contact. "Nothing is going on with me, I promise. My Nana always said I had a bad temper, so I can chalk up tonight to needing to work on that."

It's a convenient excuse, and I stop the convo right there, hoping she gets the point.

I don't have time to make anything make sense right now, but the best thing I can do right now is focus on tomorrow.

And hope that things turn out better.

Chapter Twenty-One – Zahra

I sit in my room, going over a few covers I have in my head, doing my best to stay in my zone. I need a break from doing my own songs since they aren't coming out right at all. No matter how hard I try, I can't concentrate.

I try everything, from Ella Mai and Billie Eilish to SZA and Victoria Monet. I even go back a couple of decades to Mary J. Blige and even a few songs from Mariah Carey—from her early days, of course.

None of it is working, and it's not hard to figure out why.

I'm worried about Yasir.

The music plays more as background noise than anything else, and if I'm honest, I should be doing my homework. That's not gonna happen, and it irks me that I've become so easily distracted. I don't like the person I'm becoming, and if I can't strike a balance soon, it'll all be bad.

I pull my phone to FaceTime Kendyl, hoping she's free to talk. She's been hard to nail down ever since she and Kyle went official. It's hard to blame her for getting swept up in the flow of it all. If the roles were reversed, she'd probably be checking me too. Relief washes through me the minute I see her beautiful face pop onscreen. "Hey, sis, you got a minute?"

"Hey, chica, talk to me."

I play in my braids, tripping Kendyl's curiosity over what's on my mind. No need to make her guess, though. "I'm still processing what happened at the mall earlier."

Kendyl shakes her head and rubs her temples with her fingers. "Mommy always said to watch out for the quiet ones. What was that with Yasir? I don't remember him having *that* much bass in his voice.

Not gonna lie, though. I didn't know whether I wanted to swoon or run."

She's not the only one who feels that way. "I don't know how to answer that question. When we were in the car, it's like he kept trying to calm down and failed with every attempt he made. Even when he dropped me off, I was legit scared he'd go on the hunt."

"I don't think he's that type of dude, though," she points out. "Yasir's been pretty low-key the entire time we've been around him, and while it hasn't been that long, he's definitely not like the rest of the boys at Oakwood."

"That's why he's had my attention so much," I sigh, shaking my head over the mere mention of his name. "Am I tripping? I really want to hit him up to see if he's home, but I don't want to look like I'm clocking him. It's not like I'm—"

"His *girlfriend*?" Kendyl finishes my thought whether I like the answer or not. "Nope, you're definitely not that, which means he's not your responsibility, babe."

"But how do I get this gnawing feeling off me if I don't check on him?" I want to get my way without trying to sound like I want to get my way. "He's, well, he's important to me, okay?"

"Could you be more obvious, bestie?" She can't stop laughing at me. "Everybody can see the connection between you two, but you both wanna act like it's not that deep. Do you enjoy torturing yourself? I'm asking for me."

"So, what the hell am I supposed to do?"

"Stop worrying about what it looks like if you do things and just do it." Kendyl stares right through me, giving me the whole "Big Mama" glare. "I know it's been weird because this is new for you, and you've been used to bouncing things off me or Kyle. He's told me you've been kinda off balance, and he's worried about you too."

I smile, grateful my other best friend hasn't forgotten about me. "Is it too much to ask to have you both on the line at the same time? I need his perspective on things."

"Gimme a second." She turns off the video feed to conference him in, and a few seconds later, I see him pop up on the split screen. "So, now that we're all here and such, say 'hi, best friend.'"

I crack up laughing when I notice this goofy expression spread across his face. "Hey, Ky, I need a man's opinion on something."

"Oh, good grief, don't blow his head up again, please? I just got him to come down from that massive ego," Kendyl interjects. "Bae, she's having a panic attack over Yasir. She wants to check on him, but she's obsessing over how it might look."

"I am *not* obsessing," I blurt out, blushing the whole time. Ugh, I hate them so much right now. "Okay, maybe I am a little bit, but still."

"I love you, Z, but for someone who doesn't want to belong at the cool kids' table, you act like you wanna be right in the middle of it." Kyle narrows his gaze as he focuses on me. "Us wannabe celebrities are the ones who worry about the optics, remember? You're supposed to be the anomaly in the group. You know, the one who's supposed to keep the rest of us grounded?"

I close my eyes, regretting the ask to have him here. "So, what I'm gonna do is get off the phone with you two and hit him up to make sure he's okay. There, happy?"

"Damn, best friend, no need to be hostile." Kyle breaks into uncontrollable laughter that makes us laugh with him because it's that infectious. "Tell my boy we say hello. Don't drop the hammer on him too bad, though. He's been through a lot."

I want to strangle them as I disconnect the call, but I love them just as much, so I guess I can keep them.

I hop on the bed to prepare for another FaceTime. My heart races a little as the phone trills. I almost disconnect the call when Yasir picks up, but I see a piece of his arm and what looks like boxing gear. "What's up?"

He sounds like he still has a lot of anger on him. I'm not sure how to approach him, but I decide to push through and see what happens. "Yasir, it's Z. Are you okay? I was a little worried about you."

What piece of him I'm able to see disappears as he grunts and… it sounds like he's punching something *hard*. The hits keep coming, faster and harder, and the grunting turns into growling before he stops to breathe. "I don't know how to answer that question. I'm irritated and I need to get some of this negative energy off me. I appreciate you being worried, but I'm not about to start making up lies to make anyone feel better."

Yeah, he's not in a good space, that's for sure. I don't want to give up on him, so I turn on the charm to try and pull him out of his funk. "Yasir, could you sit down for a moment for me, please? I have something I want you to hear."

Yasir keeps punching through my words, ignoring my attempts to get his attention again. He has no clue who he's dealing with, though. "Pretty please? I promise it'll be worth it. *Please*, Yasir?"

The jabs stop seconds later, and the next thing I see is his face on the screen. The scowl may have shut me down any other day but tonight won't be it. He slows his breathing a bit as he studies my facial expressions. I lick my lips as I wait for his body language to soften up for me. "It's not working, whatever you're trying to do."

"Isn't it working, though?" I tease as I let more time pass without either of us saying much of anything. I wink at him, allowing an easy smile to spread across my lips. "Can you sit there and say it's not working?"

He closes his eyes and mumbles something under his breath. He takes a few deep breaths before he opens his eyes and stares at me. He offers up a half-smile, my gaze zeroing in on that dimple of his, and I know I have him. "Nope, it's not working at all. So, what do you have for me to listen to?"

I pull my guitar from where it rests on my right hip and start strumming a few cords. The moment I start humming the chorus, my gaze never leaves his. My voice takes over the moment, its tone cutting through the air as I keep my focus on him, watching and waiting for any clue that he's relaxed. The guitar riff is soft and suggestive, with every intention of wrapping him around my finger.

Before long, he matches my rocking motion, his smile is easy and smooth, and I blow a kiss between lyrics, putting a little honey on the end of each word. I stop playing once I notice he's smiling, maintaining eye contact to see if he looks away. "So, how do you like it?"

"Beauty, brains, and a siren's voice. I think I'm in trouble." He doesn't stop smiling at me, making me wonder if he's trying to turn the tables. "I liked it a lot, just like the songstress."

I blush, taking advantage of his new and improved mood to test a question or two. "Can I ask why you needed to put some time on the bags?"

He tenses up for a moment before he settles down. "I'm trying to figure out where I fit in at Oakwood, and how I fit in your world. I'm still the new kid, and while I've managed to catch some attention, it hasn't been all good. I'm not comfortable, and it's had me on edge, especially after the last few days."

"You've been fitting in just fine. What makes you think you haven't?"

"I saw the way Kendyl looked at me after the incident at the mall. And when I was on FaceTime with Kyle and Taylor the other day, they noticed something weird that I didn't know how to explain." His voice is filled with anxiety, and all I want is to take it away. "I wish I could explain, but I don't know how to right now. I had a hard time explaining it to my grandmother, and by some miracle, she understood what I was saying."

"Yasir, just breathe with me, please?" I sense the nervous energy surrounding him, and I can only hope to get him to calm down. "Kendyl and I were concerned for your safety. Kyle's too. Baytown can be a bit rough around the edges, and we didn't want y'all caught up in a fight with them."

"So, neither one of you looked at me like I'd grown a third eye or something, huh?" He's legit shaking on the screen, and I don't know what I can do to bring him back from the edge. I can't answer his question without lying to him. "Yeah, that's what I thought. Let's be real, could you even rock with me, even as friends, knowing there's something off with me?"

Okay, I don't understand how things went left so fast, but he's not getting away that easily. "I don't know who you were rocking with in the A, but that's not how this works, I promise. I would never step away from anyone once I've decided they're my friend."

"I hear you, Z, but there's something going on with me that I haven't even had a chance to get a real word from my Nana to explain any of this madness. None of you signed up for whatever's going on with me, and I'm not sure I signed up for it, either." I see the fear behind his glare, but I'm not having it. He takes a towel to wipe his face, holding it a little longer to compose himself. The moment he removes it, it's like he's flipped a switch. "I know what I said, but—

”

“I said what I said, and you’re not about to step away like that.” I’m so pissed I feel my skin heating up. Has he lost his ever-loving mind? “If it means we head to see your Nana and get the answers you need to figure it out, then that’s what we do, okay? And I’m not taking no for an answer, either.”

He takes a few more deep breaths, pulling the gloves off and takes the safety scissors to cut the tape off his hands. “I get it, alright? I’m not used to people sticking with me when the mud gets thick. Only ones I’ve ever been able to count on was my Squad back home, and even they had to earn it.”

“I’m here for you, Yasir, dead serious.” Something comes over me in the moment. I can’t explain it, but it feels like a compulsive need to make sure he’s protected from whatever is revealed. “When you’re ready to roll up there, I’ll be riding shotgun inside Storm.”

He nods a few more times, grabbing an electrolyte water and inhales half the bottle in one gulp. He waits until he clears his throat before he glances back into the screen. “Thank you, Z, and I’m gonna hold you to it. I have no idea what to expect when I get back up there. There’s so much unfinished business to take care of.”

“Then, we’ll go take care of it, alright?”

“Say less, bestie.”

“Good, now get some sleep, we still have school in the morning.”

He chuckles, sounding so freaking cute when he does it. I think I’ll keep him—when I’m ready to claim him, I mean. “Just so damn bossy, I swear. Good night, I’ll see you in the morning.”

Chapter Twenty-Two – Yasir

They will hunt you until you give them what they want... and they will kill you if you don't.

I stifle my screams to avoid waking Unk, covering my mouth to muffle the noise as best as possible. The walls in the house aren't exactly thin, but I didn't want to have another conversation about why I can't sleep.

I haven't had a nightmare this bad for a few months. When they hit, they were bad, like bad, bad. Nana thought she would have to create batches of different herbal mixes just so I could sleep every night. They would start and stop without much of a heads up, and whether I liked it or not, I'd have to deal with it. The suffering would continue until I could figure out whatever "they" wanted, and for that matter, who "they" were. Every time, the same demand was made, and every time, my refusal was absolute, despite my insistence that I didn't know what was demanded.

"I don't know what you want. I don't have what you want!" I cry out repeatedly, each time more definitive than the last, but I can't escape reliving the same sequence of events. I have trouble making sense of why I keep saying those words. If I could have an out of body experience inside of my own dream, that's exactly where I am during this whole thing. I don't believe it's me, but somehow, it's me.

My clothes stick to my skin, dripping wet from the sweltering Georgia heat. Despite it being October, the summers never really end here. I rub my face, wishing I could rip this horrific nightmare from my mind. At this point, any relief from the attack on my psyche would be welcomed.

I check the clock on my nightstand. The glowing red light shows the time as a little after midnight. I have a few hours before heading to the boating docks, I catch my breath. Only two places exist where I can purge that energy, either the studio upstairs or the boxing gear in the basement.

That inner voice from my dream continues its assault. You know what they want, it's been inside you all along. Just give them what you possess, and this can all be over. You can live a normal life.

I sit up and stretch as I shake the voice from my head. I want to get out of bed, but my mind and body aren't on the same page. I give myself a pep talk while drowning out the critic. "Come on, bro, you have to get this out of your system. It'll be good to burn it off for a few hours."

A sudden burst of energy flows through me. A good creative session may just do the trick. I realize there won't be enough time to get things together once I finish working with Unk, so I prepare a batch of special colognes for the week. The process becomes one that I've come to enjoy, in a manner of speaking. The ritual keeps me close to my parents, even though it was my Nana who taught me once I was old enough to learn to do it on my own. Not gonna lie, though… I hope that sooner or later, I won't have to do it anymore.

I sit in front of the sink, taking care to wipe the mirror that fogged up from the steam of the hot water pooling in the basin. I open the containers which hold the ingredients I need. One by one, I retrieve the creams and oils I use to mask my unique "scent," as I was told. A scent that prevents those responsible for my parents' deaths from being able to track me down so they can kill me. Nana's quiet on the reason my life is in danger, though.

The peculiar mix of fragrances: a family recipe of myrrh, sandalwood, tonka bean, and coriander, is a part of my ritual. The original combination is supposed to be enough to repel human senses… like those who are on the hunt to find me… but not so overpowering that my teachers suggest I change my "cologne." Thank the gods the concoction isn't too offensive at first, but when I found a way to tweak the mixture, it has quite the opposite effect on most of the girls at school.

Once I finish my routine with the scented oils, I stretch and make my way upstairs to my sanctuary on the top floor of the house.

Over the door of the studio, I read a phrase Unk had drilled in my head so many times, I want to throw up: "Don't quit. Suffer now and live the rest of your life as a champion."

That quote from the greatest boxer of all time has held me together for the past few years. In fact, I'd taken up boxing, thanks to Unk, and as the rumors at school will have anyone believe, I'm that good—despite never fighting in a live match. I don't know how much longer I can last, but I do know that quitting is not an option. Muhammad Ali might have been talking about how much he hated training, but I'll take that over surviving high school any day.

Either the studio or the boxing equipment calls to me during times of stress or anxiety, and if I had my way, I'd stay lost in both spaces for the rest of the morning. After what I've just gone through, I need the release, but I still can't shake the nagging feeling inside of me. There's something there, in the nightmares, that I can't put my finger on, but it feels important. If I can break through the wall and find out, it might calm a lot of things down… at least, I hope it does.

The minute I step inside the dimly lit studio space, the familiar sea breeze scent from the candles I burn surround me, its remnants lingering in the air from the last session a few weeks ago. I take a deep breath, letting out a satisfied sigh as my mood changes in an instant.

I cultivated the space as my own over the years, a haven where I could fly free and travel wherever my heart desires… until I have the means and time to actually start checking off my bucket list. The places I've traveled always feel like home, and I paint each of them with the same passion and fervor, showing as much brilliance and detail as my creativity could muster. Egypt. Tanzania. South Africa. Ghana. Colombia. Barbados. Jamaica. Each locale holds some special meaning, whether they house a wondrous sight or the simple reasoning that I love the landscape.

They all, however, pale in comparison to a location I've placed above all others… Kindara, my Nana's birthplace, and after talking with Zahra, it's where she and her family are from too.

I stare at the most recent image I sketched on the pad sitting on the easel—a palatial estate cradled in the cliffs of Mount Kindara. Sketching always grounds me; I connect to the places that resonate most with me through my art. Nana always told me that Kindara is full of mysticism, and that magic flows through me with every stroke of the brush… or maybe that's what she wants me to believe.

I wonder if Zahra knows anything about the actual magic of the island that Nana told me about. It never hurts to ask, right?

I've never really been there, to be honest. All I have is my vivid imagination and the nightmares that I've suffered from for as long as I can remember to guide me with the imagery I create. It sounds like a wonderful place to visit, and maybe I might fall in love with the place like they have.

I carefully detach the paper from the sketchpad, rolling and taping it down to join the other completed artwork in a protective container sitting to the left of the easel. Grabbing my pencils and getting comfortable on the stool, I close my eyes and take a deeper breath. Moments later, I nod, satisfied with the next imagery I want to create.

I battle with the voice inside my head, staring at the blank page. Nana would never lie to me about what happened to my parents. I know it would have never existed, but the memories stay locked in the back of my mind, just beyond my reach, tormenting me.

As I keep myself busy with the outlines of the drawing, I hum a tune Nana frequently sang when I was a young boy to drown out the noise. The lullaby takes me away from the studio, bringing me to the shores of the massive Kindaran coastline in an instant. With each stroke, I envision the way the ocean's waves crash onto the beach before they recede. I can feel and taste the ocean breeze, tilting my head to embrace the warmth of the sun.

The beach gives way to a forest that provides a protective border that encircles the island, with thick, sharp branches and prickly shrubs that make it difficult to come out on the other side unscathed. The wildlife hidden within the vibrant, emerald foliage ranges from mesmerizing to deadly. The beautiful, yet dangerous labyrinth comes with a simple message to strangers who dare to come ashore—enter at your own risk.

From there, I'm transported through the calming waters of River Ko, named for the Vodaran God of the Seas, as the ferry traverses into the Kabila la Maji, or the Water Tribes. I wave to the other children who are learning to keep their balance while inside the boats as they pull fish from the river. I dip my fingers into the cool waves, amazed at the aquatic life traveling alongside the watercraft as they swim toward the northern savannah.

Several ospreys are in formation above me, their expansive wingspans appearing to touch each other. Some already have fish in their talons, while others are in full dive before leveling off mere inches above the water, grabbing their dinner and then flying off over the trees framing the river. I continue sketching as I hum in sync with the pencils skating across the page.

Once we disembark from the ferry, a Jeep Gladiator truck takes me through the hilly terrain, the rough ride bringing me farther into the heart of Kindara. To my right, the majestic beauty of Mount Kindara up close causes me to gasp in awe. Just above where I remember creating an estate on the mountainside, the opening to the Nyati Temple lay hidden in plain sight… something Nana has told me about so many times, and Zahra has confirmed, I swear I've been there before. According to her stories, its walls house the true wealth and nature of Kindara: sacred Vodaran magick and another world beyond this one. Only those who are chosen by the Divine Mother can travel there.

At the top of the mountain, Kindaran sculptors are hard at work carving the images of Nyati and her seven children into its side. I've never fully committed them to memory, but in this dream, I can recall them as though they are second nature: Ko, Vodaran of the Sea; Zatara, Vodaran of the Earth; Adin, Vodaran of War; Abibatu, Vodaran of Magick; Nahara, Vodaran of Fire; Ubaka, Vodaran of Air; and Ashanti, Vodaran of Love.

To my left, off in the distance, the twin volcanoes, named for Nahara, rumble in a rare show of power during this specific trip. I marvel at the spectacle, taking the pair of binoculars in the middle compartment to get a closer look at the low roiling of the lava trickling above the lip of the basins. The direction of the flow faces toward the ocean on the west side of the island, building another difficult entry point onto the countryside.

To the north, I observe the airplanes as they take off and land at the airport near Drana Tirin, the capital city, which is beyond my ability to see at that moment. I don't worry too much about it; I'll visit other parts of the island soon enough. I can't believe the splendor surrounding me, and wish Nana had the ability to take me there, but I'm content with what she'd been able to do for me while I was growing up.

I'm still sitting in my studio, a little confused over how I'm able to dream walk. I mean, it's the only explanation for what's happening to me. I'm always asleep when I travel to Kindara, but I know I'm awake this time. I would've never been able to make it up here if I were asleep. The whole thing is disconcerting, and I struggle to maintain my balance on the stool. I take a deep breath and continue through to the end, but I have no idea how I'm supposed to wake out of this when I'm already awake.

The Jeep finally comes to a stop at the gates of a village called Solara, but instead of finding peace when I gaze upon the enclosure, goosebumps cover my skin. Smoke rises above the twenty-foot-high stone walls. I move the pencil across the page at a feverish pace now, depicting the fires and explosions throughout the village. Despite the initial panic in my heart, I trudge forward in a desperate attempt to find out what was happening inside.

In the next moment, an alarm sounds, and no matter how hard I try to advance, an unknown force holds me still. My confusion turns to anger as I'm yanked away without warning from the village, from Kindara, and across the ocean at lightning speed, bringing me back to the studio. "No, don't take me away, please! I need to know what happened!"

I'm unable to get my bearings, the blaring of the smartphone alarm threatens to cause a headache I don't need. I silence the device, slowing my breathing before focusing on the canvas and the picture I had been sketching during my "trip."

Despite the weird way I traveled while awake and then get ripped away during my latest journey back to Kindara, I'm ecstatic over the richness of the landscape in my latest creation. I love all the aspects I've captured, including the legendary Kindaran sunsets that, in Nana's opinion, eclipse anything I'll ever witness Stateside. I stroke my chin as I consider my options over how I want to complete the painting. "All I need is the right color combination to paint this, and it'll be perfect."

In a flash, a tune Zahra hummed when we were in the mall during the problems we had with Beach Creek seduces my ears. The faded sound of her voice hypnotizes me, raising my body temperature to a low-grade fever. I no longer feel agitated, or overwhelmed, for that matter. I close my eyes to imagine her near me, continuing her welcomed assault on my senses. Her soothing tones, despite being miles away, warm me as nothing else has since I left the A.

What I can't figure out is where all of this is coming from. How am I able to vividly create a painting of a place I couldn't remember living, down to the most intricate detail? How in the world is that possible?

It's time to get back to Atlanta, ASAP. I have to know if what is happening to me is somehow related to the nightmares I'm still having. It's the only way to explain any of this, and how I'm able to do all these wonderfully scary things with almost no effort whatsoever.

I mean, there's no such thing as magic, right?

There are too many questions, and Nana may be the only one who can give me the answers I need.

Chapter Twenty-Three – Yasir

I'd planned on having this convo sooner, but the way things have gone since I got here, time slipped away from me.

Now, don't get me wrong, I've talked to Nana since I've been in Oakwood Grove. I make it a point to call her at least every other day, but we don't video call all that much. Today, I need to see her face, and I'm sure she wants to see me too.

Questions deserve answers, and I want her to be aware of what's happening to me. She's the only person who can tell me the truth.

I think about heading out to the back deck to talk to her, but I think better of it. The neighbors are nosey as hell, and I don't think a chat about the possible existence of magic is something regular people need to hear. I don't know how she'll react to what I have to tell her.

As I wait for her to pick up the call, I set the phone on top of my desk in my room so my hands can be free. I have a habit of explaining things with my hands, and I don't want the phone moving around while we're talking.

She finally picks up, and seeing her smiling face puts me in an instant good mood. My Nana is a stunning, beautiful woman, and no, I'm not biased. People question her age because they can't believe how old she is. Like, she and Angela Bassett could pass for sisters, and we all still have a hard time believing the Queen Mother of Wakanda is as old as she is too.

"Hello, my darling boy, this is a pleasant surprise." I can tell from the background that she is in her sitting room. She gives me a wide smile as she keeps herself busy crocheting another piece. "Is something the matter? I was not expecting your call until tomorrow."

"Well, there's nothing really wrong." I take a sip of my water bottle, feeling my throat tighten up. "I've tried to stay out of trouble, but you know how that goes."

She laughs when I mention that, putting my mind at ease a bit. "That temper was a challenge, that is for certain. I thought the boxing was meant to help give you the outlet you needed?"

"Yes, it has, and I haven't gotten into any trouble at school, I promise." I want to make it clear that she has nothing to worry about, even if I am kinda lying to her about it. Being away from me and not having any influence was one of her major concerns, and I don't want to add to them. "It's nothing that I haven't been able to handle, and Unk's been great, he's helped me a lot with how things flow down here."

"Well, that is a relief. Since he has not called to let me know anything, I can rest my mind knowing that you are doing well." She stops for a moment to get a sequence on the cloth locked in before she focuses on me again. "So, when are you coming up to see me? I have not seen that handsome face of mine in a few weeks, and the last time we talked, there was a girl you were trying to impress. How is that coming along?"

Yeah, she has a gift for understatement at times, and I thought she'd forgotten about me mentioning Zahra. "It's going okay, so far. I told her about you and maybe her coming up with me to visit."

"Well, now, that would be very interesting, and I would be happy to welcome her when you come up."

"Nana, I need to ask you something, and it's kinda important."

"Sure, baby, what is on your mind?"

I take a deep breath as I choose my words carefully. "Well, while she and I were getting to know each other, she asked about my parents and where I come from, and I couldn't tell her because I honestly don't know anything outside of what you've told me."

Nana nods slow and easy, putting down her piece to give me her undivided attention. "Okay, what questions do you have?"

"I'll get to that in a minute, but I need to explain something else," I tell her as I get comfortable in my chair. Okay, so I can't lie to my Nana. It just doesn't ever feel right. "I have been caught up in a couple of fights away from school. Before you start, I didn't instigate any of them, but… it feels like something takes over when I fight."

She continues to nod at what I say to her, and I notice she doesn't freak out. She might not have been, but it causes a bit of anxiety for me. "Okay, go on, baby, tell me everything."

"Well, after a convo with the new friends I've made down here, one of them said that my eyes glowed in a deep shade of crimson red." I keep purging, remembering that she's always been a safe space. "I didn't know what they were talking about, so I played it off like it was a camera filter. My eyes had never done that before, and I don't know what to make of it."

Nana flinches before she regains her composure, and for the first time during our talk, I'm concerned that something may be wrong with me. She offers a smile as though she could feel the rising fear flowing through me. "Okay, first, I want you to know that there is nothing wrong with you. I need you to understand that. Do you hear me, Ya-Ya?"

"Yes, ma'am."

"This girl that you've been seeing, where is she from? Is she from Georgia?"

I don't understand why she asks the question, but I don't think it would cause any harm, either. "She and her family are from Kindara, Nana, same as you."

She widens her eyes and sits up in her chair, getting closer to the camera. "How soon can you and this young lady come up to see me? I would like to speak to her too. I have a feeling, but I will not say anything until I see you two together."

"Nana, is there something I need to know about?"

"I promise, my darling grandson, if I see what I think I saw, and it matches the visions I have been having over the past couple of days, I will explain everything. It may mean more than we know." Nana gives up another warming smile, blowing kisses at the screen, causing me to blush. "When was the last time you had any nightmares?"

Last night, and almost every night. "I had one earlier this week… but that aside, there's something else that happened," I say, quickly changing the subject. Now that she's willing to open the book on Mom and Dad, I figure, why not? "After my first day at school, I had a… I wish I could understand what happened."

"Go ahead, baby, you know Nana has seen a lot in her life."

Not like what I'm about to tell her, though. "I spoke into the air that I missed Mom and Dad, and a few moments later, I felt Mom kiss me on my cheek and Dad's hand on my shoulder."

When she doesn't bat an eyelash over my reveal. I sit there, stone-faced, with more questions than answers about my own grandmother. How is she taking any of this in stride like she's done it all before? "Okay, baby, we need to sit down and handle everything that is coming at you. What I need for you to do is understand that this is normal for people like us."

"Pause, Nana… us?"

"Yes, baby, but this is not something that we need to talk about over a video call." She clasps her hands together and takes a deep breath. "I honestly thought I would have more time to prepare you, but I guess the gods had other plans. First things first, when you have a chance, and hopefully soon, please come see me, and bring your friend with you. I have a feeling this visit will change everything."

Chapter Twenty-Four – Yasir

The next morning is intense.

It doesn't take long for the word to get out about the incident at the mall, according to texts from the group, but Ian's the only one talking and wants to whip everyone into a frenzy. I have a theory, and I don't like where it's leading me; I have a feeling Ian is trying to expose me and get me into something that is liable to get me into some real trouble.

I don't have any real proof, but he's gonna slip up sooner or later.

This whole thing feels way more personal than I'm aware of, and that scares me more than anything. The game he's playing—being in my corner one minute, then being my sworn enemy the next minute—there's something else going on, and I need to pay more attention to him when he's around me. If I play my cards right, he may give me the answers I'm looking for.

The game later in the evening comes with its own level of intensity, but me being thrust into the spotlight as the side show is not what I had in mind. I did what I could to manage my emotions, but it takes longer than usual to clear my head before I can even think about entering the building.

I get out of Storm and take a deep breath. The kids are already staring. Girls smile at me, while the boys give thumbs-up signals…huh? What kind of information was shared overnight? Even the quick conversation with Zahra at my locker didn't provide much clarity, as she, Kyle, and Kendyl couldn't decipher much.

By the time I get to English and sit down with Kyle, the curtain has been raised on why everyone is buzzing.

"Uh, Yasir, you're gonna want to see this…" He holds his phone out to me, and I can almost see the sweat roll down his forehead.

A video that had gone viral on social media of me and Vonte going at it, with a lot of shares and comments comparing me to boxing champ Canelo Alvarez.

Fuck. This is not good.

Anyone could possibly have seen that video. What if I gave whoever-they-are a way to find me after Nana went through so much trouble to keep me hidden?

I bend forward and bang my head against the desk a few times, sighing deeply and breathing slow despite freaking out on the inside. I mean, it's high praise to be compared to the undisputed Super Middleweight champ and best pound-for-pound boxer on the planet, but this isn't what I need in my life right now. If it goes viral, it's only a matter of time before word gets back to my people in the A… including Nana. "So, the secret's out, huh?"

"Yeah, champ. You've been trending all morning," he says, seeming relieved with my response. "I'm surprised a few boxing promoters haven't been lighting your phone up," Kyle teases as he taps fists with one of the other boys in class. "I guess I need to see about having you as my bodyguard when I get to the next level. No one will want to mess with you after that performance."

"Bro, you don't understand. This is not good." I rub my hands together, feeling every ounce of nervous energy coursing through me. I shake my head as more notifications rattle off faster than lightning, adding to my anxiety levels big time. "I'm trying to keep a low profile, and this is gonna blow things way out of proportion."

"Don't sweat it, bro, there's perks to being the 'it' thing. Ask Ian," Kyle chuckles. "Man, he's liable to be hotter than fish grease by the time he gets wind of this news."

I don't give a damn about that right now. I may have put a larger target on my back than I planned. All the fears Nana had when I was growing up. What the hell have I done?

"Bro, I still don't get it. Why did he have our backs at the mall? He's been trying to bury me since I got here, and in the course of one night, we ended up on the same side?" I'm struggling to figure out what part of the high school survival manual I'm supposed to read that will explain how to deal with this. "Make it make sense, for real."

"Look, bro, it's like having a big brother growing up. He may give you the blues, teasing you at every corner, but the minute some of the boys from the neighborhood start bullying you, he and his boys will lay waste to everyone in sight. It doesn't exactly make sense, but that's the way it goes."

"You're right, it doesn't make sense, but I'm an only child, so, it probably won't ever make sense to me," I say. "It's fine if Ian tries to take me down or whatever, but outside forces don't get the luxury. Got it."

"Yeah, but trust me, he's still not your biggest fan," Kyle advises. "Don't drop your guard around him, even if he's still trying to be civil. Besides, after last night, I think a lot of the boys are starting to get a little tired of always having to back him up when it isn't necessary. What we can't do is constantly clean up messes we didn't create."

"I'm not anyone's cleanup crew, so, you don't have to worry about that out of me."

"Speaking of messes, I'm gonna need you to stay home for this next game, bro," Kyle leans in to whisper to me. "Those boys got embarrassed last night, and they're gonna want payback. We can't have your back when we're on the field and in the locker room during the game."

If he thinks I'm gonna sit on the sidelines, he has another thing coming. "That's not gonna fly, my boy. Who's gonna keep an eye on Zahra and Kendyl. They're exposed too, and someone's gotta be there to handle that."

"You've got a target on your back, Yasir." Kyle checks his phone and nods at something on the screen. "It's best if you stay out of the mix."

Yeah, nah, that's not what's gonna happen. I look at my dawg, flexing my fists to calm down as best as I can. "Who else is going to look out for them? I promise, whoever you're thinking about, I trust them as far as I can throw them."

"Well, whether you like it or not, lover boy, who we have in mind are the better option, and they don't mind getting caught up if the need arises," Kyle remarks. "I know you took them down on your own, but they're gonna be out for blood, for real. We can't tell you what to do, but I'm just saying."

"I'm not leaving Z, not after what happened the other night," I deadpan. "They know we're together, and I'm the only one who actually traded fists. The others will try to deal with you on the field, so you have to worry about that. Let me worry about the sidelines and the stands."

Kyle shrugs. My guess? He no longer wants to argue the point. "I don't think anyone will be able to get past security to even get to the girls since they'll be on the sidelines with us. The Grove still takes care of their own. If you're so insistent on being there, then you're gonna need backup. I just got word my cousin Quentin and his boys will be in town early for my party to come to the game. They're in the League, so they definitely have a presence. Maybe those extra pairs of eyes will help settle you down."

I tap my fingers against the desk, considering Kyle's alternative. If he trusts his family, then I guess I can try to trust them. "Okay, let's rock with that, I'm good."

"Good, that settles it." Kyle checks his phone again as another notification comes through. He can't stop laughing at the reference he saw from the video. "We will have your back once we bury these boys again. Besides, superstar, me and some of the boys might have to be *your* bodyguards to keep the masses away."

I suppress my laughter at that remark, but I wonder whether things are getting too far out of my control. It's one thing to keep things self-contained at Oakwood Grove, it's quite another to deal with the outside variables. One thing I know for certain: no matter what, I'm not missing the game tonight under any circumstances. If Zahra's going to support her friends, I *will* be there to protect her.

Being a fan in the stands of either team during this game is torture, for real, considering the sheer number of big hits the players from each team are taking. Neither team wants to give an inch, and if any of the star players are injured, they never let on to any of the coaches or medical staff.

"Kyle Channing breaks away for another long gain!" the announcer's voice bellows from the press box. "Oakwood Grove is inside the twenty-yard line!"

The Oakwood Grove fans are roaring, hoping for another score to break the tie, and I'm blending in with the crowd to keep from drawing too much attention to myself. I'm sitting in the stands, looking on with the rest of the Oakwood Grove fans at the carnage on the field. The battle of attrition has claimed casualties on both sides, but it has somehow spared the most important pieces on the field to keep the contest heated and even. I have no choice but to remain as helpless as the rest of the spectators and hope that the clock winds down as fast as possible.

As Kyle promised, his cousin Quentin and his friends added an extra layer of protection in case anyone got a little aggressive away from the field. I nod in their direction, grateful that I won't have to handle things on my own, despite the bravado displayed earlier in the day with Kyle. He has enough to worry about out there.

I cringe from yet another hit on Kyle as he tried to break free into the open field. He manages to get closer to the goal line, but he has to be carried off the field as he holds his midsection. Several scuffles break out in the aftermath as the officials attempt to settle things down.

The announcer tries to be the voice of reason as I notice several people trying to jump the protection fence. "Ladies and gentlemen, please refrain from entering the field and allow the officials and coaches to restore order or you will be removed from the stadium."

Yeah, this is gonna be a wild game, and it hasn't even gotten to halftime.

Zahra got pulled in for emergency duty to help with the medical equipment and hydration tents near the cheer section. I keep a closer eye on that more than the field, making sure that Zahra and Kendyl are as safe as they can be. I also sit as close as allowable in the stands and rely on silent hand gestures between me and Zahra to maintain the connection despite the higher-than-normal crowd noise that has drowned out any other communication.

I want to enjoy the subtle flirting between us, but with the heightened animosity I sense in the immediate area, I'm focused more on trying not to alarm her with my facial expressions. My phone rings, and when I see Zahra's face on the screen, I look out on the sideline, noticing her making the hand gesture to pick up the phone. She furrows her brow, bouncing her knee while she leans against the fence.

"I can feel you, Yasir. Calm down, please," Zahra says, taking her hands and turning them palms down and pushing downward.

"How are you able to feel what's going on with me, Z?" I cock my head in disbelief. We need to have some deeper conversations so I can understand her intuitive nature. "I'm calm, I don't have a choice but to be. It's not like I can do anything but play sentry."

Zahra blows a kiss, flashing a smile that takes my anxiety levels down a few notches in mere moments. I maintain eye contact with her through the next few minutes in the quarter, ignoring the outside noise in the process.

"That's better, bestie, you're much more relaxed now." I watch as her body relaxes too. "Keep that energy until the half and I'll see if I can get away to see about you." Zahra grins as she makes herself busy on the sideline.

I stand for a minute to stretch my legs. "I'm gonna grab something to drink, but I won't be long, promise. I don't want to leave you out of my sight."

"Hurry back, please. We'll be here." Zahra waves before she gets the other girls together to reset the cups on the table.

I climb the steps to make my way to the concession stand, passing by a group of boys I don't immediately recognize. The way they're staring at me, I wonder if I owe them money or something. Whatever, I'm gonna get something to drink, so I ignore them as I hit the breezeway to stand in line.

I stand in place for a good couple of minutes before I have the urge to hit the restroom. I check around to see if anyone from Beach Creek has been trailing me or not, then make the quick walk to the restroom to handle business and get out. Times like these I wish Dante and the Squad were here to have my back. Not that Kyle and the others don't, but they're on the field, taking care of business. I sigh in relief as I enter an empty area, giving me the chance to slip in and out without any further issues.

I step over to the sink so I can clean my hands and get back to the concession stand and back to my spot. I don't want Zahra to worry. I peer into the mirror for a few moments, keeping my focus trained on anyone who would come into the restroom. Thank the gods I could finish and leave; I have a taste for some nachos that needs to be handled as soon as possible.

I saunter out and… well, damn. The four of the boys I passed on the stairs are all leaning against the opposite wall, staring me down hard. They have menacing expressions on their faces, looking like they have nothing but pain on the menu, and I figure to be the main course.

That exit gate looks really good right now, and I do a quick calculation in my head, wondering how fast I can get to Storm to at least get a tire iron, anything to make this a somewhat fair fight. My gaze darts from the exit to the group, back and forth as I continue to weigh my options. I have no way to get at Quentin or the rest of my backup, so I'm left with no choice but to go with door number one.

In the next second, I break for the gate, opting for a power walk to keep anyone from noticing I'm in danger. Out of the corner of my eye, I can see the other boys chasing me, matching my pace with the same energy and speed.

I make it to the curb that leads to the parking lot, scanning for anyone who might be in harm's way. Once the coast is clear, I switch up, going from power walk to a brisk jog, still trying to keep the chase as low-key as possible until the last possible moment. I continue to glance behind me, noticing my would-be attackers are still in pursuit.

I make it to Storm, unlocking the doors and jumping into the back seat to snatch anything I have in the cargo area to defend myself. I lose sight of the boys while scrambling, and by the time I find something to pull, two pairs of hands grip my ankles and yank me to the ground. I try to turn on my back to get into a defensive position, but I feel a fist to the back of my head and another fist to the small of my back.

I grab for my back first, the pain shooting through my legs with a severe tingling sensation that borders on the inability to feel anything. I manage to turn over, with my back against the ground, to get a good look at them. One of them tries to kick at my stomach, but someone pulls him away as the others laugh at my vulnerable state.

"So, this is the one whose hands are supposed to be deadly? He don't look like much," one of the boys scoffs as he balls his fists. "How Vonte let this fool get the drop on him, I'll never know."

So, these boys are linked up with Vonte. Yeah, I should have known he might have had something to do with it, but I'll have to deal with him later. Right now, I need to get out of this without having to go to the hospital.

While I want to keep loudmouth at bay, my fight-or-flight instincts are in full-tilt fight mode. I turn to face the group, scanning to figure out the best way to defend myself. I try to sound like I'm not panicking, dropping as much bass in my voice as I can muster. "I guess you're gonna have to find out for yourself if these hands work or not, huh, bro? Your boy couldn't handle the smoke, so I guess you need your own lesson."

"Say less. Come on, boys, time to have some fun."

I slip by one of the boys, ducking a swing from the second boy trying to double-team me, dropping an elbow on the center of his back with enough force to hear a crack and that boy yell out in pain. I circle back to the first boy who rushed me, but I catch a punch to the ribs before he drives me into the side of one of the nearby cars.

I take a few more shots to my ribs before I find an opening. A swift left hook to the boy's temple drops him to his knee. I look to my left, ducking another swing from the third boy but catching something hard and metal against my knee. I howl in pain as I crash to the ground, grabbing my leg while looking up at my attackers, wondering what they might try to do to me.

In the middle of the fight, a gunshot rings out, and then a couple more after that.

I freeze instantly. I don't feel any pain from being hit, but I can't figure out which one of them has a gun. I better figure it out fast before I do get shot.

Darkness sweeps over my sight as I fight from getting overtaken. The only thing I can hear is the boys' muffled screams and a series of crashes. I attempt to push through the darkness so I can see what's going on, but the more I push, the darker the shroud becomes.

I shout against the confines of the shroud, but the silence that greets me is consuming. I continue to claw at it, but it doesn't help, and I scream out in utter frustration. I have no control, and it's pissing me off. I'm in the middle of a fight, but I'm not *in* the fight.

Before long, the shroud lifts, leaving me with a scene out of a horror film. I clasp my hand over my mouth as I take inventory of the four bodies on the ground. Blood is everywhere, and none of the bodies move. I'm too scared to check to see if any of them are still breathing, fearing that I'll leave fingerprints, and the cops may try to pin the crimes on me. My first instinct is to leave quick before someone else enters and draws their own conclusions.

Then I come to my senses. I can't leave them here like this.

I pull out my phone and call 911 to report the assault as I step over the bodies to get to Storm. I do my best not to sound calm, insistent on making it clear to the operator that the people I see on the ground need immediate help.

I know I finished what was started, but that doesn't mean that I can't have a heart.

But I'm not gonna stick around to make a statement, either. That's begging for trouble.

I open the driver's door and check around before I sit in the seat. It takes every ounce of energy I have to look like I'm not freaked out over what just happened… and I have no way of knowing what I did. Going back to the game is a no-go, so I push the ignition button and head out of there, determined to put as much distance between me and that stadium as I can. I send a text to Zahra, praying she gets it before she realizes I haven't gotten back from the concession stand.

I check the rear-view mirror once I reach the exit to the parking lot, stopping long enough to wipe the remnants of blood from my cheek with the towelettes I have in the middle compartment. I bang my hands against the steering wheel instead of screaming at the top of my lungs. Fear mixes with confusion, and I still can't figure out what happened.

My senses are on overdrive from the fight, and I hear the distinct screams of the people who'd happened upon the boys I… I'm not sure if I killed them or caused critical damage. I block out the frantic voices and continued screams as I push the accelerator and peel out of the parking lot. I need to get home and get myself together before I go back to campus to pick Zahra up.

I wish I could chalk this night up to a horrible nightmare, but I was awake for every second, and helpless to stop it.

Even more terrifying? I didn't want to.

Chapter Twenty-Five – Yasir

Panic comes close to consuming me.

I pos up in the parking lot, thoughts racing through my mind as my heart pounds through my chest. I struggle to keep calm, but can you blame me? I mean, after the scene I left about a half-hour ago, I'm surprised I remembered how to breathe.

I've never felt more alone.

What have I done?

The wind blowing through the trees sends a shiver up my spine, lending to the uncertainty of the moment. I keep Storm running since the weather decided to turn colder than usual, and I need to keep warm. Or maybe I feel cold because I don't know what happened at the stadium and I'm left to my vivid and overactive imagination.

I don't know who I can trust. There's no way to know if those kids are dead or alive without going back to check, and I can't take that chance. I'll give myself away in a heartbeat. I'm not a criminal, but I would've acted like I was guilty.

I play the whole thing out in my head over and over, or as much as I can recall, anyway. The howl of the wind sounds so judgmental, almost condemning me for not sticking around. I convinced myself that not checking the bodies was the right move. My fingerprints would have been all over the place.

Man, I've been watching too many episodes of *Law & Order: Organized Crime* with Unk. At least I called for help before I left the area. If anything, someone will have heard something and relayed the message that those boys aren't dead.

Even the campus rattles my nerves a bit. The forest that surrounds the school seems to roil and sway as the wind whips through it. Maybe it's my own paranoia playing all sorts of tricks on my mind, but I swear the trees are talking among themselves, judging me.

A series of rapid-fire pops causes another fight-or-flight response as I duck down into the middle console to avoid whatever was being shot. But after hearing a few more pops against the hood of my Jeep and then on the ground, I realize it's nothing more than pecans being shaken from the trees. I grip the steering wheel tight, upset with myself that I've gotten so skittish. I need to get my life quick.

I dial Dante on instinct. I'm not sure if I wanted to call him or not, but I have to get this off my chest. He knows where the other secrets are buried, and I need him to bury one more. I close my eyes as the phone trills, half expecting him to not answer. They're at a rivalry game, and the noise level has to be ridiculous.

I hear the background noise and know he's still at the game. "What's good, little bro? I didn't expect to hear from you until sometime tomorrow."

I hesitate in that instant. Do I tell him? Squad would find out the minute I do, and that might create more problems.

"Yo, you good, my boy?"

Now I'm stuck in my head, playing a quick game of chess to make sure this is the right move to make. If I tell him, then it gets back to… *her*. I'm not prepared for that at all, but this has the potential to crush me if I keep it bottled up. Every time I close my eyes, all I see are the bodies lying around me in such unnatural positions that I can't deny what I've done. I have to accept the fact that I might have taken a life.

I want to throw up.

"Diablo."

That gets my attention. Full stop.

He only uses my nickname when he needs me to focus and get things done. It's obvious he wants me to focus. Consider me focused. "I hear you, Hades."

"Good, you're hearing me, now tell me what's happened."

I hate it when he could read me like that. "Things have gotten a bit wild down here. I might have caught a few bodies. At least, I think I did… I don't know right now. It's hard to explain."

Dead silence on the line for several minutes, except for the shouting and screaming of the crowd in the stands. I don't freak out yet; this is the routine between me and my "big brother." I wait for him to sort through his thoughts before I think about saying something.

The background noise dies down, leading me to guess that he's headed away from the stands so he can hear me more clearly. "Okay, either you caught bodies, or you didn't, Ya-Ya. I mean, it's only been a month, what have you been doing down there?"

I hear a call coming through, and I pull the phone away from my ear and notice it's Zahra calling me. The game must be over, and they can't find me. Dammit. Not good. I send the call to voicemail so I can focus on Dante.

"Nothing," I snap back before I catch myself. "These boys play by a different set of rules down here, Te. All I've been doing is keeping my head down and doing me."

"Yeah, I feel you, but when you're just doing you, people get salty. You that dude." Dante starts talking to someone, but I can't make out the convo between them. He comes back to the phone to make a simple statement that's not so simple. "Let me move some things around, and we'll be down there in a couple of days."

"That's not necessary."

"It's obvious to me that it is necessary." I hear a tone out of Dante that I haven't heard since someone tried to come for Nana a couple of years ago. "I knew better than to let you talk me out of having someone watch your back down there."

"Aye, look, I can handle myself," I bark, this time not caring about how he would respond. "You got me twisted if you're gonna treat me like some rookie on the block. If you're coming down here, it's because you and Squad wanna come through."

"This isn't up for discussion. I promised Nana that I would keep you safe."

"Nope, it isn't. Leave the heat at home if you come through. I mean it."

The line goes quiet again, agitating me. I'm not backing down this time. I'm just starting to get a grip on how things work down here, and the last thing I need is my old life colliding head on with my current one. I'm not ashamed of it, not by a long shot, but I've slowly come to the realization that some things don't need to follow me.

“I got you, Ya-Ya. We’ll wait things out up here… for now.”

I exhale slow and easy, looking skyward, shaking my head over dodging that bullet. “Thanks, big bro. I mean that. I need time to work through things down here. Once I’m good, I’ll make a trip to the A. I miss my people.”

“Yeah, your presence is missed, too… by some more than others.”

Another call comes through from Zahra. I send it to voicemail again, but I know she’s gonna keep calling until I answer my phone. I don’t need her panicking and then the rest of the crew has to get involved.

That veiled comment freezes me. “I know what you’re doing, but there’s nothing I can do about that now. I’m iced out, and I can’t get around that until she unblocks me.”

“I feel you, and I’ll do what I can on my end. You need to make that right, and you know it.”

“Say less. When I’m up there next. Promise.”

I switch up my headspace as quickly as I can. There’s a lot to process tonight, and while I can’t be sure that what happened tonight won’t come back to bite me, I can’t worry about it right now. I have to make Zahra believe that I’m okay.

But if I’m honest with myself, I’m *not* okay.

Chapter Twenty-Six – Zahra

We can't find Yasir.

He isn't anywhere in the stadium. Quentin and his boys checked to be sure.

Storm's gone too.

This isn't good. I can feel it.

I panicked when I couldn't find him during the halftime period. It amplified once we received word to shelter in place on the field due to a horrific assault in the parking lot. The only thing I had to cling to was the cryptic text he sent, saying he left to handle an emergency at home, and he'd call me when he found out what happened.

Kendyl's doing her best to keep me calm, but we're too busy absorbing

the details swirling around in the stands. The condition of the boys involved makes things difficult to digest until we hear back from Yasir. Kendyl takes my phone away so I don't obsess over waiting for his call, a text, anything, distracting me the best way she can with other nonsensical things.

The officials called the game, giving us the win since we had the lead. The Beach Creek High fans booed the final score, only changing their tune once the detectives explained everything.

Now that all the confusion has died down, my concern remains with finding Yasir. "Have you seen anything at all, Kenni? He should've called by now."

She shakes her head, placing a hand over my forearm. "He'll turn up soon, babe. I'm sure he's okay. He said it was an emergency at home, right? Maybe he'll call once that's been handled."

"But what if he's one of the boys they're talking about? We need to find out what's going on."

Kendyl presses her index finger against my lips. “Don’t say those things, chica. Yasir can handle himself. I’m sure he’s far away from the area. We just need to be patient and wait for him to call.”

As we board the buses to head back to campus, Kyle and Taylor meet up with us. They both look like they’ve been through hell, with Taylor still holding his bruised ribs and walking slow enough to resemble a man in his elder years.

Kyle winces through his smile as he greets us. “We heard about the mess in the parking lot. At least we know Yasir isn’t among the victims.”

“How did you find that out? We’ve been trying to get information for the past fifteen minutes,” Kendyl replies. “How in the hell did you find out anything?”

“Ian. His father sent officers to make sure no Oakwood Grove students were harmed,” Taylor states. “They were Beach Creek kids, but from the rumors running wild, they were the rougher kids in the school. A lot of the Beach Creek players weren’t too concerned about whether they were alive or not. In fact, the way they looked, it’s almost like something did the school a favor.”

“Something?” Kendyl gives me a curious glance, and I can’t do much more than shrug. I don’t have the slightest clue. “They don’t think a person did this?”

“According to Ian, it’s being called an animal attack,” Taylor explains to us. “This is getting weirder by the minute, and no one has a clue of what’s going on.”

“None of that matters until I hear from Yasir.” I’m done being patient, and I make sure everyone in the immediate area knows it. “Give me my phone. If I have to blow up his phone, then that’s what I’ll do.”

Kendyl hesitates for a moment before I give her a scowl that’s sharp enough to cut through a diamond. I sit on a nearby bench and begin texting Yasir in rapid-fire succession. Whether he likes it or not, he’s going to hear from me.

I’ve only gotten off a few texts before my phone rings. My heart skips a few beats as I connect the call. Any anger I feel dissolves in seconds. “Yasir, tell me you’re okay, please? We heard about what happened in the parking lot, were you caught up in it?”

The pause on the other line almost causes a panic attack. "I'm… I'm okay, I promise. I'm on campus waiting for you as we speak. I'm sorry it took so long to get back with you, something weird happened at the harbor with Unk's boat, and we went to check it out."

I take the phone from my ear and press it against my chest, closing my eyes and mumbling thank you before I place the phone to my ear again. "There was an attack of some sort at the game, and some kids from Beach Creek were hurt. I was scared that you were caught up with them."

I grin as I hear him exhale over the line. "I kept my head on a swivel the whole night. Besides, we have more than a few things to do this weekend. The last thing I wanted was to add a hospital stay to the itinerary. I don't look all that great in a hospital gown."

I stifle a burst of laughter, holding my index finger up to let everyone know things are okay. "I can't wait to see you back on campus."

"Neither can I, but I have to admit, I may need to be a good boy tonight and take you straight home. We have brunch with my uncle and his new girlfriend."

I blink a few times, caught off guard by the additional guest. "Um, so, when did you plan on telling me about that?"

"I promise, it's not an ambush," Yasir stresses to me. "Remember when I told you that once I trusted you, I had no problems telling you things as I learn them? Well, about that."

I want to choke him. I still may do that when I see him, once I make sure he's really okay. "You could've set that up a little better, Yasir. So, what's going on that the extra guest is invited to witness?"

"Nah, it doesn't work like that," Yasir teases. "I promise it isn't anything too wild. Well, at least, I don't know how you might react."

"You're lucky I like you or I would cancel on you without a second thought," I giggle. "We can talk about things the minute I slide into my Jeep."

"*Your* Jeep? When did we come to that agreement?"

"When you decided to spring some epic secret on me with less than twenty-four hours' notice," I switch the phone to speaker so Kendyl can hear my next words. "That's a best friend code violation, which means your Jeep is now half mine as penance for your oversight. Isn't that right, Kenni?"

"Best friend code? Wait a minute—"

Kendyl can't play up the shenanigans quick enough. "Yes! So, when are you picking me up in your Jeep, sis? And he better make sure it's gassed up and cleaned out too. We have things to do this weekend!"

"See, you can't disrespect the code." I take the phone off speaker so I can resume the call privately. "I really am glad you're not hurt, Yasir. I wouldn't have been able to function, and I probably would've gone hunting for whoever did it to you."

"Hopefully, it won't have to come to that, *best friend*," Yasir says. I'm not sure if I want to feel some kinda way about the sarcasm in his voice, but he switches up and sounds like his normal, laid-back self. "I'll see you when you get here. I'll be posted up with Storm, and I'll have the neon glowing, so you'll know where to find me."

I disconnect the call, smiling to myself over the possibilities of what Yasir has to tell me. I wonder if it has anything to do with the changes in his eye color when he's thinking about something or when he's irritated. Or even when he's giving that "look" that makes me melt, even though he shouldn't be looking at me like that.

The next thing I hear is the quick finger snapping from Kendyl. "Earth to Z, come in, Zahra. What's going on, and can we know why you went from homicidal rage to kitten calm during one phone call, please?"

I shake out of my thoughts, leaning back in my seat as the bus pulls off. "He's okay, and he's on campus so he can take me home. We have some things to talk about. It seems tomorrow's brunch date just got a lot more interesting."

Chapter Twenty-Seven – Zahra

Sure enough, Storm's glowing in her amethyst-tinged glory, making it easy to find her—and Yasir.

Her engine rumbles as I approach, and her tall and handsome owner gives me a glance that should've melted me where I stand, regardless of how cold it is out here. By Nyati, I need to find a way to build up a tolerance to what he does to me.

He keeps his hands inside the pockets of his Miles Morales inspired airbrushed hoodie, but he looks worn down. He still has a smile plastered on his face as he waits until the last minute to take them out to wrap his arms around me. He flinches before he squeezes me tighter, and then walks me to the passenger side to let me in.

I'm not letting him off the hook, not when the bruises on his face and hands are exposed.

I sink into the leather seats as the heat inside the cabin casts its spell, warming me from the inside out. I wave at Kendyl as she hops into Kyle's truck, making the hand gesture for her to call me when she gets home. Yasir opens the driver's side door and quickly jumps in. The wind is disrespectful tonight. "Let's get you home."

We pull out onto the street, heading away from campus to make the short drive home. He has the Afrobeat rocking, bumping Ladipoe and Burna Boy as usual, but he shocks me when the tracks switched over to Ayra Starr and Tems, and then came back to the States with H.E.R. and Tyla, Chloe and Megan Thee Stallion. I don't know if he's rocking out to keep from talking about why he disappeared like he did, but I have no problems pressing pause to get answers.

No matter how much I try to ignore it, the bruises on his knuckles and the smudge of blood on his neck make it difficult. While I'm relieved he's okay, regardless of whatever he said he was doing, I'm worried that he's gotten himself into something.

I pick up the phone to pause the music, turning my body to focus my attention on him. I grab his hand before he can jerk it away, reaching into the middle console to grab some wet wipes and napkins to clean the area. I frown as he winces in pain, reacting to the stinging the alcohol has on his open wounds. "Do you want to tell me what happened?"

"Do you really wanna know?"

"I never ask questions I don't want the answers to."

Yasir nods, still jerking as I finish cleaning his right hand. He switches to give me his left hand, which doesn't look as bad, but that's not my main concern. "I don't know if I want to tell you or not. It will keep you out of the mix in case something else happens."

"Do you mean the weird scene at the game tonight?" I don't have time to play around, and this mysterious urge to protect him rises from out of nowhere. It catches me off guard, but I don't run from it, either. "The police said that the Beach Creek kids were taken to the hospital with really bad injuries."

"I'm surprised it wasn't worse."

"You're *what*?" I blink a few times to make sure I heard him. It doesn't sound like him, but it came out of his mouth. "Were you there? Tell me what happened."

He glares at me, but I don't back down from my questions. I press into his cuts, causing him to scream out in pain. "Alright, damn, you don't have to torture me, Z."

"If that's what it takes to find out the truth, then, yep, it's gonna happen."

Yasir takes a sharp breath and exhales hard. "Those boys Kyle and I ran into at the mall had some friends in the stands. They followed me out to the concession area, and when I tried to make a run for Storm, they cornered me and tried to inflict some major damage."

"So, it's safe to say that didn't happen." I find some cloths to wrap his right hand and keep it from getting infected. "How did you manage to get out of there and they caught the worst of it? I'm so confused… and low-key feeling safe at the same time."

"I didn't plan for any of that to happen, Z." His hand trembles beneath mine, and he groans when he tries to squeeze my hand again. "I don't even know if I killed any of them or not, but they weren't moving, and I got scared and ran before anyone could find out I was there."

"Well, for now, I don't think they're gonna worry about looking for anyone. They're calling it an animal attack."

I think it'll calm him down to know, but he closes his eyes and strains to keep from screaming. I release my grip, taking my hand to caress his cheek. "It might give us some time to figure things out."

"There's nothing to figure out."

"It was self-defense, Yasir."

He doesn't say much of anything for a couple of miles, waiting until he turns into my subdivision before he breaks the silence. "I'm sorry I lied to you about where I was, Zahra. I have a hard time trusting people. I'm already the new face in town, and all these different incidents keep popping up. It won't take long for someone to try to figure out if I have anything to do with any of it."

"You can trust me, okay? But I need you to keep it a buck." I turn his head as soon as he pulls into the driveway. "Between me, Kyle, Taylor and Kenni, we'll figure out something if and when the time comes. Now, tell me about this brunch thing tomorrow. Is there anything I need to prepare myself for?"

"Well, you get to meet my uncle, so there's that." He smiles for the first time the whole night. "And his new girlfriend too… okay, wait, before you say anything, it really wasn't my idea."

"Mhm, you sure about that?" I narrow my gaze as I ignore the cut above his left eye. It looks like he'd already treated it. "You sure you didn't want to show me off too?"

My gaze never leaves his, and I feel the heat from his fingers on my knee through the thermal leggings I wore under my jeans to keep warm while on the sidelines. I want him to kiss me, but I don't want to tell him to. For the sake of the gods, why am I torturing myself like this?

"Maybe I do want to show you off, but I wonder if I should invite some of the others to be there too." I can't stare into his eyes anymore, focusing on the image of Miles' face, hoping to break the spell he has me under. "That way, we won't be tempted, right?"

"Right. No temptation." Yeah, right. It won't matter having Kenni there, and we both know it. "I think we can survive without the audience, can't we?"

"I think so. I think my uncle and his girl will be audience enough." Yasir rolls his eyes and chuckles to himself. "He's gonna give me the business the minute you show up."

"He's got to be excited for you. Having a pretty girl come to the house to see about his nephew." I tease. "I can hear him now saying, 'Yo, I see you, nephew.' I can't wait."

"And this is where you get out of my car and head inside." Yasir hops out and rushes around the front to let me out. "I'll see you in the morning."

"Well, you're no fun at all."

"Yes, I am, but you'll have to find out another time. Good night."

I slide out of the car, doing my best to wipe the silly grin off my face. I'm still concerned about what really happened and what's really going on with him, but we can have that talk when we make the drive up to Atlanta.

Whether he likes it or not, he's gonna learn that there's not much he can do to make me change my mind about him.

Even if I'm being ambushed in the morning with absolutely no advanced notice.

Things could get very interesting in the morning.

And I can't wait to see what happens next.

Chapter Twenty-Eight – Yasir

"Hey, come on in. We're just finishing up the menu now."

Nova-star-level heat and nerves flow through me as I invite Zahra to come through the door. I've been looking forward to this all night, and I'm worried I've built things up to be more than what it might be in reality. This step feels right, it cements things on a different plane for me, and even though we aren't official, later at Kyle's birthday party later today could change things. Today has "EPIC" written all over it. I can feel it. The minute I kiss her cheek to say hello, though, all my other thoughts disappear in a plume of smoke.

I escort Zahra into the dining area, where Unk and Lennox, his new love, await. The food has been laid out buffet style, which surprises me a bit. I thought we were sitting down to eat. Oh well, I guess I'll shake that off to be the other host for this occasion. "Unk, Ms. Lennox, I'd like to introduce my friend, Zahra Assante. Z, you already know about my uncle, but Ms. Lennox was the other person I told you about last night."

Unk rises from his seat at the head of the table and saunters over to greet Zahra with a handshake. "I'm thrilled you could make it. I know last night was particularly rough. Even Yasir looked like he'd been through a fight or two, and he wasn't even on the field."

Zahra flashes a smile, looking over at me as if to ask if Unk knows what happened last night after the game. I shrug; I didn't plan to tell him much of anything… unless I had no other choice. "Thank you for inviting me. I've heard a lot about you."

"And the feeling is mutual. He's been floating around here the past few weeks." Unk chuckles. "Please, have a seat, enjoy whatever looks good to you. Ya-Ya and I have been at it all morning to make sure you all can enjoy."

I cringe at the mention of my nickname in Zahra's presence. No, he didn't just drop that in the middle of the conversation… *ugh.* "Yeah, I had a hand in the shrimp and grits and a few other things."

"You didn't say you could cook." Zahra cuts her eyes at me as she sits in the seat at the other end of the table. "You're just full of surprises… *Ya-Ya.*"

"You're lucky I like you—only family calls me that," I correct her. I'm never gonna live that down. If she ever calls me that in school, there goes my rep. "I'm not gonna lie, though, it sounds kinda good coming off your lips."

"Oh my God, you two are so freaking cute," Lennox gushes as she takes a bite of her pancakes. "You two are so connected, don't ask me how I know, I just have a feeling when I see you together. You just … fit."

Unk pulls Lennox to him, placing a finger to his lips. "They're just *friends*, babe. I don't know what's the hold up, but that's their story and they're sticking to it."

"I don't care what they're talking about, you two are absolutely stunning together. You are gorgeous, Zahra." Lennox sits down in the chair across from us, shaking her head as she gazes at us. "From what Xavion has told me, you've had a positive effect on his nephew. I can see why; there's a glow about you, young lady."

Zahra blushes and leans into me. "Thank you, Ms. Lennox, but I don't know if I've had as much influence as people think I have. We haven't been around each other that long, but I'll take it if you're saying it too."

"You should take the compliment, I'm awesome like that, but you'll find out soon enough. Both of you will," Lennox quips. "Look, Yasir, I've grown to care for your uncle deeply, and I hope that we will have the chance to build a friendship. You're important to him, which means you're important to me, okay?"

Okay, she pulls that card on me real quick. She's right, though. I don't remember the last time he smiled like that. It's a good look. "I hear you, Ms. Lennox. I look forward to it."

Unk does his best to cut the convo short and save me from a few more embarrassing moments. "Okay, I need to get you out of here before you really have my nephew regretting doing this get together.

Besides, they need some privacy, and we still have a series to finish streaming."

Lennox rises from her chair, grabbing some of the dishes as she makes her way into the kitchen with Unk. "Fine, since your uncle wants to leave you two to your privacy, I *guess* I can lay off the inquisition for now. Oh, and I'm really not buying that 'best friends' bit, okay? I'm just saying."

Zahra watches Lennox head outside and once she closes the door, she lets a giggle escape her lips. "Are you sure your uncle is ready for all of that?"

"Yeah, I think he is, but it's going to be a wild ride, I can tell." I rise from the couch, offering my hand for her to stand. "Would you like to see the surprise I have for you?"

"Lead the way, handsome. I can't wait to see it."

"By Nyati, these paintings are beautiful," Zahra says. "It's like you captured the essence of my home country with each stroke and color. I almost feel like I can step inside and be right there. Are you sure you've never been there before?"

"No, I created them from a few pictures my Unk had. Do you like them?" I roll up the most recent painting she viewed, moving to place it into the bin with the rest. "I think they still need a lot of work, but I've been studying some new techniques to try to give them a more hyper-realistic feel. I *want* people to feel like they can step inside them."

Zahra turns around and slips her hands around mine, gazing into my eyes. I want to turn away, but she's so captivated, I don't want to ruin the moment. "I could feel *everything*… the sun on my face, the ocean breeze, even the water near the river tribes. You made me miss home."

I smile, pressing my forehead against hers. "I was afraid to show them to you," I admit. "Outside of Unk, no one has seen my paintings before. I figured that I could trust you with some of the things that mean the most to me. I trust you, Z."

"Ugh, if you wanted me to fall for you in one singular moment, this was that moment. I'm glad you can trust me. It means a lot to me."

I glance toward the ceiling before meeting her gaze again. I will the words to come out of my mouth and pray that they don't sound like something out of a sappy *Lifetime* movie. Nothing ventured, nothing gained, right? "I know we're supposed to just be friends and everything, but the weird part of it all …"

Zahra picks up on my voice trailing off. "Tell me."

"It feels like we were made for each other, as cliché as it sounds," I confess. "There's something that I feel deep in my core every time our eyes meet, like there's more between us, but I can't figure out what it is that connects us deeper."

Zahra looks away, but I don't force the issue. I want her to feel safe, but I have to get my thoughts out before they eat me alive. She focuses her gaze on a corner of a painting on the easel in the center of the studio. She breaks from our embrace to peek under the cloth that conceals the rest of the painting.

I grab her hand in a knee-jerk response to not wanting her to see what lay beneath the cloth. "I'm sorry, it's just that… it's sort of a work in progress, and I don't know if I'm ready for you to see it yet."

"Too late to be shy now. What's the image of that has you so nervous?"

I know I said I trusted her, and now it's proving to be my downfall. Oh well, it's not like she won't see it eventually. "It's a painting… of you."

Zahra widens her eyes as her gaze falls back to the concealed painting, then shifts to my face before pivoting back to the painting. She turns to face me and slips close enough to tiptoe and brush her lips against my face. "I understand if you think it needs to be perfect, but I promise I'll love it regardless. I want to know how you see me."

I breathe deep, turning her around to face the painting. "Take off the cloth so you can see how I see you … well, at least one version of you."

She tugs on the paint-splattered cloth, watching it slide off the top of the easel. Everything seems to flow in slow motion as the painting reveals itself from top to bottom, uncovering a stunning, full-bodied portrait of Z in a formal dress and head wrap. She gasps as she sees her body adorned in golden arm cuffs wrapped around her biceps in a spiral, snake-like pattern, and rings on her index fingers and thumbs. A diamond and amethyst encrusted pendant rests against her chest, along with matching earrings that look like they drip from her earlobes.

She keeps turning her head back to me as though she can't believe what she sees. From the meticulous attention to detail around her eyes and the contouring of her cheekbones, to the way her lips were splashed in the black, gold, and purple color scheme of the Kindaran flag. She marvels at her portrait on the canvas. Her braids are swept up into a ponytail with a matching headwrap encased around her hair, giving a playful-but-serious look to her face.

Zahra covers her mouth with her hands as she stares at the dress, and I notice her fingers shaking. A halter-neck maxi dress, also in the Kindaran flag colors, shows cut-out patterns on the sides of her waist, and from the slight side profile of the portrait, it's clear to see that the dress is backless, stopping a few inches below the middle of her back. From there, the dress flows down to about three inches from the ground, where diamond-encrusted strapped heels are on her feet.

Okay, she still hasn't said anything. "If you don't like it, I can start over and rip this one up."

Her hands are still covered over her mouth, and I brace myself against the overwhelming emotions coursing through me. "By Nyati," she says, "it's like you took my essence and captured everything I wanted to exude. I can't believe that's how you see me."

"So, I don't need to change it, right?"

She turns around and faces me, wiping a tear from her cheek. "Don't you dare touch this painting, please don't change anything. It's so vivid. I feel like I'm looking in the mirror."

I exhale, bringing her hands to my lips. "You had me worried for a minute. I spent the past few nights trying to get this right before I got up the nerve to show it to you."

Zahra wraps her arms around my neck, pressing her lips against mine so hard it blurs my vision. I quickly lose myself in the kiss between us, despite the confusing emotions swirling in my head. I pull away, but she holds me in place, almost like she's determined to keep me there in the moment with her. She deepens her kisses, taking steps with me as we move backwards.

She giggles the moment we hit the wall, smiling as she gives me silent encouragement to keep going. I slip my hands around her waist, the intoxicating scent of her perfume causing near dizzy spells. She locks her fingers around the back of my neck as I lift her off the ground.

"Are you sure about this, Z?" I ask between kisses, shaking off the dizzy spells. By Nyati, her lips are so soft. "Should we be doing this? I mean… we can stop, this isn't…"

"Don't stop kissing me, Ya-Ya," Zahra whispers in my ear before caressing my neck to make a path back to my lips. "We're just kissing. *Friends* can kiss, remember?"

Before I lose my nerve, I pull Zahra closer, focusing on her lips before I close my eyes. I lose my breath all over again the second our lips touch and fight every instinct to pull away. Every nerve is on fire and getting hotter by the minute. Okay, so, um… I've never kissed a girl like *this* before, and the energy coursing through my body scares me beyond my capacity to understand what's happening.

I almost rip myself away, bringing my fingers to my lips in disbelief over what we'd done. I can't look up, can't handle her reaction. I vibrate from head to toe, willing the insecurities that want to rise to the surface to stay in the depths of my mind. I swear I feel hot to the touch and I'm close to passing out.

When I finally get my nerves together to meet Zahra's gaze, I come face to face with a confused expression I hoped wouldn't be there. "Umm… Zahra, I… I wanted to… well, that is to say…"

Zahra grins at me, placing an index finger against my lips to quiet me mid-sentence. "It's okay, I liked it. Actually, I liked it a lot."

I let out a long exhale, placing her hand against my chest to try to slow my rapid heartbeat. "It's been a minute since… let me stop lying… I've never kissed a girl before. I'm… did I do it right? I don't know what to say right now."

Zahra leans in closer, purring in my ear, "Yasir… kiss me again."

I blink a few times. Is this actually happening? "Are you sure? Like, really?"

"Yes, silly… I can show you how I want you to kiss me, if you'd like?" Zahra gives a knowing wink. "Did you like kissing me?"

"Is that a trick question?"

Zahra rubs her nose against mine, coaxing me as she stares into my eyes. "Then kiss me, Yasir."

I cup my hands around her face this time, mimicking some movie scene I committed to memory or something. I stare into her eyes again, only this time, I notice her studying them. "What's wrong? Is there something on my face or something?"

"Your eyes… they've turned colors," she says, her gaze never looking away from mine. "They're this shade of purple, like an amethyst gemstone… they're so beautiful, I can't stop staring."

The uncertainty washes over me like a waterfall. I have no idea what she's talking about, my eyes have always been a mix between amber gold and light brown. For her to say my eyes were on a whole other color spectrum has me a slight bit panicked.

I draw back again, but Zahra keeps me with her. I don't resist when she brushes her lips against mine, but I still have her last thoughts flowing through my head. What's happening to me? My eyes have never done that before. Was she playing with me?

She keeps at it, playfully kissing my chin, then my nose. "Oh, no, you're not getting away again. Kiss me… Yasir, kiss me."

Despite my best efforts. I can't concentrate on being in the moment with her. "Zahra, there might be something—"

"We can deal with that later… kiss me."

I give in to her wishes—or at least my body does—and slip my hands around her waist, losing myself in the embrace. I retreat to the recesses of my mind, intent on traveling as we continue our interlude. I hope it will settle me down so I can enjoy this moment.

I conjure the first image that comes to mind, taking me across the Atlantic and to one of my favorite places on my bucket list, Victoria Falls in Zambia.

In a blink, I'm floating above the majestic beauty of the largest waterfall in the world, its size literally forming the border between Zambia and Zimbabwe. I gaze over the expansive curtain of falling water, marveling at the columns of spray rising from the falls, almost feeling the water against my skin, providing a refreshing reprieve from the heat of the day. I smile as I locate the Knife-Edge Bridge, setting down on the platform to take advantage of the special vantage point of the Eastern Cataract and the Main Falls and the area called the Boiling Pot, where the Zambezi River turns and heads down the

Batoka Gorge. The awe-inspiring sight was exactly what I need to get in sync with Zahra.

I'm so taken with the view that I don't notice Zahra standing next to me with a stunned expression on her face. I struggle to understand how she's there, too, and can't find the words.

Let's be real. I'm at a loss for words to explain *how* she's here with me. How in the world is this even possible?

She grabs my arm, almost too scared to move. "How are we here, Yasir? We were just in your room, and now we're in… Africa? How are you doing this?"

I shrug at her questions, unsure how to answer them. How the hell am I supposed to know how she's here with me? I was in a zone, trying to balance my psyche, but I'm really worried over how I did this, and how can I get us out of whatever I just did.

Even though I'm terrified and doing my best to keep Zahra from freaking out with me, I'm happy she's in the space with me. That's probably the only reason I'm not screaming right now. It's bad enough we're floating inside my head and can feel and see and hear everything surrounding us. What scares me the most is staring into the bottom of the falls and praying that I don't lose concentration, and we end up falling out of the sky.

No point in arguing the why of it all, I'm content to enjoy the ride—even if I'm confuzzled as hell with no way to figure out how to get out of this conjured daydream. "Do you want to see more? I think we still have some time to kill."

"You still haven't explained how we're literally somewhere else other than back home in Oakwood Grove," Zahra insists as she grabbed my hand. "I feel like I should be freaking out, but I can't understand why I'm not freaking out. What's going on?"

"I have no idea how to answer your questions because this is the first time someone else has been in this space with me." But she seems to be okay. "Do you trust me?"

"Do I have a choice?" Zahra holds my hand tighter, wrapping her arm around mine. "I don't know if I'm dreaming or if this is real."

She's not the only one. I suppress the rising fear in my heart and keep moving forward, holding her tight around her waist as we lift from the bridge and take flight. In seconds, we land at the base of Mt.

Kilimanjaro in Tanzania, taking in the snowcaps that adorned the three volcanic cones and the rest of the top of the mountain. The descending sun provides the backdrop to a tide of elephants making their way across the savanna outside of the massive mountain forest that encircles it. I smile wide as I observe the captivated look on Zahra's face. We take a few more seconds to enjoy one of the Seven Summits on the planet.

"Ready for the next stop?" I'm getting a little more comfortable with what's going on, and I begin to remember how I leave when I'm meditating. That calms me down a lot more and gives me more control over things.

Before she can answer, we fly in a flash farther north into the land of the pharaohs, arriving at a location that draws another confuzzled glance from Zahra. "Where are we now?"

"Abu Simbel. It's one of my favorite places in the world." I'm beaming as we gaze up at the statue of Rameses II and the smaller statues at his feet.

"Well, don't keep me in suspense. Why?"

"Because Rameses had a temple dedicated to his wife, Queen Nefertari, and the smaller statues that surround his feet are of her and their children, along with his mother." I guide her around the base of the statues, enjoying the monument all over again through her eyes. "Standing monuments to their love to last beyond their lifetimes. Who wouldn't want that?"

I stare into her eyes, smiling over the wonder in her expression. "What's on your mind, if you don't mind me asking?"

"Ask me when we get back," she says.

One last burst across the burning sands of the Sahara with what feels like light speed, and we're back in my studio. We settle into our bodies again, breaking from our kiss and searching around to see if anything has changed around us. I hold her in my arms, waiting for her to get her bearings.

"Umm, that was one helluva kiss, boy, are you sure that was your first time?" Zahra's trying to catch her breath, fanning herself the entire time. "What would you do for an encore? Good grief."

I chuckle, keeping my hands around her waist to keep her steady. "That depends on whether you want to stick around to find out."

Zahra looks at her watch, shocked that only five minutes had passed by while we were, quite literally, on the other side of the world. "Oh, I'm definitely sticking around, but… wait, how in the world did you… was any of that real? Our bodies were still right here and… wow, all that from just a kiss?"

"I really have no clue, but it was all real," I reply. I'm serious, I really don't. "All I wanted to do was show you what was in my mind. Everything else is as surprising to me as it is to you."

Zahra plants a series of kisses across my lips over and over. "I only have one more question, in light of tonight's 'excursion,' Mr. Salah."

"Yes, Ms. Assante?"

"When can we do *that* again?"

I crack up laughing. "I don't have a problem with that at all."

"You know, we're going to have to talk about how you did all of that, right?" Zahra remarks. "My head is still spinning."

A knock on the door makes us jump.

"Ahem… Ya-Ya, I wanted to check on you two," Unk bellows through the door. "It's almost two in the afternoon, we have to get to it if we're gonna get this order to your friend's birthday party. You need time to get back, get ready, and not be late."

I break from our embrace, looking skyward, wanting to scream. "Gotcha, Unk. I'll be ready to roll in ten minutes."

"All right, bet, kiddo. Wheels spin in ten."

Zahra buries her face in my chest, shaking her head. "Do you think he heard?"

"I know he heard us, but I'll deal with that during the delivery," I counter. "Am I wrong for thinking that everything around us completely disappeared while we were… well, you know?"

Zahra shuts her eyes as she taps her forehead against my chest a few times. "You're not wrong at all. I was in that space with you, and I didn't want to come out, period. I'm still feeling some kinda way about being ripped back to reality without my consent."

She blushes for a moment, pulling me over to a mirror on the other side of the studio. "Umm, we might need to not be so obvious."

I search for a napkin to wipe the traces of her lipstick from my face and lips. "I'm with you on the rip, that's for sure, but there's nothing we can do about that now. Come on, I'll walk you to your car."

Before we leave, I catch a glimpse of what Zahra tried to explain before we kissed. My eyes have a strong purple glow, around my irises. I blink a few times, not believing what I'm seeing, and the glow seems to consume the whole of my irises now. *What's happening to me? This isn't normal.*

"Are you okay?" Zahra slips into my sight, moving her head so I don't have a choice but to face her. "Is it the thing with your eyes?"

I shake my head violently like I'm trying to get rid of whatever is happening. I breathe a sigh of relief when I look in the mirror and see my eyes have returned to their usual hue. "I think so, not sure what that was about. I guess it was some residual whatever from when we came back."

We walk downstairs, bypassing the adults as they continue chatting, stopping long enough to wave goodbye to Zahra before returning to their conversation. Once outside, the warmer-than-usual-for-fall South Georgia air hits us, which does nothing to quell the residual heat we tried to temper only minutes ago.

I kiss her lips once more before tucking her into the driver's seat. I wink and she pushes the ignition to start the car. "You know we're gonna have to pick this up again soon, right? And I don't mean just the kiss, either."

"That's an understatement," she says, then motions for me to lean down to steal one more kiss. "Now, be a good boy and get things squared away with Unk. I need you freshly oiled and looking good enough to eat later tonight, okay? See you in a couple of hours."

Chapter Twenty-Nine – Zahra

Watching Kendyl's eyes grow as big as the full moon overhead as she gawks at Storm's interior, it feels like I'm viewing Yasir's pride and joy all over again. With its deep purple neon accents that matched the undercarriage neon, she's a sight to behold. I've gotten used to it over the past few weeks, but it impressed the hell out of me when I first sat inside.

"Damn, boy, this is one of the nicest Jeeps I've ever seen!" she says as she continues to run her fingers along the seating and the doors.

The only reason she was able to get the full effect had everything to do with Kyle calling Yasir to ask if he could pick my bestie up and bring her to the party with us. When I say how much I smiled when he didn't hesitate to say yes? It made it that much harder to think of him as just a friend.

Now, if I could keep from being so obvious about it.

I turn to face Kendyl while she enjoys the wind blowing through her hair. It's a clear night, perfect for the top to be open. "Now you see why she's half mine, right?"

"Chica, like, this thang is *pretty*, pretty." She keeps playing with the neon on the door panels, then leans forward into the front seats, planting her elbows on the middle console. "You might have picked up some cool points with me, Yasir. How did you put all this together? It had to cost a few stacks, at least."

"Well, my Squad in the A helped with a lot of it," he tells us as he pulls out of our subdivision. If I didn't know any better, I'd swear he's in a showcase kinda mood tonight. And he's a lot more open than usual. That whole thing at his uncle's house must have done the trick, not to mention the thing that happened in his studio—*whew*.

"We learned from the boys at the customs shop my ace's uncle owns."

"Speaking of your Squad in the A, you haven't mentioned them much." Kendyl ramps up her interrogation, cutting her eyes at me the whole time. "Do you still talk to them? Do they know what you got going on down here?"

"Kenni."

"I mean, come on, Z, you gotta admit, it's the first time he's said anything about his life before he got to Oakwood." Kendyl turns toward Yasir and jumps back into her bag of questions. "So, what's good, bro? You gonna let me dig or nah?"

Yasir tightens his grip on the steering wheel as he drives, tapping his thumb against the gearshift. Not a good sign. "Okay, you wanna be the big, bad bestie, huh? I know why you're digging, but you wanna play, let's play. Let's start with my ace, Dante, he's been like an older brother to me. Then there's Caleb, and his older brother, Malik, and, well, there's Alyssa and Dominique."

"Oh, now we're getting somewhere." Kendyl rubs her hands together like she's struck gold. "So, what's up with the girls in the Squad? Anything we need to know about?"

"Okay, Kenni, you're getting a bit wild, what's up with you?" If I'd known she'd corner him like this, I would have thought twice about her riding with us. "Are you kidding me with these questions? Like, for real?"

"He doesn't seem to have a problem with it, do you, Yasir?" Kendyl smirks as she looks into the rear-view mirror, and she cracks up when she notices his face. "See, he's even trying not to laugh in the mirror. I'm doing you a favor, chica."

Yasir cracks up out of the blue while we're still going back and forth. He glances over at me, then back at Kendyl, and he pulls the car over so he can really get the laughter out of his system. "Kenni, you're wild, I swear. Ally and Nique are lesbian, for the record. Well, at least Nique is, anyway. I think Ally's bi."

"TMI, my boy, TMI." Kendyl leans back in the seat, crossing her arms over her chest. "I didn't ask for all that."

"Nope, but you didn't ask for specifics, either, chica." Yasir can't stop laughing through his response, wiping real tears from his cheeks.

"Man, this is too funny. Do you want me to call Nique real quick? She loves girls who have a little fire."

The way he flipped the whole sitch has me cracking up with him. I see the sour face on Kendyl and tapped the side of her thigh. "Aww, come on, babe, you know you belong to me, I'd never let anyone take you from me."

Kendyl takes my hand and pushes it off. "So, I'm trying to protect my girl and I'm being treated like that bad guy? Mhm, I see how it is now."

"You're the one trying to find drama where it ain't. It's not my fault it backfired on you." Yasir pulls off, shaking his head as he chuckles while driving. "I get it, though. You're looking out for your ace, and you should. Hell, Dante's dying to figure out who I'm trying to holla at so he can give her the third degree. Squad takes care of its own."

"I'm glad you see things my way, unlike my bestie over there in the *girlfriend's* perch," Kendyl teased as she leaned forward to kiss me on the cheek. "You're alright with me, but you're not off the hook. I got a lot more questions to ask before we get to the house."

"I kinda figured as much, and you're about to find out I'm not as thin-skinned as you might have guessed," Yasir warns her. "You might wanna be prepared for the answers to those questions, too. I'm learning you just like you're learning me, as friends, girlie."

"Yeah, that reminds me." Kendyl taps against her temple as she ponders her next inquiry. "You've gone through a whole makeover from what we saw when you first got here. You're from the A, but the way you wear the oils and scents and the way you have your hair cut, it's screaming something from overseas. Where are you from, for real?"

Okay, now she's jumping into my space, and I need to shut this down. "Wow, would you look at the time. We're almost at Kyle's anyway, I think we can pick this up another time, okay? Besides, I'm *supposed* to be the one asking these questions, remember?"

"Ugh, then you need to get to asking, chica, because if my inquiring mind wants to know, others are gonna want to know, too," she stresses. "He's a mystery to all of us, and you seem to be the only one he's willing to open up to, so, yeah, I'm gonna need y'all to get that handled and soon, okay?"

"It'll get done when we say it gets done, sis." I rolled my eyes over the hypocrisy of it all. Just nosey for the sake of being nosey. "When did you become Oakwood's Tamron Hall?"

"There's a method to my madness, chica," Kendyl points out as Yasir turns into Kyle's neighborhood. "First thing they taught us in the journalism club: if you can control the narrative, you do it before someone else does it for you. All I'm trying to do is help do that."

"So, pause, stop the presses, I'm confused." Yasir slows down long enough to locate the street number of Kyle's house since the GPS says we're already there. "One minute, you're in protective mode over your bestie, and the next minute, you want to help me control the information that gets out to the school. What gives, shawty?"

Kendyl sighs, shaking her head a few times as we finally arrive at the long driveway that leads to the estate. "Okay, here's the real, playa. My girl likes you, and you like her too. I'm willing to give you the benefit of the doubt because you've opened up more in the past few days. If you were still the brooding loner, things would be way different, trust."

"Fair enough. I admit I could have been a bit more open with people, but everywhere I've gone to school, whatever I've told has been used against me." Yasir puts Storm in park and opens the door to hop out. He slips around to the passenger side and opens the door for us to get out. "Since you're talking about controlling the narrative—I like that, by the way, I'm gonna have to borrow that—if anything comes up, I'll make sure you and Z know about it first. Sounds like a winner?"

"Deal. Now, let's see what's going on. I need to see about my baby before things get wild around here."

Chapter Thirty – Yasir

The Channing estate, in every sense of the word, personifies everything that anyone who likes to entertain would want to have in their home. The tree line alone boasts privacy on levels that even the most introvertive personality would appreciate. The waterfront, resort-like style of the pool gives the adults something to enjoy and still be separated from the teenagers, while the covered verandas speckled about the ten-acre backyard allows us kids the ability to enjoy ourselves without the overbearing gaze and interference.

For me, the walk to and from the trucks earlier to get things into the home and the backyard almost wore me out, and I swear I'll never complain about Unk's five-bedroom house ever again. Thank the gods we didn't have to cater for the event; we only provided the seafood as part of the expansive menu that's housed inside of one of the larger verandas closest to the house.

"Thank you all for coming out for my son's seventeenth birthday!" Mr. Channing says through the microphone. "I have no doubt that you will enjoy yourselves." He steps off the stage to mix and mingle.

Zahra and I stroll through the maze of tents that augment the verandas in search of the rest of the group. It won't be long before we find Kyle and Kendyl. They're in the eye of the storm, with Kyle soaking up every bit of the attention showered on him. Kendyl is posing and smiling for the cameras, too. Kyle's cousin, Quentin Channing, stands beside him in the midst of the throng of people, gushing over his younger protégé, telling anyone who will listen that Kyle is the next college football phenom.

"If anyone needed a quick reminder of whose night this was, there shouldn't be any doubts now," I remark leading Zahra to the area where Kyle told me we would camp out for the rest of the night. "This is bananas. I would've never thought things could get this interesting down here."

"See, it's not as boring as you thought, huh?" Zahra's smile lights up the night sky. "It's nice to actually be able to just enjoy things, be Kenni's cheerleader and let her step into the spotlight with Kyle. It's a beautiful thing."

"Yeah, I just hope it stays that way." I keep my head on a swivel as we move through the crowd, and I'm fighting the nagging feeling that there could be someone here who doesn't belong. In the back of my mind, I'm still thinking about whether that viral video will come back on me tonight. I know it sounds a bit extreme, but nothing's happened yet, which means something can happen sooner or later. "It's nice to not be in the spotlight for a while."

"My mom loves to say, 'Don't borrow trouble.' Let's enjoy the night, okay? There's plenty of time to worry about things another day," Zahra points out. "We haven't had a chance to have a fun night. I'm gonna make sure you do."

I notice a group of people swirling around an elder gentleman and his family but can't make out who they are. "I don't recognize those people. Who are they?"

"That would be the Mayor and Mrs. Lance." Zahra rolls her eyes. "That means Ian and Chrisette are around here somewhere. It looks like we're gonna have to do our best to make sure the plan is in motion and followed to the letter."

"I thought Mayor Lance was out of town. At least, that's what Unk told me when I asked about the VIP list."

"Yeah, so did I, but rumor has it, Ian convinced him that Mr. Channing's party was the place to be this weekend," Zahra explains to me. "He's as much of an egomaniac as Ian is. Apple. Tree."

"Okay, so we stick to the plan, then," I declare. "As soon as Kyle and Kenni get over here, we can figure out what needs to be done next and take it from there."

Before we settle into our seats and enjoy the music, the microphone screeches a couple of times, and a distinct voice sounds off through the air. I don't know who stepped up on stage, but I have a bad feeling the spotlight's gonna get shifted to someone against their will.

"Ladies and gentlemen, it is a pleasure to be here among you all to help celebrate the coming of age of one of our favorite sons of Oakwood Grove," Mayor Lance announces to the crowd. After the applause dies down, he continues as he motions for Kyle to join him and Ian. "Kyle Channing, we can't wait to see what you and my son, Ian, will accomplish during the rest of this magical undefeated season, and I will be in the stands cheering you on."

We helplessly watch as Kyle tries to find the opening to take the microphone away from the mayor. He's sandwiched between Ian and Mayor Lance, and his distressed expression can be felt by everyone except for the Lance men.

"You know, I remember when you and Ian were in little league, and the connection between you two as quarterback and tight end was evident back then." Mayor Lance continues to lavish praise on both Kyle and his son. "Who would have thought that all these years later, you two would be in a position to get Oakwood Grove another state title!"

"I'm going up there. I'm not leaving my boyfriend caught out there like that," Kendyl seethes as she attempts to get up from her chair.

Zahra grabs her arm as we watch Chrisette, Ian's girlfriend, saunter up on stage to join the group. "I know what you wanna do, babe, but it's gonna make things worse."

"How do you expect me to stand here and just—"

I tap Zahra's shoulder and smirk as I point toward the equalizer making his way through the crowd. "I have a pretty good feeling all this is all about to get shut down in a few seconds."

As the crowd cheers and roars, Mr. Channing steps back onto the stage. His face shows no emotion as he whispers something in his son's ear before stepping to the mayor. He holds out his hand, staring the mayor down for what seems like forever. I pump my fist in a silent show of solidarity, hoping the mayor gets the point.

Before long, Mayor Lance places the microphone in Mr. Channing's hand and gestures to him to take center stage. Mr. Channing then points toward the stairs, a not-so-subtle clue for the mayor and his family to step off the stage and taps the microphone a few times to make sure he can be heard. "We would like to thank the mayor and his family for their gracious birthday wishes for our son. We know he can get a bit long-winded at times, so I wanted to make sure he kept things under the mandatory three minutes before the crowd turned on him."

Man, it's the low-key shade for me. I wanna be like him when I grow up.

The laughter radiates through the crowd at that backhanded remark, and I'm there for all of it as I see the scowl on Mayor Lance's face. Kyle and Kendyl make their way down to the lawn and head in our direction. I grin as I scope the relief on Kyle's face over being saved by his father.

"Man, that was too close, bro." I tap fists with Kyle as we slip inside the veranda. "Did anyone even know the mayor was gonna pull that stunt?"

"Bro, I know my dad, and he's gonna have words for the mayor at the next council meeting," Kyle explains to us. "He's constantly trying to keep the focus on him, no matter who the night belongs to."

The glare in Kendyl's eyes is enough to melt steel. "He's lucky I'm not that chick, or I would have embarrassed him myself. How dare he bring his family up on stage like that, and that nonsense with Ian and Chrisette? What in the hell was that about?"

Zahra puts her hand up to settle everyone down. "Look, you said it yourself, chica, this is your boyfriend's night, and we're focused on that, okay? There is no need to bring the Lance family up or anything that has nothing to do with the fact that we should be partying with the birthday boy."

"You're right, Z, so let's see about doing exactly that," Kyle declares. "Now, I'm not saying I snuck wine coolers into the ice chest, but if you happen to lift the lid and find something to smooth things out a bit, have at it, you feel me?"

In the next few minutes, we're sipping and enjoying the live entertainment. For most of the night, everyone has a fun time mixing and mingling among themselves. I even manage to settle in and indulge a bit.

I place my drink on one of the side tables and kiss Zahra before heading out of the veranda. "I'll be back. I need to hit the restroom.

Are there any on the main floor?"

"Yeah, soon as you hit the back door, turn to your left, it will be the first door on your right, you can't miss it," Kyle replies, turning his attention to his social media feed. "We'll keep up with Z, bro."

I saunter through the crowd, determined to avoid eye contact with anyone to keep my anxiety tamped down. Despite my newfound semi-celebrity status, I don't feel as safe and in control around large crowds yet. In fact, I'm low-key scanning the crowd for people who don't look familiar to me, allowing my imagination to run wild, fabricating all sorts of doomsday situations and what I might need to do to get out of here. While I'm able to keep it together while Zahra was with me, dealing with it on my own is a completely different circumstance.

Real talk, I'm so out of sorts that exiting out the front door looks really good right now. Each step I take toward the house feels like my shoes are filled with concrete, and despite my best efforts, my anxiety is spiking beyond my ability to function.

I shouldn't have left the safety of the group, but I can't do anything about it now. I'm focusing on getting in and getting back and not having a full-tilt panic attack.

I get to the restroom without incident, but once I'm inside the house, I come face to face with Ian, who happens to be in a better mood than usual. I take one look at him, realizing that he's been drinking. A lot. His inability to stand up straight is a dead giveaway.

"Yasir, what's good, my guy?" Ian's speech slurs as he greets me. "This party is wild, bro. I couldn't have crashed a better situation."

I scratch my head, trying to understand the statement Ian has a hard time getting out. I play it like I'm not in the loop, but I figure he might not buy it. Like I care if he did or not. "Wait… you mean, you weren't invited to the party? How did that happen? I thought you and Kyle were cool."

"Well, I figured that *you* had something to do with that." Ian steps into my personal space, his breath reeking of something a lot stronger than what we'd been enjoying inside Kyle's veranda.

"Bro, you're drunk, and I'm not having this conversation with you. You said you aren't supposed to be here, then do everyone a favor and ghost." I push past Ian to head for the back door when he grabs my arm. "Who the hell died and made you the gatekeeper?" Someone has to be playing a joke and catching it on camera or something. He's acting mad weird right now, and I have no interest in playing along. "Look, I'm gonna slide out of your space and leave you to whatever dream world you're living in, because I'm not there."

"You aren't going anywhere until we get some things cleared up."

I glare at him. If there weren't people around, I would've thrown a few quick jabs to drop him where he stands. "We are not even close to being cool enough for you to dictate what we need or do not need to do, partner."

Ian releases his grip, standing his ground for a few minutes. "Look, I'm not trying to be your enemy, bro. You bailed me out after the game that night, even when you could have left me to… God knows what would have happened."

I cross my arms over my chest, leaning against the wall. "Oh, this should be good. What are you trying to prove, coming for me? I'm at a loss, so maybe you can give me a clue or two, huh?"

"I don't know what it is about you, dude, but every time we're around each other, I have this deep need to either wring your neck or try to find some common ground so we can at least be cordial." Ian sits on the edge of one of the couches, waiting for other people to leave the area. "Right now, I have no animosity toward you, you haven't done anything to me. What I'm not about to do is pretend like we're friends, either, but that's what's making things complicated."

Before I jump in with my thoughts about what Ian wants to discuss, Mayor Lance shows up out of the blue. "Who's your friend, son? I don't believe I've met him before."

Ian rolls his eyes, taking another sip of his drink. "Dad, this is Yasir Salah, and he and I are not exactly friends, more like acquaintances. I was asking him about some things we needed to talk about."

My anxiety shoots through the roof. I take a few deep breaths to calm things down before extending my hand to greet the mayor. "Mayor Lance, it's good to meet you, sir."

"Is this true, Yasir? Are you two not friends?" Mayor Lance

inquires, not offering his hand back.

"Sir, he is correct, we know each other from school, nothing much more than that." I narrow my gaze in Ian's direction, wondering how I managed to get caught up in this situation. "In fact, I was just about to leave and rejoin my friends, so if you'll excuse me—"

"Wait a moment, there's something about you." Mayor Lance takes a closer look at my face. He raises an eyebrow as though he recognizes something familiar. That alone makes me nervous. "Your father wouldn't happen to be Bakari Salah, would it? You favor him greatly."

I flinch. "How do you know that name?"

"Because your father was—" He stops himself from whatever he was going to say next. "Now I'm starting to understand the simmering acrimony between you and my son," Mayor Lance asserts. "Considering he told me that he helped you escape the fight with those Baytown kids, I would think you would show a little more appreciation."

"Okay, pause… he *helped* me keep from catching a beatdown with kids who didn't even know who I was? With all due respect, sir, but what alternate universe are you two living in?" Oh, no, what we're not gonna do is play stupid games right now. "I did what I could to get those kids off his back, and he all but pushed me into my car for me to split from the scene so he could handle the cops, whatever that meant. Your son was not the savior in that scenario."

"Look, it's cool, alright? I'm not sweating it, for real. I know it's rough, being the new kid in town and all," Ian jumps in to say. This Jekyll and Hyde routine is getting old really fast. "You don't have to make things up to make yourself look better. I mean, you might have been the one behind why I got jumped in the first place, for all I know."

I suppress my anger, but it's overruling my ability to be logical. I flex my fingers, balling them into fists and releasing them to temper my annoyance over the revisionist recent history Ian's spinning. I won't get the upper hand if I continue to debate, but I'm not backing down, either.

"Oh, so why didn't anyone call and ask for a statement? My uncle didn't get a call, either, or he would have told me." Dammit. I should've known I would regret not being there to tell my side of the story. "Don't you get it, Mayor Lance? None of this is making sense, am I the only one seeing that?"

"Yasir! Bro, we've been looking everywhere for you," Kyle shouts as he and the rest of the group show up. Mr. Channing is in tow, following his son and our friends to the source of the minor commotion. "What's going on here? Why do you have my boy hemmed up like this?"

"That's what I would like to know, Robert," Mr. Channing asks of Mayor Lance. "From the looks of Yasir's body language and the irritation on his face, he's not exactly happy with the way his interactions with you are going."

Mayor Lance turns to Mr. Channing for a moment before focusing back on me. "Nothing for you to concern yourself with, Asa. It seems that Mr. Salah might have incriminated himself over an incident that happened a couple weeks ago, and we were having a chat about it."

What the hell is this man talking about? I didn't do a damned thing. The last thing he's gonna accuse me of is assault. "Let's call it what it is, Mr. Channing: the mayor and his son seem to think that I orchestrated a fight. I have no idea what would possess them to want to accuse me of such things, but I think I might need representation, in case he might get a bright idea and accuse me of something I didn't do."

Mr. Channing strokes his beard. "So, you and your son decided to corner a friend of my son's, at his birthday party, that neither you, nor he, were invited to, and without a lawyer or his legal guardian present, engaged in a 'discussion,' where you admitted he might have incriminated himself, is that right?" He pauses for a few moments before he continues. "If that is the case, Yasir, it is in your best interest to give me a dollar so that I may represent you in whatever nonsense the mayor is trying to bait you into."

Oh, say less, sir. I pull out my wallet without a moment's hesitation and place a folded one-dollar bill in Mr. Channing's hand.

Mayor Lance flinches for a minute, forgetting that Mr. Channing happens to be one of the most celebrated and notorious defense attorneys in the Southeast. I didn't. I understood the assignment.

"Now, now, we don't have to go to such drastic measures."

"Oh, I believe that it has to, unfortunately," Mr. Channing counters. "And since you insist on disrupting this night with your son's petty grievances, I'm going to ask you to leave."

"Are you sure you want to do that, Asa?" Mayor Lance challenges, almost like he wants to make a scene.

"Be thankful I'm willing to politely request that you remove yourself, or would you rather I advise my client to file harassment charges against your son on Monday?" Mr. Channing answers. "I mean, you said it yourself, it doesn't need to get to such extreme measures."

Mayor Lance glares at his son, who tucks his head to keep from meeting his father's disapproving gaze. "You're right, I think we will take our leave. I apologize for any disruption we have caused tonight. I'll see you for the council meeting on Tuesday?"

"I'll look forward to it, as always, Robert." Mr. Channing sinks his hands in his pockets, nodding toward the front door. "Be safe on the way home, please."

I stare Ian down as we remain in each other's space. "Something's off with you, seriously. It might be in our mutual best interest to stay away from each other, or things could get wild."

Ian frowns as he walks away. "Honestly, you might be right, but we're gonna have to find a way to coexist, one way or the other. Even though this went a little weird… my yacht party invitation is still good."

I wave him off, turning my attention to the stunning beauty by my side, meeting her curious gaze with a mischievous grin. "Do I want to know what's going through that pretty head of yours?"

"Do I want to know why the hell Ian was trying to rile you up?" Zahra asks. "He's almost laser focused on you now for some reason, and I have a bad feeling about this. Is there something I should know? What invitation was he talking about?"

I shoo away Zahra's concerns with a dismissive wave of my hand. "You know Ian better than me. He runs hot and cold; one minute, he's trying to catch me slipping so he can make me look bad, the next minute, he wants to figure out how we can coexist. Let him try to bring the smoke; he's on a blamestorm anyway, it won't go anywhere. Now, can we get back to the party? I think we can finally enjoy it without all the negativity swirling around."

Even with the bravado to show her that I'm not concerned about Ian, the truth of the matter is harsher than I want to admit. Ian's gonna be a problem, and I know it. If I don't figure out why things are so tense between us, it could cause other issues that I don't have time to resolve.

I also have to face another unfortunate truth… that I might not survive the glare of the spotlight. For my sake, and everyone around me, I better find a way to survive.

Failure would undo everything I've tried to build.

Chapter Thirty-One – Zahra

"That was more fun than I thought it would be. Kyle and his folks really know how to throw a party," I say as I settle into the passenger seat enjoying his hand as it rests on top of mine the entire way home. I'd indulged all night with Kenni and some of the other girls, and although it wasn't heavy liquor, I was proud of myself that I kept most of my emotions in check.

Being in the car with Yasir will test that theory because I'm really feeling myself tonight, and I want to act on so many thoughts in my head it's not even funny anymore.

The rest of the night went as smooth as silk, with Kendyl and Kyle assuming the spotlight again, despite the other distraction of his cousin mixing and mingling too. Quentin did his best to deflect all attention in his younger cousin's direction, but the crowd gravitated toward him until he left. Kyle didn't care too much, he enjoyed having his favorite brother-cousin in the mix with him, being able to brag about the different records he'd break.

"Yeah, it was fun, but I need a severe recharge from the energy drain from tonight," Yasir comments. "I'm looking forward to resting as much as possible tomorrow before school on Monday."

"Speaking of draining, what was that about with Ian?" I decided to rip the band aid off instead of dragging out the questionnaire. "Do you want to talk about what went down between you two earlier tonight?"

"I don't know what you're talking about," he snaps back.

"Yasir, don't play dumb. I know he was a bit lit tonight, but—"

"But, what, Z?"

There are a few moments of silence between us, and I stare him down because I'm not letting this go. Yasir's grip tightens around my hand, a reaction I expect considering the tensions that still exist between him and Ian. He slows Storm as the traffic light changes from yellow to red, then loosens his grip once we came to a stop. "I honestly thought after everything at the mall and that madness after the Baytown game that he would just roll with things for a bit. What I'm trying to figure out is why he wants me at one of his parties?"

"Wait, what?" I sit up in my seat. I didn't expect that at all. "Where did that come from and why did he want you there?"

Yasir shakes his head as he accelerates through the intersection. "It doesn't make sense, for real. He came at me with Eric one day, wanting to relieve the pressure between us, and then he came out the blue with a party invitation. He even thanked me for bailing him out."

"So, are you planning on going to whatever party he's talking about doing?" I continue the Q&A session, trying to avoid it sounding so informal. "What type of party is he throwing?"

The answer to my question comes in the form of a notification chiming in on both our phones at the same time. Usually when that happens, it's a group message, especially if some of the same people are close by. I check my IG and, just like that, a whole group message from Ian's IG handle pops up on my screen. "Well, that's interesting."

Yasir keeps driving, switching his attention from me to the road and back. "Don't keep me in suspense, what's going on?"

"Ian's ears must have been burning," I reply as I scroll through the details. "It's a birthday party on his father's yacht, and we've been invited."

"We?"

"Yep. I see Kyle and Kenni on the guest list. Taylor too," I continue to run through some of the people on the invitation. "A lot of his crew, some of the cheerleaders and a few of the more popular kids on campus. It's not a large list, maybe around thirty or so."

"Doesn't sound like the odds are in our favor if we go," he says as he taps his thumbs against the steering wheel, as though the wheels in his head are spinning. "Is this a good idea to go? I still don't know if I trust him yet."

"It would be a different story if it were a smaller party or something, but it looks like he wants to go big for his birthday," I tell him. "Considering what he just saw being done for Kyle, he wanted to try to do something bigger and different. Being out in the Atlantic for a few hours would pretty much do it."

"Outside of you, Kenni and Kyle, I won't know anyone else at that party," Yasir counters. "Sure, I just got to know a few of the other boys, but I'm not sure how… I don't want to feel like I'm being clingy because I'll want to be with you and the rest of the crew."

I don't know if it's the coolers in my system or what, but my filter doesn't want to work tonight. "I want to be with you too. I won't be far from you during the party, I promise. I can barely let you out of my sight as it is."

"Um, Z… I can't… I can't trust what you're saying to me right now, especially when we've been a bit lit tonight." Yasir sighs as we finally make it to my house. "I can't afford to, when we're friends or whatever. Things are confusing between us, and you know it is."

I don't mean to pout, but here I am with my bottom lip poked out. I'm not used to being refused, but I helped create this madness between us, so I have to deal with the good and the bad. "But we said it was better to wait for now, right? We agreed it was best."

Yasir offers up a half-smile as he parks the car. "We can talk about it more once we've gotten some sleep. Now, get in the house so you can get settled in. I'll check in on you tomorrow."

"Fine. Can I at least have a kiss goodnight?" I insist on getting my way, one way or another. I grin when he leans over to slip a few kisses, tasting the last of the wine coolers on his lips. "Thank you. I know I haven't been easy to deal with, but I'm not doing this on purpose, I promise."

He lets me out of the car, gives me a hug and points toward the door, making it clear I've pushed my luck a little too far. "I understand, but I don't understand. It's okay, though, I'm getting used to you, and as much as it drives me crazy, I like it a lot. I like *you* a lot."

I gaze into his eyes and nod as I caress his cheek. "I like you a lot too. So, what do we do about this?"

He pulls my hand from his face and kisses my wrist, staring into my eyes like he can see right through me. "You know how I feel about you, but I'm not gonna push, not until you're ready. I'll have to be okay being your *other* best friend."

I hop out, enjoying my mini victory—even though he's a little annoyed with me—as I almost burst through the front door to do the quick wave to Mom and Daddy and head to my room.

I slip off my skirt and top and am in the middle of grabbing my robe when my FaceTime sings out. I check the ID and see Kenni's name pop up. "I hope you don't mind seeing me all indecent, sis, you caught me trying to get out my clothes."

"It's nothing I haven't seen before, so why would I complain now?" Kendyl giggles. "Besides, you know I wouldn't call if it wasn't important."

I raise my left eyebrow, sitting down on the side of the bed to get comfortable. I already know what she wants to talk about, and I'm still a little too tipsy to form coherent thoughts. "Okay, so I take it you got the invite just like we did?"

"Chica, what in the world is he thinking?" Kendyl fumes over the call. "He used my baby's party to see what he didn't want to do for his."

"I know, sis, I know," I reply. I wrap my robe around me and jump on the bed to give her my full attention. "You know how Ian is, we all do. Does Kyle know about the invite?"

"Yeah, he said he knew before it went out. He's not as heated as I am about it, but I think he's over it all," Kendyl told me. "I wish I had his calmness, because I'd be setting bombs off all over social media right now."

The way I crack up probably has her wondering what's wrong with me, but I don't care. It's funny because it's true; she sets a bomb and watches the flames burn, and depending on her mood, she might respond to the comments and reactions. "Okay, okay, now that you've gotten that out of your system, are you planning to go or nah?"

"We don't have a choice, we have to make the appearance, even if it's for a second or two." Kendyl rolls her eyes as she blows out some air. "The question is, are you and Yasir going, and if you are, how is that gonna look?"

"What do you mean?"

"The comments have been a bit wild, and some of the girls have been talking reckless all night," Kendyl explains to me. "A few of them were even scheming to holla at him when he was away from us, but that was before he and Ian got into that convo."

I want to explode right there on the spot. That's what we're doing, huh? "I see now that these girls just want to tempt fate."

"Let's be real, Zahra, and know that I'm in your corner, period," Kendyl starts in on me. "You and Yasir have been playing this 'are they, aren't they' game for the past few weeks, and more and more girls are becoming less interested in the conclusion. Amber wasn't the first to try, she was the first to act on it."

"I thought I'd made my point clear when she tried it, though."

"That probably lasted a week at best, chica." Kendyl shakes her head. "Look, I know that because you're unbothered by being in the same circles as the more popular kids in school, but they don't care if you're trying to figure it out. They're going to present Yasir with other options, and as much as I like him too, he's still a boy."

I think about it for a few minutes, and she's right, I don't know how to roll in these circles. I was good where I was, even with being best friends with Kyle, it didn't seem to come with this type of pressure. Why me and Yasir being together became such a focus for everyone around us irritates me. But he's a boy, and if someone else were to try hard to get his attention, I can't be mad about it. We're. Just. Friends. Kinda. "So, what do I do? I like him, you know that, but I'm scared of what might happen if I let my heart decide."

"Well, until we can figure something out, we may need to shield you both from all the outside noise as best we can," Kendyl advises. "But don't be surprised if there are people who might want you too, chica. I noticed a few of the boys checking for you. You don't have to put everything on Yasir."

I nod at her suggestion, wondering how to balance myself. I understand where she's coming from, but the last time I tried to play that game, it went all bad. I don't have it in me to try to pull something like that again.

As I disconnect the video call with Kendyl, I feel a strange heat flow through me. It doesn't hurt or anything, but it pulses through for a few minutes before it subsides, leaving me confused over where it came from in the first place. I don't think anything else of it, slipping off my robe and settling in for bed.

I prefer to dream about what might happen once Yasir and I have a chance to deepen our bond. Maybe this situation with Ian's birthday party could be something we need to figure out what we can be to each other. Maybe, just maybe, it could be the catalyst for something…

Transcendent?

Epic?

I don't know what word I want to use, but one thing's for sure.

Whether I want to admit it or not, I've fallen hard for Yasir.

Chapter Thirty-Two – Yasir

After the past few weekends, when there was always something going on, it's nice to have a chance to breathe and do nothing on a Sunday. Last night was a lot, and I need the break, at least for a few hours, anyway. I plan to catch up on some pleasure reading or maybe check out some shows I've been missing. I'm probably late to the game on some of them, but I've been keeping a pretty busy schedule.

Unk's at the shop, handling a large order for a client in Jacksonville, so having the house to myself is a rarity I don't want to waste. Junk food on deck, something I don't always get to do, since he's on a sugar restriction kick. Not that I crave anything sweet on a regular basis, but it's nice to have that option from time to time.

I finally get the chance to sprawl out on the couch to binge-watch, when my phone rings with a number I don't recognize. I grumble, then pick up the call. "Hello? Who's this?"

"Hi, Yasir, this is Ms. Lennox. I hope you don't mind the intrusion. Xavion gave me your number. I told him I wanted to talk with you, if that's okay?"

Now, I have no issues with Unk giving up my number, but he could've at least given me the head's up or something. It smells like a setup. "Sure, I'm game. What's on your mind?"

"Well, I'd prefer having this talk in person. Can you meet me at Fire Street Food in downtown Savannah?"

I pause for a minute, trying to figure out the angle.

She must have noticed my hesitation, because she clears her throat before she says, "It's my treat. I felt like we needed to get a chance to get to know each other a little better."

Yeah, it's a setup, but I don't feel like she's planning anything off-key. She likes Unk, and we've already had this convo. To be honest, she's good for him. The least I could do is find out more about her. It might give me a chance to pick her brain in the process.

So much for resting on a Sunday afternoon. "Cool, I'll be there. I can't wait to chat."

The oranges and lighter colors inside the restaurant put me in a better mood than I thought I would be, despite the anxiety over talking with Lennox *alone*. So many ideas run through my head over who she is, what draws her to Unk. The possibilities make me dizzy.

I get there about fifteen minutes early so I don't feel rushed, taking a seat at one of the booths near the entrance, making sure I face the exit as I run through the menu. It's a habit I picked up when Nana and I went out to dinner at times, and I feel like I need to know who's coming through the door. Nana always said it's the first time she realized that my desires to protect others shaped the person I would become.

I'm not a big sushi fan, but there's enough on the menu for me to eat and not be disrespectful of her choice of location. I don't have much of an appetite anyway, so I order a kiwi and strawberry smoothie. I spend the time waiting by people watching, and there's a lot to watch. I settle on a family, a mother and father and their two boys. The way they interact with the small boys triggers a memory I didn't know existed.

I'm with Mommy and Daddy, and we're on a beach watching the tides roll onto the shoreline. I don't recognize it right away, but the feel of the memory… it feels like I'm home. There's someone else there, and I can't make out their face, but it's another boy. He's older than me, I think. We're all wearing a mix of purple, black, and gold clothing, and the smiles on my parents' faces warm me inside unlike anything else has in a long time.

Then the confusion sets in, and I'm left with more questions than answers. Where did that memory come from? Why can't I access it when I want to? It doesn't make sense.

"Hi, Yasir, thank you for meeting with me." Lennox stands just outside the booth, pulling me from my thoughts. "You're a bit early, have you already ordered?"

I stand up from my seat and wait for her to take her seat before I sit down again. My uncle taught me better than not to stand when a lady needs to be seated. Once we settle in, the waitress takes her drink order as she places my smoothie in front of me. "Not really, I only ordered the smoothie for now. I wanted to have something to drink in case my throat got dry."

She tilts her head slightly to her left, mulling over my response. "Does this make you nervous? That's the last thing I wanted. Would it be better if your uncle was here with us, because I can call him—"

"Nah, that's alright. He's still handling that Jax order, and I want him to be able to complete it. It's a huge boost for business," I reply, then sip my smoothie. "I'm not always socially adept at things when I'm in public, but it has nothing to do with you being here. Promise."

She smiles, disarming me in seconds. Lennox has that type of vibe that seems to put anyone at ease, whether they want to be or not. She reminds me a lot of Unk's favorite actress, Sanaa Lathan, and now it makes sense how she caught his attention so quick. I also know my uncle, and it'll take more than good looks to keep him enchanted.

"Good, I'm glad. I was worried I'd gotten off on the wrong foot already." She takes a breath, leaning forward over the table. "So, I'm sure you have a ton of questions about me. I'm an open book. Fire away."

"Like that? Oh, say less, then." I grin as I rub my hands together. "How did you and Unk actually link up? I don't remember seeing you at the shop all that much."

"Actually, a friend of mine told me about his shop." She pauses for a moment as the waitress comes with her drink order. She sips a few times and nods before the waitress leaves, focusing her gaze on me again. Sheesh, she has such pretty eyes… okay, let me stop right now. "I started coming through during my lunch hour a couple of times a week at first, and we traded glances and smiles a few times. Next thing I knew, I was there every day."

"So, what do you do for a living?" I don't mean to sound so formal about it, but she said she was an open book, so… "Are you from Savannah?"

"Yeah, he told me once you had a chance to warm up, you'd be a bucket of questions." She giggles and takes another sip of her drink. Even her laugh is easy and light. "I'm an antiquities dealer, but I've been teaching college classes online as of lately, mostly in African Studies. And no, I'm not from Savannah. I was born in Barbados, but my parents moved to the States with my sister and me when I was young."

I study her face a little longer, listening to her voice a few more times in my head. Color me confused. "I never would have been able to tell. You sound like you're from the South, but another part of the South."

"Depends on who you ask. We moved to Miami. Ended up going to college at the University of Miami too."

I crack up laughing. "Thank goodness I grew up a Bama fan."

"Oh, so you're one of those delusional Tide… you know what, I was just starting to like you."

"Hey, I can't help it if it's no longer 'all about the U' anymore. You need to get you a Nick Saban, ma'am."

"Yeah, I see college football season is gonna be a laugh riot with you, but you do realize your coach is retired now? And those Dawgs up the way in Athens are now the gold standard."

I flip the convo back to the original reason we're there. "So, are you into Unk? Like, for real, for real? I'm not about to be that kid who gets all attached and then you're gone in less than sixty days."

She stares at me for a few moments, and I'm not sure if I overstepped or not. Yeah, I probably went too far. I withdraw a little bit, waiting for her to give me the "stay in a child's place" speech, bracing for the impact of the words.

Instead, she smirks at me, shaking her head a few times before she sips her drink again. "Yes, I'm very much into your uncle. There's something about him that has me completely enthralled with him. And I understand your need to protect him. He's probably had a lot of women fall for him."

"Umm, I can't speak to that, I've only spent the summers with him before moving down here over a month ago," I admit, sipping more of my smoothie as I choose my words carefully. "You're the first woman he's really had to talk to me about, which says a lot. For a minute, I thought he didn't have no game, but seeing how beautiful you… I'm sorry, should I be complimenting you like that? I mean, I don't want to… ugh, now I'm overthinking."

Lennox covers my hands with hers, rubbing her thumbs over the backs of my hands. I pull away because I'm trembling so badly, but the warmth of her hands radiates through mine, up my arms to my shoulders, and then down my spine. How the hell is she able to calm me down without so much as a whisper, in a restaurant full of people? I have more questions, dammit.

"Don't try to make every interaction with people feel like you have to be perfect, or you have to say all the right things," she advises, keeping her hands over mine. "Believe me, even adults get it wrong, and we have time and experience on our side."

I nod, not sure what else I can say without feeling like I'm putting my foot in my mouth again. I hate times like these when I want to sound like the silver-tongued devil my uncle is around people, but I end up sounding like I have no basic understanding of simple communication. "Thank you for that. I've been trying to not feel so awkward around girls and women. It seems like it's easier when I'm not trying, but I never know until it comes out of my mouth."

"What about Zahra? The way she was around you when I met her, I'd say you're doing pretty well."

"Yeah, about that." I slip my right hand from her grasp, rubbing the back of my neck to calm down the rising tension. "I don't know how to get out of the friend zone, which is where she seems to want me right now. I'm trying to be, but that's not what my heart wants."

She gives my left hand a gentle squeeze, acknowledging my anxiety. "I'm sure it's a confusing time for her too. I saw the way she looks at you, and I'll admit I spied on you two when you walked her to the car. That's not how a 'friend' looks at you."

"But every time I try to say something about it, she's all 'be patient, I'm not playing games with you.'" I thought about the incident with Amber and the way Zahra kissed me, and it irritates me all over again. "Then, if someone even breathes in my direction, she's staking her claim without staking her claim. I don't know whether I'm coming or going sometimes, and as much as it makes me miserable, I can't stop thinking about her."

"I get it, and I promise, it will work itself out, one way or another. She obviously likes you, Yasir, and she might be going through her own insecurities and 'what if' questions in her head too."

Okay, she's turning into the auntie I never knew I needed. Unk had better keep her around. "I'll try to see things her way, but it hasn't been easy. Every time we're around each other, there's this pull, this connection I can't explain, and I don't want to ignore it when it feels like this."

She gives up that smile again, and I forget all about what I want to say next. Talking with her is the closest thing to talking about things with Mommy, and as selfish as it sounds, I don't want to give that up. "Can I, like, text you when I need to vent? Talking to Unk is one thing, but I don't really have that… how do I say this… I don't have a grown woman who's young enough to understand where I'm coming from, you know?"

She leans close, close enough to whisper to me without anyone else hearing. "I'd be honored to help in any way I can. To have you want to trust me means more than you know."

Not as much as it means to me, that's for sure. "Good, because I might be leaning on you a lot sooner than you think. Thank you for the chat, I'll save the rest of the questions for another time."

"No worries at all, I'm looking forward to the next time we sit down to talk." She gets up from her chair, grinning when she notices me rise to my feet with her. We leave the money and tip for the bill, then I escort her out to her car. "I have a feeling we'll have more interesting things to discuss the next time around."

CHAPTER THIRTY-THREE – ZAHRA

I don't know what it is about the middle of the week, but it has become a bit of a pattern with us as a group to hook up in the courtyard to figure out what the weekend looks like. With the upcoming yacht party Ian has going on this weekend, at least don't have to worry about where we'll all be going. The unfortunate part is that Yasir and I aren't sure if we're still going or not.

We sit on the benches nearest to the gym, staying as far away from prying ears as possible. I get comfortable in Yasir's lap, a strategic move for me since the last time Kendyl and I talked. I figure actions and words need to sync up. I want him to know where I stand, and I can't ignore what my heart wants anymore.

What started out as a simple conversation over when to arrive to board the yacht turns into a whole debate over whether any of us are going at all. And while we're in the middle of doing that, we're also massaging the new situation between Taylor and Tania Ingram, one of my friends in my STEM circles. She and I take classes together and we work together on the sidelines during games too. I should've known she'd catch Taylor's eye eventually, but I've been a bit preoccupied.

Taylor's trying to impress Tania with his response, making it clear they're going to be there, whether we were or not. "Come on, you're turning down a whole yacht because it belongs to Ian's pops? We can't call a truce for a night and get back to it the next day?"

Kyle scowls like the mere thought of being on the boat with Ian would knock his status down a few notches. "So, we're gonna forget about the grandstanding at my party, right? Or what about the subtle shots at my ace at every given opportunity? He's flexing, and I'm not going for it like he's on my level."

I chime in while trying not to sound biased but sounding very much biased. "Ky, you're right, but he might just be trying to keep the spotlight on him more than anything. It's on brand for him, you know?"

"Yeah, but something's still doesn't feel right about any of this." Kyle takes a sip of his water bottle. Kendyl sits next to him, rubbing his shoulders. I sense the tension on him, too, and I wonder if something else is going on that we don't know about. "If we do go," Kyle says, "I'm staying in the open areas on the boat. Rumors are already rocking about others who are supposed to be there that aren't from Oakwood Grove."

Taylor nods and leans forward while rubbing his chin. "I get that, but you're sounding paranoid. There's nothing happening at the party, just like no drama went down at yours."

"We kept the guest list tight and away from random folks, bro," Kyle glares at Taylor. "The wild part about all this is he's been real loose with the invites. He's trying to play himself like he's got reach."

Yasir goes silent for a moment, and I focus on him to make sure he's okay. He returns my gaze with a nod and a half-smile, while trying to stay engaged. I whisper in his ear, "I need to talk to you when we're done with the crew."

He mouths, "So do I," before he turns back to the debate. "Aye, look, a lot of this is still out of my depth, so I'm not gonna pretend that I know the best move to make here. Kyle's got a point, though. Ian's been a bit more hyper than usual. Maybe he's angling for something, maybe he's just trying to top what Kyle did for his birthday party, but it's obvious to me that he's intent on keeping the spotlight focused on him."

I turn my attention to Tania, whose curious expressions throughout the convo have me just as intrigued. "Nia, what's your take? I know the boys are amped up, but we're gonna be there too."

Tania blushes, staring at Taylor for a few seconds before she speaks. "Not gonna lie, it's not like any of us have access to a yacht. I'd love to see what it's like to be at a yacht party, seriously."

Kendyl nods as she turns to Kyle, still massaging his neck and shoulders to calm him down. "Babe, I get what you're saying, and we can still find a way to get what we want while keeping out of the drama. As long as we stay tight and among ourselves, we could survive this and have a whole reason to people watch and be nosy for the hell of it." She kisses Kyle across each cheek and his forehead, and I low-key want to have the same influence over Yasir as Kyle softens up fast. "If one of us leaves the group while at the party, then a wingman goes with them. It will keep what happened to Yasir at your party from happening this weekend."

"I'm feeling that," Yasir co-signs. "Although I know if any of the girls go, y'all are all going together. We're not that naïve."

The boys get a good chuckle out of that quip, but it's not like he's wrong. Kyle taps fists with Yasir and Taylor, dropping a peck on Kendyl's lips before he shifts back to the rest of us. "Alright, let's run with that plan. I'm still not with it, but we can at least stay insulated and protected while we're there."

I kiss him then rise from his lap. "I need to talk to my girls for a minute. I'll meet up with you later?"

"Yeah, I need to drop by Unk's shop to see if there's anything he needs. Meet me there so we can talk?"

"I'll meet you there."

I let my gaze linger a lot longer than I want as he strolls away. I bite my lower lip, suppressing the thoughts in my head knowing I need to chat with the girls. I take my seat next to Kendyl, encouraging Tania to join us on the wider bench.

"So, now that the boys are gone, what do you really think?" I cut to the heart of the matter, especially since their collective body language tips me off. "This is Ian we're talking about, and we've all had our dealings with him in one form or fashion. And there's still the issue of Chrisette being there too."

"Yeah, a lot of the girls on the squad are buzzing about the boys that might be there from other schools," Kendyl adds to the mix. "Chris has been taking the lead, almost playing matchmaker in some cases. Turns out, Ian's been branching out, spreading his network of madness."

Tania sighs as she rubs her temples. "I feel like I just jumped into a situation that I don't know if I'm equipped to be in. How do y'all do it?"

"Don't look at me, I'm not a part of that world like that, either," I rebut. "You know me, Nia. My life is my engines, my besties, and—"

"That cute ass boyfriend of yours," Tania blurts out.

Kendyl laughs out loud. "They're not together yet, chica."

Tania fans herself a few times, staring at me with this "are you serious?" expression. "I don't know how you've been able to be 'just friends.' He's absolutely hypnotic, no disrespect, girl. I'm just getting to know Taylor, and I'm into him, but whew, I don't know how you do it."

I smirk, appreciating her honesty more than anything. While Yasir's comfortable maintaining his smaller circles, I'm not immune to the comments about him. "Kenni's right, but I'm planning on doing something about that later today and make a few statements of my own this weekend."

"It took you long enough," Kendyl announces. "Sheesh! It I had to play bodyguard one more time, I was gonna wring your neck."

"Well, you won't have to do it anymore." I stand and get ready to meet up with Yasir. "I gotta go, girls. I have a cutie I need to claim."

I opt to leave Raiden in the parking lot in front of Unk's store, then jump into Storm and settle in the passenger seat, directing him to a secluded spot so we can be alone. I don't want to sound nervous while we ride, but I can't stop trembling in anticipation.

We stop at Prentiss Park, a location I use whenever I want to be alone to create music. We get out of the car and walk to one of the empty pavilions. He's carrying one of his parkas with us, since we're in a wooded area in the park and the weather has turned cooler than expected.

Being wrapped inside the fabric and inhaling the faded remnants of his scent puts me in a mood. I take a deep breath and sigh as I turn my gaze to meet his curious stare. "Look, after what happened last weekend, and before we agree to go to Ian's party, I'm just gonna come out and say it before I lose my nerve—I'm ready to be your girlfriend, if you still want me to be."

I search his widened eyes, noticing his amber-golden irises develop a pulse all their own. I take his hand, feeling that same pulse racing through his grip, which seems to sync with my own rapid pace.

"I-I mean, are you… yes, of course I want you to be my girlfriend." The way he stammers out the words before he finally smooths out his tone makes me want to reach out and wrap him in his coat with me. "I'm serious. Are you sure, you swear?"

"I swear, baby." I lean in and kiss him. "I want us to be together."

"Now I feel like what I needed to talk about kinda pales by comparison." He licks his lips to moisten them, pausing for a moment as he continues to stare into my eyes. "My Nana wants to see me this weekend, and she's asked if you could come with me to visit."

Umm—what? "Well, that was sudden. Why this weekend? What's the rush? Wait a minute, is she ready to have that talk about where you come from?"

"I understand if it's too soon. I can tell her we'll come up another time if you want." He backtracks a little quicker than I want, but—yeah, we've just solidified our relationship seconds ago. "I know you said you wanted to go when we were just friends, but this is something completely different. You're my girl now."

Hearing him say that causes this heat to course through me. I have to take off the coat so I won't faint. By Nyati, what did I get myself into? "I still wanna go, baby. I promised I would help you see this through. What time do you want to head up there?"

"I wanna make it a day trip, get down and back before nightfall so we have enough time to prep for the party on Sunday night," he tells me. He keeps staring at me, making me blush and bury my face inside his coat. "You're my girl. You have no idea how long I've been waiting to say that."

"Well, get used to it, pretty boy, because I'm yours."

I don't want to sound like I'm all doom and gloom, but this is coming out of nowhere, and as much as I'm happy that we can finally define what we are now, I can't escape this nagging feeling in the pit of my stomach.

I just hope I'm wrong.

CHAPTER THIRTY-FOUR – YASIR

I've only been gone from the A for six weeks.

Six weeks feel like years to me.

Everything I remember as we travel up I-75 to get to my Nana's exit… well, it looks different for some reason. Maybe it has more to do with getting used to Oakwood Grove than anything. Still, by the time we exit and head up University Avenue to turn into her neighborhood—Pittsburgh community—I've settled back into my groove.

Paradise Drive is only a few turns away. The only place I've ever known and felt safe.

The row of houses on that dead-end street comes with an interesting story I was told when I was younger. The houses used to occupy the land where the highway exists today. So, the city and the state governments, according to Nana's neighbors, negotiated to have all the houses on the street relocated. The foundations were extracted, set up on blocks, moved to their new plots of land, and resettled.

I always thought it was a cool, but irritating, piece of history. Still, whether by divine invention or just the pure goodness of the people, that street managed to be a haven of sorts for anyone who lived there, and for those who visited. Almost as though the minute you turn onto the street, it becomes a "fortress" of sorts, like nothing else matters, and you can leave your troubles at the corner. I don't know how else to explain it. Chaos may swirl in the rest of the Pittsburgh community, hell, the rest of the world, but it never touches "paradise."

Maybe that's what I miss most… feeling safe despite everything.

Zahra and I had been vibing the entire drive, stealing glances during the five-hour trip, stopping in Macon to grab some food and gas up. I make a mental note to grab the special fuel blend I have at Nana's when we get there, since I only run Storm's engine on ethanol blends when I don't have time to mix the fuel for longer road trips.

I keep glancing at her, grinning over the beauty who's making herself comfortable in the passenger seat, playing with the music selection that became the soundtrack for the trip. I can't believe she's here with me. I mean, yeah, she said she wanted to go a while ago, but this… it hits different.

"Your whole energy is different, baby." Zahra breaks through my thoughts as we make the final turn before hitting Nana's street. "It's aggressive, edgy."

"Oh, really? How do you mean?"

"It feels like you had to match the vibe surrounding us. I noticed you started scanning the area more, like you were putting your head on a swivel to see every angle you could." She keeps studying me like she's never seen me before a day in her life. It makes me a little uncomfortable, but I adjust quickly. "I'm trying to decide if I like this look on you… ruffneck."

I hide my grin. Okay, let's stop playing, I can't hide my grin, and I don't want to, either. She has a point without realizing it. I kinda remade myself a little bit because I didn't want my past to follow me to Oakwood Grove. What I failed to account for was having to come back home, and with someone who never knew or had seen that other side of me.

I shrug off those thoughts as I wink at her. "I hope once you've seen this side of me, you don't go running for the hills."

She leans over and kisses my cheek, sending waves of heat down my spine. "I'm a big girl. I like to think I can handle a few things."

"You haven't met my Nana yet."

We pull into the driveway, making sure to turn the music down low. While Zahra is confused over my insistence, she doesn't understand what the streets already know. If anyone came to Ms. Johari's house for anything, the music had to be turned down or turned off. She always said it upsets the ancestors who commune with her, but I know better.

I take a deep breath once I put the car in park, gripping the gearshift tighter than I planned. I've been asking, and asking, since I was thirteen, to find out about my family tree. Now that the moment is here, I want to back out. The unknown freaks me out, and I fear whatever it is that she might have to tell me.

A soft, soothing hand covers mine while it remains on the gearshift. When I shift my gaze, her eyes pierce through to the very core of my being. I can't tear myself away, even if I want to. "It will be okay, promise." She rubs her fingers across the back of my hand, sending shockwaves through my arm. "This was a long time coming, and you're ready for this."

I get out of the car, moving around the back to the passenger side to make sure Zahra hops out in one piece. Okay, so I want to sneak a kiss in before we walk up the stairs arm-in-arm to the front door. I'm gonna have to calm down. I'm about to introduce a girl to my grandmother for the *first time* in my life, on top of learning information that has the potential to shift my whole life.

Even though I have a key, I ring the doorbell and step back to wait for her to go through her usual routine. I look to my left, where I notice the familiar rustling of the curtains, suppressing a smirk because I know what comes next. I'm not prepared for how far she's about to go, though.

"Now, why would my grandson ring the doorbell when he knows he has a key?" She shouts through the heavy, lacquered, and polished oak door. Her accent comes through with all the richness of a thick batch of molasses. Man, I miss her so much in this moment. "I do not think I should open the door, since I was not expecting any strange visitors today."

"Nana, I would have used my key, but I have a special guest with me." I chuckle, cutting my eyes at Zahra, who stifles a giggle of her own at the spectacle we're putting on in front of her. "I know my grandmother would prefer that I make formal introductions before she welcomed the special guest into the house."

"They had better be special, or I am giving them the business."

"Nana, come on. Why would I bring someone to the house if they weren't special?"

"You have a good point, grandson." Nana taps her knuckles against the other side of the door. "They had better be pretty, or I will disown you. And you better be wearing your necklace, or I will have another reason to cut you out of my will."

Zahra breaks out into laughter, bracing one hand against the wall and holding her stomach with the other. "I love her already. She got you shook."

"Nana, I would never go anywhere without my necklace." I roll my eyes, intent on breaking through the stone wall she insists on throwing in front of me. She knows I don't go anywhere without my amethyst teardrop necklace. That's a karma I don't want. "She's stunning, and she's also the one I told you about."

"Wait… what?" Zahra whispers in my ear. "You told her I was coming with you? I thought you wanted this to be a surprise."

Nana opens the door in grand fashion, causing both of us to jump. She gives me the once over, then throws a sideways glance at Zahra. "Oh well, since you put it that way, let me get a good look at her for myself, make sure you are not slipping."

"Nana!"

"What? I have to make sure that you have good taste in girls, Ya-Ya."

Zahra keeps laughing at the "show" my grandmother puts on, unable to stop, even with her standing in front of us on the other side of the wrought-iron outer door. I want to die on the spot. This is not the way I envisioned things to go at all. "Oh em gee," Zahra says. "This was worth the trip and then some. I can't wait to find out what happens next."

I clear my throat so I can get my life together. "Nana, I would like to introduce my girlfriend, Zahra Assante. Z, this is my Nana, Mrs. Johari Salah, known in the neighborhood as Ms. Johari or Mama Johari."

Zahra blushes for a moment, extending her hand out to shake. "It's a pleasure to meet you, Ms. Johari. Yasir has told me a lot about you."

Nana takes a long look at Zahra and her eyes light up. In the next moment, she rushes us inside, taking Zahra by the shoulders and studies her like she's connecting the dots in her mind. This smile… I mean, this *smile*… shows up out of nowhere. I have no clue what to make of it, and Zahra looks a little uneasy the whole time.

Nana keeps going into this trance, like she's looking through her and off into the distance. Her hands start trembling, and I do what I can to calm her. I don't want Zahra completely freaking out. First impressions and all that.

By the time I get the chance to shake Nana out of whatever is happening to her, she just snaps right out of it. Her gaze is strange, like she doesn't want to say what she's seen, but there's no way I'm about to let that ride. In the next moment, her facial expression turns again, this time she's all smiles again. "You are Kua Tribe, are you not, little one?"

Zahra's eyes flash, and I stand there confuzzled as all get out. "Yes, ma'am, I am. But how did—?"

"Yeah, Nana, how in the world could you have figured that out just by staring at her?" Why do I get the feeling this all ties into a lot of what she wants to talk about? "And what's that whole thing you just did where you blanked out on us? I think we need to sit down, for real, for real."

She ushers us into the living room, moving with a sense of urgency that triggers my anxiety. She takes each of our hands in hers, grinning the whole time as she sees the two of us together. "Yes, baby, we do… I had no idea… please, you two, make yourself comfortable on the couch, I will grab some sweet tea and lemon and explain as much as I can."

We've spent the last two hours talking about my life in Kindara, and I'm sitting here reacting like all the things that happened that night before I was brought to Nana were happening to someone else. Every word she speaks feels like I'm sinking deeper and deeper into a rabbit hole, with no chance of coming out of it as anywhere near the same person. Nana has been an oral storyteller her entire life, so, everything that comes from her sounds like it was written for fiction.

Except, not one word of it is fiction.

"You, your parents, and your older brother, were selected by the Kindaran Council to be a part of the Kindaran Nine families," Nana began weaving the next part of the fascinating tale that is my life. "You were charged with knowing the location of, and protecting, something very sacred to Kindara, because the Vodaran priestesses who brought you into the world saw what the Divine Mother had gifted you."

My head is spinning, trying to make sense of everything she's told me and Zahra so far.

My parents were… *murdered*?

My bloodline is Kindaran, and I wasn't born in the States.

I have, or had, a big brother?

I was supposed to die that night during an invasion—the Bralba invasion.

"That night was one of the worst nights of my life," Nana continued, wiping tears from her eyes like it all happened last week, much less over ten years ago. "Hassan brought you to me and gave the devastating news that your father and your mother had been killed to protect you and get you out."

"What happened to my… my brother?" I ask her, doing my best to keep my hands from shaking. "Has anyone been able to find him?"

"No, my child. Bomani, your older brother, was a part of the Kindaran military at the time of the invasion," Nana answers as she continues to rock in her chair. "I fear he is dead, possibly killed during the invasion. When efforts were being made to identify the bodies in the aftermath, the only thing found were his identification tags around the neck of a body found outside of Drana Tirin."

Tears streak down my face, and I'm sad and confused at the same time. Somewhere deep in my core, I feel the loss of family, another person who could've helped me figure out who I am. I just can't figure out why I'm so distraught over it. I don't remember him, except for a memory triggered out of the blue before I met with Ms. Lennox for lunch a few days ago.

But she still doesn't explain why she blanked out into a trance when she held Zahra's hand. That's gonna bother me for a minute, but I'm in too much shock from the other revelations to pay any attention to it right now.

"I know that this is a lot for you to learn in one day, but I promise, we will take everything one step at a time, one day at a time." Nana leans in, taking my hands in hers, focusing her gaze into my eyes. "I am sorry that I could not tell you before now, but there is a reason we had to keep the truth from you."

I force tears back as best I can. It's more than I thought I'd hear, and more than I can handle in one short burst. I wanted to know, but now I don't know what to do with it all.

"So, I'm… Kindaran? Like, I'm from the same country as you, as Zahra?" I struggle to get the words out. It's not every day that your world, your history, is split into pieces and put back together again to look like a whole other picture you're struggling to understand. "So, what Tribe… what Tribe are we from?"

"We are Solara Tribe, my darling." She keeps rubbing my hands, but I can't stop shaking. "And unfortunately, we were ground zero for one of the worst atrocities in Kindaran history."

"By Nyati… Solara was where everything happened." Zahra gasps and clamps her hand over her mouth. I'd almost forgotten that Zahra sat right beside me while she listened to everything I heard coming from Nana. It doesn't even register for me over what she might be thinking right now. "My father is a Kindaran historian. I've read about what happened, and I was a little girl when we were evacuated to the States, but I never thought I would ever meet anyone who survived the attacks. We were told that almost everyone was killed."

"Well, my dear girl, as you now realize, that was not the case." Nana nods as she glances at her. "I have a feeling your father and I may need to have a longer conversation. If for nothing else, we may need to update his recollection of historical data."

"So, I have another question," I interject. My head is still spinning, and I try to find some way to balance. "What about what I told you about the way my eyes turned red. And Zahra said she saw my eyes turn purple when we were alone. What does that mean? Is there something wrong with me?"

"No, there is nothing wrong with you at all, of that I am certain." Nana's eyes smile before the rest of her face follows. She places her hand against my cheek. "Nyati has placed something special inside you. What that is, and why the Divine Mother chose you, even I do not know. But I do know how to find out. I will contact Hassan. He has been on a separate mission for the Kindaran Council."

"Who's Hassan? Is he part of the Solara Tribe? Or was he part of another Tribe in Kindara?" It sounds so foreign to me, the way it's coming out of my mouth. I have to get used to saying it, though… it's my heritage now. "Does he know where our kin who survived might be? Does anyone else know if they are still alive, and if they know my parents? I have so many questions."

Nana closes her eyes for a moment, clasping her hands together and mumbling something I can't make out. When she opens her eyes, I can tell it pains her to have to explain things. "We had to… tell a different story… for the Solara Tribe to have a chance to rebuild. The truth of what happened there could only be entrusted to the Kindaran Council and the elder Vodaran priestesses. Not even Hassan knows the whole truth. All he was told was to find you and get you somewhere safe. That's how you were brought to me that night."

"But if I lived there, how am I not able to remember? I keep having these strange dreams that don't make sense to me." I blink a few times to try to access some of the images to describe to her. "I mean, I kept seeing different parts of the island, and I thought it was more because of the stories you told me when I was younger. I even told Zahra that I didn't know the island, and I still don't know if I do or don't."

"A priestess suppressed your memories. As I was told by Hassan, you were in so much shock, you could not speak," she replies, wiping a tear from her eye. "She warned that you might still have nightmares of that night, but we had hoped that they would not happen at all, at least until we had time to prepare you for what I have told you today."

"How soon can he get here? It sounds like he holds the key to a lot of my past, and I need to know it ASAP."

"These things take time. I do not know where he is on the planet right now. If I can get him to come to Georgia, I will tell him to come as soon as possible," Nana says. She leans back in her chair, rubbing her hands together. "There was no way to know when your subconscious might awaken. Now that we know it has, we need to unlock what has been hidden from you."

"Did you or Unk know what's going on with me?" I narrow my gaze, unsure of what answer I'll get from her. "Did you know the truth and kept it from me?"

"Ya-Ya, take a breath, okay?" Zahra rubs my shoulders. I knew I was tense, but considering the information being laid at my feet, I want to explode. "We will get you through this, but you need to breathe. Breathe with me, slow and steady."

"I need answers, that's what I need." I massage my temples, feeling Zahra's hands moving to my back. "I don't why I'm even asking. Who knows how much more of this I can handle right now? Everywhere I've been, I've felt like I was out of place. Now, I kinda know why, but I don't know why."

Zahra presses her lips against my cheek and hums a tune in my ear, pulling me closer so only I could hear it. It's so hypnotic, so soothing, I almost forget where we are. Our eyes meet when I turn to face her, and she doesn't speak a word, the only thing I hear is the tune she continues to hum. I take deeper breaths, falling into a Zen-like trance, concentrating on the melody more than anything.

She smiles as she hums, her eyes darting back and forth. I wonder if she notices something in my eyes and pray they aren't changing colors again. I'm already hanging by a thread, the last thing I need is to have something else that I can't explain.

Zahra places an index finger against my lips, her silent cue to stop worrying over whatever is happening to me. It's easy for her to say, she's not the one whose eyes are glowing… who knows what hue they are this time around?

The moment she stops singing, a cloud lifts from my mind. I grin at her, mouthing "thank you" as I caress her cheek. She whispers, "We'll handle this, I promise."

"Yes, that is what I thought." Nana claps softly over what she'd witnessed. "The gods placed you where you needed to be for their own reasons, and this is one of them, Ya-Ya."

Zahra smirks a bit, shaking her head a few times as she waits for me to give her any idea that I'm okay. I nod placing a small kiss across her lips. "I wouldn't exactly say the gods had anything to do with it, Ms. Johari. Your grandson is quite the charmer. He had my attention from the moment he stepped on campus."

Nana doesn't say anything. She just continues to stare at us, crossing her arms over her chest. "My dear girl, first, you no longer have to call me Ms. Johari. It's Nana. Second, there is a fine line between coincidence and fate. Only time will tell if the gods were right or not."

I check my watch, realizing we better head out and make a few more stops before we make the drive back to the Grove. More than likely, the streets have already caught wind that I'm back, and it's only a matter of time before certain people check in to make sure I know that they know.

I kiss Nana's cheek, giving her a long hug, smiling when she cups my face and then squeezes Zahra so tight, I think she won't be able to breathe. "Now, I expect you to come back and see me sometime. There is so much more we need to discuss, you hear?"

"Yes, Nana, I hear you." Zahra giggles as she takes my hand to leave. "I promise, we will have more conversations soon. I have to find out more embarrassing stories about Ya-Ya, and you're the perfect person to get that from."

"Yeah, nah, it's time to go, for real." I almost drag her to the door, coming close to picking her off the ground to carry her to Storm. "We have some other things to do and people to see."

"Yes, you do, Ya-Ya. You have been gone too long, and you might need to get things back in balance." Nana winks as she sits in her favorite rocking chair on the porch. "Things have been a bit off for the past few weeks."

Zahra's ears perk up, turning her attention to my concerned expression. "What does she mean by that? Is there something you're not telling me?"

The distinctive rumble of several engines catches my ears. It's faint at first, but the sounds get louder within minutes. I can deal with them if I'm by myself, but having Zahra with me complicates things, and there's no way I can talk my way out of the situation. Not when *she's* with them.

A few minutes later, the line of muscle cars, a mix of Mustangs, Camaros, and Chargers, pop up in front of Nana's driveway. Zahra surprises me by stepping in front of me, almost like she wants to protect me. Nana notices it too, but all she does is continue to rock in her chair. If she had access, I'm sure she would have a bowl of popcorn in her lap, ready to watch whatever is about to unfold.

Dante exits from his Charger, walks around the front, and leans against the hood. The rest of the Squad follow his lead, blocking the driveway—and our ability to leave.

Yeah, this is gonna get really interesting, really fast.

Chapter Thirty-Five – Zahra

What in the *Fast and the Furious* is going on out here?

I've never seen so much chrome, and the low-profile tires and twenty-eight-inch rims are a little gaudy, but who am I to criticize? I hope it's all for show because they can't possibly be racing these cars.

If their plan is to intimidate either of us… epic fail.

If they want to impress with the display in front of me and Yasir—yeah, nah.

Maybe if I weren't into cars like that, I probably would've looked all mesmerized or whatever, but I spent more time calculating the amount of money they wasted on aftermarket upgrades they didn't need.

I'm already in front of Yasir before they hop out of their cars, and while it might not have been the best idea on the planet, it feels good. He can handle himself, but that doesn't mean I'm not ready to ride for my baby, either.

The expressions on their faces make it seem like he's done something to piss them all off, which has me confused. *This* is the Squad he's been bragging about? The only thing I can do is let the convo play itself out, because it's obvious they have some things to get off their chests.

Yasir wraps his arms around me, inserting his thumbs inside my jean pockets. Not gonna lie, it sends a surge through us that I don't want to go away any time soon. I slip my hands over his as he focuses his attention on his Squad. "Dante, what's good, my boy? I told you I'd come holla when I was done visiting with Nana."

"Yeah, well, I figured we'd bring the party to you, in case you decided to, shall we say, take a few detours," Dante says to him. Maybe it's my imagination, but he sounds aggressive. Like, really aggressive. "Seeing the little baddie in front of you acting like she's trying to protect you, I guess that might explain why you've been MIA for the past few weeks."

Yasir squeezes me a little tighter than I expected, and I take that as a silent clue that he's agitated. A low growl escapes his throat, and I caress his hands to keep him calm. "Forgive my manners, I'd planned on making more formal intros in a different way. Zahra, this is the Squad I told you about. The boys in the back are my brothers, Malik and Caleb; the girls in front of them are Dominique and Alyssa. And of course, my Day One, Dante."

I don't appreciate the way Malik and Caleb are eyeing me like I've committed some unforgivable sin against them, but I have no intention of letting them know it's bothering me. I scan the group, catching the scowl on Alyssa's face, and make a note to see what that's all about if the convo shifts in her direction.

Dante, however, takes the lead on how things are about to flow. He looks past us, waving toward Nana to acknowledge her. "Hi, Nana, how are you doing this afternoon?"

"Things are fine, baby. I am hoping you and the Squad were coming by to have a civil conversation." I hear her still rocking in her chair, subtly setting the tone for how she expects everyone to act. Watching everyone straighten up when she speaks gives me a greater appreciation for the respect she wields. "I would hate to have to intervene to ensure everyone plays nicely."

"Yes, ma'am, I guess the Squad and I wanted to make sure we didn't miss him. There's no telling when he might be able to come through again," Dante explains as he returns his glare in Yasir's direction. "He's usually a man of his word, but he's been distracted lately."

"Okay, well, I will head back into the house. I have some other business to attend to," Nana says as she slowly rises from her rocker and shuffles inside. "Make sure you let me know when you leave, grandson."

The moment the iron door closes behind her, any hope for civil discourse goes up in smoke.

"When have I not been a man of my word, Te?" Yasir still doesn't move, but he's vibrating so intensely. I squeeze my hands tighter around his palms to let him know I'm still with him. "I said what I said when I texted you. There were some things I needed to talk to Nana about, and it would take some time."

"Chalk it up to some within the circle who felt they wanted some sort of closure," Dante says. He turns around and looks at Alyssa—who still hasn't wiped the scowl off her face—in a not-so-subtle attempt to explain who has the most pressure to release. "Since you had to skip out of the city at a moment's notice, right?"

"So, you wanna do this here, huh? Real classy, but I guess I shouldn't be surprised." Yasir removes his hands from my waist, then steps around to the passenger side of Storm and takes my hand to follow him. He leans against the door, motioning the rest of the group to come closer. "So, let's get this over with, I ain't got all day."

"Yasir, you don't have to do this right now, okay?" I interrupt. "We've been through a lot over the last few hours, and you don't want to say anything that you'll regret."

"It's cool, Z, they have pressure they need to get rid of, so, we can get that handled and let the chips fall where they may." He keeps his grip on my hand, pulling me closer to him. "I'd hoped to do this somewhere else, but here we are."

"Yeah, here we are, and from the looks of things, she doesn't look like much. I don't care what Te says." Alyssa frowns as she steps in front of me. "Damn, Ya-Ya, I thought you had better taste than this."

"Ally, stop being salty for no reason," he says. He follows my gaze, realizing I haven't taken my eyes off Alyssa the whole time. I flex my fingers to keep from balling them up. Yeah, I'm spoiling for a fight. "I told you before I left that we were better off as friends. Why are you popping off like this?"

"Is that what you're trying to convince yourself of what happened that night, bro?" Alyssa scoffs at me, which trips my trigger to respond in kind. "Don't flex in front of your 'girl,' playa. We know you better than she does, trust."

Yasir takes a sharp breath, tapping his fist against Storm's hood. "Whatever Ally told you about that night, I'm telling you right here and now, that's not what went down, alright?"

"Why don't you do us a favor and tell us what happened from your point of view, then, Diablo?" Dante spits out. "Because you know the drill, and you know how things rock within Squad too."

"Wait a minute, what are they talking about, Yasir?" This whole situation is going in a direction I'm not sure I'm ready for. "What happened between you and Alyssa? She's looking like—"

"Oh, don't act like you're concerned now, shawty," Alyssa cuts me off before I can finish my thought. "But, let me tell you about the boy you're dealing with so you can make up your own mind. Yasir—the boy we all lovingly know as Diablo—was willing to risk betraying Squad by getting with me before he had to leave, knowing it would screw things up."

"That's not what happened, and you know it, Ally." Yasir's pulse is racing, and I can feel it through my fingers. I'm caught in the in-between, suddenly desperate to separate fact from fiction, but in need of all the information before I can say another word. "You pushed the issue while we were working on your ride. I never gave you any idea that I was interested in anything. That's bad for business."

"So, you didn't try to stop me when we were kissing that night?" Alyssa throws in that tidbit, watching my reaction with a smirk. "You didn't tell me to put my clothes back on, either."

"Yes, I did. You were upset because I didn't tell you before I told Squad about what happened and that I had to leave." Yasir's voice never rises an octave, even though I feel him shaking. This is getting way out of hand, and he's struggling to keep his composure. "You'd been drinking when you came over, and I even made you sleep in my room while I crashed on the couch because I was scared you weren't thinking clearly."

"You took advantage of my feelings for you and promised me once you got where you were going that you would come back for me!" Alyssa screams. "I was willing to be with you over Squad because you told me you loved me. And like a fool, I believed you."

"Wait… what the hell?" I twist around and stare at him. I search his eyes, hoping to see the truth. "Is any of what she's saying true? Do you have feelings for her?"

"No, I never promised—"

Dante inserts himself into our exchange, leaning against the front of Storm's hood. "You're like a brother to me, Yasir, and even I had a hard time believing Ally for a minute, but it made sense when I thought back on it. You were gone only hours after you told me you had to jet. Then Nique called me, saying that Ally was at her house, crying her eyes out."

"You're bugging out, Te. I don't know what conclusion you think you've come to, but that's not what happened, dammit," Yasir flat out states. "She tried to kiss me, that part is true, but I smelled the alcohol on her breath, bro. I made her sleep it off, and then—"

"And then you were gone by morning, right? And you left her in Nana's house alone and confused," Dante points out, turning his attention to me. "Real talk, I'm sorry you had to hear about your boy like this, but he's not who you think he is. He's just like me, and the rest of the boys in the crew. We're players, which is why we all agreed that Nique and Ally were like sisters and off limits."

"I didn't have a choice in the matter. Don't you get that?" Yasir insists as he rubs the back of his neck. "I tried to stay until morning to make sure she'd sobered up, but Nana rushed me out the door because there were some—you know what, never mind, nothing I say will change your minds."

"You're right, and the fact that you're trying to drop Nana in the middle of your bullshit is low, even for you, especially when she isn't out here to speak for herself." Dante jumps in his face, but Yasir doesn't flinch or blink at all. "I don't know if you're even Squad anymore if you're gonna act like you didn't do anything."

"Then I guess I'm not Squad, but I'm not gonna sit here and cop to something I didn't do," Yasir counters. "If you can't trust me as your Day One, big bro, then there's nothing more for us to say."

"Yeah, I can't trust you right now, and I expected more from you, to at least be a man so we can squash this and move on." Dante steps away from him, making the motion for everyone to get back to their cars. "When you're ready to come clean, shout and I'll listen. I owe you that much to hear you out as my Day One. Until then, don't holla."

They all get in their cars, leaving the front of the house one by one until the street is clear. Not one of them even bothers to say goodbye.

"Yasir, I-I need to know what happened. Are you willing to talk to me about it?" I don't know what to think. Confusion swirls around me with no real way of knowing what, or who to believe.

Yasir's eyes are closed so tightly I can see the muscles in his jaw twitch. "I'll tell you everything you wanna know. It's not pretty, but it's the truth, I promise."

It takes about an hour of driving before he calms down long enough to say anything regarding that night. We're not entirely quiet during that time. I mean, we still talked about everything else that happened with Nana. I'm trying to be patient with him, despite every fiber in my being wanting to run. I want to believe him, but the way his framily just turned on him is hard to ignore.

"Alyssa and I started out as friends. She became friends with me when I first got to Douglass, the last school I attended before I came to Oakwood," he begins, switching between glancing at me and keeping his eyes on the road. "I'd kept her at arm's length for nearly the entire semester, but she never gave up on trying to be my friend."

"Go on," I choose to listen to him purge instead of asking questions while he's talking. I want the whole story and then I can ask away.

"Once I got over my anxiety of dealing with anyone outside of Squad, things took off fast between us. She became a best friend of sorts, helping me learn Doug and how things flowed, helping me with homework. We bonded over her Mustang and Storm. I learned how to work on her car, and she learned Storm." His shoulders relax a little bit, but his hands never leave the steering wheel. "Eventually, I introduced her to Squad, and it actually felt good to have her there. Nique was already Squad, so having another girl for her to vibe with, it felt like a win-win, you know."

I turn my body toward him as we cruise down the highway, my focus solely on him. I'm still not saying a lot, but my anxiety is ramped up and then some.

"Before the school year started, Nana had been getting these strange calls, and she told me it was nothing at first, so I didn't pay any attention." He groans in frustration, then mumbles something I can't make out. "Then, I overheard a tense convo one night when she thought I was asleep. She was angry—like, white-hot angry—and told whoever was on the phone that it wasn't fair to put me through it again."

I can't resist asking a question now, it's getting too intense. "Put you through what, again?"

"Before I finally settled at Doug, I had a history of temperamental outbursts, getting into fights, all that." He turns on the windshield wipers as we're riding through an unexpected rainstorm and taps the brakes to disengage the cruise control. "I'd moved through so many schools, I'd lost track over the years, but Nana managed to help me through it. I eventually found boxing through Unk, and I was starting to even out and not let my temper get the best of me. I was so angry about my parents and everything that came with it."

"What about the night that Ally was talking about, the night I assume you two had sex?" I'm having trouble even speaking those words into the air. It's not out of jealousy, at least, I don't think it's because I'm jealous. Am I? "What really happened?"

"Ally and I never had sex, and that's the truth." He sounded so emphatic that the force of his words pulses through me. "But thinking back on it now, I guess I see why she might have thought so."

"What do you mean?"

"That whole night was a nightmare," he recalls as we weave through traffic. "Nana called me, panicked, and said that I needed to get some clothes together and be ready to leave at any moment. She was out of town, and I was home alone. When I asked her what was wrong, she wouldn't tell me anything, just that I needed to be ready to head down to Unk's when she called again. None of it made any sense."

I'm completely enthralled with the story he's spinning. It sounds like a whole movie, I promise. I'm hooked on every word, waiting for everything to be revealed. "Keep going, I'm still listening."

"I told her I had stuff to do the next morning, and she said that I had to cancel it all, and to tell whoever I needed that I had to leave the city. She hung up before I could ask anything further." He blinks a few times, taking his right hand off the wheel. The rainstorm starts to let up, so he accelerates to keep up with the traffic around us. "I ended up calling Te, telling him that I had to leave town, and that I couldn't explain right then. We had a tense exchange, but I stuck to my story and told him I'd explain when I got settled where I was headed."

I nod, silently letting him know I'm locked in. How can I not be? Whew.

"While I was getting some clothes together, thinking it would be nothing more than a weekend trip, someone was banging on the door. Not knowing who would be at the house after midnight, I grabbed the stun gun and headed for the door." He shakes his head, almost like he doesn't want to remember any of this anymore. "I heard Ally's voice, yelling for me to let her in. Her eyes were red, and she looked like she'd been crying. I asked her what was wrong, and she yelled at me, asking me why I was leaving Squad—and leaving her."

I freeze, thinking back to the scowl on Alyssa's face when she looked at me. "Did you kiss her?"

"She tried to kiss me, yes, but I smelled the alcohol on her breath. I assumed she'd gotten the call from Te and got upset. She kept yelling at me, telling me that I should have told her myself, that she shouldn't have heard it from him." He blows out a sharp breath, taking a few calming breaths where he can. "She started crying again, and I went to hug her to try and settle her down. I kept telling her that I couldn't explain what was going on, but that I would tell her myself when I got where I was going. She had her arms wrapped around my neck, and when I tried to break from our embrace, she reached up and tried to kiss me."

"Okay, slow down, take a breath," I say, but I wonder if *I'm* the one who needs the break. "How did it go from her trying to kiss you to her saying that you didn't tell her to put her clothes back on?"

"When I made her sleep in my room, and I grabbed some blankets and a pillow to sleep in the living room, Nana called again. Ally was half naked by the time I got back to her," he utters. "I told her that Ally was there, and she said she would be there before Ally woke up, and she would explain everything to her after I left, but I needed to go right then and there because they had found me."

"Who's 'they'? Who found you?"

"Beats the hell out of me. It wasn't until I got to Unk's that I got part of the story that tied into the oils and scents I'd been mixing, and that it was to keep whoever wanted me dead from finding me." Yasir shrugs, pausing for a few more seconds before he picks up where he left off. "When I tried to call Ally back to make sure she was okay, she said she hated me and didn't want to see me again. It wasn't until I called Te back to give him the update that he asked about what went down with me and Ally, and that she was upset about what happened at the house."

"So, for the past few weeks, while you and I were trying to figure things out, you left all that going on without trying to make it right?" I ask in earnest. I can't be mad with Alyssa until he answers that question.

"She wouldn't take my calls, Z."

"What about Te?"

"He told me to give it time to blow over, and that he would work on Ally to get her to at least hear me out."

"So, that means you never tried after she stopped taking your calls."

He snaps his head in my direction, his eyes widening as he notices my irritation. "What could I have done? I can't force someone to talk to me."

"Would you have given up on me so easily?"

"No, I would have tried to get to you no matter what."

"Because you have feelings for me, and not her, right?" I cross my arms over my chest, turning my gaze toward the road. I can't even look at him. "How do I know that you won't do the same thing to me if these 'people' who are trying to do you harm find you again and you have to move to who knows where?"

"I don't know what I can say that will convince you," he replies. "Yes, I have feelings for you, but you know I have feelings for you."

"I don't know if there is anything you can say right now." As much as it hurts, I put myself in Alyssa's shoes, realizing the why of it all. I wipe a tear from my eye as I consider my next words. "I think it's best if we just stay friends for now, and we can see what happens down the road. I can't go through what she went through, even if you didn't encourage anything."

"Zahra, please." Hearing his voice crack threatens to break my heart. I don't want to do this, but what other choice do I have? He reaches out to take my hand, but I push it away. "I tried to reach her. She blocked me in every way possible. I didn't have a choice."

"Yasir, just take me home. I need time to think. Give me the space to do that, okay?" I still won't look at him. I can't. "I promise, we will talk about it once I've had some sleep, but right now, it's hard to understand your side of things."

"But, what about the yacht party tomorrow?"

"I'll ride with Kenni and Kyle. I'll understand if you're not okay with that."

Maybe I'm not being fair, but I really do need time to think, and I don't want my feelings for him to cloud the issue. If he's in my personal space, I'll cave on general principle. I need a clear head to make the best choice for me.

He doesn't try to argue, and I guess it may have more to do with exhaustion than anything. He just focuses on the road, not even bothering to look in my direction until we get to my house.

I want to say something when I get out of the car, but he refuses to look at me. I don't force him, I simply close the door and head into the house, watching with tears streaming down my face as he pulls out of the driveway and out of sight.

Chapter Thirty-Six – Yasir

So, remember a while back when I said I'll never figure girls out?

Add today's unexpected series of events to that list.

I wake up to a series of messages from Zahra, saying that she overreacted, and she would rather ride with me to the party. The other messages are a string of "I didn't mean what I said," and "We need to talk this through," among other things I'd rather not talk about because it's liable to make my head hurt and my heart ache.

The minute I finish reading the texts, I almost throw my phone against the wall.

Between the lack of sleep from feeling disconnected from her all night and making a surprise run with Unk to pick up some extra inventory for the shop because it's a holiday weekend, I'm completely exhausted before noon.

Oh, and speaking of the holiday weekend, we all should've known that was the reason why Ian would throw a party on a Sunday night. No school on Monday, which opens the door for all types of madness, with enough time to recover before school on Tuesday.

Now, I gotta figure out whether I wanna ask for… wait, what the hell am I asking for? To be forgiven? I didn't do anything. She's the one freaking out over something that I had no control over and decided that we don't need to be together, and in the span of less than twelve hours, she wants to find a way to work things out?

Just throw the whole damn weekend away.

Never mind the mess with my—former?—Squad in the A, and the fact that Dante turned his back on me over something that I know isn't true. Ally twisted everything up to keep from going out bad, and I'm the convenient villain in the story.

Okay, yeah, I didn't handle things all that great, and that's on me, but not enough to get labeled a traitor.

I can't worry about them right now.

The more important matter at hand stands about five-foot-six with hazel-green eyes that take me prisoner every time I gaze into them.

I know what I'm not gonna do, though. I'm not caving. Nope.

I text her and tell her before I jump in the shower that I'm running late and to catch a ride with Kyle and Kenni so she doesn't miss the boat. I'm still at war with my emotions over whether I even wanna be there when she and I aren't on the same frequency.

I step out and towel off so I can get my oils rubbed into my skin. I think about what I want to put on for tonight. The petty in me rages to the surface, and I remind myself that, while Zahra and I are trying to figure where we stand, she and I aren't together, together. She made that decision for the both of us.

Laid out on my bed are two distinctly different outfits, and as I consider my options, I have a YOLO moment. I put away the hoodie and jeans I planned to rock, choosing to go with a two-toned, black and gold turtleneck sweater to pair with relaxed black jeans and matching Timbs. This feels like a bold look that would get the attention I'm in the mood to command tonight. The bomber jacket completes the combination, and I can't resist pulling out a gold curb chain necklace and my prized black-and-gold trimmed Black Panther helmet pendant.

I check things over in the mirror once again, and I have to admit, I look good, if I do say so myself.

Unk and Lennox are downstairs in the living room, watching some movie I'm not interested in.

Lennox whistles her appreciation of the fit, and I'm blushing in seconds. "Well, well, well, look at you, handsome. I like that outfit, it looks really good on you. Zahra's a lucky girl."

I bypass part of her compliment, smiling over the fact that a grown woman thought I put together a look that looks good to her. I hit the remote to ignite Storm's engine, then slip the jacket over my outfit. Even though it's still a bit mild out, once we are on the water, the temperature drops a good ten degrees, easy.

"Have fun tonight, kiddo," Unk says as Lennox snuggles back in the crook of his hip. "We won't wait up, but don't get home too late."

꩜꩜꩜

I guess I can cross being on a mega yacht off my bucket list.

The sheer size of this boat is enough to make me wonder *how* Mayor Lance is able to afford something like this, much less allow his son to just take it without parental supervision.

I'm not complaining, though. Outside of the crew members to make sure this 200-foot monstrosity is traveling safely, I'm good with no adults being on board.

I step onto the aft landing, and it's like I've entered another world. Hardwood floors as far as I can see toward the bow of the ship. Enough lighting around the railing to make it look like it's daylight. The buffet table looks like it's at least a good twenty feet in length, loaded with everything: fruits and cheeses, seafood and chicken, chips and dips.

And that's just the *first* floor.

I take in all the kids that are on the yacht, and my anxiety kicks into high gear. I make a mental note not to bother with being on the bridge on the top level. Nope. I'm good. The amount of people I'd have to walk through is more than I'm willing to deal with tonight.

Not like I'm gonna have to worry about doing that. The crew has already spotted me, and from the expressions on their faces, I already know I'm gonna catch all the jokes.

"Oh, you two decided you had to take the spotlight from the rest of us, huh?" Kyle's giving me the business, but not in a bad way. I'd been trying to catch up to his fit game for a few weeks, and to get the seal of approval from him, and the rest of the boys in the clique, makes all the difference for me. "I don't know how you managed it when you haven't talked to each other, but I'm not about to make sense of it. Y'all fire."

I have no freaking idea what he's talking about… until Zahra appears from behind Kyle and Taylor, and *dammit*.

I should've stayed in the car. I wasn't ready.

The sweater dress she's wearing compliments her body so well, I wonder if someone knitted it just for her. We didn't have the chance to really talk about what we were planning to wear, but it's scary seeing the golden speckles woven into the black fabric. She finishes the outfit with a pair of black leggings and matching, knee-length, faux-fur-trimmed boots.

Whether we meant to or not, even though we'd barely said two words most of the day because I was still mad at her, we managed to sync up our outfits.

I don't know how to feel about that.

She glances up into my eyes, and as much as I want to be mad at her, by the gods, why can't I stay mad at her? She comes close to breaking my heart, and all I can do in that moment is take away the pain I see in her eyes. What the hell is wrong with me?

Zahra must have sensed the conflict in me because she slides her fingers against my cheek, her eyes never leaving mine. She whispers, "I'm sorry," with the familiar trembling of her lower lip.

I hate repeating myself, but I'll forgive her anything as long as I see her smile.

We stand there for what feels like hours, stuck in the moment, each of us waiting on the other to say something. I'm sticking to my vow of silence for now, even though she apologized first. I can't take my eyes off her, reacting to every movement, every embrace, every time my lips caressed hers, as though I met her for the first time. She already has me captivated, no matter what I do to keep it from happening.

She makes me sick. And I like it. "Why can't I stay mad at you?"

She gives up a slight grin as I pull her in for a hug. "The same reason I couldn't stay mad at you."

"So, what are we gonna do about whatever's going on between us?"

Zahra shrugs as she rubs the back of my neck. "Let's just enjoy the party for now. We can figure out the rest later."

I put the head-to-toe scan of Kyle's fit to change the vibe, realizing that he wants to make sure his physique and height are on full display. "You and Kenni are ones to talk, my boy. You pulled out the hoodie game tonight, and I see the logo is on blast. Starting the branding already?"

"Yeah, Quentin made it clear now that the NIL endorsement deals are out there, it helps to already have the following," Kyle replies as we tap fists. I turn to get a tap from Taylor, one of the other boys hanging with us tonight. "Me and TK hooked up with this graphic artist, and he got us right. We might need to get you to him soon, see if we can't turn you into a walking billboard."

"I'll leave that to the ballers, bro. I'm but a humble fan and supporter." My laughter is born more from nerves than anything else. "Besides, I probably look better promoting y'all than I would myself, anyway."

"Sooner or later, bro, you're gonna realize that you've got juice, too. Your ride speaks to that," Taylor points out as the boat rocks, letting us know we're in motion. "And don't think you haven't been getting attention, either. Eyes have been on you and Z the whole damn time."

Kendyl saunters into the space we carved out near the back of the yacht. Kendyl makes herself comfortable quick, dropping into Kyle's lap, while Tania finds her spot next to Taylor as he leans against the railing. Kendyl cuts her eyes in my direction, huffing like I missed an appointed time or something. "You were supposed to be here a half-hour ago. You're lucky Ian has a tendency to start things late. You can't have my girl out here solo, alright?"

Zahra blushes, glancing at me for a few moments while she plays in her hair. "Well, Ya-Ya and I, we… we had some things to handle."

Yeah, she gave a good cover excuse, but I don't have the energy to play make believe. "Yeah, some things went down in the A with my grandmother, and I'm still trying to sort through that information."

"Whoa, sounds intense," Kyle muses. He gives me a curious glance, then taps Kendyl on her thigh. When she pops up from his lap, he nods toward Taylor before he heads for the bar. "Yo, we're gonna grab something to drink real quick, do you ladies need anything?"

"Wait, we're not about to bypass the fact that Z just called Yasir by a nickname we hadn't heard before, are we?" Kendyl snaps her gaze in my direction. "When did my bestie learn that, and when did you plan on telling us, *Ya-Ya*?"

"Okay, first, yes that's a nickname my fam gave me when I was younger." My temper's boiling to the surface, and I'm ready to find somewhere else to be with the quickness. "Can we talk about that after we get the drinks, please? There's a lot going on that we need to let y'all in on."

Tania kinda takes the hint, but I get the feeling from her body language that she doesn't want to be separated from Taylor for a long period of time. I don't care either way, I'm focused on putting some space between me and Zahra right now. "Yeah, just a water for me, thanks. I'm sure we can find something to do while you're… at the bar."

We finally get out of earshot of the girls, and Kyle cuts to the white meat before I have a chance to react. "So, what's up with you and Z, bro? And don't say it's nothing because she's tiptoeing just like you are. Talk."

Well, since he wants to keep it a buck, let's keep it a whole buck. "She's in her feelings because when we got to Atlanta, there was a mess I thought I'd handled that blew back on me. A girl who… we were friends, and she wanted to be more, but we had rules in the crew we were in about coupling up. She got salty about me being with Z and got in her head about us being together."

Kyle frowns, and I prepare to catch a fade. After all, she is his best friend. "There's something you're not saying, my boy, so come with it, or you will catch smoke."

"Are you sure you want it all? I'm still trying to sort it out."

"If it means we don't get to scrapping on this boat, yep."

"Alright, here's the rest… my grandmother dropped bomb that I'm not from Atlanta. I was actually born in Kindara."

Kyle's eyes light up, realizing the significance of what I'd just said. "Pause, so that means…"

"Yeah, it means that Z and I are from the same country. Born in different tribes within the country, but we're both Kindaran." I rub the back of my neck a few times, the weight of the information still sitting on my shoulders. "That was already hard enough to deal with, and then she went and told me that I've had heat on me since I was younger, but she won't say what that means right now. All she said was it was the reason why I had to move around a lot and deal with so many different schools."

"And now, Z's thinking you might get snatched up again, and she's pulling away." Kyle puts on the detective hat, drawing the conclusion before I could say anything. "Whew, that's a lot. No wonder she's so off-balance."

"She's not the only one, bro." We finally get to the bar to order the non-alcoholic cocktails … I'm not about to get caught up, nope. "I don't know what to say to her to tell her that she doesn't have to worry about that. If my Unk gets a call and I have to jet ASAP, it's out of my control."

"Maybe we need to get her head right," Taylor says. "I mean, we're getting to the point where we can insulate a little bit. Our girls are starting to get along, maybe between Kenni and Nia, it might keep her hopeful for the time being."

"I hear you, bro, and for now, I'm content with trying anything." I look at Kyle. "I'm really feeling her, and I can't see being able to exist at Oakwood if we're not together."

"No cap?"

"No cap. I've been off-balance and low-key hurting all day."

"Then let's see what we can do to get you two back in sync. It's obvious by the fits you wore that you're already in each other's heads." Kyle chuckles as we grab the drinks and head back to where we left the girls.

Until we see Zahra talking with some random dude who's trying to flirt.

All I can see is black.

"Yo, ease back a bit, don't overreact," Kyle advises as he presses his palm against my chest. "This is a party. I can't have you going off script because things aren't back in the flow with you two."

He's right. It's a party, and if she's good with idle chit-chat, then I can do the same thing. "Look, I hear you, but if I go over there, it won't be pretty. I'll be back when I clear my head," I say as I break from Taylor and Kyle and head to the front of the yacht.

I take a few sips of the drink in my hand, wondering when the anger in my heart would calm down. I've only been in this section of the boat for a few quick moments, but I can't settle down. My instinct is to drop ol' boy overboard and deal with the consequences, but I don't want to let my temper and anger rule me.

The events of the past day-plus have me in a tailspin. I thought I had things on lock, only to find out how sloppy I let things get. As I slow my breathing and think things through, I realize that the whole thing with Alyssa was a bad look… I mean, a *bad* look. Would I have even given her a shot to explain herself if the roles were reversed?

I turn to walk to the back of the boat, when Chrisette and Amber startle me, stepping into my path. From the look in Amber's eyes, she's already had more than a few *real* drinks tonight. Chrisette's lit too, but she's hiding it well… or so she thinks. "Um, excuse me, ladies, I need to get back to my group."

"What's your rush, Yasir? I know Z is a little occupied at the moment, I'm sure she won't mind if we're talking, right?"

Amber slips into my personal space, and to be real, I don't push her away this time. It's a party, right? "I'm sure we can find a way to entertain each other until she's done with her convo."

"Yeah, but I don't know if that convo needs to happen between us, especially when Chrisette is here to stir up mess." I glare at Chrisette, hoping she gets the point. "Where's your man at, anyway? I thought he'd be helping to steer the boat or something."

"Yeah, he's handling all that up there, but why does it matter?" Chrisette puts her hands in the air in mock surrender. "Fine, maybe I need to see what my baby is up to. I'll check up on you two in a bit."

I lean against the wall, almost finished with my drink, and Amber takes the glass from my hand. She examines the half-empty glass and stares at me with this slick grin on her face. "I think you need another one, don't you?"

What does she take me for? "I'm not done with the one I have right now, thanks, but no thanks. Besides, I need to get back to my folk, for real. Z and I have some things to talk about."

She gives the glass back to me, standing against the open doorway as I down the rest of the drink. I don't have time to really worry about whether I hurt her feelings, I need to get back before someone sees something that could make me look bad.

I turn to make my way back toward the area Zahra and the crew are when I start to feel dizzy. I attempt to take another step, and things start spinning.

"Are you okay, Yasir? You don't look so good." Amber props me up against the railing, her eyes roaming all over me as I struggle to maintain eye contact. "Maybe I need to tell Ian to take the boat back to shore so someone can check you over."

I hold my hand up in protest, insisting that nothing is wrong. If I paid attention to my body, "fine" is the last thing I can profess to be right now. "I'm good, for real, I just need to sit down and clear my head."

"Here, let me get you into one of the rooms so you can lie down."

That's not an option. I don't care if things are iffy between me and Zahra, I'll go out bad if I get caught up with Amber on this boat. I can't allow that to happen. Even in my compromised state, I know who I want, and she needs to know.

I have to find a way to make things right, so we can get back to being together, the way we want to be. If I could simply apologize, have the type of convo that will clear everything, and kiss and make up.

Amber tries to pull me into the room, but I refuse to go. There's no way she can overpower me, regardless of how weak I feel. We're fighting when I sense us moving backwards. My head is still swirling, so I can't tell which way is up. I fade in and out during the scuffle, and when I finally have a clear moment, I see the concern on her face, but it doesn't quite register over the why of it all.

"Yasir, stop fighting me, you're gonna… oh my God!"

I'm not sure what happens next, because everything moves in slow motion, but the only thing I hear is Amber screaming, which I find odd when I haven't touched her. I swear my mind is playing tricks on me, because it feels like I'm falling, and then there's a rush of water that surrounds me in seconds.

After that, everything fades to black.

Chapter Thirty-Seven – Zahra

"Why are you still here, Giovanni? I said what I said and you acting like you heard something else."

"Yo, I'm just trying to see if you got room on your team. A few girls are already trying to put a little pressure on your boy, so I'm trying to see about you."

I search for anything I can get my hands on to stuff in this boy's mouth. He has his mind made up that he needs my attention when I have nothing to give him.

I catch a glimpse of the boys walking back from the bar, and I know I'm busted in seconds. Dammit.

I can't get this knucklehead away from me fast enough. By the time Giovanni's gotten the point, Kyle and Taylor arrive—without Yasir.

"Where is he?" A heat rages through me that I try to ignore. "I know he saw what he saw, but that's not what it is."

"I feel you, Z, but he's not hearing anything about anything right now," Kyle says. He scoffs, shaking his head as we scan the area. "What the hell happened to y'all while you were up in the A? Yasir told us a lot of stuff went down, but you're on one tonight."

I play in my hair for what feels like the fiftieth time this weekend, flipping a coin in my head over which way to answer. "Look, it's been a long weekend, and I'm not trying to mess up the vibe."

"Um, chica, the vibe is already a little off to say the least," Kendyl chimes in. "We need to know what you know. How else are we gonna help y'all through this?"

"Alright, fine." Now that I think about it, they may be able to help after all. "Yasir's Kindaran."

"Yeah, he put us on to that info just a few minutes ago," Kyle says. "Talk about a plot twist."

"Hold on, are you for real right now?" Kendyl looks like she's been dropped in the middle of a super-secret reveal. "I really didn't see that coming. Is that what his grandmother told him?"

"Yeah, and that's not all of it, but it's hard for me to explain because it's specific to our country. Trust me, it's wild, but it makes so much sense over why we connected so quickly, despite the both of us trying to just be friends." I think back to when he and I were first in each other's space. Whew, even then he gave me chills. Ugh. "But the girls in his crew that hang together, one of them caught feelings and got salty when she saw me. She got in my head for a second, but I needed time to think things through."

"What's there to think about?" Tania expresses her point. "I don't know Yasir all that well, but he doesn't act like the rest of these boys. Nobody's perfect, but from the outside looking in, he's worth the effort."

I wink at her as I sort through my emotions and the information in my head. Tania's right, it feels real. I can't walk away, even if I wanted to. "He's worth the effort, and I need to go get him before someone tries something stupid."

The next thing we hear makes my blood run cold. "Yasir! Nooooo! Man overboard! Help! Help!"

The engine stops almost as soon as we hear her screaming, and most of the kids run toward where the hysterical screaming is coming from. We rush in the same direction, and we find everyone crowding around Amber, visibly shaken from whatever the hell happened. I don't care about her in that moment; hearing her yell Yasir's name has my attention.

Kyle pushes us through the crowd to get to her. "What happened? You yelled for Yasir. Where is he?"

Amber can't speak, she just points toward the water, tears streaking down her cheeks. Chrisette stands with her, helping her hold on to a blanket to keep her warm.

Kyle and Taylor lean over the railing, trying to get any kind of sign that he's popped up out in the water or something. "Yasir! Come on, bro, where are you?!?!"

I can't breathe for a few seconds.

If something happened to him—there's too much that I need to say. I whisper to no one in particular, *By Nyati, please protect him.*

Kendyl cuts through the fog building in my mind, almost shaking me to bring me back to the present. "Z, do you have any cell reception? We need to call for help."

I don't remember saying if my phone works or not, but I give it to her and race to the back of the boat. Since the engine isn't running, I have a chance to not get caught up in the current. I pray he cleared the hull, but there's no way of telling what condition he may be in when we get to him.

Not seeing his body at least float to the surface scares me the most.

I take my boots off and tie my hair back, with only one thing on my mind. I ignore Kyle's screams for me not to jump off the boat, diving in feet first and swimming in the opposite direction. I shorten my strokes, working with the current and using it to help conserve as much energy as possible. I stop every few seconds, hoping I can see anything resembling his body above the water line.

"Yasir! Baby, where are you?!" I keep swimming in the direction I think the current may have carried him. I fear he's unconscious, which would be all bad, especially if we don't hear him screaming for help or anything. "Come on, baby, tell me where you are."

I dive underwater, realizing that it's foolish since I don't have a flashlight or anything to see through the darkness. I have to try something. I can't let him die out here.

I rise to the surface to catch my breath, hearing someone splashing toward me. I wipe my eyes as best I can, hoping it's Yasir trying to swim toward me. I float in one spot as the splashing comes closer, and I want to yell out again, but I feel a strong pair of hands grab around my waist, holding me still.

"I should choke you, scaring us like that, girl," Kyle growls as we continue to bob above the water. "What the hell were you thinking? I know you can swim, but we can't possibly find him in dark water."

"We have to try, dammit," I insist. I tremble as the cold water begins to affect me, but I refuse to leave. "Help me, please. I'll never forgive myself if we don't try."

Kyle nods, keeping his arm around mine as we swim further away from the boat. "Ian's keeping the boat in place until someone can get to us. We need to get to him quick. He could still drown even if he's unconscious."

I really don't want to hear that part, but it only increases the urgency to locate him before it's too late. We swim in as much of a straight line as the current will allow, shouting Yasir's name in hopes that he'll hear us. The longer we stay in the water, the more I try not to panic.

Frustration takes over, and I'm scared that we won't find him before more help shows up. I close my eyes to try to calm down and think, even for a few seconds. I start humming, although I don't know why or understand why I'm doing it, but I just keep humming, trying different frequencies as I maintain my energy.

"Yo, what are you doing, Z?" Kyle must have felt me vibrating, but I can't think about that now. My focus is on finding the right pitch to reach Yasir. "Yo, Zahra, are you awake? Talk to me, don't blank out on me."

I shut everything out, hearing a faint moaning in the distance. I can't be sure that it's Yasir, but I swim in the direction of what I hear. His voice is faint and fading fast. "I can hear him, Ky. Follow the direction I'm swimming, we don't have much time."

"How in the hell do you—"

"Not now, Kyle, just trust me."

We quicken our pace, and I hear his groans getting louder as we get closer to him. The sounds stop as soon as we're on top of where I heard his cries. "He's right here, I swear I heard him in this spot."

Kyle looks around, his eyes locking with mine in disbelief. "He's not here, Z. What did you hear?"

I hear my name again, but this time it's coming from directly under us. I don't explain, I just descend and reach below me as I kick down as far as I can go. I scream for Yasir to reach for me, almost letting the air out of my lungs.

I feel fingers, but they're not grabbing mine, so I grasp with both hands for his wrist, using every ounce of strength to drag him to the surface. Another pair of hands grab my ankles, and I know it's Kyle trying to pull me up. He wraps his arm around my waist, kicking toward the surface, while I hold on to Yasir like my life depends on it.

We finally break the water, blinded by floodlights coming from the shoreline. Kyle takes Yasir from my grip, swimming as quickly as he can as I struggle to keep up. I hear men yelling out at us, encouraging us the entire way, thanking the gods that we were able to find him.

The paramedics meet us as soon as we exit the water, taking as much care as possible to get him onto the stretcher. I reach for him, but the medics block me, assuring me that they'll do everything they can to revive him.

As they continue working on Yasir, Kyle holds me tight, repeating that Yasir will be okay and that he'll come back.

"He's not breathing. I couldn't feel a pulse when we got to him."

"He's strong, Z, he'll get through this. We have to believe he can."

I jump when I hear the shock of the defibrillator against his body, gasping at the way he flinches, pushing down the fear in my heart. So many things were left unsaid between us, and the regret threatens to send me into a tailspin.

They ask us if we want to ride with him to the hospital, and I almost fly into the ambulance before they can get the question out. Kyle follows me in, grabbing the blankets offered to us while they load Yasir him inside. I don't realize the adrenaline has been keeping me warm the entire time, and when it subsides, my body grows ice cold, and I wrap the blanket tighter around me to get my body heat back to some form of normal. My eyes never leave the scene unfolding in front of me. He never once opened his eyes during the entire ride. Not even a flicker or fluttering of his eyelids. I'd have been grateful for a grunt, anything to let me know he's still with us—with me.

I overhear one of the medics say that Yasir's "coding," whatever the hell that means, but when the machine goes from rapid beats to one long signal, my heart stops too. They charge up the defibrillator again, sending another jolt to restart his heart.

Nothing else matters until I know he's alive.

I need him to come back to me.

I need to tell him that I love him.

##*#*

Kyle and I sit in the waiting room at Oakwood Grove Memorial

Hospital, doing our best not to bother the staff every few minutes to get an update. I keep warm with him under the blanket the nurse gave us when we arrived, noticing that we were still soaked from being in the river. The sterile nature of the space disturbs me in ways I don't know how to say at that moment. I manage to keep to myself, despite all the other kids that make their way to the hospital. If I had my way, I'd tell them all to go home, nothing to see here, but I suppress my petty and focus on being grateful that any of them bothered.

Kendyl, Taylor and Tania are the first to arrive. Seeing them helps ease my nerves a little, and I don't even care that Ian and Chrisette showed up too. Knowing him, he's more interested in making sure he doesn't get blamed for anything. Or maybe, just maybe, he may be concerned about another human being, regardless of how he feels about them.

Hey, stranger things have happened.

Unk and Nana rush into the area, and the shock of seeing her here only lends more to the urgency of the situation. I'm at a loss over how Nana made it here so fast, but I'm in too much shock to care, I'm just glad she's here.

Lennox finds me, pulling me into a warm and tight hug I didn't know I needed until she squeezes me tighter. "Are you okay, sweetheart? Do we need to call your parents and let them know you're okay?"

"No, I called my mom. My dad is overseas handling some business affairs, but I told her to let him know that I wasn't hurt," I reply as I hold on to her for a little while longer. Her energy is so warm I almost forget I have the blanket wrapped around me. "I'm just worried about Yasir. The medics in the ambulance said they had to bring him back twice before we got him here."

Lennox nods as she kisses my cheek before she lets me go. "Yasir's a strong young man, I'm sure he's gonna pull through just fine."

Unk walks over with Nana, their expressions reflecting the mood I'm already trying not to be in. He gives me a hug, whispering in my ear, "Thank you for helping to save Ya-Ya, sweetheart. Are you okay? What happened?"

I cut my eyes at Chrisette, who avoids eye contact from the

distance she maintains with Ian. If we weren't in a public place with security around, I'd break her neck. "He was away from me when it happened. A couple of the other kids said he was with someone else trying to get away from the convo they were having when he fell overboard."

Nana focuses her attention on me, not really saying anything, but she somehow knows that I'm holding something back. She's not wrong, but this isn't the time, and I'll handle that once I get an update from the doctors. I nod as I match her concerned expression.

Kendyl jumps in, backing me up with what she knows. "One of the other girls on the boat wanted Yasir's attention, and he tried to leave. According to some of the kids who saw what happened, he looked like he was drunk."

"That's impossible," Kyle shakes his head, emphatic about what he saw. "We all ordered sodas, there's no way he got a drink. Something's not right."

We're interrupted by the doctor coming out into the area and heading in my direction. I stand, bracing myself for whatever she might have to say about Yasir's condition. Her facial expressions give nothing away, something that always irks me whenever I've had to deal with medical professionals. I understand they can't be too emotional, but I need a cue or something, dammit.

"Ms. Assante, I'm Dr. Forrester, thank you for your patience while we worked on your boyfriend," she says as she shakes my hand. "We were able to stabilize him and get him settled into a room. He's still unconscious, but we have active neurological function, which is a very good thing."

Unk steps into the convo, placing a comforting hand on my shoulder. "Dr. Forrester, I'm Xavion Okafor, Yasir's uncle, and his grandmother is here too. What happened to him?"

"He took a blow to the head, and it was a miracle that he didn't drown, thanks to the efforts of this young lady and her friend." Dr. Forrester smiles when Nana ambles over. "He didn't require surgery, and we're waiting for the toxicology screens to come back."

"I do not understand. Why would a toxicology screen be needed?" Nana inquires. "My grandson does not drink or do drugs. Do you think something else happened to him that you are not telling us?"

"I understand your concern, ma'am, but it's normal protocol." Dr. Forrester takes Nana's hand and gives it a gentle squeeze. "The reality is that with any holiday parties that happen on any of the rivers, alcohol can slip in, even if the parents are on board. We're not accusing your grandson of anything, but his pupils were dilated, which could also be a sign of the concussion he suffered, but we can't be sure until we can rule out every possibility."

"Can we see him, please?" I found my voice in the midst of all the adults in the group. I don't think I'm prepared for what I'll see when I get in there, but I'm hoping for peace of mind. Nana turns her attention to me, nodding in agreement. "I just want to make sure he's comfortable before I go home."

Dr. Forrester pauses for a moment or two, and I hold my breath, hoping she'll say yes. I can't accept anything else right now. "It might be good for his friends and family to be around him, but I can only allow two of you to go in at a time, until we can get him into a larger room."

Unk glances at me and Nana, a smile spreading across his lips. "You two go. Zahra, I imagine your mom is worried about you. You need to get home as soon as you can."

I take Nana's hand and follow the doctors to Yasir's room, saying a silent prayer that he's not hooked up to tubes or anything like that. That'll break me.

She taps my arm, sensing my hesitation when we get closer to the room. "He is Kindaran, baby. We are strong and stubborn. Trust me, it works for us when we need it to."

Walking into the room feels like a slow-motion movie scene sequence for me, and I half-expect to hear the familiar beeping of the machine that monitors his vital signs. Sure, I hear that, which isn't a surprise, so I brace for the other things that come with it—the IVs in his arms, the tubes to help him breathe and get pure oxygen in his system and finding him sleeping.

What we find instead causes Dr. Forrester to gasp out loud and drop her clipboard. She rushes toward the nurse's station to alert the staff. Nana clasps her hand over her mouth, and she's not the only one who stifles their screams.

Based on what Dr. Forrester told us before bringing us back here,

I can't believe my eyes. How is this possible?

Yasir's awake—and only hours after he'd been fighting for his life.

"Yasir?" I want to say something more, but words escape me.

He glances at us, flashing that smile that makes me warm and gooey, and sits up in bed. "Hi, Z. How did I end up in the hospital?"

Chapter Thirty-Eight – Yasir

I'm in and out of consciousness, and everything feels like a dream.

Voices swirl around me, all of them panicked, but I can't really see anything. It's like I'm stuck in the darkness, with no real way to escape.

I hear monitors, and I feel something sharp being stuck in my arm. I'm trying to ask questions, but even though I hear myself, it doesn't sound like anyone can hear me. I'm almost yelling into the ether while trying not to panic at the same time.

What in the world is going on?

"Yasir, come back to me, please!" Zahra yells at me. "I need you to fight!"

I muster as much strength as I can to push through and get to a small light that looks like it's miles away. As I get closer, the light gets bigger, and I see a doorway, and the light shines through the cracks around it. The closer I get, the further away it moves, frustrating me the entire time.

I don't understand what's happening, and I'm legit freaking out that I can't find a way out of whatever is surrounding me. I have to get back to Zahra, no matter what it takes.

Out of nowhere, all these memories start flashing in front of me, almost like I'm playing a highlight reel of my life, but the things that I see are confusing me, to the point where I feel like they're someone else's memories. They can't be mine, can they?

"Let's get him into triage and get him stable while we still can," I hear one of the medics explain as I watch the scenery change from the top of the ambulance to the blinding lights of the hospital hallways. "Zahra, sweetie, we're going to need you to wait in the reception area until one of the doctors can update you."

No, I want her here with me. *Don't take her away from me, please!*

I fight with everything I have to get back to the doorway, but my energy is completely spent, and I feel myself falling into the darkness again.

But not before I hear a voice I don't recognize calling out for me.

"It is not your time, Yasir."

Who in the world is that?

I have no idea who the hell decided to make such a statement, but whoever they are, they need to keep their opinions to themselves.

And how are they able to speak to me when I'm stuck in literal darkness?

"I know you can hear me, Ya-Ya." The accent is thick, but I can still make out what they're trying to say. Not that I want to listen, anyway. *"Ignoring me will not help matters. I am here now, and there are some things we will need to discuss, once we get you out of here."*

Yeah, I'm ignoring him. This is unreal.

I'm not sure what sounds more unbelievable though… hearing another voice in my head or having a full-blown convo with that voice. I have to get a grip on things, for real. It's obvious he wants my attention.

The sooner I could deal with him, the sooner I could dismiss him and move on.

"I'm trying to figure out how you're so familiar with me, and how you know my nickname my guy. Who are you?"

"We can have that conversation soon. Right now, you need to wake up."

"And how do I do that, huh?" I shout back, but the voice doesn't respond right away. *"Oh, nothing to say when I need something useful, huh? Typical."*

I continue to wander in the darkness, not knowing which way is up, trying not to freak out. The isolation I feel… this ain't it. For the first time in my short life, the concept doesn't work out so well in its actual application. I'm getting out of here, and right now isn't soon enough.

"Wake up, Yasir." The voice returns, repeating the command.

"How?!" Frustration makes itself clear and present, and fear

begins to take up residence. *"How in the hell do you expect me to just wake up like I'm in a dream that I can control or something?"*

"Trust me, Ya-Ya. Just wake up," the voice insists. *"Just follow my voice. We need to get you out of here."*

In the distance, a door opens, and an ambient light illuminates the doorway. The warm glow is soothing, and I hear Zahra's voice as I move closer. I feel itchy, like I'm shedding an old skin and slipping into a new body.

The light flashes as I step through, bringing a sharp pain with it. It only lasts a few moments, and I'm grateful for that because… whew. It takes a few more minutes to open my eyes and adjust to the brightness of a… a hospital room?

How in the fraggernackle hell—Unk's phrase, not mine—did I get here? I was on the boat with Zahra and the crew and… how long have I been here?

Where's is everyone? Where's Zahra?

The next thing I hear while I sift through the myriad questions in my mind is the answer to one of them. "Yasir?"

I swear, hearing her voice… Best. Sound. Ever.

Whatever anger I had? Gone. Yep. Iced. Over with.

The fact that she's here tells me everything I need to know.

But what's the answer to the million-dollar question? A little help, please? "Hi, Z. How did I end up in the hospital?"

Zahra gives me this look like I'm supposed to know the answer to my own question. I return her confused expression with one of my own, and I do my best to suppress the growing fear rising deep within. "Do you remember anything before you fell overboard?"

Pause. *What?* "What are you talking about? Is that how I got here?"

Nana slides out from behind Zahra and into my field of vision. How is she here? She's supposed to be in Atlanta. Zahra and I were on a boat earlier tonight before… wait, I was arguing with Amber when I started feeling dizzy.

It's coming back to me now.

Events come flooding back, almost overwhelming my senses. Amber's attempts to coerce me into a private area while on board. Her taking my glass to try to get me another drink. Trying to get back to Zahra and having her block me. “The last thing I remember was getting away from Amber.”

“Yasir, you fell overboard, and we heard Amber screaming. Kyle and I jumped in to get you.” Zahra wipes tears away as she attempts to fill in the gaps. “We almost lost you twice on the way to the hospital. You almost drowned.”

That hits me hard.

Puzzle pieces start to come into focus. So, that’s why I was stuck in the dark? I don’t know how to process that information, but seeing Nana struggle to hold back tears of her own almost shatters my soul. Being in that void inside my mind, with no way out, comes close to the scariest thing I’ve ever experienced in my life.

I glance at the clock on the wall across from my bed, and while it reads that it’s a few minutes before midnight, I can’t get a quick gauge of what day it is—is it still Sunday or nah?. “How long have I been out?”

“That is what does not make sense, Ya-Ya,” Nana speaks up for the first time. “The doctor told us that it would be another day or two before we had any idea that you would awaken. It has only been a few hours. How do you feel, grandson?”

I must have really taken a few hits while I was in the water. “I feel fine. I don’t have any headaches or anything like that.” I check my wrinkled fingertips, the only real indication that what they’re telling me actually happened. “I feel like I’ve been in a long-distance swim event, but that’s about it.”

“I’m going to get your uncle and let him know what’s going on,” Nana tells us before she steps out into the hallway. “I will also tell the nurses to go get Dr. Forrester. She is liable to be in as much shock as we are right now.”

Nana disappears in seconds, leaving me and Zahra alone in the room. We stare at each other like we haven’t seen each other in, like, ever. I ache for her to come closer. I’m desperate to feel her fingers on my skin.

Whether she senses my urgency or not, I don’t care anymore, but in moments she’s at my bedside. The anticipation kills me, dying with every second she takes to grab my hand, caress my arm, anything to put me out of my misery. The moment her fingertips trace a line from my ear and across my cheek to my lips, I want to combust right there on the spot. It feels so electric, like I'd been awakened. I mean, I'm awake, but something else inside me senses her and reacts to her.

Reacts to her touch. Her energy and essence.

What in Nyati's name is happening to me? And why am I speaking of the Divine Mother like it's second nature?

"You gave me quite a scare, pretty boy." She cuts through my thoughts, keeping her hand on my cheek the entire time. "If you wanted my attention, all you had to do was ask me."

Even the sound of her voice enchants me. "I did ask you, but you took your time answering me."

"Well, then, ask me again."

"Are you sure? I mean, I probably look like I feel right now, and I feel like I've been hit with a steel beam. By Nyati, I probably look like pure trash."

"Okay, I'm gonna have to get used to you saying that," she confesses as she slides her hand from my cheek to interlace her fingers inside mine. Damn, I feel better already. I only hope she doesn't let go. "Trust me, Ya-Ya, you're still my sexy one."

My eyes grow wide. "I'm … *yours*?"

The grin on her face triggers all types of thoughts I shouldn't be having, especially when I'm wearing a whole hospital gown and very little else. "Yes, you're mine, Mr. Salah, if you still want to be."

"Keep playing with me if you want to." I pull her down to steal a kiss or a dozen. I want to hold on to this moment for as long as I can in case I'm dreaming. "You've been mine, well, in my head you've been mine since the first time we met."

Zahra blushes, and I swear I notice her eye color change from their usual hazel-green hue to the most stunning shade of platinum and a smoky white color. I couldn't explain it if I tried, but I don't want to take my eyes off them.

When did she have the ability to do *that*?

She catches me gawking at her, blinking the entire time. "Baby, are you okay? You're… by Nyati, stop staring at me like that. I shouldn't be thinking what I'm thinking when you stare at me like *that*."

"Ahem—I would say he's better than okay." Dr. Forrester interrupts our moment. Ughhhhh, I want to scream. Doesn't she know how epic this was about to get? "Mr. Salah, I don't know how you managed it, but welcome back, young man."

"Thanks, doc, I appreciate it." I keep Zahra close so I can prepare for my next question. "So, when can I leave? I really would like to get out of here."

Dr. Forrester gives me a curious look, and I've already braced myself for the "medical speak" over why I have to stay. "I wish that were possible, but there are some abnormal results in your bloodwork that we need to understand before we release you. Not to mention your CT scan came back with no damage. After the fall you took, and the concussion the paramedics reported when you arrived, in addition to the bruises and lacerations you suffered… nothing's adding up."

Nana and Unk come in with one of the nurses as Dr. Forrester explains things to me and Zahra. The worry on Nana's face gives me chills. "What was that you were explaining to my grandson about his bloodwork without either of his guardians present?"

Dr. Forrester clears her throat, turning to face them. "As I was telling Yasir, Mrs. Salah, we found some abnormal markers in his bloodwork, and we need to run some more tests, just to make sure things are okay. I also want to order a follow up CT scan. I can't make sense over how he has no head trauma."

Nana winks at us before she switches her attention back to the good doctor. She stares into Dr. Forrester's eyes for a few moments, and Dr. Forrester adjusts the collar on her shirt. "I do not believe more tests are needed, doctor. In fact, the blood needs to be discarded. Yasir can be released tonight."

Dr. Forrester nods, confusing everyone in the room. "Yes, I believe Yasir can go home. Just make sure that he gets plenty of rest and that he hydrates properly. And have him follow up with his primary doctor within the week. There's no need for the blood to be retained."

What in the Jedi Mind Trick just happened?

"We will do just that, Dr. Forrester, thank you." Nana shakes her hand as she instructs Zahra to grab the bag with my clothes so I can get dressed. "We will make sure Yasir is properly cared for."

Nope, what we're not gonna do… did my Nana just… come on, now?

Nana slides over to the other side of the bed, plants a kiss across my forehead, and gives a knowing wink. "Nana has a few tricks up her sleeve when the occasion calls for it. Now, you get dressed so we can get you home."

"I'll make sure that the paperwork is handled, and Zahra gets to her car in one piece," Unk ushers them out of the room. "The nurses will probably wheel you out instead of letting you walk on your own."

Zahra stops Unk for a few seconds, skipping back to my bedside to steal another kiss. She stares long… longer than I think she would, and I'm here for all of it. "Please take care of yourself tonight. I'll be back in the morning to see about you. We still have things to talk about."

I take a few moments after they leave to get my head together. As I receive different pieces of what happened to me earlier in the evening, I don't know whether to be angry about what Amber tried to do to me or if I should be upset with myself. Being in the room gives me a little too much time to think, but at least I can be alone for a few minutes.

Or so I thought. *"I like her. We should definitely keep her."*

I snap my head in the direction of where I thought the voice came from. There's no way I could be hearing voices in my head right now.

"Yes, you are hearing what you think you are hearing, Yasir."

I flinch, covering my ears with my hands, willing the noises away. I couldn't be hearing things. I'm not going crazy.

"No, kiddo, you are not going crazy. There is a conversation we need to have, and soon."

"Who are you? What do you want?" I shout to the empty room. "Where did you come from and why are you here?"

"Go look in the mirror, and I'll show you who we are. Once you see for yourself, then we can go and have that conversation. Do you have somewhere that we can go?"

"If… and that's a big *if*… I see what I see, and it's something we need to convo over, then yeah, I got somewhere we can go."

"As you kids love to say, say less."

I'm completely out of my skull, listening to a voice in my head. I have to be dreaming or hallucinating or something. I didn't hear whoever this was before, why am I hearing him now?

Wait… pause a moment. *Think, Ya-Ya, think on it.*

I *had* heard him before, I just ignored him.

And I heard him before I woke up from my concussion, but it took a minute to connect those dots.

It's obvious to me he wants my attention for real, for real.

So, he wants me to see who "we" are, whatever that means. Okay, let's see what he's talking about.

I go back to the mirror, and at first, I don't see anything that would freak me out.

And then I notice someone standing over my left shoulder and—nope, I'm not seeing this right now. My mind's playing tricks on me. The doctor said I had a concussion, remember? Yeah, that's what we're gonna blame this on, right now.

I rub my fingers over my eyes, try to focus, and take another look in the mirror. Now I see someone literally standing behind me. Like, a whole person in the reflection, and the minute I turn around, he's standing right there, but he's not—*there*.

Is he a ghost or something? And if he is, how am I able to see him right now?

I stifle a scream to keep anyone from coming into the room to see why I'm legit freaking out. Make no mistake, I. Am. Freaking. Out! How in the hell is this happening? This isn't possible. There's no way he's standing in front of me right now.

His eyes glow bright purple, almost like pure amethyst stones—the same way Zahra described the way mine looked. In the calmest voice that sends chills down my spine, he waves at me like it's normal for him to be there and introduces himself with two simple words.

"Hi, kiddo."

In the next second, he just—disappears into thin air.

Chapter Thirty-Nine – Zahra

"Oh, thank the gods you're okay." The hug my mother gives me is exactly what the doctor ordered. "Mr. Okafor told us Yasir was in an accident."

That feels like a bit of an oversimplification, but if that's how Unk spun the story for my parents, I'm gonna go with that, too. I'm already having a hard time wrapping my head around what happened tonight, but I'm off balance, and I knew it. The only thing that matters to me is making sure that my baby's home and resting.

So many other thoughts are in my head, not the least of which have more to do with stringing Amber up by her ankles and finding out what she did. While it would make me feel better, I'm sure it'll get me the answers I'm looking for. Oakwood Police might have their own questions, and considering it's the mayor's yacht, I doubt if they'll get much out of anyone, either. The last time something happened at a party he hosted, Ian coordinated a rather impressive effort to get rid of the liquor that was at the house.

Smart money says whatever liquor that was on board now resides at the bottom of the Savannah River.

Mom shakes me out of my thoughts, making me face her. Her eyes search mine, studying my facial expressions. "Talk to me, babygirl, I need to know what really happened. Your father doesn't have to know the details, he's just relieved you're not harmed. I heard the panic in Mr. Okafor's voice, so I know it was serious."

I don't know if the adrenaline has finally worn off or if I'm tired of spinning the story all night, but I collapse into her arms. The tears flow as the worst-case possibilities flood through. "Mommy, tonight was crazy, and I still don't know how to explain it. He almost drowned and, I mean, I couldn't lose him, and—"

"Shh, hey, hey, it's okay." Mom holds me close, and I lose it. I need it so much that I wrap my arms around her tighter. "Okay, let's go sit down so you can let it all go. You've been off since you got back from Atlanta with Yasir."

We sit down in the living room on the U-shaped sectional, and I lay my head in her lap, exhaling as I do my level to keep more tears from falling. Mom just rubs my head, humming the song that usually calmed me whenever the world got too crazy.

"Yasir's Kindaran, Mom."

She flinches like she's been shocked with an electrical prod. "Say that again?"

I nod while she plays in my braids. "It was a shock to my system when I found out. His Nana dropped a lot of info on us the whole day."

"What is his Nana's name? It is safe to say she is Kindaran, too, if she told you this information without giving you the third degree." Mom keeps shifting under me like she's trying to get comfortable all over again. "What else did she tell him?"

"Nana's name is Johari Salah, but she asked me to call her Nana." I have no idea why that has any importance, but I don't think it'll harm anything to tell her. "Yasir's last name is Salah too."

Mom sort of pauses in the middle of the convo, and I turn my head to look up and see what she's thinking about. She snaps her fingers out of the blue, like she had a whole lightbulb moment. "That last name—there were Salahs we knew a long time ago, when we all lived in Kindara. If Mama Johari is his grandmother, then that means Bakari and Nasira were his parents—Nyati rest their souls."

I gasp for a moment. The way she speaks of them—nope, it can't be. "How do you and Daddy know them? And how did you know she went by Mama Johari? Please don't say that we're related to them, that would kill me right now."

Mom claps her hand over her mouth, and my heart drops. I almost want to scream, worried that she's answering my question without answering my question. She keeps shaking her head, whispering something that I can't make out. "How is it possible? We were told the entire family was killed during the Bralba invasion. How is he here in Oakwood Grove? It doesn't make sense."

"Mom, you're freaking me out. Can I know what's got you tripping right now?" I reach for a pillow, preparing for the worst. "Spit it out, so I can get to my mourning period that the one boy I've been this deep into is a blood relative."

She presses her hands against both sides of my face, her eyes welling with tears as they dart back and forth. She offers up a smile that confuses me more than anything. "The Salah's are not blood-related to us, so, let's get that out of the way. But there's so much more to the story, sweetheart, so many questions your father and I have to ask. We need to get with his uncle as soon as possible."

"Okay, what's going on, for real? You're more cryptic than usual, and I feel like I'm being left in the dark." I sit up on the couch, turning to face her. I need an explanation, and she's not helping at all. "This is directly affecting me, so I need to know."

"Babygirl, I promise, it is not my or your father's intention to keep anything from you, but we were convinced that Yasir died along with his parents." Mom wipes a tear from her eye. What I want to know is why is she so emotional about someone who isn't family? "Okay, I need to call your father. He's going to freak out when he finds out that Yasir has been in the States this whole time."

"Okay, a little help, please?" Yeah, like what the hell is going on that she's bringing Daddy into things? "You sound like this revelation is earth-shattering or something."

Mom dials Daddy's cellphone, leaving the speakerphone on so we can both talk. That eases my anxiety attack a little bit, but I still don't have much more information than before she made the call. "Hi, Beloved, I was just getting out of the meeting with the Kindaran Council. Is everything okay? Is Zahra safe? What about Yasir?"

"Yes, Daddy, I'm okay," I reply, smiling over his concern for Yasir. "He was discharged earlier tonight. I'm hoping he's home resting."

"Thank the gods for that. Now, what else is happening? I can sense it in your mother's voice," Daddy asks. He always seems to be able to tell when something is happening with either of us. "Can I know so I can get in on the fun? I do hate when I miss out on things."

"Um, okay, so Mommy and I were talking about what happened tonight and everything, and I told her that Yasir's Kindaran." I brace myself all over again for his response. If it's anything like Mom's, I'm in for another storm of emotions. "When we went up to Atlanta to see his grandmother, she revealed his actual bloodline. Yasir's last name is Salah, Daddy."

The line goes silent for a few seconds, and then I hear him clear his throat a couple of times. "Wait a moment, am I hearing that name correctly, sweetheart? I mean, are you sure the last name is Salah?"

I want to pull the pillow up to my face and scream all over again. I know Yasir is special, but the way my parents react to things, we're going into a whole other category. "Yes, I'm sure, Daddy. I mean, I met his grandmother, and from what Mommy told me, y'all know who she is, too. What I need help understanding is why you both are reacting like that name evokes—wait, is Yasir Kindaran royalty or something?"

"Mama Johari is his grandmother? By Nyati, this changes everything," Daddy replies. "He is not part of the royal family, in a manner of speaking, but he is important—so very, very important. His family was part of the Kindaran Nine, a set of families who were tapped by the Kindaran Council to keep specific secrets hidden and safe within the island."

"What secrets? Now I have more questions, like, does Yasir even know what they are, and would he even be allowed to tell me what they are? I'm so confused right now." I need to get my life together. This is more than I'd thought possible. "This is a lot to handle. Help me understand, because none of this is making any sense."

"I'm sorry, babygirl, I can imagine that you're confused over our reactions to this news." He sighs for a few moments. "I'll tell you what, can you invite Mr. Okafor and Yasir over for dinner? It might be better if we all sit down and they can understand what's going on, too.

"Daddy—"

"I promise, your mother and I are not keeping you in the dark, not anymore." I know he wants to try to reassure me a bit, but I need answers. "This is information that Yasir needs to know, and the Kindaran Council needs to know that Yasir is alive. We'd been trying to find him for years when his body wasn't found with the rest of the dead at Solara. To realize that he had been in the States—that he is in Oakwood Grove—it is mind-boggling. How did Mama Johari keep him hidden for so long? Can you invite them over for dinner next weekend? I'll be home by then and we can all figure things out together."

A week? Ugh.

Okay, settle down, Z. Yasir has been kept in the dark way longer than you have. You can handle a week. "I can try to wait, but I'll be heading over later in the morning to help take care of him. I can ask them to come over once I'm there. Now that I think about it, maybe it's best that I don't know a lot right now. I won't be able to look into his eyes and not tell him what I know."

"Thank you, darling. Believe me, there is a lot that needs to be explained, and it is not something that can be done lightly," Daddy explains to me. "In the meantime, I will inform the Council so I can get guidance on what to explain to Yasir. This is liable to be a lot that will get thrown at him at one time, and we need to be there for him as Kindarans. But for you, our precious girl, I will say this: there is so much more that this means for you."

I hate it when they're cryptic.

But what else can I do?

I just hope I can keep it together for a little while longer, at least for Yasir's sake.

Chapter Forty – Yasir

We get home from the hospital and settle into the normal routine—except, tonight hasn't exactly been all that normal. Having a whole other whatever-the-hell-that-was show up and engage in a conversation with me in the hospital room is the total opposite of normal.

There's something that needs to be handled, and I can't have my parental figures interrupt what I have to do. Thankfully, Unk's so consumed with making sure that Nana is comfortable in one of the spare bedrooms that I'm able to slip out without either of them noticing.

I pull into the parking area at Wright Square in the heart of downtown Savannah. I figure it'll provide the best possible hiding place on such short notice. I would've preferred to head down to Driftwood Beach, but that might have been pushing things a bit too far. We don't have that kinda time anyway, and the way this day has been going, I don't want to compound the issues I'm already facing. This whatever-the-hell-this-is needs to be sorted out before I can move forward.

I send a text to Zahra to let her know I got home in one piece and that I'm gonna crash soon. I hit Kyle to tell him the same thing, hoping I get some privacy to hash this out. With those bases covered, I beeline to the first location I can think of that'll provide the type of isolation needed: the granite stone of Tomo-Chi-Chi, the leader of the Yamacraw Tribe. He's the man responsible for negotiating the treaty that gave General Oglethorpe the land that would eventually become the city of Savannah.

Hey, I happen to be a history buff, what can I say?

The spot I chose has a tinge of mystery and a haunting beauty, much like the rest of the city. Considering we're under the cover of night, this would be the perfect location for me to have what might be one of the scariest convos of my life with an entity I had no idea resides inside me.

I mean, how the hell am I supposed to react, huh? One minute, I'm a normal kid, and after a wild accident and almost dying—well, the doctors told Zahra and Nana that I died *twice*—I come out of it with the ability to see specters and Nyati knows what else at this point. All I know is I don't feel normal.

There's no need to scan the surroundings. No one's around this time of night to listen in on me having a whole convo with myself.

Except, I'm not. I'm chatting with a specter who, as far as I know, showed up the minute I came to Oakwood Grove.

Not that the spot isn't already an odd choice to begin with. The large granite stone—a chunk that was taken from Stone Mountain decades ago—has its own superstition attached to it. As the legend goes, if a person runs around the stone while chanting Tomo-Chi-Chi's name, his ghost will appear. His remains were not relocated with the memorial, which gave rise to the urban legend.

While I don't exactly buy into the ghost stories that surround the memorial stone, and in light of what's happening to me real-time, I'm willing to make a huge exception over my initial skepticism. The fine line between myth and truth could be blurred at any time, all someone has to do is read deep enough between the romanticized lines of history to find what they wanted to see.

The lightning bugs flicker against the darkness, their bioelectrical impulses seeming to sync with one another. The light show, using the trees surrounding me as a backdrop, helps soothe the uneasy thoughts roiling through my mind. I can't resist focusing on the captivating display, as dozens of the fascinating insects keep things appealing.

I take a deep breath and let out a long sigh, bracing myself against whatever happens next. I close my eyes and allow my body to relax. "Okay, we're alone now. Show yourself."

For a few moments, nothing happens, and I sit for a few more moments, wondering if I should try it again or just pack it up and head home. I make another attempt, closing my eyes tighter to concentrate and remember what I did to bring the voice to life in my head. "Show yourself. I don't have the time for the grandiose entrance or anything like that. That time has passed, for real."

Again, silence.

"Look, if you don't show yourself, you disrespectful son of a bitch, I'm heading home and ignoring you until I feel like dealing with you," I yell into the air. "If you think this is some type of joke, I'm not the one for it tonight. Show yourself, dammit!"

After a few more moments, the voice roars to life, making himself known. *"I can only imagine the questions you have right now, Yasir. I sense the anxiety and confusion in you. Let us get to it."*

I let out a mock chuckle. "Yeah, that's putting it mildly. I'm still trying to understand who, or what, you are, for starters. And how in the world are you in my head is at the top of the list. How was I not aware of you before?"

The voice bellows out a laugh of its own, causing me to roll my eyes, annoyed that I wasn't in on whatever the inside joke might have been at the moment. *"Okay, let us see if we can get the important questions out of the way. I just wish there was a Vodaran priestess to assist with the transition, but we will have to figure things out as we go along."*

"Vodaran priestess? What are you talking about?"

"Are you not Kindaran? I would have thought you would be versed in the traditions," the voice questions.

"I just found out I was Kindaran a couple of days ago."

"Hmm, interesting." The voice begins knocking on different walls inside my mind, which only confuses me further over what it's trying to find. *"It looks like a priestess has conjured a barrier around your memories. We are going to need to do something about that soon."*

I still have no clue what he's talking about. I shrug, moving back to my original questions. "So, out with it, mystery being… who are you, how are you here with me inside my head, and why are you here now?"

"My name is Gamba. It is a Kindaran name that means 'warrior.' I was hoping to make a more formal introduction when you were ready to acknowledge my presence."

I rub my hand over my face. These answers are leading to more questions, and I can barely understand the answers he's giving. "So, when was that supposed to happen? Considering my parents have been dead for a full decade now, would this conversation have ever happened? And who's to say I'm ready to acknowledge it now?"

"Yes, it would have happened, but I believe the barrier is the root of the problem," Gamba explains to me. *"If the Divine Mother did not believe you were ready, I would not be here right now. I would have stayed in the recesses of your mind until I was brought forth. This is why a priestess would have been a better medium for this conversation."*

"And why is this happening… no, pause, I need the other questions answered first, because I'm completely confused. What are you?"

Gamba continues with the rapid-fire responses like he's been waiting to drop all this on me for a minute. *"I am, or was, a Vodaran priest, Ya-Ya. I was brought back into the mortal world, in a manner of speaking, to serve as a guide for a machari once they have been awakened."*

"And how did that happen? I don't think this is something I would have chosen to have happen." My mind's swirling, but I'm trying to keep it together. "What is a machari, anyway?"

Gamba sighs, taking a breath before he responds. *"Machari are a part of a metahuman bloodline, the mwali duati, or the Sageborn, identified at birth through a special gene passed on from generation to generation. The gene activates after times of great tragedy or loss. Even though your memories of your parents' deaths have been shielded from you, the trauma of your death and resurrection would qualify as the tragedy that activated the gene."*

"Yeah, you think?" I scoff at him. "I can't even see you, for all I know, you're a side effect of the concussion and near-death experience. I don't even know if you're real."

"I know this is a lot to take in, Ya-Ya."

"How long have you been rattling around in my head, Gamba? Only family knows my nickname."

"While I have just made myself known to you now, I have been around since you lost your parents," he replies. *"I was only in my infancy too, so, in a sense, I grew up with you, but I did not possess*

the strength to make myself available to you until now, although I was able to come when you needed me most."

It takes less than a few seconds to put the puzzle pieces together. "The ambush during the Beach Creek game… that was you?"

"Yes, most of it was me. I only followed your lead, feeding from your instincts and emotions. I had to conjure your zamwani to deal with that situation."

"The authorities said it was an animal attack, but it wasn't. I was… I was the animal. I'm a monster."

Something lets out a growl in the distance that shuts me down cold. Gamba pauses for a moment once the growling stops. *"A zamwani is your protector, Yasir. It was serving its purpose. I know you can handle yourself, but that situation would have ended in your death."*

"How am I supposed to excuse what happened, Gamba? Those boys that the… zamwani… decimated at the game, they could've been killed," I say. "All I saw were bodies on the ground. I didn't know if they were hurt bad or worse, and you were nowhere to be found to help me make sense of it all."

Gamba changes his tone this time around, and I take some comfort in that small victory. He at least understands my point. *"I am learning how, and when, to appear so I can use the zamwani to keep you out of harm's way, Yasir. That time at the game, you were in danger of being badly hurt. My purpose is to guide you until you fully realize your abilities."*

I take deep breaths, trying to focus on the questions in my mind, but my emotions are on tilt, and I really want to scream instead. All of this is happening too fast and bordering on overwhelming. "So, how are you doing this? I need a frame of reference to wrap my head around what's happening to me."

There's a rustle in the trees, and before I know it, Gamba steps from the shadows, making his human form visible to me again. He bears a striking resemblance to Aldis Hodge, the actor who plays Alex Cross in the new *Cross* television series. I'd almost swear that he can be his father. He's wearing a black button-down shirt and matching slacks, making his salt-and-pepper goatee stand out that much more. He has a bald head, which is a good look for him, no cap.

He leans against the stone and gives up a knowing smile. *"It is by our link that I am able to be here, but it is by the Divine Mother's grace and power that I am able to help you do other things. For example, this is what happens when we have to conjure the zamwani from the depths."*

Gamba stretches and waves his arms, making some foreign movements that look like circular and infinity symbol motions, and the next thing I know, this creature materializes out of thin air. Its arms and legs grow to their fullest length, and fangs jut from its mouth as its snout makes room for the rest of its teeth. Its paws are huge, and its razor-sharp claws gleam against the darkness that enshrouded us.

By the time the transformation is complete, the zamwani has to be something like nine feet long, and despite its undeniable mass, I swear it's floating above the ground, or it at least barely leaves any sort of footprints. It looks like a mashup of a Komodo dragon and a hila monster, but its face looks human-like, which is freaky in and of itself.

"So, what do you think?" he asks. *"It is magnificent, is it not?"*

Man, listen.

I take one look at the zamwani, then Gamba, and for the first time in our convo, I give up the most mischievous smile possible. All the Merlinian lore I've ever consumed, combined with my curiosity over what Dr. Strange can really do as Sorcerer Supreme… it all manifests itself into the most fearsome creature I could've ever imagined.

And I can imagine a lot!

"What do I think? By Nyati, I don't know whether I should have a fit that I can conjure this magnificent creature or be scared out of my mind that it even exists." I can't stop staring. Like, I'm legit scared and excited at the same time. "How the hell am I… there's no way I can tell anyone about this. My uncle? Nana? By the gods… how will Zahra react to this?"

Gamba motions his hands and creates this warm, orange glow. He projects it toward me, and it somehow puts me at ease. I have to get used to it now that I finally know where it's coming from. *"I know it might not feel like it right now, but I promise you, it will all work itself out. If you want to go fast, go alone. If you want to go far, go together. You're not alone, kiddo, and there's a pretty girl at the end of this journey. We need not disappoint her."*

Oh, wait, we're playing those games? "Since when did we start worrying about pretty girls? And how did you know about Zahra to begin with? By your admission, you've been around for the last day or so. She's been around since I got down here a few weeks ago."

Gamba gives up a satisfied grin. *"When she managed to calm the storm inside you, for starters. And she did save your life before I had a chance to step in and do something to help. There is something there, and we need to see what it is."*

"I can already see that this is going to be a challenging relationship between us, Gamba."

"It does not have to be," Gamba insists. *"Sure, there will be growing pains, but there are some advantages to being a machari."*

"Oh yeah? Like what?" I ask.

"Take a glimpse skyward. The night sky is crystal clear, and you might be surprised at what you find."

I hesitate for a moment, then stare out into the night sky and marvel at the constellations. Gamba chants something I don't understand and then everything looks—*different*. I recognize all the Kindaran clusters: the Ikba Scales, named for the Vodaran God of Justice, within the batch of stars just south of Ursa Major. Another glance to the east, and I locate the form of Nyati, the Divine Mother, looking down over her beloved Kindara. To the west, the distinct wildfire constellation of Nahara, its flames pointed toward the sun. I remember the last time I went stargazing, but they were never *this* clear and bright as when I peer through Gamba's eyes. I even search for Adin's Bow again, marveling at how brilliant it looks this time around.

Now, if I could just figure out how I know where to look for constellations I've never studied, much less recognized, that would be great too.

All of it stuns me into silence. The further I peer into the night sky, the more I see, beyond what I thought I would observe through a telescope. It threw me into a state of disbelief that I have vision beyond the naked eye. "What else am I—are we—able to do? There's so much I need to know."

"What did I tell you? Beautiful sight." Gamba grins as I resemble a whole kid playing with a new toy.

"I swear, I didn't know how beautiful things could be through your eyes. We have to do this more often," I declare. "Real talk, what else can we do? I have so many more questions now."

Gamba shakes his head, changing back to his human form. *"I think that is enough for tonight. There is a lot to take in as it is, and we need to figure out how this all works, we do not have much time. For now, I am content that you are not having a whole meltdown right now. We can have another conversation as soon as possible, but we do need to have a Vodaran priestess to help with the full transition so we can realize everything you have at your disposal."*

In a snap, I forget that Nana has already said someone would be informed of my "awakening."

At the same time, I'm trying to wrap my head around something Gamba just said. "What do you mean, we don't have much time? Is there something happening that I don't know about?"

"Yes. Now that you have been awakened, we have to get you ready."

"Ready for, what, exactly?" The riddles are killing me, and I'm not in the mood to decipher. "If I'm in danger, then I need to know so I can figure out my next moves."

"We are in danger, which is why we need to have a Vodaran priestess to assist," Gamba stresses. *"There is a lot to do in a short period of time, but I have watched from the shadows as you have grown. You will be ready when it is time."*

"I think I can arrange for a priestess, but I'm going to have to tell someone about you to get him to bring who we need. It's a risk, since he's not family, but he's the only one who can do it. My Nana trusts him, so I think we can trust him too."

Gamba nods. *"If that is what we have to do, then we need to get it done. The priestesses can unlock everything within us, and that is important for whatever we might have to face down the road. We will have to trust him until there's no other reason to trust him. Either way, my duty is always to protect you... no matter what."*

I open my eyes, getting my bearings after using Gamba's eyesight.

I check the time, realizing I'd taken the past hour sorting through everything. I can see so much clearer now, more than I'd ever known before. I walk back to Storm, working through all the scenarios in my head over how I would explain this new revelation to Unk and Nana. Zahra will have to wait until later; things are still so new between us I can't worry about that right now. I need more time to get her comfortable with the idea that I am—well, metahuman, or whatever the term is nowadays.

First things first. Get home before someone realizes I've been gone all this time.

I'm grateful that Storm has a hybrid engine as I approach the driveway at a gods-awful time of morning. The whisper-quiet EV part of the engine comes in clutch when I need to not be noticed or caught. Normally, I park in the garage, but that's not a good look right now, considering I'm not supposed to be out of the house after suffering a concussion and all sorts of other bodily injuries.

I purposely disengaged the alarm before I left the house, praying that Unk or Nana didn't check on me while I was gone. The moment I slip in the back door and notice the main level is dark, I exhale with relief, then tiptoe upstairs to my room so I can rest as best as possible. My body is still sore and hurting, despite my need to converse with Gamba and make some sense of what's happening to me.

Instead of heading straight to my bed, I fire up my laptop, and Google is, hopefully, gonna be my friend for a few minutes. I'm trying to find as many keyword combinations as I can to figure out where I want to research, but the only thing that keeps coming up is Merlinian and Arthurian myths and legends. After everything I've seen tonight, nothing I've found matches up.

What in the world am I becoming?

I continue my deep dive until exhaustion finally takes over, whether I want to stop or not. The deeper I go, the more I want to find out, and the more I need to understand so I don't feel so scared. I resign myself to the fact that if I don't get some rest, I'm not gonna be any good to anyone tomorrow, least of all myself, and there's a lot of questions I have to ask and answer.

I peel myself away from my desk and slog to my bed so I can

stretch out and get as much sleep as my mind will allow. Easier said than done, especially when the lasting images I see before I close my eyes are glowing orbs staring back at me, and I hear a voice in the dark assuring me that everything is gonna be alright.

As much as I want to believe that, I'm really not so sure anymore.

Chapter Forty-One – Zahra

This isn't how I'd planned to be in his bedroom for the first time. Still, I can't think of a better place I'd rather be this morning.

I half expected to step into a war zone the moment I opened the door to check in on the patient. Clothes would be everywhere, there would be posters on the wall of Chloe and Halle Bailey or Zendaya or Coco Jones or insert resident hot girl of the moment. I braced myself for Nyati knows whatever I might find, preparing not to judge because, after all, he's still a boy after all.

What I find instead makes me swoon.

The room isn't immaculate—there are clothes on the floor, but it looks like they're the ones he wore last night, and maybe a couple of other shirts. His L-shaped desk sits in the far right corner, where I notice papers spread out among the books on the desktop. His laptop screen displays a Google search that strikes me as odd—Merlinian magic?

Above the short end of the desk sits a bookshelf that looks like it's built into the wall. I pad over to be nosey, wondering what books he has on the shelves. From *Black Sands* comic books to, of course, the Miles Morales arc in the *Spiderman* comics, and I see the *Ironheart* comics too. Then I move over to the hardcover books, reading the spines that catch my attention. *Percy Jackson. The Witcher. The Lord of the Rings.* All three books in the *Legendborn* Cycle series by Tracy Deonn. The *Beasts of Prey* series by Ayana Gray. *Blood at the Root* and *Bones at the Crossroads* by LaDarrion Williams. There are even nonfiction books that caught my eye. *Letters to a Young Brother* by Hill Harper. *The Mamba Mentality: How I Play* by Kobe Bryant. To top it off, I saw a hardcover copy of *Native Son* by Richard Wright and *A Collection of Poems of Langston Hughes.*

On his closet door is a full-sized poster of Chadwick Boseman as T'Challa. The poster only shows his head and shoulders, and the image is split down the middle, with one side showing his head encased in the Black Panther mask, and the other side showing his face. Underneath the striking image were the familiar claws that made up the necklace always worn by the warrior king.

That's not what makes me clutch my proverbial peals, though.

Sitting in its own corner away from everything, propped up on a stand against the wall, is a remote-controlled F-22 Raptor jet, painted all black with purple and gold accents throughout the fuselage and wings. Considering it's nearly five feet long and the wingspan looks around four feet long, and he has space to keep this beast in his room, it's safe to say that, outside of Storm, this has to be his pride and joy.

Be still my STEM girl heart. He's gonna teach me how to fly it. Period.

I step over his Timbs, still marveling over all the reminders of Wakanda—including the life-sized Panther mask on his nightstand that tugs at my heart strings. I roll the desk chair along with me, settling at the side of his queen-sized bed, watching the sudden object of my affection as he sleeps.

I stare at him, studying his face, wondering if the frown I notice has anything to do with the pain he must still be feeling. His hands are balled into fists, and he groans and jerks like he's still in a fight. Not loud, but enough for me to hear him from where I sit. But there's one glaring change—make that two, now that I take a second glance—that gives me pause and makes me wonder if I'm seeing things.

The bruise on his left cheek and the cuts above his right eye are gone.

That's not possible. He died in front of me—twice—and now he looks like he hasn't gone through anything he's been through over the last twelve hours. I try to touch the spots without waking him, just to make sure I'm not dreaming or wishing that last night didn't happen.

Last night happened, but how are the bruises not there? It make no sense.

"You know, when I imagined you being in my bedroom for the

first time, this wasn't what I had in mind."

I jump, rolling the chair a few inches away from the bed. "By Nyati, you scared the hell out of me, boy."

He chuckles, but I don't find it all that funny. "I'm sorry about that, I didn't mean to throw you off, but I was trying to figure out why you were staring at me like I'd grown a third eye or something."

"There's a reason for that." I pull up the camera on my phone and place it in his hands. "Tell me what you see, because I'm literally trying to understand what I'm looking at when I see you."

It takes a few moments for it to register, but as his eyes widen with the revelation, I begin to freak out a bit with him. He drops my phone in his lap, lifting up into a sitting position, checking other spots on his body. "Wait a freaking minute, how in the—?"

"How did you manage to heal almost overnight from bruises and cuts that would've taken weeks to heal?" I finish the question for him, hesitating to touch his skin. I'm scared to touch him because if I do, I'll want to kiss him, and since no one has really checked on us for at least twenty minutes, getting caught in a compromising position would be a bad look for the both of us. "What's the last thing you remember from last night? Did Nana do something to you before you went to sleep?"

Yasir hesitates for a few seconds before he answers, and I can't tell if he's trying to remember or if he's trying to come up with a different explanation. He shakes his head a few times, looking like he's mumbling something to someone, but the only ones here are me and him. "I-I'm not sure how to explain any of it right now. I remember coming home, and then Nana gave me something to drink to help me sleep. From there, everything feels like a dream, but it doesn't. I don't know if I'm making sense right now."

"Yeah, you're right, it doesn't make sense. How are you feeling, are you hurting at all?" I lean toward him, feeling his forehead to make sure he doesn't have a fever. He shivers under my touch, but I'm not sure whether he's reacting to my touch or if he has a fever. "I'm still trying to understand how you don't have any bruises or injuries from last night."

"I can offer a few ideas, but that might require explanations that you may or may not be ready for, grandson." Nana creaks the door open, holding a coffee mug in her hands. She smiles, but I see the sadness in her eyes. Things might have gotten a little bit more complicated. “How much are you prepared to learn?”

Like she needs to ask? “Everything.”

Chapter Forty-Two – Yasir

Nana brings me and Zahra down to the living room, where two strangers sit on the sectional with these pleasant smiles on their faces. I assume they're here to see me but based on the confused expressions coming from Unk and Lennox, it's safe to say no one got the memo. Unk shrugs when I stare him down to get a silent cue that I don't need to freak out, which simply puts me on high alert.

While the stunning woman wearing a purple sleeveless pant suit with a black and gold corset belt and absolutely flawless copper-bronze skin is not familiar to me in the slightest, the man wearing a black two-buttoned suit to almost match his sable toned skin and long, flowing dreadlocks sitting next to her is very familiar. He's been in different parts of the nightmares when I'm visiting Kindara.

Zahra pulls me down to whisper, "They're Kindaran, babe. Something serious must be happening if they're here."

Don't have much of a choice but to take her word for it, now, do I?

Considering I just found out about my true bloodline less than a week ago, all I can do is take everything that comes at me with a grain of salt.

"Good afternoon, Yasir. I have been told a lot about you. I know my appearance might come as a shock to the system, but I promise you, this meeting is long overdue," the woman says as she rises from her seat on the sectional. "Please forgive the abrupt interruption. My name is Kynani. I am a Vodaran priestess, sent here to help clear up some of the confusion swirling around you."

Okay, good. Unexpected intervention isn't on the to-do list today. Great job.

"Thank you, and welcome to the Grove," I reply, and then switch my attention to the gentleman still seated. "From the look on my Unk's face, I don't think anyone was expecting you. I hope one of you will be able to help me understand what's going on."

Nana steps in front of me, taking my hands in hers. I search her eyes, looking for some sort of comfort. Having strangers around only amps up my anxiety, and she knows it. "Listen to me, Ya-Ya," she says. "This is the man who saved you during the invasion in Kindara. His name is Hassan, and he brought you to me when you were younger."

I flinch after hearing that part of the story, shooting my gaze in his direction. "Is this true? You were the one who brought me to my Nana? I vaguely remember you."

"Yes, I am." Hassan rises from his seat, then walks toward me until he stands a couple of feet from me. He studies my face, staring up at me as he gives a knowing smile. "It has been so long since I have seen you. You have grown so much over the years."

"That's funny, because I don't remember ever seeing you."

"Yasir," Nana frowns at my lack of tact. "That is no way to speak to a guest in your home."

I take a deep breath as I turn to face my grandmother. "Nana, I get it. I'm supposed to be indebted to this man for saving my life, but where has he been all these years? If he's been in contact with you, why couldn't you have at least put me in front of him so I can have an idea of who he is, instead of staring at the stranger in front of me?"

Kynani slips into my field of vision, almost commanding my attention without so much as a word. "My apologies, Yasir, as it is obvious that no advanced notice was sent to alert you to our arrival. Upon my awareness of your recent awakening, I needed to get to you. time is now of the essence, and I am hopeful that you will agree to meet with me to begin your acclimation process."

I don't know how she's able to stare into my eyes and melt away every ounce of aggression inside me. Despite her doing that, I wonder why the conversation between us now feels so rushed. "Okay, can I ask a question? Is there some end of the world ploy happening that you're not telling us? If you can explain it to me like I'm a six-year-old, that would be great."

"I assure you, everything will be revealed to you," Kynani nods as she keeps eye contact the entire time. "I do not mean to sound vague, but there is a lot to discuss, and I am hopeful that it can be done as soon as possible."

I feel like I'm in the middle of a bad movie. I turn to Zahra, matching her hesitant expression, sensing every bit of the chaotic energy that's suddenly swirling around us. "How soon are we talking? I mean, I was kinda in the middle of something before y'all showed up."

Kynani raises an eyebrow, switching her glance toward Zahra. "You have already found a suitable mate? Is she aware of your awakening?"

"Yasir, maybe we can talk after whatever is happening here is handled." Zahra squeezes my hand, taking her free hand to get me to look at her. "This is all a bit… we can find time to sort through things later, I promise."

"Um, nope, not when I literally went through hell last night to come back to you," I protest. "We need to talk now."

Kynani places a comforting hand over my forearm, looking into my eyes again before nodding. "This is an intricate process, Yasir, and we need to get to it as soon as possible. Allow me to ask this question: is this young lady standing next to you a fellow Kindaran? This is important information for me to help with the acclimation."

Zahra grins, blushing as she stands in front of me. "Yes, I am from the Kua Tribe, as is the rest of my family. My father, Kairo Assante, is a Kindaran historian, are you familiar with him?"

Kynani smiles. "Yes, I am familiar with your father. If it is okay with him, I would like to reach out. There is much that I may need to discuss with him, too. The stars are aligning more than ever imagined."

Hassan clears his throat to insert himself into the conversation. "I may need to be involved with these discussions, Kynani. In fact, Xavion and Mama Johari need to be involved also, as Xavion is Yasir's current legal guardian. Yasir is still a minor, and this is too important for it to be left up to him."

A minor? My dude, I'll be seventeen in February, and by certain American laws, I can declare independence and leave y'all in the dust. Who the hell does he think he is, trying to act like he has say in what happens to me?

Kynani turns to Hassan, then glances at Unk. "You are correct, his legal guardian is needed for such matters, and as such, I will bring him up to speed. However, as you are aware when we spoke to the Kindaran Council, your presence is not required. You are needed in the field with the rest of the priests and priestesses to continue with the primary objective of locating the remaining Kindaran Nine."

There's something in Hassan's irritated expression that rubs me the wrong way. I'm not sure what it is, but I file it away into a mental note to follow up later. "I'd prefer my uncle is involved. He's been the one dealing with everything in Oakwood Gove. I can't see doing this without my family."

Hassan shakes his head. "Come on, kiddo, there might be some things that I can help with during your acclimation. I'm sure the Council can find someone else to assist the priestesses. This is too important for me to remain in the field now."

Yeah, that's a no. "So, for years, you've been in the field while Nana was going through a confusing time with me, and now, when you realize that whatever I'm about to go through is taking you out of the mix, you feel like being in the field isn't important anymore? Thanks for your concern, but I'm not feeling it. I don't know you."

He protests further, but I'm still not hearing it. "There is too much at stake for me not to be involved. There are things I can do that can help you."

My anger rises to the surface, but I suppress how I want to react despite all of this putting me on edge. "Since you swear you have influence, can you find out why I have no knowledge of my homeland, and how it happened? Or maybe why, since I'm supposed to press pause on my life, I haven't been able to go back to Kindara after all these years?"

Hassan winces, but then nods in agreement. "Fair enough, Yasir. You deserve answers to those questions."

Unk walks over to put his hand on my shoulder, giving a knowing wink as he turns his attention to Kynani. "I'm in. This will be a good thing for him. Everything will open up for him, and hopefully it will give us a clue of what's been going on all this time."

"Very well. We will get started as soon as possible." Kynani takes her seat on the sectional near Unk and Lennox. "Xavion, there are some other matters that we need to discuss, especially if Lennox will be a constant in your life. I will also need to secure a temporary location until Yasir's acclimation is complete, so I do not impose on your space."

Well, it looks like my work here is done. "Good, now that things have been settled, Z and I have some things to work out. I'll leave you to work out the details, and I'll catch up later. I know I sounded a little off, but I'm down with whatever it is that I have to do. There's something big happening, I can feel it."

"Whatever you have to figure out, do it quick," Lennox opines as she slips her arm inside Unk's. "There's a glow, this aura that swirls around you when you're in each other's space. It's addictive, and I, for one, want to see more of it."

I notice Kynani's inquisitive stare as Lennox continues gushing over me and Zahra. Her eyes dart back and forth between the two of us and triggers my curiosity.

Zahra smirks as she taps my chest. "From what I've been told about Vodaran priestesses, once they began studying their subjects, it's only a matter of time before an interesting convo pops up. I have a feeling that things are going to get a little more interesting around here."

"Yes, Zahra, Ms. Lennox is correct. There is something swirling around you two, something—ethereal." Kynani continues her assessment as we stand there looking all kinds of confused. "I sense the Divine Mother's around you. That has not happened in quite some time whenever I have observed Kindaran children or young adults."

I start tapping my watch, almost yanking Zahra out the door with me. "Whew, would you look at the time. Appreciate the extra pressure, we'll talk later, okay?"

I escort her to Raiden, my nerves completely frayed thanks to the added voices in the house throwing their collective energy behind us, when we haven't had a chance to put our energies into each other. All I know is that I can't let her go without telling her how I really feel. Everything else will have to fall the way they fall. I send up a silent prayer for strength for whatever happens before I stop her.

"Are you okay? I know things were a little intense in there."

"Intense isn't even the word, but I don't scare that easily. Why do you ask?"

"I feel like I have to apologize for what you had to see just now." I rub the back of my neck, feeling the anxiety tingling up my spine whenever I think something bad is about to happen. "I mean, I'm still trying to process all that in there. It's obvious that something big is coming. I need to find out how deep this goes."

"Then let's find out—together," she replies. "I know you want to figure out what this thing is between us, but it feels like there are some other issues that might be more important."

"But we just got a chance to… never mind." Who am I kidding? My life has gotten complicated in two seconds flat. "I understand if you still want to be just friends. All that's going on in there—that's a lot to deal with."

The look on her face throws me off-balance. "I said what I said. I'm yours. My soul has chosen you."

Hearing her say those words somehow clears all the clouds in my mind. Here I am acting like the sky is falling—let's be real, it's still falling—and she's the one telling me she's ready to face down the apocalypse with me.

"And mine has chosen you." I softly kiss her, wrapping my arms tight around her waist, not wanting to let her go. "I want you with me when we figure this all out. Will you be there?"

"That's not even a question, babe." She kisses me a few more times before I tuck her into the driver's seat. "Whatever is going on with you, I'll understand."

"Call me later, you have a whole house to clear out." Zahra closes the door and starts Raiden's engine. "I'll be waiting for you. Promise."

I turn to head back inside the house, sensing a combination of anticipation of what's to come and apprehension over whether this may be more than I can handle.

Still, I've never backed down from a challenge.

I'm not about to start now.

Chapter Forty-Three – Zahra

My parents are waiting for me in the foyer the minute I step through the door.

By their facial expressions, they have a lot of questions.

The way I play with my hair right now, I have a whole lot of tea to spill.

I recap everything that happened in my head—so much happened in such a short amount of time—while making sure to leave out the small detail of being alone with Yasir in his bedroom. My parents are liberal, but not *that* liberal. I figure if I keep my story straight before telling them, it'll make it more believable during the actual convo.

I better keep it consistent too. Kendyl's liable to have everyone on a conference video call once she wakes up, and she's more thorough than an assistant DA when it comes to her Q&A. Outside of a few texts to her and Kyle, I still haven't had a chance to catch the crew up on Yasir's improved condition. How the hell am I going to be able to explain that?

I meet my parents in the kitchen, where my father has already poured himself a two-finger shot of small-batch bourbon. Mom has a full glass of Moscato in front of her too. "Hi, Daddy, how was your trip back home?"

"It was going well, until I received the truth of what happened to you from your mother." Yeah, today has the makings of revealing the whole truth whether I want to or not. "You jumped out of a moving boat after Yasir into dark water? You had no way of knowing if you could find him, and you took the risk of drowning yourself. What were you thinking?"

I should've known Mom would snitch, but I can't blame her. Once I had a chance to think about it, it wasn't the most thought-out idea.

"Daddy, before you jump to conclusions—"

"What conclusions are there for me to jump to, hmm?" He downs the bourbon shot in one gulp, pouring another one seconds later. I knew he'd be upset, but not back-to-back shots upset. "Yasir fell overboard, you jumped in without any concern for your own safety, and by Nyati's grace, you were able to find him and get him to the paramedics, with Kyle's help. Does that sum it up?"

Well, damn, he's got me there. "Okay, when you put it like that, it does sound a bit foolish, but Daddy, I couldn't leave him out there to drown, not when I know he would risk his life to save mine."

"Okay, you two, we need to take a beat look at this from a different perspective." Mom steps between us, sipping her wine, and rubbing her finger along the rim of the glass. "Darling, our daughter has every bit of the impulsive nature of her father, and she is just as fearless. In your heart, you know I am right."

"But it is our job to keep her safe, my love," Daddy counters. "We got lucky last night, but as much as Nyati tries to protect her children, she cannot see what they are doing all the time."

"We also know that this day would come once Yasir was found," Mom grins as she considers her words. "After all, there is a connection that cannot be denied. Ashanti had foreseen this before they were born."

"Okay, can I know what was just said right now?" Once they start speaking about the other Kindaran gods, especially when they're referring to me, I have to slow them down so they can explain it like I'm a six-year-old. "What do you mean there's a connection between me and Yasir?"

Daddy cuts his eyes at Mom, shaking his head as his gaze turns to me. "This was part of the reason that we wanted to sit down with Xavion and Yasir for dinner, baby girl. While I was in Kindara, a message was delivered that there was a possibility that Yasir had been discovered. The Council kept this information as discrete as possible, but as important as he is to our country, it would not be a secret for much longer."

I nod like I have a clue, but I don't understand a word he's saying. "So, is that the reason why a Vodaran priestess was sitting in his uncle's living room today? It feels like coincidence, considering

Yasir almost lost his life yesterday, that they would show up today looking to help him."

Daddy's eyes widen, leaving me even more confused. "Did you say Yasir almost lost his life yesterday?"

"Yes, they had to use a defibrillator to bring him back." I wipe tears I thought I was done shedding as I recall everything all over again. "He flatlined twice while we were on the way to the hospital. I was there in the ambulance when it happened."

"How soon can we meet with the priestess?" The urgency in his voice startles me. "Do you remember her name?"

"Yes, her name is Ms. Kynani."

Daddy nods. "She's one of Mama Johari's most gifted priestesses in her downline. The stars are aligning in ways that we didn't expect."

"Okay, this is a lot to take in, I need a few to process." He's rattling off so much information so fast that I have trouble keeping up. "I know Ms. Kynani asked to reach out so that you can compare notes or whatever. Can I go to my room, please? It's been a crazy day, and it sounds like it's about to get crazier before the weekend gets here."

"Sure, baby. Go and rest, I will let you know when dinner is ready." Mom pulls me in for a hug, kissing my cheek before letting me go. "Your father and I have a lot to discuss before we reach out to Priestess Kynani and Mama Johari. Once we do that, we can coordinate through you and Yasir to get the time and date done for next weekend."

I don't have the energy to respond. I need to process what I've just heard before I get myself together to watch my friends' collective heads explode once they see my boyfriend shows no signs of being hurt and almost dying last night.

I hope he has answers because I'm fresh out.

I make sure the door is locked so we won't be interrupted. The worried expression on his face causes me to do the same, and that's not how I want this convo to go. I've been getting texts from Kendyl every few minutes, asking when they can see us because they're concerned too.

I'm anxious for both of us, to be honest. Can anyone blame us?

We've both been on a social media blackout since the accident, and if I have my way, wc won't say much of anything until we get to school tomorrow. All the kids who are pressing our friends for information are, let's face facts, prying more to be nosy than wanting to know if my baby is okay or not. I couldn't care less when they get their updates.

Besides, I know two people who are sweating the outcome more than anyone else, anyway. The last thing Ian needs is bad press when his father is still running for reelection. This incident has spectacle written all over it.

I don't care. Our inner circle deserves to be brought up to speed, and that's all that matters.

"Are you ready for this?" He has the look of a boy who's grasping at any lifeline he can get to help him stay afloat.

"Nope, and I can sense how anxious you are. Do you wanna talk about it before we holla at the crew?"

Yasir plays with his hands, something I've learned he does whenever he's really nervous. "I'm trying to make sense of so much new information, and it still feels like I've only scratched the surface. It's like my whole life has been hidden from me, and now everyone wants me to remember it all overnight. How, Sway?"

His eyes turn bluish-grey, showing me how sad and alone he feels. While I want to comfort him, what I have trouble understanding is *how* I can sense his emotions seconds after he does. "Did Ms. Kynani get the chance to explain what happens to your eyes when you show your emotions?"

Yasir blinks a few times, leaning into the camera and notices what I see. He frowns, looking like he doesn't recognize his face. "See what I mean? How am I supposed to explain that when it happens? I'm legit scared of what's happening to me, Z. My injuries heal in less than a day or two, with no believable reason as to how it's possible. Kenni's liable to flip out and wonder if I'm a freak after all."

"Shh, relax, I can handle Kenni, and Kyle too, for that matter," I say as I search for a way to calm him down so his natural eye color can return. "We will figure this out together, okay?"

Yasir takes a deep breath, closing his eyes and mumbling

something that has me wondering if he's talking to someone off camera or something. Whoever he's speaking to, when he opens his eyes, the amber-golden hue has returned to his irises, and he looks more like himself again. "Yes, we will. Now, let's get the rest of the crew on the video call so we can try to explain everything as best we can."

"Okay, chica, what in the world is going on? Are you and Yasir okay?" Kendyl's in rare form already, and that's putting it mildly. "Oh, and you can answer too, pretty boy. Social media has been lit since y'all blacked out."

Having Kyle, Kendyl, Taylor and Tania on a group video chat helps to ease the tension from the last few hours. I mean, sure, we're trying to figure out how to deal with everything swirling around me and Yasir, but it beats feeling like we're stuck in a bubble.

Tania nods on screen as she continues to check her phone. The texts come almost back-to-back, and she shakes her head over the sender. "Amber has been blowing up my phone, like I have info or something. Have you been avoiding her texts, Kenni? She's wearing me out."

"Yep, absolutely I am," Kendyl proudly proclaims. "How you gonna be all sometimey when it benefits you, and now that you might get caught up in drugging somebody and almost getting them killed, now you wanna be besties? Nah, sis, you can sweat it out over there on read."

I tilt my head over that reveal. Amber did what? Let me find out if that's true. "Pause—when did she try to drug him?"

"Not try, babe, there's at least three witnesses that know she had something on her before she cornered Yasir," Kendyl says. "It was a coordinated setup to get her alone with him. Yasir's the new flavor of the month. Even when Giovanni tried to holla at you, it was done to get Yasir riled up. Chris read your body language and thought there might be trouble in paradise."

Chrisette. I'm gonna wring her neck. She doesn't even like Yasir like that. What sense would it have made to have him and Amber as a couple inside of that clique? As much as I want to be upset with her over what she tried to do, I have to look in the mirror. If I wasn't so undecided about whether Yasir and I should be together, it wouldn't have looked like we weren't and someone else could holla.

I switch topics to keep my anger under control. "So, the other reason we needed to talk has a lot to do with everything else that happened in Atlanta."

Kyle pipes up for the first time in the chat. "So, don't keep us in suspense. What happened? Something was off between you two when he came onboard."

Yasir jumps in on that question. "I had a bit of a run in with my Squad. Things went left with the quickness."

Everyone gets quiet as Yasir settles in to explain himself. "Yeah, it was interesting to say the least. My folk don't trust outsiders, and I guess I turned into one when I left."

My smile disappears in seconds as the memories of the confrontation at Nana's house rages to the surface. He had so many places he wanted to show me that day. The last high school he attended before he came to Oakwood. Some of his favorite restaurants. The Georgia Aquarium. All that got ruined when that so-called Squad turned their backs on him.

"Damn, that's cold. You've only been gone a couple of months." Kyle grabs an apple slice and takes a bite. "Z told us one of them was your Day One. I wouldn't turn on mine like that just because they had to leave."

Yeah, I won't drop Kendyl like that, either, but not everyone rocks like that, I guess. My heart hurts for him, but I hold out hope that maybe he and Dante can find a way to get past whatever happened. Alyssa read the situation wrong. I have to believe that. Everything in me swears that Yasir's not that type of boy, and after finding out he's Kindaran, it only strengthens my resolve.

"Dante and I have gone through this before. We've found a way to remain brothers, but only time will tell." Yasir pauses for a moment, tapping his fist over his heart four times. "He loves my Nana too much to let things die like that."

"Then when y'all do, let him know you got aces down here who have your back," Taylor chimes in. "You're good people, and they'll see that when they have a chance to get out of their feelings."

"So, now that we've gotten that out of the way, what do we do about the madness at school tomorrow?" Tania asks as she checks the notifications on her phone. "I'm catching it from just about everybody now, wanting to know if Yasir is dead or alive and whether Z is in mourning. That blackout has people shook, for real."

"Then they'll find out in the morning when we show up," I announce. I'm getting sick of the messages I've been ignoring the whole time. They weren't worried about me like that before, so all this faux concern just pisses me off. "Until then, y'all don't know anything more than you know. As far as you're concerned, Yasir is still in the hospital."

"Say less, bestie." Kyle fires off a status message. "Hashtag prayers for Yasir. Sounds like a plan. That should keep Ian sweating for another day or so. His pops has been doing some damage control, according to my dad. He'll probably be a bit subdued in the morning, so, you should use that to your advantage, my boy."

"We'll see y'all in the morning, bro," Yasir nods as everyone shuts off their video feed. "Be easy."

I can't resist asking the one question that burns in my mind once they're off the call. "Are you sure you're ready to deal with everyone tomorrow? I don't know if you have the energy for all the madness that may swirl around us."

Yasir gives up a smile that warms my soul and makes me melt. "As long as we're together, I can handle anything."

By Nyati, I adore this boy.

Chapter Forty-Four – Yasir

From the moment I step on campus, I'm bombarded with all sorts of questions, and I already wanna turn around and go back home. Half of the people are asking about what happened this weekend, and the other half are asking about something I've put out of my mind. My nerves are on edge with each question being asked, because all this is doing is making things more difficult for me to stay out of the spotlight.

"Yo, Yasir, I didn't know you had hands like that. You should hit Michael B. Jordan up for the next *Creed* movie."

"You're blowing up on social media, bro! I heard a few Beach Creek girls been trying to see about you."

"Wow, we thought you were dead, my guy. We didn't hear anything from your circle the whole time you were down."

"Is there anything we can do for you? We heard you're still suffering some side effects from almost drowning."

"Man, Ian and Chris must be breathing a sigh of relief that you're alive. I'd be finding a way to sue, seriously speaking."

What in the entire hell did I just walk into this morning?

Zahra was right. I should've followed my first instinct and stayed home a few more days until I was ready.

I don't wanna think about any of this nonsense, especially when there wasn't much of a reprisal after what I did to them. Disappointing. Would've had to keep my head on a swivel in the A, but then again, Squad would've had my back.

For a fleeting moment, I almost wish they were here, or at least that they knew I almost died.

I shift those thoughts out of my head while dealing with another wave of people coming through to check on me. I've never had so much as a passing greeting with most of these kids, and now they feel the need to come through and… I mean, I'm trying to understand what half of them are so hyper about, while the other half are on some fake sympathy train.

I shoot a text at Kyle while in class, asking if he's seen or heard anything I didn't know about, waiting for his response to be the usual benign-slash-nothing-to-see-here. What I get doesn't resemble the usual, not by a long shot, especially when he jumps me into the group chat with the rest of the clique.

Bro, I don't know how that managed to get bigger, but you're all over the net today, Kyle replies. *Can't get away with anything, since everyone is recording it all.*

Yasir, you good, bro? Taylor chimes in. *I know this ain't what you asked for, and hopefully we can find out who posted that out there. You got enough going on with the boat incident stuff floating around, too.*

Yeah, I wanna say I'm good, but that's a whole lie.

I get caught between wanting to burn everything to the ground and hiding inside the nearest out-of-the-way location to escape everything. I text back, *Someone obviously wanted me to see that, and they wanted the world to see it, and it wasn't a good thing. I'll be alright for now, but nah, I'm not trying to get used to the spotlight.*

I feel that. Let me and TK get to work a bit and see what we can find out, Kyle responds. *I think I have a clue who might have done it, but I need to be sure.*

I avoid the stares that no longer have anything to do with the war that Ian used to wage when it came to my physical appearance and the scents I wear. That's dead now. Hell, I almost welcome that negativity over the adulation being heaped on because I helped handle some idiots from a rival school. And this BS about wanting to make sure I'm okay? Yeah, that needs to be deaded soon, too, because I'm not here for that, either.

"Is everything okay, kiddo? You\re a lot more agitated than usual."

I jump in my seat, but not enough to draw attention. I completely forgot that Gamba's still roaming around in my head. I take a quick breath and scan around me to make sure everyone is still paying attention to the discussion on the book we'd read and retreat to the recesses of my mind. *"I got caught on camera when we were dealing with those jokers from Beach Creek."*

"So, what is the problem? Any publicity is good publicity, right? Especially when Ian has been off your back for the past few days," Gamba points out. *"As I understand it, he has more important things to worry about, right?"*

I can't have a conversation with Gamba in the middle of class. I'll look like I'm completely spaced out. I ask Mr. Trice, our English teacher, if I can go to the restroom, making up an excuse that I'm not feeling well due to the side effects of the medication. Once I step out into the hallway, I search for the first empty classroom and duck inside. The minute I think I won't be interrupted, I sit in a chair and journey into the recesses of my mind.

We settle into a sitting room in my mind that I created whenever we need to have a convo, and I grab a lemon iced tea while Gamba drinks water. I take a sip or two first, working through the chess game in my head. *"Ian's found a new angle. I can feel it. We need to find out more about him, and I don't mean what the fluff pieces of the town newspaper do on him and his family."* I'm getting tired of being on the defensive. It's time I become the hunter instead of the hunted. *"From the day I hit Oakwood Grove, he's been trying to ruin whatever reputation he thought I had, and I haven't been here that long. It's become a borderline obsession. Not to mention how weird his dad acted when he learned who my father was..."*

Gamba strokes his beard, studying me. *"Let your friends do the digging for you for now. There is no need to get caught up. Besides, if he is still on you, he will feel the counterattack coming and try to blame this on you."*

"You might be right. I do have friends now. I should trust them to have my back."

"Yes, you should. No one can handle anything alone. It is a blessing that you have people around you to help." Gamba leans back in his chair, chuckling. "*I know it is not an easy time, there are so many questions that have yet to be answered, but until they are, just take things as they come."*

I offer a chuckle and a shrug. *"Every day might not always be good, but there is always something good in every day."*

Gamba smiles. *"I like that. You should keep that when you are feeling stressed, and I cannot get to you quickly. It is perfect."*

I disengage and head back to my conscious mind, realizing that I have enough time to get back to class without causing a stir. I take my seat, taking a deep breath before I find out where we are in the discussion.

"Mr. Salah, is everything okay?" Mr. Trice inquires with a furrowed brow.

"Yes, sir, I'm okay."

"Good, now that you're back with us, can you please explain the significance of *Black Boy* by Richard Wright? The first question from last night's discussion homework?" Mr. Trice states as he leans against the front of his desk.

So, all eyes on me to answer the question, huh?

Okay, let's do this.

Gamba whispers from the recesses of my mind, *"You've got this, kiddo. Blow them away."*

I give the question some thought, smiling as I feel Gamba sending a warm and comforting energy through me. Yeah, Mr. Trice wants my thoughts on the book, he should be careful what he wishes for. "Mr. Wright was convinced, through his fictional accounts, that the true problem of racism is not that it exists, but that it is woven so deeply inside the fabric of American life, that it may take generations to extract its influence, but not without destroying American culture altogether. Is that what you were looking for, sir?"

The class erupts in oohs and ahs over the response, and the smile I see coming from Mr. Trice shows I had gotten the answer to my question. I sit at my desk, soaking in their appreciation for my words, and for the first time this school year, I flash a genuine smile.

There's always something good in every day.

It takes the rest of the school day for Kyle and the rest of the boys to find out who's behind the viral video, but the wild part is that Ian had nothing to do with it. It doesn't make sense. We've been on this whole frenemy arc since I got here, and he's been trying to pull me into a spotlight I didn't want to be bothered with, and he has every reason to do it. He needs the attention off his party debacle and what happened to me.

But the clique did find out that we weren't off the mark entirely… Jordin put the video out there, not Ian. I guess he thought if it came from another school that it wouldn't come back to bite him. Yeah, right. But that's not the funny part about all of this.

That video managed to convert a few of Ian's crew into begrudged fans, each of them showing a tempered respect for my ability to hold my own against hated rivals. The boy that I put down had me by at least a hundred pounds, and the rumors flew around both schools. He ended up becoming the subject of memes and all kinds of other embarrassing status messages all around social media, adding fuel to a wildfire I had hoped to not have to handle.

Things hit a fevered pitch by the time I meet Zahra in the courtyard, and I've had about enough of the circus atmosphere that I didn't ask for. Several different "promoters" want to try to turn me into the next Jake Paul and put me up against the Beach Creek kid for a boxing match. I got hit up during class, and I'd just told one more that I'm not interested before I even get to our spot under the Oak.

Never mind the approving glances and comments from the girls around school. It would only be a matter of time before someone catches smoke from Zahra, and I don't need her to get suspended over nonsense. Kendyl turned into a whole bodyguard to keep her bestie from chopping anyone's head off.

"Z, baby, let them go. They're only seeing me because I'm the hot flavor of the day." I cup my hands around Zahra's face. "I'm not stupid. Half of these wannabes are doing nothing but developing selective amnesia right now."

"I don't care, they don't get to be all reckless and I can't do anything about it," Zahra counters. "I swear by Nahara, I'll set these little girls on fire if they even breathe in your direction."

"I love that you're territorial, I wouldn't expect anything less from a Kindaran girl, but I promise you, there's nothing any of them can do for me." I press my lips against her forehead, giving up a smile when I hear a soft sigh escape from her mouth. "That's better, now, we need to focus on more pressing matters, like why is Eric trying to raise my profile and what does he hope to gain from it."

Kyle walks up with Kendyl in tow, tapping fists with me as the girls group together. The expression on Kyle's face worries me a bit more than I want to admit. "That had to be the worst bait and switch I'd ever seen in my life."

Kendyl shakes her head, adding to the lead in from her boyfriend. "Ian was pulling the strings, trying to make it look like he had nothing to do with it. My friends in the IT club were able to figure it out within a couple of hours. It came from Eric's account, but it was done on Ian's phone."

"I'm getting tired of this game he's playing." I grit my teeth, almost vibrating as I try to keep it together. "I didn't ask for this zoo swirling around us, but he's insisting on making this all about me."

"He's trying to take the spotlight off him. What happened to you at the party was a bad look, and he knows it," Zahra points out. "He still thinks that he can't be touched, but maybe we need to find a way to put some cracks in that wall."

Kyle jumps in, "His father had to pull some major strings to keep the drugs that were found on board from getting into the press. Turns out there was some harder stuff being used outside of the Molly and marijuana that we avoided the whole night."

"Yeah, he's been real quiet most of the day, which is not like him. He's rattled because he has no idea what you plan to do," Kendyl says. "A lawsuit would put a major crack in that Lance wall, for real."

"What y'all might need to worry about is making sure the new superstar on campus can handle the spotlight." Ian pops up, interrupting the conversation. Chrisette stands by his side, a smirk spread across her face. "I mean, by the time we get done with him, he'll be the hottest thing in town."

I take a step toward Ian, but Kyle steps in front of me. Kyle glances back at me and mouths, "we got you," before turning his attention to Ian. Kendyl stares Chrisette down, almost daring her to speak. Zahra makes herself the last line of defense, posturing in front of me with a scowl on her face.

Ian smirks over the show of solidarity. "What's all this for? I was simply stating the obvious. I mean, he can destroy anyone he wants in a fight, so it's not like he needs any of you to protect him. Isn't that right, killer?"

"That's funny, I was thinking the same about you, bro," Kyle interrupts. "Damn, I thought you were smarter than this, yo. My ace almost lost his life because of you and your clique, and you wanna act like you didn't do anything, right?"

"I didn't have anything to do with it, and you can't prove otherwise," Ian sneers. He tries to step to me again, only to get blocked by Kyle in the process. "Why don't you step from behind your muscle and holla at me, man to man. Show everyone in this courtyard who you really are."

"Nah, I'm good, besides, it wouldn't be a fair fight for you. Haven't you seen the video *you* posted?" I crack up laughing for a minute as I watch his face contort. "I mean, you must be losing your grip on reality or something. I was fine where I was, and you decided to pull me into the spotlight. This is what that comes with, remember?"

"You're supposed to be the baddest on the block, but you won't step to me?"

"You might wanna look around while you're busy trying to make me out to be some simp who can't handle himself." I smirk as I see the stares in our direction. The ones who are close enough for me to hear what they really thought almost have me feeling sorry for him. "Remember, I still have you over a barrel. It's only a matter of time before my toxicology screens come back. I wonder how much longer it will take before Amber cracks under the threat of a drug charge. You might wanna quit while I'm in a mood not to bury your football career."

Chrisette pulls on Ian's arm, trying to get his attention. She frowns as she stares me down. "So, who's the bully now, Yasir? How does it feel to be the one causing the pain?"

"Are you really forming your mouth to say anything?" Zahra steps away from me and gets in her face. "You can't possibly be that brainwashed, there's just no way."

"I have a clarity that you could never understand, Z," Chrisette stands her ground, furrowing her brow as she keeps her gaze trained on Zahra. "If you actually took the time to understand the stress that he has been under this whole time, you wouldn't be so hostile toward him."

"And what stress would that be? He's been at the top of the food chain his entire life. His father has been mayor for as long as we can remember. Stop before you hurt yourself," Zahra deadpans.

Ian turns to quiet Chrisette, taking control of the conversation. "Let's be real, and you might want to let your new 'friends' know before it's too late. You're a menace and a monster, and the truth will come out sooner or later. I know about your rep in the A, 'Diablo.' You're gonna need the support around you when it does, playa."

"Thank you, but no thank you. I know you don't have my best interests at heart, so why should I take any advice off you, huh?" I wrap my arm around Zahra's waist to bring her close. "There's nothing you're gonna be able to do to rile me up, bro. You have to get close enough to do that, and why in the hell would I allow it?"

"Whatever, man, it's your funeral."

As Ian and Chrisette leave the group and the rest of the crowd disperses, Zahra turns to me, focusing her gaze into my eyes. "Are you okay? I felt you vibrating when you pulled me to you. How did he know about your nickname in Atlanta?"

Gamba chimes in, confusing me over the timing. *"Everything is okay for now, kiddo. I did what I could to keep things under control. There's something about Ian that is triggering something darker in us. Until we can figure it out, there's nothing to say to anyone."*

I stare into Zahra's eyes to reassure her. "I'm good. I'm not about to concern myself with how he figured that out. It's been a weird day, and I need to take my mind off things for a bit."

"I can think of a few ways to make that happen," Zahra coos in my ear. "It is a bye week, after all, so I'm sure we can find a few things to do."

"You two need to get a room," Kendyl chides, then plants a kiss on Kyle's cheek. "Seriously, though, Ian's becoming more of a problem than we thought, and now he's got Chrisette turning into a hype woman. And what's this 'Diablo' business that he was spitting?"

I grab Zahra's hand, making our way to the parking lot. I have other, more pleasant things to think about. "We'll figure them out later. Right now, Z and I need to get over to my uncle's shop to pick up something for dinner. He and Ms. Lennox are going out on a date tonight, and we'll have thc house to ourselves for a few hours."

"Oooh, I think I like where this is going. Having a man cook for me sounds absolutely lovely." Zahra grins as she waves goodbye. "We'll catch up with y'all later."

As we head toward Storm and Raiden, I can't shake the feeling that Ian knows more than he's letting on, I just wish I knew who he found to give up that information. I tap on Gamba's door, letting him know we need to start digging into Ian's past and find something we can use for leverage. *"I'm gonna have to keep him at more than an arm's length. He's got it out for us, and everything in me is telling me he's playing a long game. We need to be prepared."*

"I'm with you, Ya-Ya, but that can wait until tomorrow." Gamba peers through my eyes and sees Zahra next to me. *"Right now, I need to make myself scarce. Based on the grin on your girlfriend's face, you will have a need for privacy tonight."*

Chapter Forty-Five – Zahra

Yasir's preparing the crab legs and fried shrimp we picked up from Unk's restaurant. Whether he realizes it or not, he understood the assignment, and I'm here for every bit of the catering being done for me. It's not until Yasir places the steaming hot plate in front of me and waits for my approval of the dish that I can relate to my mother's "look" whenever my father cooked and cleaned up afterwards.

He couldn't have been more attractive to me than in this moment.

I don't know about him, but tonight feels like… more. Despite the intimacy of the night, this has connectivity written all over it. We haven't had a chance to really learn each other and understand what it all means for us. I also want to catch him up on Kindaran culture, now that he knows where he comes from.

I wonder if I have to do more teaching than learning, though. If what Nana told us is true, there's suppressed information and memories that he doesn't have access to. That may keep him from understanding everything I have to tell him about our country. And what if he knows more than I do about our country once his mind is unlocked, for lack of a better word?

So many questions, not enough answers.

He catches me in my thoughts as I consume this delicious dinner. "Penny for your thoughts, pretty girl?"

I wink at him, popping a shrimp in my mouth. "I have a few thoughts, but it may cost you more than a penny. Who taught you how to cook? The shrimp are to die for."

"Well, I mean, Unk is one of the best on the coast at what he does. I picked a few things up over the years, and between him and Nana, I had to learn quick." He pours some apple juice into a glass for me before he sits next to me at the dining room table. "I'm sure I'll figure out more things as I continue to practice, but I'm glad you're enjoying it. I was low-key nervous. You're the first person I've cooked for outside of them."

"You keep cooking like this, and I'm gonna have to watch myself. If anything, I'll need to return the favor." I crack open a crab leg to slide the meat from its shell. "How do you feel about what's happened so far? I know it has to be a lot to process."

He pops a piece of crab meat into his mouth as he ponders my question. "I'm still trying to get over the fact that I'm Kindaran. I've been processing the meaning of it all ever since Nana dropped everything on me."

"What do you remember about Kindara?" I start off slow, not wanting to upset him by what he can't access. "I've read on people who have suppressed memories, and sometimes they manifest themselves in dreams. Have you had any dreams or anything?"

Something I say must have triggered him because he taps his index finger against his temple. "I'd been having, like, nightmares, I guess. It's hard to explain, but I travel to Kindara, and I see different aspects of the island. Then I—"

I take his hand in mine, placing my other hand against his cheek, and gently nudge him to meet my gaze. "We don't have to talk about that if you don't want to. My parents told me of your parents' bravery to help repel the Bralba invaders. What I do want to talk about is how you were brought into this world by the Vodaran priestesses—if what Nana's saying is true, that means your family was one of the Kindaran Nine."

Yasir shrugs, and I can tell it's another piece that he's not aware of. "I still don't know what any of that means. I feel like I have so much to learn. Unk might know a lot, too, since he's my mom's brother. I don't even know what Tribe that side of the family is from. And now I have to deal with Hassan, who was supposed to be a friend of the family, but I have no idea what he's about. Who knows what family I might have and if they survived the invasion like I did?"

"Maybe Daddy can help with that," I offer. "He is one of the foremost Kindaran historians in the world. There's nothing he doesn't know."

“I don’t know, Z, what if your father isn’t too keen about me dating his daughter?” Yasir shrugged. “Hell, maybe I’m overthinking all of this, I don’t know how to act right now. All of this is just so amazing—and scary.”

I smiled bright, melting when he smiles with me. “My father will be thrilled that we’re dating. He never liked any of the boys I might have been interested in because they weren’t Kindaran. He almost came to blows with one boy I was dating and his father one time at a dinner at their house.”

“Whoa… well, I don’t think that will be an issue with my uncle. He’s never met a stranger,” Yasir grins. “Maybe talking to your dad might help connect some of the dots in my mind. The gods know I need a basis of understanding. It might help with so much more.”

“Well, now that we’ve gotten that out of the way.” My smile turns more suggestive, as other thoughts make their way to the surface. “I’m still waiting for you to explain our first kiss. I know I have to be patient, but I don’t think you realize how epic that was for me.”

Yasir blushes, and I giggle when he turns the camera away. “I guess it’s my turn to try to keep from being so flushed that my skin feels like it’s on fire. It was epic for me too, and honestly, I don’t know how to explain what happened. I was so nervous that I wasn’t kissing you right that I did whatever I could to stay in the moment with you. I may need to reach out to Ms. Kynani so she can help explain how I did it.”

I sigh, fanning myself over the memory as I take a sip of my juice. “If that kiss was any inkling of what is to come, I’m gonna need you to get with her as soon as possible. I’m completely floored that you even have access to the priestesses to begin with.”

Yasir tilts his head to the side. “Why is that? Doesn’t everyone?”

Yeah, I have a lot to teach him until we can unlock his memories. “According to Daddy, there’s never been anyone who wasn’t already picked by the Kindaran Council to have that type of access to any of the Vodaran priestesses.”

Yasir scratches his head as he tries to connect the dots the best way he can. “Is it because my family is one of the Kindaran Nine? I’m still trying to figure all of this out, and you’re the first person I’ve been able to even have this type of conversation with ever. I hope I’m not bending your ear off."

"No, not at all, I'm loving this," I assure him as I crack open another crab leg. The sweetness of the meat nearly took me into a different headspace. "There's so much we can learn together now … and learn about each other, too. I can't wait to find out."

"Neither can I… it feels so right when I'm around you," Yasir smiles wider this time, showing off dimples I hadn't noticed before. "We need to finish things up so we can enjoy dessert before Unk and Ms. Lennox get home."

"Yes, absolutely. I'll be waiting in the living room." I kiss his lips soft and slow before I pad into the living room. "You know, a girl could get used to being spoiled like this. I think I'll keep you around after all."

His cell phone rings, startling both of us. He picks it up, and we notice Nana's number pop across the screen. He answers it and places it on speaker so we can hear the call. "Hi, Nana, is everything okay?"

"Yes, grandson, everything is faring well." Her voice sounded soothing, steady. "I have been able to speak with Kynani at length since we arrived, and I was wondering if Zahra is with you."

"Yes, Nana, I'm here," I chime in.

"Wonderful. I have already contacted your uncle and his girlfriend. Zahra, we have contacted your parents as well. We would like to bring you over to Kynani's rental property tomorrow night." We hear the smile in her voice, but the cryptic nature of her message throws us off. "It is time."

"For what, exactly?"

"To show you both who you are."

Chapter Forty-Six – Yasir

Nervous doesn't even begin to describe my feelings as Kynani invites us inside. "Good evening, Yasir, Zahra, please come in. I am pleased you could make time for tonight's occasion."

The heat we're generating might as well be calculated for nova-level radiance. I've been looking forward to this for so long, I'm a little worried that I've built things up too much. I squeeze Zahra's hand, tempering my emotions, realizing that I could bring Gamba to the surface before I'm ready to show him to the group.

That may be what Kynani and Nana have in mind, though.

I breathe a sigh of relief that everyone else who needs to be here has already arrived. I'm not exactly ready to see Zahra's parents just yet, but these aren't the most normal of circumstances, either. That means more to me than anything, and it also means we won't have to wait around to do whatever it is that they need to do to bring everything out of me.

And that's the scary part… what the hell is inside of me?

Kynani escorts us into the dining area. Unk and Lennox, and Kairo and Kesi, Zahra's parents, all sit at the table, along with Nana, who can't stop smiling when she sees us walk in.

"Just have a seat, enjoy, since we didn't have to cook today, and let's let Ms. Kynani and Mama Johari explain why we're all here," Unk says. "This is a bit, well, unexpected, to say the least, especially when we could've planned a more formal introduction with Zahra's parents."

Zahra clears her throat to sort of cut in as she looks at her parents. "Mommy, Daddy," she announces, "I'd like for you to meet my boyfriend, Yasir. This is his uncle, Xavion Okafor, and his girlfriend, Lennox Alvarez. And this is Ms. Kynani, the Vodaran priestess who is here to help Yasir with… well, I'm still trying to figure that out."

"Yasir, it is a pleasure to meet you and your uncle as well," Kairo states as he extends his hand to Unk. As they regard each other, Zahra and I can't help but see how similarly they resemble each other. I mean, Unk's Kindaran too, but it's like they're from the same area. Kairo has a low-cut fade and a well-kempt beard, and he's a little bit smaller than Unk in size, even though they're the same height at six-feet-tall. "I'm looking forward to finding out more about you all, including the young woman who I didn't expect to see outside of Kindara."

Zahra grins as she motions for Kynani to stand next to her. "Ms. Kynani has told us a lot about what's going on with Yasir, and she's hopeful she can provide more insight."

Kairo takes Kynani's hand and politely kisses it before switching his attention to Yasir. "And, if I may ask, what are you here to provide insight on, Kynani? I'm a bit confused over why a Vodaran priestess is away from our home country. Has the Council even verified Yasir's identity to warrant such attention?"

His thinly veiled questions put us on edge, and I can only imagine what's going through Zahra's mind. She tries to put me at ease over her father being difficult, and I want to dismiss it as nothing more than him being overprotective for no real reason.

Kynani flashes a small smile, but in a blink, her eyes change from their hazel-brown hue to an amethyst tone that happens to me when I'm a little agitated. "Mr. Assante, I understand your apprehension due to others you have encountered who provided false witness to our shared bloodlines, but I *assure* you, I am not here on some whim or an unchecked rumor."

Kairo raises an eyebrow before his whole demeanor changes. He drops his head in reverence to Kynani, allowing a moment of quiet between them. In the next breath, his tone changes quickly. "Priestess, I apologize for my misstep, I do not mean to question your presence here. There is a reason why I am hesitant."

Kesi holds her hand up, interrupting her husband's further attempts to speak. She walks over to me, giving me a warm and inviting hug that catches me off guard. "I apologize for my husband, everyone. Yasir, Zahra and I have had a few conversations about you, and while we did not find out your last name until a few days ago, I am happy to see that the young man in front of me has the aura that I expected to see around him. It has been such a long time, child, and you have no idea how much we prayed to the Divine Mother that you survived and were safe."

Umm, that escalated quickly. Zahra switches her gaze between her parents so fast it makes me dizzy. "Wait a minute, you both know about Yasir? What in the world is happening?"

Yeah, let's change the subject, shall we? "So, why are we here, Ms. Kynani? Nana was a bit cryptic over the phone."

Kynani smiles as she sits at one head of the table, sharing a glance with Nana at the other head of the table. "The reason why we asked you and the women in your lives to be here has everything to do with what has happened to you over the past few days. It is time to bring things full circle, in a manner of speaking."

I rub the back of my neck, unsure how to elaborate what Kynani led with. "I assume you mean the *other presence*, right?"

Zahra snaps her head in my direction, along with Unk and Lennox and my parents, who look as confused as I am. "Um, what *other presence* are you talking about?"

Nana interrupts Zahra before she can really crank up the interrogation. "We will explain things as best as we can and as quickly as we can, my child. Right now, we need to focus on Ya-Ya. Before the end of the night, much will change."

I squeeze her hand again, turning to kiss her lips. I whisper, "It'll be okay, promise," before I turn my attention to Kynani. "I trust her completely with whatever happens tonight. Now, what do you know about the *other presence*?"

Kynani nods, focusing her attention on me. "The *other presence*, as you are calling him for now, has already made up his mind about the persons in this room before I have had the chance to commune with him."

I'm sorry, what? "How are you able to know that he's okay?"

"You have not had to retreat into yourself to chat with him. He always tries to make an appearance whenever there is a threat surrounding you, in case your *zamwani* needs to rise." Kynani smiles as she peers toward the others in attendance. "I believe he knows there are no threats here, especially when he has grown quite fond of Zahra. Not as fond as he is of you, of course, but fond enough to declare that she is also under protection. He has sensed something within her that he recognizes. What that is, I do not know at this moment."

Zahra takes a sip of the mimosa in front of her then clears her throat. "Um, can I, Ms. Lennox, and my mom, get a clue of what you're talking about right now? What *'other' presence*? Yasir, do you have Kindaran bodyguards following you in the shadows or something? And what exactly does this presence sense in me?"

Considering I had a chat with Gamba already—and he's being *real* obvious with his silence, now that I think about it—they all deserve some sort of answer.

"I think it's best if we had this conversation in the great room. I think we will need to be comfortable for this part of the process. I can't really tell you… I kinda have to show you."

##*#*

"Breathe, Yasir. Focus on my voice as we prepare for your guardian's arrival."

I focus on the instructions Kynani gives me, but it becomes more difficult with each moment that passes. It may have had something to do with the quick convo and Q&A we had before we started this part of the process. It didn't get worse as the layers were taken off the proverbial onion, but by the time we'd finished, the looks on Zahra's and Lennox's faces were a mix of shock and disbelief.

What unnerves me more is that Kairo and Kesi, Zahra's parents, don't look as out of the loop as I expected them to be. They simply whisper between themselves like the proverbial lightbulb has gone off or something.

"You can't be serious," Lennox says as she sits with Unk. The confusion all over her face makes me chuckle, but that's more of a nervous laughter. "Are you telling us that there's some sort of specter, a ghost, inside of his nephew's subconscious? And we're supposed to just accept it like monsters actually exist?"

Kynani is undeterred by the incredulous looks on their faces. "To take a quote from Mr. Spock: 'If you eliminate the impossible, whatever remains, however improbable, must be the truth.' Is it so hard to believe that supernatural beings exist?"

"Yes, yes, it is." Unk glances over at me, shaking his head in the process. "All this time, the information that Mama Johari tried to explain to me, the advice from the Kindaran Council on how to keep Yasir hidden from the world. All of this was real?"

I turn to face Zahra, desperate to get an idea of how she feels about what she's hearing. I look into her eyes, searching for anything that'll keep me from regretting the decision to trust her with such a closely guarded secret. "Z, talk to me, please?"

Zahra caresses my face, tracing my eyes with her fingertips, biting her lip as she continues to move over my skin. "So, this *other presence*… has he been in there this whole time?"

I shake my head, closing my eyes to lean into her touch. By Nyati, she feels so damn good. "Kinda yes, but not really. I wasn't fully aware of him until after the boat accident. Why do you ask?"

"Your eyes… every time they changed colors to match your emotions. I couldn't figure out what it meant." Zahra keeps staring, almost like she's waiting for them to turn another shade while we talk. "I was so hypnotized by them that I didn't think they could have meant something more … mystical."

I narrow my eyes and think back to the incident with Squad. Then again, when we first kissed in the studio after I showed her the portrait of her likeness. "So, now that you're about to find out what I am—what I truly am—do you still want to be with me?"

Zahra grabs my hands and holds them in hers. "I guess I always knew what you were. I just didn't think it would be this beautiful. You might not know this about me, either, but I'm a Marvel girl, so, I can't resist thinking that the boy that I've fallen for could be… yeah, the whole possibility that there's a bit of Dr. Strange inside you… the idea sort of intrigues me."

"Wait, you're into comics too?" I wait until Zahra opens her phone and shows me the Marvel Comics app on her phone. "Okay, I'm officially in love, love with you right now. But wait a second… does that mean—?"

"Yes, it means that whoever or whatever is inside of your head doesn't scare me." Zahra kisses my cheek as she continues to trace my face with her fingers. "I don't know how else to explain it. The connection between us scares me more than anything else. But I still wanna know what Ms. Kynani means about whatever the other presence senses in me."

Kynani clears her throat to interrupt our private side convo. "I can help clarify things in that manner soon, but right now, we need to focus on Yasir and his acclimation process. Once that is complete, we will be able to explain things with you."

I tremble as I shake off the chill racing down my spine. "We can talk about things after this is done. I want to get to know Gamba, figure out where he came from and how we ended up together."

Zahra stops me for a moment and whispers in my ear, "I want to be there with you, if it's allowed. You shouldn't have to do this alone."

I nod as I kiss her fingers. "If it's allowed, I will ask. Promise."

I take my place in the middle of the living room floor opposite Kynani, crossing my legs to shrink the space I've taken. I close my eyes before the process begins, sending a silent prayer to the Divine Mother for strength through the process. *I know I'm not supposed to be afraid, but this whole process has me completely freaked out. Guide me through this as best you can, Divine One, and help me understand the importance of all of this.*

Kynani begins chanting in her Kindaran dialect, lighting candles that surround us. In the next breath, she closes her eyes, encouraging me to do the same. From there, her octave changes, the tone sounding like that of a soothing parental figure, coaxing whatever hesitant spirit lay in the depths.

"I can feel your presence within your protégé's conscious mind. I encourage you to come forth, you are in a safe space here," Kynani declares, keeping the sing-song cadence in her tone to summon Gamba to the surface. "Yasir's uncle is here, and two new friends are here to speak with you. You can come out and say hello to them, they are a part of him, they are not threats to him."

Gamba emerges through the darkness, taking his time to break through to my conscious mind. Our eyes meet as Gamba nods, opening the "door" to walk through and make his presence known. *"Do you think they are ready to see the full picture? They are going to be in for a shock."*

"I have a feeling they'll still be shocked, but the more they see it, the more comfortable they'll be okay. We have to normalize it sooner or later, right?"

He answers by giving a subtle and proverbial tip of the fedora. *"After the process is complete, we will be able to sense everything. Everything will feel different."*

"Then, let's give them a show."

Gamba's noncorporeal form takes shape next to us, and I hear an audible gasp from more than a few people. He recognizes Kynani first, acknowledging her with a wry smile. "Good evening, Kynani. It has been a long time since we have seen each other. You have gotten stronger in that time."

Kynani returns his smile, but she raises her right eyebrow as she stares at him. "I apologize, you have me at a disadvantage. May I ask your name? I recognize the cadence in your voice, but your features are foreign to me."

"Forgive me, my friend, I have forgotten that you remember me as an older man," he says. In the next moment, he switches his features, resembling an elder gentleman, gray beard and all. "Do you recognize me now, my former student?"

"Gamba. By Nyati's grace, I had hoped—" Nana gasps as a tear falls. "If you're my grandson's guardian, then that means—"

"Yes, the fates were not kind to me on that side of the veil." Gamba offers up a comforting gaze and smile. "But the Divine Mother saw fit for me to be of service in the most honorable way possible now."

Kynani does her best to manage her emotions, but I see a small tear streak down her face. "Gamba, I am elated that you are here but saddened over the reason why. Yasir is a strong one to have you. How have you been able to survive for so long without communicating with him?"

While I listen in on the conversation between Kynani, Nana and Gamba, I keep a sharp eye on the reactions from Unk, Lennox, and Zahra as things unfold in front of them. Unk looks like he's gonna have a million questions as everything is happening, and he's rubbing his hands over and over again, which is a dead giveaway that he's uncomfortable with what's happening, but he's helpless to intervene.

Lennox, on the other hand, gives me the impression that she's taking mental notes, which has me wondering why she isn't completely flipping out. There's no way she's seen something like this before. I've never been through anything like this before, and I know I'm not calm. At. All.

I zero in on Zahra's surprised and inquisitive facial expressions and the wonder washing over her. I smile as I guess what could be going through her mind in the moment and can't wait to get her alone to find out what she's thinking.

My Nana's reaction to Gamba raises more questions over who he was, and why she regarded him with such… love?

Gamba takes a deep breath before he speaks. "It has not been easy, but he has had a lot of growing up to do. I had time to commune with our ancestors to assist me on how best to guide him. I am impressed with how he has handled everything he has endured all this time, despite what was hidden from him. I feel a shift in the winds."

"As do I, my friend, now that I see that you are here. For that shift to come full circle, it is time for you and Yasir to complete the acclimation process," Kynani stresses. She looks at Zahra, Unk, and Lennox and grins. "For the rest of you, this process will be foreign to you, but I promise I am not hurting him. I understand if there are concerns, but this will help him more than you know."

Unk grabs Lennox's hand to keep her close. "Yasir hasn't been in touch with his true roots and bloodline. If this helps him figure things out, then I'm staying with him to see it through."

"What does that mean?" I ask. "No one really told me what this all means."

"All will be revealed very soon, kiddo. I promise, what comes after will be life-altering for the both of us."

Okay. I'll have to trust the process despite the growing fear rising through me. "Then, let's get to it."

Chapter Forty-Seven – Yasir

Before we have any further interactions with the rest of the group outside of the circle Kynani created, she moves her hands to create what feels like a bubble between the two of us. It catches me off guard a bit, but it also gives me a chance to have her undivided attention.

I'm hesitant, but I find my voice quickly. "May I ask a question?"

Kynani smiles like she's reading my mind. "Yes, young one, you may include Zahra in this process."

"Wait, how did you—?"

"In due time, I promise. You will soon learn how to do these things yourself." Her expression turns serious for a moment. "Are you certain that you would want her to see this part?"

"Yes, I am sure. She is important to me, and I can't explain it, but I know she won't be afraid of what she sees."

Kynani takes my hands in hers. "Very well. Let us get back to the group so we can bring her inside."

The moment we emerge, I blink a few times to get my bearings. The next thing I do is reach for Zahra. "Are you ready?"

"I thought you'd never ask."

I glance toward her parents, who are still calm throughout this process, and I don't know what to think. It's almost like they know a lot more than they're letting on about this whole thing. I can't worry about it right now, considering what I'm about to do.

Zahra joins me inside the circle of candles, nudging herself as close to me as she can before she takes my hand. She whispers, "I'm right here. I'm not going anywhere."

"I know," I mouth in response.

Kynani takes her place across from us, scans the audience around us one more time, and begins the process again. "Allow me access to your mind, Yasir. It is time to sync your essences to help you work better together."

Silence consumes all four of us. I wait for the next few minutes, wondering what's supposed to happen next. The shroud fades away, slow and easy, until I see Kynani, Zahra, and Gamba.

I hold up my hand to pause things one last time, studying Gamba's face again. "Did I know you when I was younger? I feel a deeper connection to you, but I'm having a hard time understanding how we are connected."

Gamba smirks, nodding as he settles into his space within the circle. "Yes, as a matter of fact, you do know me—well, your younger self knew me well."

I lean closer, recognizing familiar features in Gamba's face. I can't quite place them, but I swear they resembled those of Dad—at least, from the pictures I've viewed a thousand times. "Who are you to me, Gamba? Are you a part of my bloodline?"

Gamba grins. "In a manner of speaking, yes and no, Ya-Ya."

"I don't like riddles all that much, even though I'm good at solving them when the occasion calls for it."

Gamba moves closer. "I am a close friend of your father, and I am also your godfather. He and I were best friends. He has spoken of you often and has kept watch over you this entire time."

I take a couple of steps back, reaching behind me for the back of the chair so I can sit down. I'm stuck between wanting to believe what Gamba is saying is true and writing it all off as one bad joke. "You knew my father? How is any of this even possible? I don't remember you… I don't remember anything from that time."

"You have my word, we will sit down and have this conversation after we're done with the acclimation, kiddo," Gamba says. "I believe it will all come to you once Kynani is able to lift the suppression spells. I would never lie to you. I never did, even when you were smaller."

Kynani places her hand on my shoulder, giving it a gentle squeeze. "There is much for you two to discuss, Yasir. As your priestess, it is my duty and honor to help along the way. Now that you have the one important answer, are you ready to continue?"

I remain fixated on Gamba, taking in every contour of his face, the same golden-amber color in his eyes, the way his lip curls on the left side when he smiles. I've been so detached from Kindara. And now, to find out that my protector was my godfather?

I snap out of my musing long enough to acknowledge Kynani with a nod. "I'm ready. I've been waiting for this my whole life… at least, that's what it feels like, deep down."

Kynani claps her hands three times before rubbing them together to create a spark. When she separates them, we are consumed in an amethyst-hued flame that glows brilliantly against the darkness that surrounds us. She takes each of our hands, watching as the flames snake down our arms to where we connect, forming a triangle between us.

Seconds later, the flame consumes us all, but it doesn't burn us.

Kynani keeps her eyes closed to concentrate. "Gamba, do you pledge your life to your godson, to protect him from all enemies, foreign or friendly?"

"I pledge my life to my godson, and to protect him from all enemies, foreign or friendly," Gamba repeats.

Kynani continues. "Yasir, do you pledge yourself to your godfather, to ensure that you do not place yourself in any unnecessary peril, and when called upon, you both will do what is best for Kindara?"

"I pledge myself to my godfather, to ensure I do not place myself in any unnecessary peril, and when called upon, to do what is best for Kindara," I repeat, just as Gamba had done.

Kynani focuses her energy among the three of us as the color of the flames changes to a brilliant crimson before dissipating. She opens her eyes and releases her grasp. "Yasir, Gamba, the acclimation has now taken hold, the merge is complete. You should be able to move freely within Yasir's consciousness, but there are still limits. You cannot take over unless he is in severe distress, and he still can override if he sees fit. Any suggestions you make can be heeded or not."

I feel like I'm connected to something magical inside my own body. The rush of energy flowing through me—I swear I want to run for miles as fast as I can. And if we're connected, then that means I can view things the way Gamba does any time I want. It's like a whole different world has opened up for me, and I'm still scratching the surface of what we can do.

Gamba nods while I'm still scanning my subconscious like I've never been here before. "I understand. I know the limits of my power. My godson has the final say, regardless."

I give up a nervous grin. "How am I supposed to dictate to my godfather? I was always taught to defer to my elders."

Gamba claps his hand on my shoulder. "I am bound by Kindaran law to protect and guide you, kiddo. It will be an adjustment, but we will be fine. It will give me a chance to learn this mature version of you."

Zahra, who has been a quiet bystander the entire time, finally finds her voice. "That… that was amazing. I don't know what to say right now."

Gamba turns his attention to her and smiles. "My dear girl, this is only the beginning. Just wait until it is your turn."

"My turn? What do you mean—?"

"It is time to return, I imagine there are a few people who are wondering what we have been up to this entire time," Kynani advises before Zahra can say another word. "It has been my honor to facilitate this transition, and I look forward to guiding you further. The next step is imminent, as I feel the other presence making herself known."

We all open our eyes, taking a moment to regain our bearings. I chuckle at the captive audience in front of us and their collective confusion. I turn to Zahra, who has the widest grin on her face, giving me a curious look that I keep a mental note to ask about later.

Unk stares at me, his gaze darting between me and Kynani as he holds Lennox closer. "I… I have no idea what to make of what I just saw. One minute, you both were covered in this… fire, but nothing was burning around you. The next minute, the fire is gone, and y'all just wake up like nothing happened. Did it work or was that just a magical display?"

I share a knowing wink with Kynani, realizing the next half-hour will be entertaining, to say the least. "Yeah, it worked, Unk. We're good to go."

Chapter Forty-Eight – Zahra

As much as we want to get back to some semblance of normal, there are still a lot of unanswered questions lingering in the air.

Unk wastes no time in getting the ball rolling. "I'd love to know the answer to that question myself. How do you know about my nephew, Mr. Assante?" Unk hardens his stance once we've all had a chance to settle in. "I was under the impression from the Kindaran Council that Yasir's whereabouts and identity were kept under the strictest of confidence."

Daddy takes a closer look, glancing into Yasir's eyes while ignoring Unk's question. He studies his face, and a tear rolls down his cheek. He shakes his head over and over again, wiping more tears as they continue to fall. "I-I cannot believe it. We searched for you for years. No one knew where you had turned up. We feared the worst. You look so much like Bakari. By Nyati, you're alive."

I pull him away from my father, stepping in front of him as I give my father the most curious look I have. "Daddy, what are you talking about? You searched for Yasir for what reason? You've got everyone, including me, confused and then some. What's going on, and I think I deserve the truth this time."

Kynani places a comforting hand against my arm. "What your father is trying to explain is that there is a connection between you and Yasir that neither of you were made aware of. Your father's knowledge of it is based only on historical reference, but even he could not be informed of what would happen once you were connected. Until now."

I close my eyes and start vibrating in place like I'm on the verge of exploding. "I'm as good at puzzles as the next person, but this one's so wild that I'm gonna need the Riddler to help unravel it. Can you dumb it down for the uninitiated, Ms. Kynani?"

"Well, to 'dumb it down,' as you say, the short version of what I mean is that you and Yasir are connected in more ways than the romantic relationship that you two have forged. Ashanti, the goddess of Love, foresaw your link many moons ago, and Nahara forged your bond in fire, as Nyati, the Divine Mother, decreed."

I grin at the confused expression on Yasir's face, and he's really trying to get on the same page with me and Kynani. There are so many things I can file under "getting to know you better" now that Kynani has scratched the surface of what I've been feeling deep down all along.

Kynani pulls me close, giving my hand a subtle squeeze as she whispers, "We will need to speak alone when you have the opportunity. I sensed a presence inside you during Yasir's acclimation. An introduction is warranted."

I nod to acknowledge her veiled request. I go along with it, figuring that it'll come out later. I shift my attention back to the convo at hand. "Um, Daddy, you never did explain things about Yasir."

Daddy regards Unk's body language, rubbing his goatee as he considers his words. "We were approached by the Kindaran Council while your mother was pregnant with you, baby girl. They told us about Bakari and Nasira, Yasir's parents, in Solara and our connection to them. They were vague on the details until you kids were born."

Kynani chimes in, helping to fill in the blanks. "You both have a tattoo on the inside of your left wrist. Yasir, yours is in the form of a wind image, specifically a hurricane symbol, as you were born under the viewing of Ubaka, the Vodaran God of Air. Zahra, yours is a fire symbol, a phoenix to be exact, as you were born under the viewing of Nahara, the Vodaran Goddess of Fire. The balance between you is based on Yasir's ability to feed your energy and vice versa, and for one *specific* purpose once you have reached maturity."

"The protection of the Kutokufa Scrolls," we utter in unison, as though someone—or something—embedded the phrase inside our minds.

I tilt my head to the side for a moment, wondering how I've recited something I've never heard of before in my life. "Wait a minute, how did Yasir and I remember that phrase and knew to recite it at the same time?"

Mom shakes her head, matching Kairo's incredulous expression. "When we could not find you, and we feared you were dead… there was no reason to believe… we should have continued looking for you, Yasir."

"Okay, hold on a second. Can we get in on what the hell is going on right now?" Unk trades concerned glances with Lennox before he focuses his gaze on Kairo. "As his legal guardian, I deserve to be involved in the conversation as much as they are."

"You are correct, and you will all be involved. It is very important that you are," Kynani offers. "For now, there will be some conversations I need to have with the kids, separate from you. Once they have a full understanding of things, then they can bring you into the larger conversation so that you can comprehend the depth of their journey together."

"May we ask when we will have the opportunity to know?" Mom inquires. "I am sure Xavion and Lennox will need to know how to support Yasir as we will need to understand how to help Zahra through this next phase. If my husband's research is accurate, there is a lot more to absorb."

"I think this would be a good time to have dinner, so we can continue this conversation with good food and new friends," Kynani announces. "I believe that things will clear themselves up once we have had a chance to eat."

I sit outside with Kynani and Yasir after dinner is over, inside of the gazebo that's out of earshot of the main house. I want to be calm, but I'm bubbling over inside, almost silently begging Kynani to explain herself before I combust.

The clouds above us provide a captivating backdrop, projecting a brewing storm on the horizon, but I refuse to believe that whatever Kynani brings to light will be anything short of game changing. Ever since she showed up, it's like different layers have been peeled off of Yasir's exterior, revealing a different truth each time.

I guess today is no different, as Kynani's first question throws us off. "I know you both have questions for me, but for now, I will be concentrating on Zahra. My first question is simple, but not quite so simple: have you sensed another presence within your mind?"

I snap my gaze in Yasir's direction, and all I see are question marks in his eyes. I turn my attention back to Kynani as she takes my hand in her grip. "Um, no, should I have sensed a presence? I'm not quite sure what you mean."

Kynani studies my face and ponders her words. "Okay, let me try a different question: do you realize how influential your singing ability is over others? How soothing it can be, or how you're able to have an audience bend to your will at any time?"

I get quiet for a few moments, squeezing Yasir's hand as our shared incident comes to mind. "Yes, I think I do. I even have moments where I just whisper into the air when I want someone to do something, and they seem to listen to me."

Kynani rests her palm against her cheek as she considers her answer. "Indeed. There is a reason for that, my child. Your parents would have been told, and they might have been told, but they could not know the depth of the meaning of it all. That is where I come in."

"I know this sounds like I'm being impatient, Ms. Kynani, but… what am I?" I ask. I admit, I'm trying to understand where this is all going myself. "You were cryptic before dinner, and it's been on my mind for the past couple of hours. Can we get to the heart of the matter, please?"

Kynani smiles as she pulls a stray hair from my face. "Your generation, always in a rush. But I understand your desire to be given all the information needed to make sound decisions. Allow me to accommodate your request: you are a *mwali duati*, Zahra, otherwise known as Sageborn. You are metahuman too. Your abilities unlocked the moment," and Kynani stares directly at me, her eyes boring into my soul, "your betrothed's abilities began to fully manifest."

My mouth drops as I grasp the meaning of Kynani's words. "Wait, so, how was I supposed to know about my abilities before now?" The elevated pitch in my tone is a combination of confusion and excitement. "And… *betrothed*? I mean, I like Yasir a lot, like, *a lot*, but I wouldn't say it's gotten that deep between us yet."

"Consider all the facts, young one, based on what I have learned. You sensed his scent, almost entranced by it when others were repelled by it before he adjusted the mixture so it would not be so offensive," Kynani explains, smiling at us the entire time. "You have had a deep-seated need to have him close and want to keep him safe as of late. You even risked your life to save him, as I was told by Mama Johari. According to the sacred temple texts, once a machari is born, a trillsage is born as its mate."

"Pause, time out. A trillsage? Another kind of Sageborn?" Yasir asks. "And she kinda has a point, Z. You stepped in front of me when you thought my Squad was a threat."

I give up a nervous giggle. My mind is swirling. "Okay, so, things have been a bit intense between me and Ya-Ya lately."

"Um, you think?" Yasir can't avoid blurting out. "I almost flew into a rage when you told me Kyle had to protect you from one of the boys in Ian's crew when he tried to holla."

"I am enthralled at the banter between you two." Kynani giggles before she continues. "Nyati, Ashanti, and Nahara… the Divine Mother and both Vodaran goddesses placed this in motion long before you were both born. You are fated in this life to be together, and in the next life. It is the reason why no other girls have been able to capture his attention, and no other boys have been able to, shall we say, stay on your level."

"Whew, okay. That makes sense. So, now that we've gotten that out of the way, what are my abilities, exactly?" The questions are coming rapid-fire now. "I kinda knew about my voice, so, does that mean I'm like, a siren? There's so much in my head right now."

Kynani taps her chin with her index finger. "There is more to your voice, child… if ever you are in extreme danger, you have the ability to emit a scream that produces a miniature shockwave that keeps your attackers from advancing any further."

"Um, I've never had the—"

Kynani pats my hand, keeping her gaze focused on me. "We can get to your abilities soon, but I needed to make you both aware of what you are to each other. You are a trillsage, Zahra. It is written in Kindaran mythology that every few generations, a Sageborn pair are born—a trillsage and a machari—and while they are made aware of each other as small children, once they reach puberty, they are betrothed, as willed by Ashanti, to each other and to their shared purpose and responsibility to the Divine Mother."

I switch my gaze back to Yasir, caressing his cheek as I stare into his eyes like it's the first time I've laid eyes on him. "So, Yasir's Sageborn, and the whole acclimation ritual we witnessed… is that what I'll be going through? Will I become a Sageborn once that happens?"

"I know this is a lot to absorb, and I promise I will be here to help you both work through all the questions you have," Kynani advises. "If I need assistance from another priestess, then I will make the request of the Council. They will be more than accommodating once they have been advised that you both have been made aware of your other selves."

"But I have not been made aware of anything, or anyone, at least, not that I know of," I respond. "You're making it sound like I have a mental illness or something, or Yasir, for that matter."

Kynani raises an eyebrow. "I assure you, you do not have a mental illness, but I will advise that if you both have trusted friends, you will need to take great care explaining to them what is going on with you," Kynani cautions us, leaning in to keep our attention. "This is not an easy path to travel, and this is the first time that Sageborn will be guided away from the confines of Kindara, and we may have to adjust protocol as we progress."

My lip trembles, and my mind is flowing into overdrive now. "When will I get the chance to talk more with Gamba?"

"Soon, my child, but first things first, we need to set up a time so that I can facilitate the introduction to your other self… the physical manifestation of your guide, much like I did with Yasir. But we must do it quickly."

"So, do I have a *zamwani* like Yasir? Will I be able to conjure too?"

Yasir chuckles, unexpectedly throwing me off. "Okay, I wasn't expecting you to be so hype to figure all this out. Am I reacting wrong to this whole thing?"

"Well, what would you call it, Ya-Ya?" I widen my eyes as the fear seeps into my stare. The reality is setting in, and I'm legit trying not to freak out. "This is something that we're gonna have to prep Ky and Kenni and the rest of our circle, because if either of us—"

"I see you and your betrothed consume a great deal of comic books and graphic novels," Kynani smirks as she shakes her head at us. "This is not like anything that you might have read about. While Yasir does have a *zamwani* at his disposal, your guide will help you conjure your *ajanzi*. Its primary directive is to protect you, and to help protect your betrothed from harm, much like Yasir's *zamwani's* primary directive, when conjured, is to protect him and you from harm."

"Sheesh. This is a lot," I admit while I play with a braid. "So, what happens now?"

"Difficult to say at this point, but until I have a chance to get your guide merged within your psyche, helping Yasir through his acclimation process is priority," Kynani instructs us, although she's focused on me. "He has a lot that he is working through, so his learning curve is a bit deeper, at least, until we're able to unlock his memories. I am hopeful that you can help, so that when the time comes, he will be able to help you through your own acclimation."

Kynani rises from her chair, opening her arms to offer a hug, grinning when Yasir and I embrace her tightly. As we trek back to the house, she continues to look at us, her smile maintaining its energy until we make it to the front door. "I have a good feeling that you two are bound for extraordinary things. I look forward to watching it all unfold."

Chapter Forty-Nine – Zahra

Yasir and I sit across from Kynani as Lennox and Unk enjoy some time to themselves on the deck in the backyard. Nana has already retired for the night, and my parents headed home too, so it leaves us and Kynani together to chat. Kynani explained after the acclimation was finished that she needed to sit down and get a gauge on how things have progressed between Yasir and me. The more she stares at us, the more her curiosity shows up in her facial expressions.

"How long have you and Yasir been, shall we say, dating?" Kynani asks.

"Um, we've been, like, together for about a couple of weeks, so to speak, Ms. Kynani."

It's interesting that she's asking about how long we've been together, together, and I have a funny feeling she's digging for a specific reason. What that might be, it'll reveal itself soon enough. All we can do is answer the questions and take things from there.

"There is something special I see between you two." Kynani observes us as we sit on the sectional. She nods. "While I was able to connect you with your Godfather, there is much work to be done to break through the spell that was cast to erase the traumatic experience from your memories."

"I have a question, if I may ask." I gaze into his eyes, grinning at the changes I've noticed in him. "What happens to us now? Do we just go back to our normal lives—if there is such a thing?"

Kynani giggles at the question, but I'm legit interested in the answer. "The truth of the matter is that, in a manner of speaking, nothing will be normal for either of you from now on. It is my hope to help keep things as simple as possible, but there are things that you both will need to understand."

Yasir interlaces his fingers with mine, taking a deep breath and exhaling slow and easy. “As long as we don’t have to leave Oakwood Grove, I think the rest of it is doable. That’s the one thing that I’ve dreaded since I was old enough to understand what Nana was trying to tell me.”

Kynani offers a knowing grin, holding up her hand to slow the stream of questions. “I believe we need to have a deeper conversation sooner rather than later. But I need to speak with your parents first, Zahra, and with Xavion and Lennox as well.”

“Is it too soon to bring my parents into the rest of it? I mean, I’m just now trying to wrap my head around what happened today. It’s all so wonderful and confusing at the same time.” I tighten my grip on his hand, then smile when he raises it to his lips to kiss. “I don’t know that they even understand what happened, either. It might complicate things.”

“Your father is a Kindaran historian, he understands more than you realize,” Kynani says. “What he might not understand is the application of the history he has been researching this entire time. That will take time for us to help your parents work through their initial confusion.”

“So, how soon can we figure that out?” Yasir asks her. “I don’t want to sound selfish, but I just found Zahra, and for the first time in my life, things are starting to make sense. I would like to keep that ball rolling, after suffering for so long.”

“I understand the need to speed ahead, young ones, but I must ask for as much patience as you can provide. All will be revealed in time.” Kynani rises from her seat. “I will need to speak to your parental figures now, Yasir, since they are together at this moment.” She leans down, whispering low enough for us to hear her response. “Between you, me and the gods, she is what your uncle has needed in his life this entire time. He has sacrificed a lot more than you realize. There is something swirling around Lennox, something that will be good for him, and for you.”

She walks to the back door, leaving us a moment to ourselves. I turn to kiss his cheek, adjusting my body to face him, tucking my legs under me to get comfortable. “How do you feel about all of this? Do you trust me with what you are? Do you understand what I've become? I admit I don't know how to feel about everything, but I want you to know I'm not going anywhere."

He takes my fingers and kisses them. "I trust you completely. More than you know, and I'm not going anywhere, either." He offers his hand to help me up from the couch. "I need to get you home. We still have school in the morning."

"Lead the way, handsome. It will give us some more time to talk."

"Okay, so, outside of hearing Gamba's voice through you, I really don't know what that looks like, either. I mean, I've seen your eyes change at times, but you know about that."

We take the long way to my house so we can have some extra time to ourselves to vibe. Our phones are on vibrate, and the way they keep buzzing against the middle console, we'll have a lot of texts to deal with once he drops me off and heads back home.

"Well, I kinda know what that looks like, but it's hard to explain." He gives up a chuckle. "The first time it happened, I was literally left in the dark. Like, it feels like a dark shroud covering you, keeping you from seeing anything at all. It wasn't until Ms. Kynani finally merged our essences that I might get a chance to see what exactly has been manifesting itself through my body and mind."

"Well, it can't be that weird, right?" I question out of the blue. "I mean, you're gonna learn how to conjure soon enough, right? Is there any way that we can get an idea what Gamba knows about it?"

"I don't know how to answer that question. The thing that scares me the most is that you see what my *zamwani* looks like in real time, or Unk or Ms. Lennox, if I ever have to bring him out." He grips the steering wheel tight this time, while trying to keep a comfortable grip on my hand. "Nyati forbid if it happens in a public space and people would rather kill something they don't understand or fear than to try to ask questions to figure things out."

"You make it sound like… like…"

"Like, what, being a Black person in America?" He throws out the conclusion that I didn't want to voice out loud. It has to be said. "Not like it isn't already a struggle to go out into the world on that front, and now I have to worry about being a metahuman on top of that."

I massage his palm. The convo has gotten way too dark. "Then we'll do what we can to keep that from happening, okay? I meant what I said, I'm here, and I'm not afraid."

"Well, I don't know if I should be or not, but I guess I won't know until I know, right?"

"Okay, let's try to take this in a different direction, Ya-Ya." I move up to his forearm to keep him in the moment with me. "Tell me about Gamba. Is he aware of what happens when you're dealing with other people?"

"Yes, he's told me as much, although he says he tries to avoid things and situations that are more… private for me," Yasir explains. "In other instances, I can shut him out if the need arises."

"So, that means he wasn't there when we almost… well." Thinking about what happened that day in his studio almost triggers me, and not in a bad way, either. "I want to believe that moments like that belong to you and me. I may have to have that talk with Imara, now that I think about it."

"Yeah, those moments belong to us. There are no witnesses whatsoever." I squeeze his hand and breathe a sigh of relief. "Like I said, I can shut him out if the need arises. It isn't complicated in that sense. Ms. Kynani made it clear that I can still live my life, but my Godfather is there when I'm stressed or in immediate danger."

"What else have you had the chance to chat with him about? Has he, like, talked to you about other things? Does he give advice at all?"

He grins, making me blush. "I found out that he was my godfather when he was alive, and that by some form of Vodaran magick, or by Nyati's will, he was, I don't know, inserted in my psyche. I still don't know how it all works, or what abilities we have. I can only imagine it might be the same with you and Imara."

"You keep saying *we*, Ya-Ya. I get a little confused when you say it like that," I confess. "How will I know the difference between you two, besides the cadence and tone of your voice? I mean, would you even know the difference between me and whoever my guide will be?"

He thinks about it for a moment, and then he snaps my fingers. "Since they're not here to hear it, how about this: if you want to be sure it's me, and if I want to be sure it's you, we need to come up with a word or phrase that is unique to only me and you."

"Okay, so what word or phrase would we both know that will help me tell the difference?"

He mulls over my question as he pulls into the driveway. "If you ever need to bring me to the surface, no matter what is going on, get our attention and say the word, '*karasu horo*.' It's a Kindaran phrase that, roughly translated, means 'return to me, my chosen.' If you have to repeat it, repeat it. It's something neither would know to respond to, and they'll have to bring us back."

"I love it, but I'm confused now. How did you learn that phrase?"

"Umm, I've been learning a few words and phrases ever since Nana told us that I'm Kindaran." He reaches over to softly kiss me. "I'll see you tomorrow at school."

I'm not ready to let him go just yet. "What do you think about Lennox? She's definitely growing on me, and the way Unk is around her… it's like he's carefree."

"Yeah, she's definitely had a positive influence on him, and that makes me happy," he smiles as he puts Storm back in gear. "Now, get in the house so you can get settled in."

"Ooh, so forceful." I blow a kiss before getting out of the car. "You're lucky I like you, or I'd have to do something about the bossy tone in your voice."

"Mhm, no you won't. You like it too much to make me stop. Now, off to bed, young lady. See you in the morning."

He pulls out of the driveway, winking at me as he opens the sunroof, and I'm doing my best to coax him to come back. Suddenly, he stops and looks at his phone. The curious expression on his face makes me rush to open the door to figure out what's going on.

We quickly notice an unknown number calling. He doesn't think anything of it, and sort of waves it off as perhaps Hassan or someone else calling to give him an update or something. "Hello?"

There's silence on the line, and we're confused over why the person won't respond to Yasir's greeting. "Hello? Is anyone there?"

"I know who you are, and I know where you are," the voice on the phone sounds distorted, like someone is purposely trying to disguise themselves. "I'm coming for you, and I'm going to destroy you."

Before Yasir can respond to the threat, the call disconnects.

Chapter Fifty – Yasir

I should've known the incident earlier would trigger another nightmare. The only thing I can do is brace for whatever comes and focus on what I can control as it happens.

Things start off differently this time around as planes touch down at Drana Tirin Airport. I'm a bit confused over how I manage to arrive through the capital, but I take it as an opportunity to learn something new. I scan the area, not really sure what I'm searching for, until I find a placard being held by a driver who has my name scrawled across it. I've been used to arriving on the island through the usual route, so coming through the capital city presents a new set of challenges.

Or maybe it might provide an opportunity to find a different clue to help me unravel the puzzle that, through these dreams, I guess I'm meant to solve.

The driver recognizes me, shakes my hand, and signals me to accompany him to the idling Jeep Gladiator truck awaiting us in the staging area. As with my other dreams, no one really speaks, but I can't figure out if it disturbs me or if I prefer they not speak. If we are heading toward Solara, I need to brace myself for the emotional turmoil that'll greet me once we reach the gates to my home.

I keep my wits about me as I survey the landscape from this new angle. Even in my dream state, the chance still exists that I can be killed. Sure, it might be a remote possibility, but I've watched enough of the *Matrix* movies to know better than to tempt the theory that Morpheus made famous: that the body cannot live without the mind, and that the mind makes the dreams real.

The Jeep makes its trek over the hills, coming in from the north side of the island, the driver making the approach with skill and care as the vehicle begins to traverse across the cobblestone roadway. The move is neccssary; this time, storms sweep over the landscape, making the stones slippery. Kindara is “enjoying” its annual rainy season, and though it’s on the tail end where the storms aren’t as prominent or frequent, what does show up comes with its own wallop.

I hope I’m able to see something new during this recent sequence. I’ve made this normal trek from the south, so I take the new trajectory as a reason to scribble as many notes as possible on my notepad. Something has to happen during this ride that’ll trigger something new for me to research. The wind shifts the storm to a diagonal downpour, and if I concentrate hard enough, I can see the turtles slip-sliding their way through the grasslands.

The moment arrives when I normally witness the smoke pluming from behind the gates, but the storm has all but suppressed the fires from the battle. I notice a shadowy figure, something that I didn’t notice during the last sequence. What I also haven’t experienced from the last time is the torrential downpour that further obscures the person from my view. I can’t make out the features of the person, which is frustrating me. There’s only so many of these I can take before it leaves me hesitant to bother anymore. I’m not ready to give up, as I’m more concerned over figuring out who this person is, and why are they so important?

I get out of the jeep and climb the first hill that leads into the village, hearing the commotion that I’ve grown so familiar with as the rainstorm calms to a drizzle. I could tell how heated the fighting is just by the pitch and the cadence. I steel myself against the oncoming battle and its inevitable conclusion, although I have to admit that it never gets easier, no matter how many times I’ve gone through the torturous event.

I watch my younger self being led away from the fight, but I also notice something I didn’t expect. “I” was fighting against Hassan, almost like I’m fighting for my life on a different front. Hassan eventually picks me up from the ground and runs to safety, ignoring my cries that I don’t want to leave the fight. I wonder why I would fight Hassan when I needed to be brought to safety.

Then… the figure from another nightmare emerges through the

rain, rushing toward me with those same menacing crimson orbs. *"Find the artifact, or I will destroy you!"*

I wake up screaming just as the figure reaches to grab me, slapping my hand over my mouth to keep from waking up the house yet again. I sit up in bed, taking a hand towel to wipe the sweat from my forehead and the back of my neck. This new clue is unexpected and understanding it will take some time. I tuck it away in my journal for later to compare what I've found in earlier trips. There's gotta be a connection.

Between this latest nightmare and the mysterious caller threatening to end me last night, I feel like I need to take a mental health day, hit the reset button, or anything to clear my head. I'm not gonna do it, though. Too many things are happening for me to just check out right now.

I text Zahra good morning, grinning when the response comes back a few minutes later, the heart emoji conveying more than any words are needed. I send a few emojis back before I switch gears to text Kynani, asking for her counsel for the nightmares I'm suffering from, hoping she'll have the ability to help me either control what I'm witnessing or at least develop a deeper insight into what I find.

Kynani responds to my message, requesting a time to visit and assist. I glance at the time on my phone and realize it isn't quite seven a.m. yet. Fuck. I didn't pay attention to the time; she could've been resting… I apologize for texting so early, asking for her to come over after school. She mentions something about being up before dawn to confer with someone on the Kindaran Council before she confirms that I can come and see her.

Now that I've gotten through that minor embarrassment, I switch gears again to check in with the boys when a call comes through, interrupting my messaging.

I recognize Hassan's number and freeze. Not because he has my number, but why he is calling so early in the morning. And after the last dream sequence that revealed him struggling to take me away from the battle scene, it now has me questioning everything about him. "What's up, Hassan? Is there something I can do for you?"

He chuckles, although I can't understand what's so funny. "I wanted to make sure everything has gone smoothly with Kynani. She requested to assist, so I wanted to make sure she is handling things properly."

I start to answer Hassan when Gamba slips into my ear. *"Something is not right, Ya-Ya. He is a little too interested in what is going on with you."*

I pause for a moment, checking with my Godfather to figure things out. *"He's been dealing with other issues that took precedence. He had one of the priestesses come down when Nana asked at a moment's notice. Why are you telling me we shouldn't say anything to him now?"*

"Everything okay, Yasir?" Hassan inquires. "I want to make sure the connection is still solid. We are out in the Mediterranean."

"His motives are not pure, Yasir," Gamba insists. *"He is fishing to find out what you know and what has been brought to the surface. Feed him something that will keep him happy for now until we can find out more."*

"He's not a threat, Gamba."

"I cannot say that for sure, I can only tell you what I feel. He is not a threat, but he does not have your best interests right now."

I clear my throat before I offer a response. I have to think quickly; Gamba hasn't been this agitated since we became aware of each other. "Yeah, things are fine, Hassan. Ms. Kynani has been great so far, I've been learning a lot from her, including more on Kindaran culture and tradition."

"That is great, I am very glad to hear it." Hassan's tone remains upbeat, but I detect something underneath—it sounds like annoyance—that makes me wonder if Gamba is on to something. "Was she able to help with the more pressing issue you needed handled?"

I exhale slow, doing my best to measure my words. I'm not sure if it's factual or not, but it sounds good to try out. "Ms. Kynani made it clear that anything that I discuss with her can only be divulged to the Kindaran Council, so they can figure out who else needs to know what's going on with me. I can't even tell Unk right now."

"Sure, I understand," Hassan sighs. I feel like he's trying to placate me, but I'm hopeful the paper-thin explanation will work for now. "I had hoped that more would have developed, but I will abide by the Council's order. Let me know when they reach out to you or Kynani."

"Will do." I disconnect the call, tapping my knuckle against my right temple. "Gamba, we need to talk. I need to understand why I can't trust the person who got me out of Solara and was able to get me to my grandmother when I was little."

Gamba steps out from the shadows in his noncorporeal form, taking a seat at my desk chair as he offers for me to sit on the edge of the bed. "First things first, kiddo, we need to make sure there are no interruptions."

I send a text to Unk to let him know I'm up and getting ready for school, and about the meet with Kynani later today. I slip inside again, getting comfortable for the chat at hand. "Okay, we should be good for about a half hour. Do you want to explain what's going on?"

"As much as I respect what Hassan did for you, there is a story you should know," Gamba says.

"Well, we've got time, so, let's get this done."

Gamba takes a deep breath like the story he's about to recount will hurt him as much as it might hurt me. "Before you were born, your father and Hassan were friends and rivals. It was a difficult space to build a relationship, but somehow, they made it work. That all changed when your mother came along."

I nod, acknowledging the story as it unfolds in front of me.

"We were all friends, your mother, your father, Hassan, and me. Your uncle was much younger, which is why he didn't immediately recognize my name. As we got older, the rivalry between your father and Hassan intensified." Gamba sighs as he continues to recount the memories. "Your mother was deemed the prize at the center of it all, but after a while, your father won your mother's favor and attention, much to Hassan's irritation."

I feel like I already know the punchline. "So, let me guess, Hassan did what he could to make things difficult, right?"

"Well, not exactly." Gamba shakes his head. "Your mother enjoyed the attention she got, so she asked your father if Hassan could be extended family along with me. Since your father and I were best friends growing up, it caused a bit of tension… until your mother became pregnant with you."

"And that calmed things down? That's a bit convenient, isn't it?" I scratch my head, trying to understand the why of it all. "So, let's skip the details that will make things a bit boring for me. Why are you skeptical of Hassan's motives? My parents are dead, and from what I'm gathering, you also perished, and he got away from the invasion to get me to my Nana."

Gamba pauses again, regarding my skepticism. "You pose a fair question, and at the moment, I cannot provide a real answer that will make sense. I would never steer you wrong, kiddo, I want you to understand that."

"Could it be that you're salty because he's still alive?"

"That is not fair, Yasir. I chose this path on purpose. I was the one who was made your godfather, and I promised to protect you, whatever it took, even if it meant my life."

I wipe a tear from my cheek as I take Gamba's words to heart. "A lot of what has happened has left me here on this side of the veil damn near all by myself. Unk and Nana are the only family I have on this side, and I still don't know how he managed to get evacuated, but everyone else had to die. I understand the sacrifices you all made for me, but I don't know why you did it, and the only other person who can is Hassan."

Gamba leans forward, tapping my fists, offering up a sympathetic smile. "Your parents loved you more than anything in this world. If there was any way they could have escaped with you, they would have, but there was something else that was just as important as making sure you lived, even at the expense of their lives."

"What? What was more important than their sons?" I'm getting sick of this same narrative of "my parents had to make a choice." "I have almost no memory of them, and the little that I do have is locked away from me. How am I supposed to be okay with all of this, huh? Tell me."

"Okay, let us take a beat for a moment, kiddo. I think there is a way to answer your question and help fill in some of the blanks." Gamba takes a deep breath, nodding to himself. "Can you wait until Kynani arrives? She has access to the Kindaran archives and information that very few people can get. I promise I am not stalling, just try to be patient."

"Easy for you to say, you have information that I don't."

Gamba claps his hand on my shoulder, staring into my eyes. "You have had information withheld for a long time, kiddo. I promise, between Kynani and I, we will get you straight."

I open my eyes, shutting Gamba out for a moment. My temper's flaring, and I need the time away from him so I can get my head together, since the night terrors manage to mess with me, too. I look skyward, praying to Nyati for strength to temper the anger in my heart. I've got to get a grip before all of this consumes me.

If I don't, things could get much worse.

Chapter Fifty-One – Yasir

We're at lunch with the crew, going through the usual convo and planning for the next few weeks. Halloween is coming up, and I can't wait. Zahra and I put rush orders on the Black Panther suit and Storm's matching black cutout jumpsuit and thigh-high boots. When she showed me the white wig she'd found and ordered to contrast with the black suit?

Yeah, I can't wait!

Still, there's something that I can't shake, and I'm doing my best to not spoil the excitement that swirls around all of us. I keep my eyes closed for a few moments, retreating into my subconscious mind, hoping I can settle whatever anxiety trying to creep to the surface.

Gamba notices too. *"What are you anticipating, kiddo? I thought this was supposed to be the fun part of the year."*

"I'm not sure, and that's what worries me," I reply. *"Whatever is scratching at my subconscious, it doesn't feel right."*

Zahra gently pulls at my forearm, which brings me out of my meditative state. "Are you okay, babe? You're on edge, I sense it on you."

"I'll explain later, when we have a chance to be alone."

We are intent on outshining everyone during the costume party that weekend, but the girls are more hyper about something else entirely. From the annoyed looks on my boy's face, I have reason to be worried.

"I can't wait for the Bicentennial Ball." Kendyl's bouncing in her seat like she's won the lottery as she stares at Kyle from head to toe. "I get to see you in a tux, looking all… whew, let me calm down."

Did she say *tuxedo*?

Man, is it too late to get off this train before it leaves the station?

The dreamy stare Zahra gives me answers my question before I can get it out of my mouth. By the gods, why? "I haven't had the chance to see you cleaned up yet, baby. The ball is the perfect time."

"Um, prom, anyone?" I protest. "Where does it say in the rule book that I have to wear a tux twice a year?"

"Bro, don't. Resistance is futile," Kyle groans as he shows his outward disgust. "Just accept that you're going to be assimilated into the Borg and get in line to get your tux like the rest of us."

Kendyl punches his arm, giving me a glare that has me put my hands up in surrender. Nope, I'm not about to get caught up in that power struggle. "We don't ask that much of y'all, and you get to see us at our sexiest too? Win-win."

"Listen, bro, I'm feeling it at prom time, but I don't know about this." I'm still in protest mode, and I'm not about to back down, either. "Is this one of those Oakwood Grove things that I should've been warned about way before now?"

"Look, as much stress that Z and I are gonna be under getting things planned out for Anniversary week, the least you two can do is get your lives together and be the eye candy we need you to be," Kendyl huffs, which completely throws me off.

Did I miss the memo or something? "What stress are you talking about? All you're doing is coordinating outfits, right? Okay, I get that, but what exactly are the events for Anniversary Week. Can the uninitiated get an entry level information packet or something?" I'm disturbed by the "thought you knew by now" glances from everyone around me, and I drop my head and bang it against the table top a few times to get my life together. "So, what's this madness with Anniversary Week anyway?"

Kendyl pipes up quick like this whole week has been her idea the whole time. "This is the week when the founding families came and settled Oakwood Grove two hundred years ago. We rock all kinds of events, but the one that means the most is the Anniversary Ball."

"So, what has you and Z tripping right now, though? It sounds like y'all got caught up, and I'm trying to figure out who needs to bleed."

Zahra sighs, gritting her teeth as she glares at Kendyl. "Mayor Lance blindsided me earlier in the week. He wanted Oakwood Grove student participation in planning the Anniversary Week festivities. I got Kenni to tag along with me to see about the details, and as it turned out, it was an ambush. Chrisette was there, all smiles and whatever, and Mayor Lance asked the three of us to coordinate other events."

"Wait, he has to know that you aren't vibing with Chris like that," Kyle jumps in, with a concerned expression splashed all over his face. "That's a recipe for disaster, that's for sure."

"I want the record to reflect that I warned her that Chris was behind this setup," Kendyl announces. "Out of all the kids at school, and he singles you out? Come on, babe, we willingly walked right into that buzzsaw."

"And it was worth it, if I remember correctly," Zahra claps back as she pulls out her phone. "Let's see, we managed to get a large budget to get all the events we wanted to have completed, including the parade, the carnival, and Theater in the Park, something we'd been wanting in the town square for a while now, and we got him to make calls to Atlanta to get first-run advanced copies of a few movies to keep things interesting for the Theater in the Park idea you and I came up with on the fly."

"Okay, okay, okay, you got what you wanted, but so did he. We still have to work with that twit," Kendyl points out. "My pimp hand is already twitching at the first sign of her slick shading anything we do."

"We can handle her, trust. She's outnumbered, and she can't run back to 'Dad' because she can't get what she wants. Eww, it still makes my skin crawl when she called him that," Zahra mentions, gagging at the mention of Mayor Lance. "We have to suck it up for the ball, and we get to do what we want in the park. Gotta give to get."

"Remind me to hire you as my agent when I'm ready to go to the pros." Kyle's in shock, and so am I. I never realized how ruthless she could be. "You'll have these GMs shook."

"Yeah, yeah, enough of all that, I still haven't gotten what I want for the ball, so I'm about to correct that right now." Zahra leans in close, cooing in my ear low enough for the rest of them not to hear. "If you're a good boy, I promise I'll let you see what's underneath the dress I'm wearing after the ball."

I close my eyes tight, shivering when she kisses my earlobe. She ramps up her attack, ignoring my wave of the white flag. "Nod so I know you'll get your tuxedo for the ball, pretty please?"

Kyle lets out an exaggerated grunt when I comply without hesitation. "See? No fair, Z. I had a shot to at least get an honest protest from my ace."

That quip earns another punch from Kendyl. "Keep it up, and I'll change my choice of Halloween costume from Wonder Woman to the Wicked Witch of the West."

"Okay, damn, you don't have to play so rough."

"So, now that that's been settled, I need to know what your color schemes will be, so Ky and I don't clash or copycat." Kendyl pulls out her phone to jot down notes. "And I'm deadass too. I'm not about to get dragged. Nope."

Zahra pipes up for both of us before I have a chance to say anything. "Black, Gold, Purple. We're Kindaran, girl, anything less would be blasphemous."

Kendyl glares at her, irritated over the choices. My girl's right, though. Anything other than those colors, and there would be hell to pay. "I hate you, chica. Fine. Crimson and Silver. You're lucky I love you, sis."

Zahra sticks her tongue out at Kendyl, putting her head on my shoulder. "You'll be alright, promise. Besides, I didn't get to show up and show out last year because my date flaked on me. I'm flossing this year, and it's gonna be in home country colors."

"I hope you're able to find a corsage in those colors, bro," Kyle points out. "Otherwise, you may have to go outside the city to get what you want. The last thing you wanna do is have the parents give you the business because you screwed up tradition."

"Yeah, first impressions are everything, pretty boy," Zahra stresses to me like I don't already know the drill. "Although I've been told that you'll be getting that out of the way this weekend."

"Uh oh, you get to meet Mr. and Mrs. Assante?" Kyle leans back in his chair. "May the gods have mercy on your soul."

"Stop it, Ky, my parents are not that bad." Zahra shakes her head. "The worst part's over, remember? That *other* thing we did with them and Unk and Lennox?"

"Yeah, I remember, but we still have to do the same with you, whenever that happens. Besides, I have something I need to ask him… alone."

"Bro, that's not the move, I promise." Kyle says as his expression turns serious. "Don't listen to her, she's trying to sugar coat things. But if you're gonna go and talk to him alone, be on point from the jump, my boy. Her father makes my father nervous every time they're in each other's space."

Yeah, that makes me feel *much* better.

"Don't let Ky put crazy thoughts in your head, baby. I promise, my dad is hard on everyone…who *isn't* Kindaran."

"That's that BS, for real." Kyle scoffs. "We've been best friends for years, and that's the reason he gave me hell when we were growing up?"

"Sorry, bestie, but you survived it, right? Did you die? You're still alive."

"That's cold, girl. I'm heading to class before I get abused again." Kyle kisses Kendyl before he leaves the table. "I'll get with you and TK to set up the tux fitting time. Holla."

Heading to our next class, Zahra pulls me into a cleared hallway, pinning me against the wall, studying my facial expressions. "Don't let Ky get in your head, okay? I'm serious."

"That's not freaking me out." I'm lying, but I find the convenient excuse to throw her off the trail. "I had another nightmare last night. I'm not sure why they're happening more frequently, but I've been distracted all day."

She caresses my face, massaging my neck to relieve some of the tension. "Have you told Ms. Kynani?"

"She's supposed to be heading over after school."

"Okay, I have volleyball practice. Playoffs are coming, and we need to be ready." She kisses my lips before she trots off toward her class. "Call me after you're done so I can prep you for whatever you're planning to talk with my father this weekend?"

"Yeah, hopefully Ms. Kynani doesn't take too long."

Zahra's phone rings, and we're both surprised to see Kynani's number pop up on the screen. "Yes, Ms. Kynani? Is everything okay?"

"Yes, child, everything is better than okay," she almost sings over the speaker. "Your guide has communed with me. It is time to make the proper introductions."

Zahra doesn't really react, but I sense the shock of the sudden revelation racing through her. She's as surprised as I am. "Um, okay. So, when can we do this?"

"The sooner, the better, Zahra. She has been anxious to speak to you."

She presses the mute button and stares into my eyes, almost like she's searching for me to agree to what's going on inside that pretty head of hers. "This weekend?"

"Yep. We can wrap a few things up so we can move forward," I reply. "I guess the gods have been having a few conversations, huh?"

Zahra unmutes the call, taking a breath before she finally says, "This weekend will work out fine. We'll be ready. I can't wait to meet them."

She hangs up the call and immediately presses her forehead against my chest. I play in her braids for a few moments to try to settle her nerves a little. I know that anxiety well, and I slow my breathing to encourage her to do the same.

"Are you sure you're ready?" I ask. "I mean, it's one thing to watch me go through it with Gamba. It's a whole other thing to go through it yourself."

Zahra nods her head, but she doesn't lift her face to meet my gaze. "I'm as ready as I can be, but if I can have you there with me, I'll be fine."

I kiss her forehead, reassuring her as best as possible. "I'll be there. Nothing can keep me from it. Promise."

Now, if I can settle my nerves when it comes to dealing with Kairo this weekend.

I mean, it's not like I'm freaking out or anything. *Ugh.*

"Thank you for coming by, Ms. Kynani. Unk and I wanted to ensure you were with us before we headed over to my girlfriend's home to visit with her parents this weekend."

My anxiety levels spike the moment those words are uttered. The "formal" visit with her parents? I'm not ready for anything like this yet, we've only been together for a short time. No matter how I try to spin it, I can't avoid working through the worst-case possibilities in my head. I'm coming close to getting physically ill and the dinner isn't for a few days. Never mind the added part of her acclimation process with her guide, and we have a whole lot of things to sort through.

Not gonna lie, Unk kept the conversation between us light, explaining that everyone has gone through the "meeting the parents" phase at one time or another. After a few minutes conversing, even he's convinced that I've built things well beyond the realm of it turning out positive. Gamba did what he could to emanate as much energy from within to help balance me, but nothing's working.

Kynani's become the last-ditch effort to settle things down before we make the trip. I'm probably asking a lot, considering the original reason she's supposed to be here, but I can't worry about that. Getting through the dinner is more important to me.

"Yasir, I want you to sit down with me for a few moments," Kynani escorts me to the couch, motioning for Unk and Lennox to step out of the room. "Now, why are you building this meeting up in your mind as though it were going to make or break your relationship?"

"I mean, put yourself in my shoes. If I was your child, wouldn't you be skeptical of the girl I was dating?" I flip the situation, playing a real-life version of devil's advocate. "He's a Kindaran historian, among other things. I did my homework on him; he's one of the most well-respected professors in the world. I have no idea how I'm supposed to hang in a conversation with him."

"Have you had a conversation with him?"

"Well, no, but—"

"Then, until you have a conversation with him, how will you know if you can keep up with whatever subject matter he may bring up at dinner?" Kynani invited an alternate version that somewhat settles me down. "You have yet to meet the man, and you have him built up like he is going to take one look at you and deem you unworthy. What if he likes you immediately? Have you thought about that?"

I open my mouth to form a response, but then I sit with her last words. “Well, maybe you’re right, Ms. Kynani. All of this is new to me, I just don’t want to mess things up. I really like her a lot, and that’s probably the first time I’ve said that out loud to anyone.”

“Listen to me, Yasir, you are a son of Kindara, you are a newly realized Sageborn, and you have the support of an uncle and grandmother who have raised, who I believe, is a well-adjusted young man,” Kynani asserts. “Not to mention you have a Vodaran priestess who can help you realize your true purpose in this world. He cannot possibly deny the greatness in you.”

I blink a few times, absorbing every word she’s saying, and my energy shifts in the moment. Confidence courses through me like an electrical current, and it removes all the doubt I had before. I don’t know how she’s managed to do it, but I’m grateful on several levels.

“See, I already sense the shift in you, young one. Now, when we meet your girlfriend’s family,” Kynani extends her hand, taking my hands and squeezing them. “I am sure they will be very pleased to meet you.”

I breathe a sigh of relief, feeling my heartbeat slow down. “Yes, I’m ready. I just hope they’re ready for me.”

“Good, now, let us see what we can do about those nightmares.”

Chapter Fifty-Two – Yasir

"Mr. Assante, can I talk to you for a moment?" I peek into his office, hoping he's alone for this talk. "It's kinda important."

Finding out the truth of what happened to my parents during the Bralba invasion is an important piece that's missing from my memory. He is the closest credible source, and until I could get Kynani to unlock that part of my mind, he can fill in the blanks.

He's opened a few books on his massive desk, writing something down and then checking the information in the book, switching up every few seconds. He barely acknowledges me as he continues his work. "Sure, Yasir, what is on your mind?"

I don't feel like beating around the bush. Here goes nothing. "The Bralba Invasion."

He stops writing, looking up at me like speaking that into existence sends a shock through his body. He removes his glasses and motions for me to take a seat. "I guess, sooner or later, you would want to find out more about that time. Are you sure you want to hear about what happened? I do not want to drudge up any bad memories for you."

"Well, I've been told that my memories were suppressed and that it'll take a Vodaran priestess to unlock them, so, I think we might be safe." I'm doing my best to keep my rising fear at bay, but the closer I get to hearing about it, the more I don't want to move forward. "No one will tell me what happened to my parents. I don't know if they were heroes, or victims, or anything."

"I don't know if I'm the right person to—"

"Sir, with respect, you're probably the best person to tell me what happened. You knew my parents, and you know all things related to Kindara," I rub the back of my neck, hoping I can handle whatever he has to say. "It will help me connect with them, if that makes sense."

Kairo gets up from behind his desk, then ambles over to the bookshelf on the left side of the office. He thumbs through the spines of each book on the shelves, sliding from left to right until he finds what he's looking for. "Here it is, the Bralba Invasion, including timelines, major figures involved, everything you need to know."

He can't be serious, right?

I almost throw the book against the wall. I don't care if Gamba awakens, this is an insult to my intelligence. "Mr. Assante, I can do a Google search and find what I need if I had to do a social science project. Had the invasion never happened, you would've been the closest person outside of my father as any man in my life. I need your help. Please."

Kairo sighs, sitting in the chair next to me, resting a comforting hand on my shoulder. "I do not mean to be dismissive, Yasir. That day… it is still hard for many of us to talk about. It was hard for me to compile the information you have in your hands. I can promise you that you cannot find what I have learned in a Google search."

"But I lost almost everyone I loved. My culture, our culture, was hidden from me for reasons that still don't make sense." My voice cracks, and I feel small for letting it happen. "This is another piece to a puzzle that might help me learn more about myself."

Kairo leans back in the chair, exhaling sharply. "Okay, I still feel like this might not be the best idea but ask whatever questions you have in your head."

"Okay, thank you." I pause for a moment to figure out where to begin. "Why was Solara chosen as a target during the invasion?"

"Your village, as we found out after the fact, held one of the Kindaran Nine families. Your family, Yasir." Kairo sighs again as he takes his time to find the words. "Each of the Kindaran Nine had a responsibility to protect the location of the Kutokufa Scrolls, sacred scrolls hidden on the island that hold the secrets to immortality and resurrection. Only the Kindaran Council knew the location of the Nine."

"But why are people invading Kindara? Are the Scrolls public knowledge or something?" I don't mean to sound like school is in session but, seriously speaking, school is in session. "I've never heard of them before the past few weeks."

"That, unfortunately, is the byproduct of the American school system. To answer your question, several different countries have tried over the years, but one in particular—Bralba—has been a centuries-old enemy of Kindara," Kairo replies as he leans forward in his chair to maintain eye contact. "We've done our best to make the rest of the world thinks the Scrolls are nothing more than a myth, but Bralba has been after them based on information they believe is true."

"And that is?"

"That the Scrolls belonged to them." Kairo flatly tells me. "And to answer the next possible question in your head, the Scrolls have always belonged to Kindara, but the Bralbans stole them three centuries ago. We were eventually able to get them back, but it took almost another century to do so. By then, Bralba had falsely claimed that the Scrolls were theirs. That's what started the ongoing conflicts between our nations."

I have other questions, but I don't want to overwhelm myself. A lot of this is making my head hurt. "Okay. So, back to my family being a part of this Kindaran Nine. How did we get chosen?"

"It was because of your bloodline, Yasir, and the gene you carry," Kairo answers. "There are nine bloodlines, the direct descendants of the original nine Sageborn. These metahumans helped colonize this island with our ancestors."

"And you're saying that my family line was targeted because of this gene?" I have to be careful with what I say. I'm in the middle of a legend being told to me, except I'm the legend, and I didn't even know it. "This gene comes from which side of the family line? Was my father's? My mother's?"

"Hmmm, the last one we knew of that we knew carried this gene was more likely your paternal grandfather, or perhaps his father before him," Kairo continues with the information dump, and frankly speaking, I'm here for all of it, no matter how much it scares me. "Your gene could have been triggered during the invasion, but it is difficult to know for sure, since it is active now."

"So, is it possible that the priestess who suppressed my memories tried to keep the gene from being activated because I witnessed my parents' deaths?"

"Yes, it is possible."

"Well, there's no need to worry about that anymore." I chuckle, but I'm not sure if it's from being nervous or the sardonic humor. "Considering what happened to me recently, I have to deal with whatever is happening to me, without a user's manual or something."

"It will be okay, Yasir," Kairo offers a reassuring word. "Considering your priestess is here to help with your transition, it should clear up any further confusion, once your memories are unlocked."

I'm not completely convinced, but I'll have to step out on faith. "Do you mind if I take this book home so I can continue my research? I promise I'll have it back in one piece."

Kairo smiles as he pulls me in for a hug. "Let me know if you need anything, or if you want to have a longer conversation, my door is always open. You are right, I am the closest thing to a male parental figure outside of your uncle, and we need to guide you the best we can."

Kesi cracks the door open, giving up her usual warm smile as she notices us chatting. "Ms. Kynani is ready to begin."

Well, this should be an interesting experience.

All I need to do is sit back and watch it all happen.

Who knows, it might be kinda cool.

Chapter Fifty-Three – Zahra

I relax in a chair in the great room, trying to wrap my mind around what may be discussed over the next few hours. Now that my parents are on the verge of learning everything in real time, I have this overwhelming urge to have them stay in the dark a little while longer.

Having the extra audience doesn't make things any less stressful, but I have a feeling that the shock value of watching Yasir go through his acclimation would make mine a little easier to handle.

We all spend a short time engaging in idle chatter, which does nothing but irritate me. I do my best to not be disrespectful, but I'm gonna explode if Kynani doesn't get the information out in space so everyone can digest and understand what's going on with me. I wish they would hurry up because this is turning into borderline torture.

"It won't be long now, Zahra, this has been a long time coming." A voice rises from the depths of my mind, making itself clear and present. *"I have been waiting a long time to see you again."*

I nearly jump out of my chair, startling Mom, and alarming Daddy into action. Yasir pulls me close, ignoring everyone around us while he caresses my face to calm me. I continue to check my surroundings, holding a hand up to let my father know I'm okay.

"It's safe to say this is going to be quite the experience for you, my darling girl," the voice continues to speak into my ear. *"Don't worry, you'll get used to me after a while, but the first couple of times can be quiet jarring to the senses."*

"Zahra, are you okay, baby girl?" Daddy inquires as she continued to check around my chair and the immediate area. "What is it? What's happening to you?"

"I believe I can explain that, once she calms herself and we can begin the conversation." Kynani moves toward me, placing her palm against my forehead before closing my eyes. "Sleep for now, warrior. We will call for you when it is time."

"That's my cue, little one. I'll see you soon." The voice dissipates into the depths, leaving me a bit disoriented. I shake out of it as best as possible, wondering how Kynani quieted it almost on command. I don't know why I'm tripping, she's a Vodaran priestess, duh!

Once the haze clears, I rejoin the conversation in progress, offering up a smile to my concerned father's gaze. "I'm okay, Daddy, for real. I think there's something Ms. Kynani can help with to get that under control."

"If you say so, baby girl," he replies, switching his attention to Kynani. "Now, can we finally know why the impromptu visit?"

Kynani shifts her focus toward me again, smiling as she notices I've finally settled down. She returns her attention to Mom and Daddy, placing her hands in her lap. "What do you know of trillsages?"

Mom shrugs, while Daddy nods his understanding. "Outside of what information is available in the Kindaran Archives and the Central Library, there is not much common knowledge on the subject. We know more about machari than we do trillsages."

Kynani nods as Yasir and I get comfortable for the coming history lesson. "The reason why there is not much knowledge is due to the fact that, except in very rare instances, Sageborn do not venture far outside of the Temples inside of Mount Zatara."

"What information do you have on the subject, Ms. Kynani?" I inquire, shifting my body forward as the subject offers more interest to me than I originally thought. "If trillsages are rare away from the temples, what does this have to do with anything here in the States?"

"Before I answer that question, Zahra, I must provide a quick back story and history," Kynani expresses to everyone in the room. She leans back in her seat, waving her hands in a circular motion. In the next moment, images began to form out of thin air, begging our attention. "As your father knows, machari can only be brought into awareness of their powers through a traumatic event. They come from specific bloodlines, which is how the Kindaran Nine Families came into being."

"Yes, this is true, Kynani," Daddy confirms.

"What you may not know, Kairo, is that when a machari is realized, in a manner of speaking, a trillsage is realized at that same time," Kynani continued. "A trillsage is, from birth, bound to their machari mate, by Ashanti's will and power. The trillsage becomes the guide, the machari, the guardian."

Mom and Daddy gasp at the same time. Daddy grabs Mom's hand to pull her close. "I did not think that was possible. We would have been told by the priestess who helped bring Zahra into the world, right?"

"Sometimes the priestess who assists with the birth is not made aware of the Sageborn gene inside the baby when they are born," Kynani explains further. "In your daughter's case, it lay dormant for some time because her mate's gene had also been dormant, until—"

"Until Yasir had to be revived during the incident at that boy's party," Mom finishes the sentence. "It is almost like we are having to make up the rules as we go along. There is nothing in the texts that can even explain what is going on. We were told by one of the Vodaran priestesses a few weeks before the invasion that she had been having visions that Zahra's betrothed was nearing his awakening," she explains as she stares at me. "We were to have made the trek from Kua to Solara to meet with Bakari and Nasira in person. However, the details were vague."

"Wait, what?" I can't resist nervously playing with my hair as I consider the implications of what my parents are saying.

Daddy turns to face me for a moment. His gaze feels warm, and I bask in its radiance. "Baby girl, you were supposed to have met Yasir over a decade ago. When everything happened in Solara, we were forced to escape to the States while the Kindaran miliary and Mipaku Tribe—the border tribe—extinguished the Bralban threat. We did not know why we were singled out, but now it is starting to make sense."

"I am still trying to wrap my mind around our daughter being a trillsage," Mom mentions out loud, incredulous over the possibility. "I mean, how would we know if she were or not?"

Kynani turns to me, finishing the glass of water and placing the base of the glass on top of her palm. "Zahra, concentrate on this glass and sing. I believe high-C should do the trick."

Daddy's confusion is written all over his face. "What are you talking about, Kynani? Zahra can sing, but that octave is out of her range."

I tune out the conversation around me, focusing on the glass in Kynani's hand. I close my eyes, using my other senses to focus. I feel the pitch rising from my core, coming up strong and unbridled. I grin as I allow the frequency to build, opening my eyes with purpose.

"So, should I cover my ears?" Yasir asks before he mockingly holds his hands up. "I mean, I do have a whole nonhuman entity that I haven't learned how to control yet that is sensitive to higher frequencies."

In a voice I don't recognize, I give an advanced warning to Yasir. "Yes, cover your ears, this could get a bit loud. I don't want to trigger anything."

I open my mouth, unleashing a note and frequency that, at first, doesn't seem to cause the concern my warning advised. Soon, the volume rises, causing the windows in the loft area to vibrate. I'm still focused on the glass, narrowing my eyes as the octave amplifies. The windows stop shaking as the glass in Kynani's hand becomes the sole focal point of my singing voice. Before long, the glass pulses, and a few seconds later, it shatters into several pieces onto the carpet.

Kynani maintains her grin, turning toward Mom and Daddy. "And that's only one of the ways that you could tell that she is a trillsage."

I admire my handiwork, grinning at Yasir as he sits there in shock. I can break glass!

I blush as I meet everyone's expressions. "So, I've been practicing a bit."

Kynani lounges in the backyard with us after finishing the conversation with my parents, and if we're being honest, there's gonna be several more conversations on the horizon.

I stay busy with Yasir as Kynani instructs us where to place the candles around the space we cleared out on the lawn, my mind going back to what happened with Yasir when he met Gamba. I never got the chance to ask him what he experienced, but the way things were playing out in front of us, we'll be comparing notes soon.

"I heard a voice in my head earlier. Was that my guide trying to communicate with me?" I ask as we close the circle around us. "It was the same voice that I heard come out of my mouth when I started singing."

"Yes, that was her," Kynani answers. "We will be meeting them 'in the flesh' quite soon. I am pleased that she waited to reach out to you until it was time to complete the acclimation ritual."

"So, will I have the same control over mine that Yasir has over his? This is all exciting and scary at the same time." I place the final candle on the grass before meeting Kynani in the middle of the circle. "What does this mean for the future?"

"That will be answered in time, but for now, we need to get you comfortable with your guide." Kynani holds out her hands, nodding for me to take them. Seconds later, the candles catch fire in a circular sequence, their blaze surrounding us and almost shielding us from view. "Are you ready to meet her?"

"Yes, Ms. Kynani, I'm ready." I'm saying the words, but I'm not really sure I believe what I'm saying. It's a little too late now. "As ready as I'll ever be, anyway. One more thing: is it possible for Yasir to come with us? I know he allowed me, but can I allow him to come?"

"If your betrothed is willing to delve inside, if only as a silent and invisible spectator, then he is welcome to travel," Kynani states as she glances in Yasir's direction. "It is by her wish, but this is an intimate ritual, as you are well aware."

"I understand, and I will find a quiet corner and watch." Yasir rubs the back of his head like he's not sure he's supposed to be there. "I'm hoping not to freak out."

"That makes two of us." I take a deep breath and slowly exhale. "Okay, now I'm ready."

"Now, take a walk with me, deeper inside your mind, so that we can meet your guide," Kynani directed. She chants a few more words in our Kindaran dialect, and I grin as I understand what's being asked. "You have the control to create the outward surroundings to which we can meet her. Whatever you create, it will manifest itself in a space inside your mind."

I already have a location in mind to conjure, and it doesn't take long for me to create the space. In a flash, Kynani and I are sitting under the Live Oak on Oakwood's campus, on top of an oversized blanket in the colors of the Kindaran flag. We're sipping strawberry lemonade slushies as we enjoy the late afternoon sun. Kynani looks around at the serene scene and smiles as she spots a figure in the distance walking toward us.

"This is quite the backdrop for your first meeting, dear girl," Kynani opines. "I believe this will be more than suitable, and she is arriving as we speak."

I notice the woman too, stunned at her striking features as she draws closer. In fact, they're as familiar as they are striking, so much so that I swear we're sisters—except, I'm an only child. I continue to study her face, and the moment she smiles, something clicks in my head. I turn to Yasir, wiping a tear as I realize who I'm about to meet.

"I know you, don't I?" I remark as I make space on the blanket for the woman to sit. "You look so familiar to me, but I can't place your face."

"You do know me, little one. I used to babysit you when you were a little girl," the woman says to me. "You've grown up to be such a strong, beautiful young woman. Your parents should be proud of you."

"Imara?" I clasp my hand over my mouth as I recognize the woman in front of me. "You're my older cousin. You were my favorite cousin. I was so heartbroken when my parents told me you died while fighting off the Bralba invasion."

"I know, but the strangest and most wonderful thing happened. Nyati deemed me worthy to be your trillsage because I protected you in life… at least, to some degree." Imara moves closer to me, giving me the tightest hug, wiping the tears streaming down my face. "I didn't want to leave you, and I think it was that desire to find a way back to my favorite little cousin that had the gods smile on me and bring me back to you."

"I can't believe you're here," my voice breaks as I continue to hold Imara close. "I still don't understand, but I don't care right now. To have you here with me… I don't have the words to say how happy I am."

"Not as happy as I am. The gods are smiling on us both, baby girl."

Kynani smiles, watching as Imara and I continue to banter,

making the necessary preparations for the final step in the process. "It is time, ladies. Are you ready?"

"I'm ready, at least, I hope so," I tell her.

"I am ready, Kynani. I have been waiting for this for a long time," Imara answers. "We will have time to catch up on everything once the merge and acclimation has been completed."

Kynani focuses her energy among the three of us as the color of the flames change to a brilliant sapphire before dissipating. She puts us through the same ritual as what Gamba and Yasir went through, which feels strange now that it's my turn.

Satisfied that the process is complete, she opens her eyes and releases her grip. "Zahra, Imara, the acclimation has now taken hold, the merge is complete. Imara, you should be able to move freely within Zahra's consciousness, but there are still limits as her trillsage. You cannot take over unless she is in severe distress, and she still could override if she sees fit. Any suggestions you make can be heeded or not."

Imara nods. "I understand. I know the limits of my power. My cousin has the final say, regardless, unless it causes her harm."

I flash a mischievous smirk. "Ooh, I get to boss her around? You have no idea how much fun this is going to be for me."

Imara shakes her head, giggling along. "I see now that this is going to be an interesting time for the two of us, baby girl. I am your guide and bound by Kindaran law to protect you. I am looking forward to catching up with all the things that make up who you are, including… the young man in your life, as I understand?"

"It is time to return, as Zahra's parents will need to be informed of tonight's revelations," Kynani advises. "It has been my honor to facilitate this transition, and I look forward to guiding you further."

Once we come out of the depths of my subconscious, Kynani extinguishes the candles with a swipe of her hands. She glances at me, nodding at my new body language and the aura that surrounds me. "There is one more thing that I will need to prepare you to deal with, in due time."

"What else is there, Ms. Kynani? You have already done so much at this point."

Kynani gazes into my eyes to express the importance of the words in her mind. She pulls Yasir into the conversation to make sure she doesn't have to repeat herself. "You and Yasir will be tested. There is a storm on the horizon, and you cannot give up. That storm will be relentless, and it will do everything it can to make you submit."

We recognize the severity of her words as Yasir shrugs. The obvious conclusion is evident, and we both know it. "If that's the case… we're gonna need backup."

"I would not have it any other way. You will need every resource at your disposal to get you through. But make no mistake; before this is all over… it may take a machari to save us all."

Chapter Fifty-Four – Yasir

Why in the name of Nyati and her children did I agree to get a tuxedo for this madness that's about to happen this weekend? I must be out of my mind to think—on second thought, let's get this done before I change my mind.

I make it into the town square, heading toward the tuxedo shop. The store is part of a line of essential businesses—Oakwood Grove Pub & Grille, Ogletree's Drug Store, Feelin' Saucy Pizza, among others—that make up the heart of downtown Oakwood Grove. I park in the diagonal spaces just off the street, getting out of Storm to get this out of the way as soon as possible.

I greet all the boys who are on the way out with their suit bags, channeling the energy I feel as I wait outside for a few moments to get inside. I'd gotten about halfway through the line when I hear a voice that pretty much has the potential to undo all the positive vibes I've gathered.

"Just when I thought my day couldn't get any stranger, I had to run into you." Ian's hostile tone throws me off, and I struggle to understand what I did to tick him off this time. He's been gone the whole week. "I figured you were too bougie to hang with the townies."

"Bro, I swear, not today. I was having a great week, let's not spoil it with some nonsense, okay?"

"It looks to me like someone's in a bit of a predicament. The last place I expected to see you showing your face would be at a shop renting a tuxedo," Ian says. "I wonder if you're just a glutton for punishment or something."

I wonder sometimes whether Ian has a GPS tracker on me, so it'll tell him to be in the same place at the same time so he could start some drama. If it's not for the fact that I dropped a non-refundable deposit on the tux I needed to be fitted for so I could look presentable at the anniversary ball, I would've turned on my heels and found another location.

Who am I kidding? It's Thursday night, and the ball is Saturday. I don't have the luxury of switching up so late in the game. I'm gonna have to grin and bear it, no matter what he may throw in my direction.

The team has been back from the bye week minicamp since yesterday, but I can't get around how he knew I would be here at this moment. A quick snap of my fingers triggers my memory; Kyle's appointment is thirty minutes behind mine, which means most of the team may have scheduled theirs around the same time frame. If I can tolerate Ian for the next twenty minutes or so, backup will be here to help me deal.

I agreed to keep my distance as a promise to Mr. Channing, but I should've known better than to think that would have been an easy task to maintain. There are only three decent shops to rent tuxedos, and two of them were marginal, which left K. Tyler Ltd. as the go-to for cutting-edge fashion. If anyone wants to be seen, Mr. Tyler is the man to help them be *seen.*

Oh well, I'll just have to roll with it. "I'm not in the mood for your nonsense today, bro. Let's just get these rental fittings over with and let it be at that, feel me?"

"Man, there's no need to be all amped up, yo. I was simply pointing out that maybe you had more pressing matters that required your attention." Ian spreads his arms out as the tailor continues to work through his measurements. "I mean, I know I wouldn't want to act like nothing's popping off soon."

Gamba stirs awake, recognizing my spiking irritability. *"We have got to move to a bigger town or something. Is there anywhere that this man does not turn up?"*

I smirk at Gamba's comment as I take a step onto the platform to be measured. "I'm gonna break this down for you real quick. Whatever drama that you've created, it ain't gonna stick, all right?"

"I've no idea what you're talking about, playa," Ian responds. "Are you projecting your troubles or something? I mean, you look a bit disturbed right now."

"You know exactly what the hell I'm talking about," I remark. "Keep playing dumb, it suits you, for real. Did that take a few years to perfect, or did that come naturally to you?"

"Damn, you got all this energy, I see. They say a dog barks when they sense a threat, so what you barking for?" Ian chuckles. "What's the matter, do I make you nervous?"

Gamba growls from behind the door to my conscious mind. *"Why did we agree not to drop this idiot where he stands? It's like he knows we can't lay a finger on him or something."*

"Times change, and your time is up, my boy." I focus on the image in the mirror as the tailor makes sure the measurements are true to fit. "You're about to find out what it's like when you're not on that pedestal you love so much."

"I don't know, bro. The way those charges sound, from what I've heard anyway, you might be looking at getting off that pedestal before you got a chance to get it warmed up," Ian stifles more laughter. "You're looking at real time, for real."

"And I won't see a day of it, trust." I tilt my head toward the ceiling to give the tailor a chance to get the neck size correct. "Witnesses tend to be so damn unreliable."

"Yeah, and so are defense attorneys." Ian stares me down. "Don't trust the wrong one, and I'm sure the right one will run you something serious. If you want, I can take that Jeep off your hands if you can't afford the retainer."

I wait for the tailors to head to the back as I glare at Ian. The moment they disappear into the warehouse part of the store, I grab Ian by the throat and slam him against the wall.

Ian can't stop smiling. I know he's baiting me, but I don't care right now. "Woo, I think I hit a nerve."

Gamba tries to rein me in, but every nerve he soothes is white-hot to the touch. *"Ya-Ya, I need you to settle down, okay? This is not going to help matters at all. Step away from the wannabe pro athlete and be smart about things."*

"What the hell is your problem, huh? You've been riding me since I got here, and I don't remember doing anything to warrant the bullshit." I've reached the point where all I want is to shut Ian up. "You got something against folks who ain't from Oakwood? Is that it?"

"I'm not from here, either," Ian corrects me. "Just like you, I'm from another country."

I release my grip on Ian, taking a step back, regarding his facial features. "Wait a minute … how did you know I was from another country? And for that matter, you're from what country, exactly? I know you're not Kindaran, you're not built for that life."

"I'm not from your wannabe utopia, but you'll be okay." Ian frowns as he adjusts his shirt. "Not everyone wants to be a part of your island paradise, even if you keep wearing it like some badge of honor."

"So, where are you from, then?" I repeat. "No need to keep the cheap seats in suspense, playboy. Speak your peace, it can't be that bad."

Ian closes his fists, almost ready to throw a punch. "My family is from Bralba. There, you happy now?"

I freeze, unsure which emotion would rise to the surface first: anger or shock. He's … from … where???? "I stand corrected. It is that bad. All bad."

"I don't follow." Ian turns to face me, stepping down from the platform to take a seat. "What does where I'm from have to do with anything?"

"Damn, bro, you really don't know your country's history when it comes to mine, do you? You can't be that thick. I just found out, and I'm still trying to make sense of it." I'm fighting every urge I have to throttle Ian within an inch of his life. "You and your pops need to have a serious conversation. I have a sneaky suspicion he's got a lot of information that you need to be aware of."

"Are you suggesting that my father is hiding something from me?" Ian gets defensive, his anger rising by the second. "You seem to know a lot more than me about whatever you're spitting, so, get it out. Tell me what you know."

"It is time to leave, now, kiddo," Gamba implores me. He notices the amethyst hued flames rising around us, which isn't a good sign. *"He is trying to rile you up. We are too emotional after the bomb he just dropped on us. Let us go."*

"Ask your father about your country's history. I'm not doing that labor for you. If I do, I'm liable to say something I won't regret." I step back a few feet, keeping a close eye on Ian's movement within the store. "I think I'm gonna put some space between us, it's best for everyone."

"Nah, bro, we're gonna finish this right now." Ian grabs my arm, trying to hold me in place. "You're not about to drop something like that about my father and leave. I was seven when we left, and I still don't know why."

Kyle and a few of his teammates happen to slip into the store and witness the scene unfolding. Kyle makes a beeline for me, which makes Ian loosen his grip enough for me to slip away. Taylor keeps Ian occupied while Kyle grabs me, literally lifting me off the ground to remove me from the store as we hear Ian ranting to Taylor about needing to finish our conversation.

I'm vibrating and pretty much raging as I work hard to move around Kyle. "I can't even get a damn tuxedo without this fool coming in to gum up the works, bro."

Kyle waits for me to calm down a bit before he says anything. "I just got off the phone with my dad before TK and I got here. This is definitely not the meaning of 'stay as far away from Ian and crew as possible.'"

"So, I'm the one who has to play keep away while he gets to trigger me at every possible corner? How the hell is that supposed to work?" I pose the question that I know has no logical answer. "We have things to do this weekend, and as much as I would love to be a hermit for my own sanity, I have a whole girlfriend that I can't let down."

"Believe me, I feel you, and I told Dad that, so we're gonna have to find a workaround so our girls don't kill us all." Kyle chuckles at the thought. "We got you, my boy. Let's get through this weekend and then we can deal with the madness on Monday, cool?"

I'm already over it all, switching gears to the last thing Ian said to me before things went left. "I think I might have figured out why Ian has been so fixated on me for so long, but I don't think he even knows why."

"We can't worry about that now. What's more important is that TK and I and the rest of the boys get our measurements handled so the tuxedos can get back in time for the ball." Kyle taps my fists before heading back into the shop. "For now, let's focus on what's in front of us and take care of them as they come up. I'll hit you up after we're done."

I make it to Storm, shaking off the rising anger over Ian's offer to "take it off my hands" before settling into the driver's seat. I start the engine, closing my eyes for a moment to gather my thoughts. *"Gamba, we're gonna be on high alert all weekend, you know that, right?"*

"Yeah, kiddo, I did my best to keep your anger at bay. There is a lot more to this thing with Ian than we thought, and we might have to keep an eye out for anything and everything." He pauses for a moment, and I sense his meditative energy. *"We will have to dig deeper, figure out if there is a connection we are not seeing, which means a conversation with both Kynani and the Kindaran Council."*

I agree, but unless it has anything to do with spending time with Zahra, I'm comfortable ignoring it. It can wait until after the weekend.

And speaking of spending time with Z, what we have to do later today isn't what I had in mind, but it's important.

We have some things to tell the rest of the clique, and I honestly don't know how they'll respond.

There's only one way to find out, but I'm not sure if I wanna know.

Chapter Fifty-Five – Zahra

I have no intention of sounding any alarms, but after our conversation with Kynani, there's no choice but to lay all the cards on the table with the rest of the clique. I know Yasir's going through a lot of the same emotions as I am, but I've got my best friends here to help us through it. As much as I know he would like to lean on his people—or at least his former people—that's no longer possible, not after everything that happened when we were up there last time.

Now I've put him in the anxiety-filled position of trusting people on the strength of my connection to them. It's not exactly a bad thing, though, at least I don't think so. He's gotten attached to them, and some of the others in our circles at Oakwood Grove, but there's something about that built-in trust that's always been there. Still, this is a huge bomb to drop, and we have no idea how they may react to it.

I told Yasir before everyone arrived that they might be a bit confused over where the chat would take place. Any time something serious needed to be discussed, Kendyl and I would camp out in her bedroom, door locked, with the explicit request from my parents to not disturb them until we got whatever crisis had been calmed down. If that's the case, Kyle and Yasir being in the room will really throw Kendyl off.

Not to mention, we won't be in my bedroom to talk this time.

The minute Kyle and Kendyl walk through the door, all my concerns are realized. All we can do is get them where they need to be and try to keep them from freaking out.

We're camped out in the basement, all sorts of pillows and blanket pallets sprawled all over the floor. We even put the fruits and pastries that Yasir and I brought from the grocery store out on trays to cushion some of the blow of what we have to say.

Once everyone is settled in their spaces, my anxiety levels shoot through the roof.

I'm not ready. Nope. This is a bad idea.

Yasir taps my shoulder and whispers in my ear, "Are you okay? I sense your hesitation. I'm here with you, baby."

"I was about to ask you the same thing," I utter in a low, hushed tone. "I understand if you're not ready to trust them. I can just tell them about what's going on with me."

He shakes his head, letting me know we're in this together. "I'll be okay, I have to trust them sooner or later, right?"

I kiss his lips and nod before I turn my attention toward Kendyl and Kyle, noticing the confuzzled expressions on their faces. "What?"

Kendyl's never one to beat around the subject. "Girl, get your life together and let us know why we're here, and why it's not in the usual spot?"

I exhale slowly, grabbing Yasir's hand to brace myself. "Okay, so a lot has been going on that we haven't had a chance to tell y'all about. It's going to seem unbelievable, but you're my best friends, so there's no way we could hide this from you. And I'm hoping Yasir can trust you with this too."

"You're starting one of your famous rants, chica, just spit it out," Kendyl says. "I promise, we can handle whatever it is that you're dealing with. What's going on with you two, and why are you both looking like it's the end of the world?"

"Yeah, when we got done with our tuxedo fittings, I'd never seen him so focused on making sure Anniversary Week goes great for you," Kyle chimes in. He glances at Kendyl, then back to us again, confusion spread all over his face. "So, what's really good, and why are we just now hearing about it?"

I flinch for a moment, placing my hands over her ears to calm herself. I can't go through with this, there's no way I can tell them what's happening. I'm out of my mind thinking I can pull this off.

Imara senses my distress, and she vibrates against the walls of my mind, radiating a soothing energy to get me under control. *"They will understand, baby girl, I promise. I need you to settle down so you can get it all out."*

I nod to no one in particular, which probably has everyone confused as hell. *Okay, Z, let's do this.* "Kenni, remember that situation at the mall with those Beach Creek boys, when I tried to get Yasir's attention?"

Kendyl nods, looking up at Kyle before she turns her attention back to me. "I remember. We always knew you could sing."

I sigh, offering a small smile. "Yeah, but I didn't know how to answer your questions back then. I know now, and I'm scared that you'll see me differently once I tell you."

Kendyl reaches over and pulls us to where she and Kyle are to join in a tight group hug. "Z, we've been damn near blood for over a decade. You are my sister. We love you too much to worry about what you're having a hard time telling us. And Yasir… I know I gave you the business when we first met, but you mean the world to my girl, which means you're my people, too."

"You know you're my ace, bro, so you know I got your back, whatever it is." Kyle adds his piece. "You're my dawg. We might not be Day Ones, but it's felt like it since we had a chance to really hang."

Why they're making this so damned easy, I'll never know.

"If you tell me that you've developed superpowers, I'm gonna scream," Kendyl interrupts me. "Just get it out, I wanna be right, so spit it out, sis."

"Okay, okay, okay, sheesh. Yes, Yasir and I are metahuman. Happy now?"

Kendyl just smirks like she unlocked the cryptex from the *Da Vinci Code*. "Yes, I'm happy now. You made it sound like it was something we needed to be afraid to know."

I smile big and breathe out a sigh of relief. "I'm so glad you're my aces. You have no idea how much I stressed over telling you about any of this."

"Of course, only you would have best friends who could, and would, understand any of this and not run for the hills," Kendyl expresses as we burst into laughter. "But now the question is, how do we keep this under wraps with the rest of the cliques we run in, and what does this mean for all the Anniversary Week shenanigans? I mean, you're both whole enhanced beings now, doesn't that come with a secret identity or some other nonsense that we're supposed to keep hidden?"

"Yeah, we've really been reading too many comic books." Kyle breaks out into more laughter. "I mean, it's obvious that you both have abilities, when will you find out what Yasir's are?"

"Well, I've sort of seen what he can do already, but we're learning things with someone who can help us develop and master our abilities. But considering that he's supposed to be the bodyguard-slash-sorcerer with a whole beast guardian that he can conjure in the equation, I'm wondering what that might look like," I continue. "I do have a thing for boys who know how to handle themselves and take the lead."

"Yeah, it's the reason Ian got to you freshman year, before it all fell apart," Kendyl points out. Yasir gives me a hard glare, and I simply shrug. "What, you know it's true. I'm just glad you came to your senses before things got out of hand."

It gets *quiet* in seconds. Like, "pin drop on a hardwood floor" quiet.

Yasir shifts his gaze between the three of us, and we're all having a hard time maintaining eye contact. Kendyl and her big mouth strike again.

This can't be life right now.

"Wait, what was that?" Yasir just keeps looking around like someone needs to say something quick. "Is that the reason why Ian's still so fixated on me? Y'all used to go out?"

"Damn, Kenni, did you have to drop the anvil on my head like that?" I say. "I'm still trying to get that idiot out of my atmosphere, and he still manages to show up like a bad rash. His fixation with Yasir is just begging for more drama."

"It's begging for more than that, baby. He's trying to get me locked up," Yasir growls, and I sense his *zamwani* rising, swirling around his aura, turning it into a deep shade of blood orange. "I would've been able to at least sidestep a lot of his weird energy and idiotic behavior if I'd known this sooner."

"Speaking of bad rashes, how are we supposed to deal with him and his girl Chrisette tomorrow night at the Theater in the Park event?" Kyle asks.

"She will be with Ian the rest of the night anyway, and as long as they're boo'd up, that will be less stress on all of us," I reply. "What we need to do is let them pick a spot and then pitch our spot way away from them instead of the other way around. The minute they see us camped out, it gives them control."

"Say less, I'm with that plan." Kyle grabs a donut. "Any other drama that we need to see about? I'm sure that we can't be the only ones going through it."

I nod at Kendyl. "I have one thing on my mind, considering the ball is a couple of days away now. What we need to talk about is how we better outclass the entire town at the ball. The dresses we finally were able to pick up from the seamstress are fire. And what about the tuxedos that the boys ordered, though? Let's talk about that for a minute."

Kyle quickly kisses Kendyl and rises from their spot. "Yep, I'm about to head out, this is not the part of the convo that I signed up for. Until you say it's cool, I'm leaving my boys out of the mix, but I'm not gonna lie, I'm gonna end up looking at my dawg a little differently from now on. I mean, you're a whole sorcerer, bro."

"I'm still the same, my boy, but yeah, I get what you're saying. Believe me, I have a whole other appreciation for Dr. Strange now," Yasir replies, tapping fists before he kisses me and follows him out the door. "We're gonna let you ladies hash out whatever you need to for the ball. All we need to do is show up and look boss."

I stand to give Kyle a hug, laughing at his impromptu exit just when things are getting interesting, and I encourage Kendyl to escort him out while I take Yasir's hand to head up the stairs. "Believe me, things are going to be a lot different from now on. There's no such thing as normal anymore."

CHAPTER FIFTY-SIX – YASIR

Being inside Carrington Park and witnessing the spectacle of the Theater in the Park event, and this whole setup is fire. The girls did their thing with all the decorations and other pieces speckled throughout the park. I wonder what other talents my girlfriend has in her tool bag to be able to put something this large together.

I remember the conversations after Zahra and the rest of the girls handled different tasks to get things completed, and I had to do my best to calm her down almost every time. Chrisette whittled her nerves raw, and it doesn't take a genius to figure out that Zahra needed a break from her, and by indirect extension, Ian.

My creator's eye absorbs every aspect of the location, and I beam with pride over her attention to detail. From the various large movie screens that are showing at least five different movies, to the marked rows and the specific spaces that were created to protect each viewer's line of sight, I couldn't find anything I would alter to improve the atmosphere. How in the world they pulled this together in such a short period of time, I'll never know.

Zahra and I stroll arm-in-arm through the park, waving to familiar faces, stopping to speak to others as they're all jockeying for position in front of whatever screen showed the movie they want to see. The concession stands have a good number of people in line, the volunteers coming from Oakwood Grove High, and, in a surprise move, Baytown High also came through to pitch in for the special occasion. The proceeds from the event, as agreed upon by Mayor Lance, would benefit both schools to improve their respective campuses.

All in all, everything is running with an efficiency that keeps the adults quiet and happy.

"So, what do you think?" Zahra asks as she wraps her arm around mine, leaning over close enough to sneak a kiss on my cheek. "I know you have something that you would change."

"Nope, I'm not changing anything." I scan over the entire landscape, smiling at everything they've created. "It all looks so good. I could stay here all night."

Zahra taps my chin to get my undivided attention. "Are you sure you want to be here all night, handsome?"

I blush at the not-so-subtle hint. We really haven't had a moment to ourselves in a while. "Well, not *all night*, all night. We can at least stick around long enough for one movie. This is your pride and joy of an event, you know."

"Good recovery. Besides, I've had enough of people this whole week." Zahra kisses my cheek again, then we continue our walk-through. "Specific people especially. Ugh."

"I thought that was supposed to be my thing. You know, not wanting to be around a lot of people?" I chuckle at her smirk.

"After dealing with Chrisette over the past couple of days, I really don't want to have to deal with her tonight," Zahra looks more fatigued than usual, and that worries me. Maybe we should head home so we could both recharge. "I almost wanted to choke her out last night because we couldn't agree on the final movie listing. Between that, getting ambushed into working with her in the first place, and enduring her passive-aggressive shots at me the entire time, if she so much as looks in my direction, it's gonna be a problem."

"You said it yourself, all we have to do is stay out of their way, and we can get through the night in one piece." I return her kiss on my cheek with a kiss across her lips. "Now, let's find the rest of the crew and camp out so we can have some fun tonight."

We meander through the crowds, bypassing the screens playing movies we want to watch later, spotting our group in the area where we preplanned to meet up. There are others around them, but I don't mind the extra company tonight. I feel good about the way things are going, so much so that I tell Gamba to keep a minimal watch over things in the background.

"There are too many people around, and we still have unresolved

issues with Ian that have not been handled. I cannot see taking the night off, having you defenseless is not what is warranted," Gamba says.

The last thing I want is to stay in a "doom and gloom" headspace all night, and I need him to lighten up a bit too. *"I understand, but I have to be able to have fun sometimes. We can't be in a constant state of emergency,"*

Gamba moves from the shadows and into my sight. *"You can have fun, but I will keep an eye out for other threats. I have a feeling that things are not entirely safe here. There are too many spaces where people can cause problems. I will be right here if you need me."*

"Okay, old man, I hope you're wrong, but I can't tell you to stand down."

We finally find our spot already laid out for us where we're greeted by Kendyl and Kyle first, dropping into the space between them and our other friend Taylor and his date, Tania.

"Has anyone been able to track where Ian and his crew has settled?" I ask the group. "We want to stick to the plan to keep things peaceful tonight."

"I saw them a while ago outside one of the other movies," Taylor says as he settles back in place with Tania. "They're chilling out over there, so, we have a couple of hours at least to enjoy the rest of this movie before we move to another screen."

"That sounds like a plan." I welcome Zahra to sit in my lap as the movie continues. "What else have we missed?"

"Thankfully, nothing," Kendyl tells us. "It's been pretty smooth for the most part. Even the adults have been relaxed. Kyle's dad and Mayor Lance, though… they've been eyeballing each other all night, but I think that has a lot to do with the constant power struggle."

"Yeah, they don't like each other, that's never been a secret in this town," Kyle adds as he sneaks a glance in his father's direction. "It's like my dad has something on him that he can use at any given moment. I'd love to know what that is so I can hang it over Ian's head. He's gotten bolder since we got back from minicamp."

That part has my attention. "What's going on, bro? I don't want it to sound like it's all about me all the time when it comes to that dude, but I don't have a choice but to wonder."

"My uncle is one of the sheriffs working the case of those boys who got assaulted at the game against Beach Creek," Taylor says. "They're comparing notes with some claw marks the Oakwood sheriffs found when Yasir covered Ian with those Baytown boys. They still think it's an animal attack of some sort, but they can't figure out what type of animal fits the claw marks. They do know that the claw marks match up."

I tense up, causing Zahra to turn to face me. I give a subtle shake of my head, putting my index finger to my lips before she can ask a question. "So, they still don't really know what's going on at this point, got it. What does this have to do with Ian?"

"He's still focused on you, thinking that you're the one responsible for the attacks," Taylor says. "The reports from the victims said they saw a flash of light before whatever attacked them showed up. They still don't know what happened to them. All they know is that when they finally woke up, you were nowhere to be found, and they were in the hospital."

"Which reminds me, no one's still not saying much of anything about that night to anyone," Kyle recalls. "Do you know what happened, or what they were talking about? I mean, they tried to hurt you bad, and they're wrong as fuck for that, but something saved your ass."

Gamba stirs, knocking against the door to my conscious mind. *"The less they know, the better, Ya-Ya. This is not the time or place to have that conversation. We can sit them down after we have a conversation with Zahra to get our story straight."*

"She deserved to know long before now, Gamba," I scoff at him, but I realize he's only trying to protect me. I feel the aggression rising to the surface, but it's not needed. Not tonight. *"We need to tell her later tonight. Keeping her and Imara in the dark is a bad move."*

I turn my attention back to Kyle so I can focus on the situation in front of me. "The last thing I remember was blacking out. One of them had a lead pipe in his hand, so I must have gotten hit over the head or something," I explain away as much of my appearance as possible, even if it does sound thin as hell. "When I woke up, I saw them on the ground and bugged out of there, but not before I called 911. You know how this town is, bro. I would've gotten blamed for whatever happened because I was the one standing, and they were the ones hurt instead of me. All this crap didn't start happening until I got into town. I've been in enough trouble to know how this can get framed."

"Yo, no need to get defensive, Yasir, for real. We're on your side." Kyle holds up his hands to keep me from ramping up. "My dad is repping you against anything they might try to pull, so that's gotta count for something, right?"

I move my gaze from Kyle to Taylor, trying to understand their expressions, unsure what to believe. Even the comforting glances from Kendyl and Tania aren't enough to assure me that I'm not being ganged up on.

Kendyl adds to the supportive voices to keep me calm. "Yasir, look, we know you were the victim, there's no doubt about that. You're right, this town is screwed up with the way it treats certain people. We got you, but more importantly, my best friend has you. That's all that matters right now."

"Thank you for that, seriously." I breathe a bit slower as I check my watch and then up toward the screen before I tap Zahra's shoulder. "I'm gonna get some drinks. Do you want anything else while I'm up?"

Zahra grabs my hand to stop me before I can get to my feet. "Do you think it's a good idea for you to move like nothing has happened? What about what Mr. Channing told you? You're taking a chance of dealing with Ian and something going wrong."

"Don't worry, Zahra, he's still got Squad, and Squad takes care of its own."

Hearing Dante's voice freezes me in seconds. They couldn't have possibly dropped into town without a head's up. "Whiskey. Tango. Foxtrot!" I shout more out of reflex than anything, but I had more profane words that threaten to flow out of my mouth.

I rise to my feet so fast it almost makes me dizzy. Kyle and Taylor are on their feet too, not recognizing the group of people who just pop into our area without much of an invitation.

But my Day One never needs an invitation, not when it comes to his "little brother."

I stare him down, noticing Malik and Caleb in the background, standing behind Alyssa and Dominique. I notice the formation they're in, and I don't know whether to add fuel to the tension or to defuse the situation. I choose the latter, wondering why he's down here in the first place. "Long time, no hear from, big bro. I thought you were waiting for me to call you when I wanted to talk."

"That was before Nana told us you were almost murked before we had a chance to make things right." Dante moves in close enough to tap fists and give me a hug. "I wouldn't have been good with you being gone and saying what I needed to say to a gravestone."

Kyle steps in, glaring at Dante, waving a finger at Malik and Caleb when they tried to move in to protect him. "Yo, Yasir, are these your folk from the A who turned their backs on you?"

Dante frowns, switching his gaze between me and Kyle. "I have a feeling you've been hilariously misinformed. We never turned our backs on him, but there were some things that needed to be cleared up."

"I'm never misinformed when it comes to my boys," Kyle barks as he moves closer to Dante. I don't want to get between them, and content to let things play out, but if I need to get a little rough and tumble, neither one of them would be left standing. "And how do you think you know me, playa?"

"Because my Day One told me about all of you," Dante announces. "He told me that you've been his aces down here. On the real, you've had his back, and I appreciate you looking out."

"It's obvious we've been looking out better than *you* have." Kyle focuses on Malik and Caleb the whole time. "Enough with the pleasantries, why are you here?"

"I wanted to come and apologize," Alyssa steps in front of Dante, causing Zahra to stand up to slow her approach into my personal space. "I was so pissed at you, and when I saw Zahra, I saw red. That's not fair to you when you tried to do everything in your power to preserve our friendship. And after we heard what happened with the yacht—I just couldn't have that on my conscience."

Is she serious right now? Things have been icy for weeks, and *now* she wants to clear things up. A piece of me considers hauling off and cracking all three boys' jaws for playing me like I allowed Alyssa to be compromised. The other pieces of me are relieved that they even took the effort to come down here and find me.

"I appreciate that, real talk. I'm still salty that it took y'all this long to get at me." I battle with my conflicted emotions, wanting to choose violence so badly, my whole body shakes. Doing it in public, though? Yeah, not a good look. "You're still like family to me, and I'd never turn my back on family. But since you're here, you might as well have a seat and get to know my new family down here."

"You're right, Ya-Ya. And yeah, we're cool with doing that, if your people don't mind?"

"Yeah, have a seat. If Yasir says you're cool, then you're good with us." Kyle and Taylor make some space for them to sit down. "This is my girl, Kendyl, and TK's girl, Tania."

"Okay, so now that that's settled, I'm going to go grab those drinks."

"Ya-Ya, I'd feel better if one of us was with you." Zahra presses the issue. "We don't know what to expect right now."

"I'll be okay, I promise," I repeat, pointing at the concession stand. "See, direct line to the spot and back. You can keep an eye on me the entire time, but Ian's not stupid enough to start something with all these witnesses around."

I kiss Zahra and hop up before she can offer up another protest. In the next minute, I'm already in line to grab the bottled drinks.

"You know, she is right. We are taking a risk without backup." Gamba peeks through my eyes, scanning through to ensure no continuous threats surrounded us.

"We're good, godfather, I made sure to keep things on a swivel the entire way here. There are two other people in front of us, and we'll be back before we know it." I wonder why he insists on creating trouble where none exists. *"What's with all the heightened alarms? Besides, my Squad is here too, there's nothing to worry about."*

"Because you were right. Things got out of hand during that incident in the parking lot. We have to be more careful and keep a cooler head."

"Well, we can keep the cooler head, starting Monday. We still have other events to attend, and things will be okay." I approach the window to place the drink order and pay. I turn for a minute to check on Zahra and the rest of the crew before I circle back to get the

bottles, realizing they're back to watching the movie. *"Which reminds me, I'll probably need you to make yourself scarce later tonight. I'll need privacy until morning, once we're safe at home."*

I turn to walk back to the movie when I bump into someone and drop the bottles to the ground. I frown as the person I collided with remains in my personal space. Anger radiates through me. "Yo, you didn't see me… damn, I'm not in the mood for you or any of your clique, my boy."

When I look up, I take in his school colors and realize I'm in trouble. Jordin stands mere inches from my face with his hands balled tight. "Well, whether you're in the mood or not, you're about to deal. You can bet that, playa."

Before I can find a way around Jordin and clear out, the other boys from that first encounter, Mark and Reggie, show up quick and block my escape routes. I size up yet another potential situation that I'm probably not gonna get out of, and the only option I have available would expose me.

Gamba springs to life, trying to get through to me. *"Do not let them bait you, kiddo. We have to find a way out of this mess ASAP before something bad happens."*

"I'm open to ideas, and I don't wanna hear, 'I told you so,' either." I don't even bother to pick up the bottles I dropped. I can't afford to have either of them to get the drop on me. If anything, I'm doing my level best to get anyone's attention. *"If we don't come up with something, I'm gonna have to make a scene."*

"Well, well, well, I didn't think you'd have been stupid enough to roll out in public knowing what you have over your head, Yasir," Jordin utters. "I guess you aren't as smart as I thought you were."

"What in the hell do you want now?" I keep my tone as even as possible, but I can't avoid the adrenaline spiking. It won't be long before Gamba makes his presence known to everyone around us. "Am I making you nervous now? You got all this backup like you're worried I might get the best of you… again."

"Do not antagonize them, Yasir. They may trigger your zamwani, and that will not end well. We need to get your friends' attention."

Gamba's right, and I know it. While no one is looking, I press the preset button on my phone to call Zahra and pray she hears what's going on so she can get my boys over here ASAP. As soon as I hear her say hello through my ear buds, I'm back to being inside the eye of a storm that I didn't create. I know she'll sense my agitation. I just hope it's not too late.

"Man, you're really feeling yourself these days, I see." Jordin's smirk widens to a sinister smile. "That's okay, I actually want you to act up a bit tonight. All these people around, they'll get to see what you really are."

"Do us all a favor, bro, and leave while you still can." I cut my eyes toward Zahra, and I see a chance to stall these boys out just long enough to make things very interesting. "Oh, I get it, you want me to throw the first punch so you can say it was self-defense, right? Not gonna happen. I got better things to do than to get arrested over something else I didn't do."

Ian shows up with Eric and some of their teammates. Great. It's a party now. "Yo, Yasir, what seems to be the trouble?"

I let out a growl that slows everyone down for a moment. My attention remains fixed on Ian. "Step away, now. This one doesn't concern you."

"Nah, bro, these Baytown boys need to understand they're in Oakwood Grove territory this time around," Ian balks at my request. He's making things worse, and he doesn't even know it. Or worse… he knows exactly what he's doing. "If these boys need to be reminded, we have no problems knocking it up across their heads."

"What, my guy? You're running your mouth when he had to bail your ass out. What are you gonna do?" Jordin taunts us as he moves into my personal space, close enough to point a finger in my face. "What can you do? You lay a finger on me and you're going to jail for assault."

I close my eyes, feeling the heat resonating through me, and I allow every ounce of fury to rise to the surface. I no longer care what happens, all I want is for everything to burn. When I open them, everything I see has a dark crimson hue. "I'll give you one last warning. Walk. Away. Go and enjoy the night. What happens next will be on your heads."

"Put this man out of his misery, boys," Jordin commands the other boys around him. "He wants the smoke."

"If you know Diablo like we know Diablo, you'd be thanking God for your life, playa. If he really wanted to choose violence, you wouldn't be standing right now," Dante chimes in as he, Kyle, Taylor, Caleb, and Malik all surround the Baytown crew. "Since you swear you know him as well as the information your plug provided, then you should know that you need to raise up before something bad happens to you."

When I say I'm grinning like I just won the light heavyweight boxing title right now?

My eyes turn crimson as I take a step in their direction, smirking when the group takes a collective step away from me. "I'd listen to my brother if I were you. He doesn't like repeating himself."

Jordin looks around him, realizing that the odds are no longer in his favor, along with the commotion that the scene has attracted, and he sneers at me with every bit of malice in his heart. "Sooner or later, you're gonna get caught slipping, and I'm gonna be there when it happens."

They slink away before any of the security officers or the OGPD can come through and break things up. Not that there would be anything left for them to break up. Just saying.

I don't bother with a response. They're not worth it.

"You good, bro?" Dante taps fists with me as I nod toward the rest of the boys. "Do we need to do a sweep and make sure the place is sanitized?"

"Nah, I think they'll stay away from us for the rest of the night." My body is vibrating and in fight mode, even though there is no threat. I quickly turn inward, assuring Gamba that I'm okay and that we'll talk about things once we get home. "They honestly thought they had me cornered, that's the only reason they came at me."

"Yeah, nah, something's off with them, and I'm not entirely sure Ian was there to have your back, either," Kyle says to me. "I'm really starting to wonder if we need to keep a sharper eye on things the rest of the weekend."

Before I can respond to Kyle's concerns, Zahra jumps into my arms, with the rest of the girls following her into the middle of the group. In the next minute, she punches my arm. "That's for not listening to me and almost getting yourself caught up and scaring me half to death."

I rub the spot, even though she didn't hit me hard. "I promise, it wasn't on me this time. I didn't even know they were going to be here."

"I'm not worrying about that right now. We're still here to have fun for the rest of the night," Kendyl announces. She takes Kyle's hand and pulls him back in the direction of our area. "Get whatever you gotta get so we can make sure that happens, and the next time your girl says you need backup, listen to her, okay?"

Ugh, I'm not gonna live this one down at all. I turn my attention to Zahra, and I can't resist kissing her forehead and hugging her tight. "I'll do my best to keep something like this from happening any time soon. Forgive me?"

She kisses my lips a few times, caressing the spot she just hit with every bit of care she can muster. "You're forgiven, now, can we get back to our spot so we can finish the movie so I can keep you out of trouble? Please and thank you."

Chapter Fifty-Seven – Yasir

I let Zahra drive Storm to her house tonight, giving me a chance to relax for a change. After the earlier incident, I need to decompress. Besides, she's been wanting to drive her, considering she's been allowing me to drive Raven lately.

I drift in and out of sleep while she's behind the wheel. Yeah, it's easy to trust her to handle my pride and joy enough to rest the entire ride. I'm still trying to process what all of this actually means for us, but I'm putting all that to the side—we're still in the middle of Anniversary Week.

I want to enjoy—and make sure she enjoys—everything that this week has to give.

Her phone buzzes in the holster, and I peek over for a brief moment as she tries to keep from waking me. She's whispering into her air pods, but she might as well be speaking in her normal tone. My senses are so dialed up that I can hear her from a mile away. "You good sis?"

I can hear Kendyl trying to speak in a hushed tone as she responds to her bestie through her pods. I'm legit starting to enjoy these abilities and then some. "I'm checking on you, chica. Wait, why are we whispering like we're about to commit a crime? Is there something you don't want your boyfriend to hear?"

She softly giggles. "Nah, tonight took a lot out of him, so I'm letting him sleep until I get home."

"Well, aren't you being the wonderful, doting girlfriend? That's sooo cute." Kendyl makes gagging noises over the phone, causing Zahra to laugh a little louder. "Did you two get a chance to talk about this ongoing beef with Baytown and what Ian has to do with it?"

"Nope, and I'm not going to, either," she states flatly. "We're all gonna have fun this weekend, I don't care if the rest of the world is burning to ashes."

"Oh, I'm with the shenanigans, trust, baby," Kendyl's voice kicks up a notch as her excitement builds to a fevered pitch. "I'm not trying to lower the temperature at all, know that."

"Good, then we can ignore all the adulting that we'll have to do once Anniversary Week is over. Sound like a plan?"

"Yep! So, now that that's settled, did you two at least get some practice time in for the trap waltz that we're all supposed to be lighting up the ball with tomorrow?" Kendyl sounds ready to kill us both if Zahra says we didn't. "You know we gotta show up and show out, since it's the Bicentennial and everything. We get to really leave a mark and have the whole town talking for weeks."

Even though I've been working at Unk's almost all week, she still managed to sweet-talk me into practicing after work. It gave us a chance to bond and find out more about each other—at least as much as we can until my brain gets unlocked. I gave up everything I knew about my life in the A, and she taught me as much as she knew about Kindara as we perfected the steps of the waltz.

I had to let her lead for the bulk of the week, but before long, I was leading her, which put a smile on that pretty face. We even had a chance to create our own steps, just in case the spotlight found us during the routine.

"Oh, I think we might surprise a few people tomorrow night," Zahra boasts as she accelerates through another intersection.

"Good, because I'll be damned if Chrisette and her clique try to make us look bad. She's already split the cheerleading squad because some of the girls wanna step with me," Kendyl huffs through the earpiece. "She swears that this week is only for her and the rest of the Founding Families. I wanna make sure she has no choice but to bow down to the queen."

"I love it when you get like this. You get hyped when the lights are brightest."

I sit up in the seat, and she places her index finger to her lips to keep me quiet while she tries to finish her chat.

"Tell her majesty we won't let her down," I say with a smirk. "The last thing we want is to make her look bad."

Kendyl gasps as Zahra puts her on speaker, causing my girl to crack up laughing. "How in the world? What else did he hear?"

"I didn't hear anything you wouldn't say to me face-to-face," I say, freaking her out even more than she is already. "Oh, and I'll deal with Ian once I'm out from under this mess from the Beach Creek game. I can't set another fire until I've put out the current one."

Zahra's having a hard time keeping Storm on the road, she's laughing so hard.

"I thought you said he was sleeping, sis?" Kendyl shrieks. "Did you have me on speaker the whole time, trick? Ugh!"

Okay, now I'm struggling to breathe now, but I had to show off a bit. Thanks to Gamba, I have a whole other level to all my senses.

Zahra calms down long enough to answer Kendyl. "I promise, Yasir was asleep. I can't explain how he's been able to be engaged in our convo the whole time, but this is too funny."

"No, the hell it ain't, girl. That's scary on so many levels. Can he read minds or something?" Kendyl's having a whole meltdown and Zahra's trying to calm her down and not laugh at the same time. "Put him on speaker, I wanna know how he knew what we were talking about."

"I'm pretty much peopled out for today, Kenni," I say loud enough for her to hear. "You know, that whole introvert battery and everything? Today was a lot, and I still have to get myself together for tomorrow night, you feel me?"

Zahra jumps in quick to keep things from getting too far out of hand. "Okay, bestie, I'll see you in the morning when we have to go grab our dresses. Love you, mean it, bye now."

"Love you too, baby. See you in the morning, and get your life, Ya-Ya."

Zahra disconnects the call as we pull into her driveway, and she puts the car in park before she shifts her body in my direction. "So, did you have fun freaking out my bestie, baby?"

I burst into laughter all over again, holding my stomach the entire time. "Yeah, a lot of fun. It took my mind off the emotional roller coaster I was on all night."

She caresses my cheek, pulling me in for a quick kiss. "Yeah, tonight wasn't supposed to go like that, but I'm glad that it ended well. Your Squad has your back again, that's a good thing, right?"

"Yeah, I'm happy about that, but Kenni's right. Sooner or later, I'm gonna have to deal with the smoke from the Baytown crew. I've made them look silly on two separate occasions." I stretch to really wake myself up, then slide out of the passenger seat and literally trudge around to meet her on the other side of the car. "If they're smart, they'll come for me when there's not so many people around. I've gotta make sure I don't make it easy for them."

"Shhh, no need to think about that right now, okay?" She wraps her arms around my neck, encouraging me to pull her up so she can stare into my eyes. "Your only job for the rest of this weekend is to keep a smile on your chosen's face. Can you do that for me?"

I slip soft kisses across her lips, then set her down on the ground and kiss her forehead. I move a stray hair from her face, watching her blush. I flash my eyes, giving up a knowing grin and then exhaling slow. By Nyati, I love this girl. "Anything for you, my chosen. Anything for you."

My phone rings out of nowhere, taking us out of our moment. I lean in to see who it is, and the same "unknown number" pops up on my screen. I allow it to ring a few times, hoping that whoever it is gets the hint that I'm not gonna answer the call.

"What's that about, Yasir?" Zahra asks after I close the door and get my head together. "Is something wrong? Who was that?"

I blink a few times to buy myself some time to reassure her that there's nothing for her to worry about. "It's probably Dante calling, making sure I'm safe at home. I'll call him back after you're in the house."

"Are you sure? You look a little unnerved."

"I promise, I'm good. I'll call you once I'm home."

Zahra narrows her eyes like she doesn't believe a word I'm saying, but I don't want her to press the issue. At least, not yet. "Okay, I'll talk to you when you get home."

The phone rings again before Zahra gets in the house, and I realize I better answer it before it becomes a situation. I hop inside, accidentally hitting the speakerphone button as I answer the call, silently encouraging her inside the house. "What do you want?"

"I bet you felt real safe having your little crew around to get you out of that situation," The same distorted voice booms loud and clear across the speaker, causing a chill to creep up my spine. "It won't matter, though. No one will be able to keep me from ending you."

"Who the hell is this, and how did you get my number?" I let out a frustrated growl, desperate to regain some control. "And why are you using an auto tune to hide your voice? Are you that scared of me?"

I don't understand why any of this is happening. What did I do to this person? I don't remember doing anything to anyone—I mean, not anyone who didn't deserve it.

I better figure it out fast before I fuck around and find out the hard way.

One thing's for certain, and two things are for sure… they'll be in for the fight of their lives if they think about trying to run up on me like I'm some rookie on the block who can't handle himself.

"Don't worry, Yasir, you'll find out everything in due time. I fear no one, not after what I've been through," the voice lets out a chuckle that boils my blood. They're intentionally mocking me, and I don't like it. "I'll see you soon."

Yeah, not unless I find a way to see them sooner.

Chapter Fifty-Eight – Yasir

I wake up the next morning with the biggest smile on my face.

I can't remember the last time I've felt this good, and I don't want to lose this feeling at all. Even with everything that happened last night, the way it ended and all the good vibes that came through as the sun breaks through the clouds, it feels like it's gonna be a great day today.

I'm intent on putting that phone call out of my mind too. I can't worry about things that I can't control. Whenever the person who's threatening to kill me shows up, that's when I'll handle it. That's it, that's all.

Being in the middle of both of my cliques and having them getting along the rest of the night before Squad jetted back to the A had me beaming with pride. It couldn't have gone any better, and it's been a minute since I've had a chance to really feel comfortable. I don't want to let that feeling go.

Dante, true to his word, personally escorted Nana back and called me to let me know she's safely tucked away and under constant watch. Having that off my mind helps more than I can even say.

I pop out of bed, connecting my phone to the speakers as I skip into the bathroom to shower. I have to head to the shop to pick up my tuxedo, and then slide over to the flower shop in Savannah to get the corsage for Zahra that I had to special rush order in to have it ready in time for the ball tonight.

Even Gamba is in a whole good mood, which adds to my excitement.

"Today's gonna be a good day," I tell my godfather as we vibe to Burna Boy. *"I can't wait to cut loose a little bit and just be a kid for a while."*

"It is gonna be lit, as you kids love to say." Okay, I'm enjoying the way Gamba's trying to get on my level with the slang and popular phrases. *"You are right, today should be fun and magical. I am looking forward to seeing you smile and enjoy life."*

I step into the shower, enjoying the heat of the water on my skin. I go through the to-do list in my head again to make sure that everything is covered. I'm not gonna lie, I'm legit nervous and I can feel the rumblings of my anxiety threatening to push to the surface. This night has to go perfectly.

Steam fills the bathroom, adding to the mystical vibe I'm feeling right now. If I concentrate hard enough, I can peer through the fog and allow my mind to take me anywhere I want to go. I imagine being in either Ghana or Senegal, enjoying the landscape and the beauty of those countries, or even traveling north, across the Mediterranean Sea and check out Italy. I haven't had a chance to see the Leaning Tower of Pisa yet, and I can only imagine what it looks like in person.

And to have Zahra with me every step of the way? Pure bliss.

"I wish I could be there to help you with your first big function, my son."

I jump and quickly take a look in the mirror, suppressing an audible gasp that makes me wonder if I'm hallucinating. I spin around and exit the shower, wrapping a towel around me like I expect to see someone leaning against the counter. It's like when I first came to Oakwood Grove, and somehow Mom and Dad sat inside Storm with me, telling me that everything would be fine.

"Dad? Is that you?"

"Yes, my son, I am here."

I rub my eyes, blinking them several times over, almost wishing that I can see him as clear as the hand in front of my face. I turn off the shower, still in disbelief. *"How is this possible? Am I able to actually see you for a little longer this time?"*

"I believe I have a theory." And sure enough, my father is leaning against the counter, a smile spreading across his lips. *"I think that because the days are getting closer to Fete Gede ... the Festival of the Dead, celebrated in parts of the Caribbean, and in Kindara too. As the holiday gets closer, the veil between the afterlife and the living world thins, and we are able to pass through, if only for brief*

moments, to visit those who are able to see."

"I don't care how it's possible, I'm just happy to see you." I sit in the chair believing what I see and grinning the whole time. He's actually here. *"There's so much I want to talk to you about, including everything with Zahra. Have you and Mom been able to see what's going on from where you are?"*

"Yes, we have, and we are so proud of what you are becoming." He pushes off from the counter, moving closer to where I'm sitting. *"I am sorry that we can't be more help with the trials that you will go through. I imagine you have a lot of questions, and perhaps we can have a longer conversation soon."*

I slowly nod. We're on borrowed time, so I don't waste a second of it. *"Do you know about Gamba? Is he able to communicate with you at all? You're right, I have a lot of questions."*

"Save them for the next time your mother and I are able to see you together." He studies my face, another smile beaming through. *"Tell me about Zahra. She seems like a wonderful girl. The gods are smiling on the two of you, pleased at their work."*

"Dad, she's unlike any girl I've ever met." I blink a few times. I still can't believe it sometimes. *"She's as smart and as pretty as Mom, and she ... by Nyati, she's all I can think about sometimes. I know it sounds ridiculous, but—"*

"She fits you." Dad finishes my thought before I can say it out loud. *"Ashanti and Nahara knew what they were doing when they paired you. You are meant to do great things together."*

I switch the subject before time runs out on us. *"Dad... I can't remember things about our life in Kindara. I mean, I see flashes of things when I was little, but it feels like there's so much more that's locked away."*

"I understand, my son. All will be revealed soon. Trust your Nana and the Vodaran priestess to help bring all of that back." Dad glances at his arms, and I notice that he's starting to fade away. *"I have to go, but I promise we will try to see you soon. I love you, my son."*

"I love you too, Dad. Kiss Mom for me." I shed a tear as his form dissipates inside the fog, then a grin spreads across my face. I know I'll see them again. I just have to prepare for the next time.

❂❂❂

I step out of Storm, enjoying the mild afternoon, marveling over the way the clouds move across the sky for a few moments. Yeah, today is a good day, and it's gonna stay that way. The sun peeks through long enough for me to stand and bask in the warmth before it ducks back behind the clouds. It isn't until then that I realize I can't remember the last time I sat down to ground myself with the earth.

Mental note: get that done ASAP.

I open the door to the tuxedo shop, observing all the activity going on around me. If I didn't know any better, I swear it's prom season instead of Anniversary Week festivities. All the boys are in full-blown showcase mode, dropping videos on TikTok left and right, running the poor employees through it with their last-minute changes to their accessories.

Nah, I'm good on all that. I'm sticking to my plan: get in, get my tux, and get out. Simple.

Kyle's already working his way in my direction, grinning ear to ear as he shows off the crimson and black tuxedo. "Yep, I'm gonna be ridiculous tonight, on God."

I burst into laughter, stopping long enough to give the consultant my name so he can grab my rental. "Oh, but you were giving me the business when Z was whispering in my ear about going all out for this ball. Now look at you."

Kyle stares me down, causing another hilarious outburst. I'm legit holding the wall to keep from falling on the floor. "Yo, we ain't gotta bring all that up, my boy."

"It's all good, for real, but as long as we can get up outta here so we can get ready for everything later, that'd be great," I shake my head, still holding my stomach from another fit of snickering. "I still got some other things I have to pick up so I don't rush."

"Yeah, and I see you got Storm looking shiny, shiny." Kyle whistles as we glance out in the parking lot. He's one to talk, though. His F-150 looks like it went through an extra coat of candy-coated royal blue paint. "You gonna light up the neon too? Just show out, then."

The consultant finally returns with my tux, and the minute I pull it out of the covering, all eyes are on me. The next thing I know, there's this collective buzz swirling through the shop. A few of the boys are elbowing each other as they gawk at the black, purple, and gold pattern in the vest that peeks out from under the black suit coat.

"Wait, you mean we could've rocked something like that?" one of them remarks to the consultant standing next to him. "You got anything like that in the back? I wanna cop it if you got it."

Nope. I'm not stepping in the middle of any of that. "Time to raise up outta here, bro. I'm not about to get caught up in whatever is about to happen."

Kyle chucks up the deuces and follows me out of the store, weaving through the foot traffic still entering through the door. I breathe a sigh of relief, thankful that it didn't get any wilder than it could've been. I tap fists with my dawg then carefully lay the garment bag on the back seat and reach for the remote so I can start the engine as he jumps in the truck and pulls away.

That is, until I get rudely interrupted by the usual suspects. "Looks like you got out without too much of an issue, Yasir. How wild is it in there?"

So, let's set the scene so we can figure this out, shall we?

Ian and Eric stand in front of Storm when they should be trying to work their way into the store so they can get their tuxedos. They have these non-threatening expressions on their faces like they don't have an ounce of pressure to release toward me. And I'm not supposed to interact with them in any way because Mr. Channing said it would complicate things.

What am I supposed to do in this situation? What would you do?

I can tell you what I'm gonna do… I'm opening the door, getting in Storm, and getting out of here before something goes left.

But Ian holds the driver door open, preventing me from closing it. Dammit.

I pull a little harder to get him to release his grip, but he's insistent on keeping me here for whatever reason. Yeah, this isn't gonna end well, and I better find a way out before something else happens and I get blamed for it. "Dude, what's up with my door? Are you trying to cause issues?"

Ian sort of shrugs, then he lets go of the door. "I stopped to say I don't want any problems. Tonight is too important to my father for anything to go wrong, alright?"

I raise an eyebrow, still skeptical over what angle he's trying to come at me from. "Okay, so, if that's the case, why are you in my space? This is the exact opposite of not wanting any problems."

"Yeah, but I'm serious this time. I wanna call a truce, just for tonight," Ian says. "I need this to go smoothly. My dad's reelection campaign is riding on the success of Anniversary week."

I want to believe him, but he's been coming for me at every opportunity, and now he wants to act like, what? Are we supposed to be cordial or something like that? That's just ghetto.

"Okay, say I believe you, that means no BS tonight, right?"

"Yep. No BS tonight."

"You'll forgive me if I'm looking for the trap door." I lean back in the seat, glaring at him with every bit of irritation I have in me. I'm keeping my temper in check, despite every fiber of my being telling me to act a fool.

Against my better judgment, and to stick to the "good vibes only" type of day I'm gonna have by any means necessary, I close my door and start up the engine. Before I leave, tell him, "I feel like I'm gonna regret saying this, but I'm gonna hold you to it. I accept the truce. Be easy."

I know what he's saying, but actions speak louder.

If he's smart, he'll honor the truce.

And if he doesn't?

It won't end well for him, and that's a promise.

CHAPTER FIFTY-NINE – YASIR

I finally get home after picking up everything I need for the night, and to be real, I'm legit trying to find a way to summon some extra energy to handle people later. It isn't that I don't want to do people, but it's *certain* people I don't want to be around. I'm a bit wary of whether Ian can keep his word—all signs are pointing to *no*—but I'm not about to let that ruin my good mood.

If anything, I'm leaning toward the extrovert side of my personality tonight. It feels good too.

I lay the garment bag with my tux on my bed, making a beeline to the bathroom so I can freshen up and get this fit together. There's a stunning beauty who's expecting me to flex so she can watch the other girls be high-key irritated that the spotlight will be focused on us. I even mixed a special batch of oils to have the desired effect.

Yes, I want her to swoon even more than she already does.

I check my phone before I jump in the shower, grinning as I see the text from Zahra. She leaves a series of flirty emojis and a "I can't wait for you to see what type of dime you have on your arm" message that has my imagination on tilt. She's been secretive all week, not even giving me a hint of what her dress looks like. All she would say when I asked was that I wouldn't be able to wipe the smile off my face the minute she comes down the stairs.

She rarely disappoints, so there's no need for me to worry that it won't be something that's ripped off the runway. She's particular like that, and I love every bit of it.

I'm about to start getting ready, when Unk knocks on the door. "You good, kiddo? I wanna make sure you don't rush out before I can get some pics for your Nana and Lennox."

"Yeah, I'm good, but wait… Where's Ms. Lennox?" My senses

are tingling. I smell a setup. "I thought she was already here to hang with you tonight."

When he opens the door, I shake my head in disbelief. He's in a pair of suit pants and a button-down dress shirt, and I already know where this is going. He leans against the door frame with this smirk that lets me know the fix is in.

I groan as I continue to apply the oils on my skin. "Let me guess, y'all are chaperoning tonight at the ball. You couldn't give your nephew the head's up or nothing, right?"

Unk chuckles as I pull my pants on and reach for my shirt. "Sorry, I had to keep this one under wraps until the last possible minute. We're not gonna be there the entire night, just long enough to see y'all rock this trap waltz I've been hearing about."

Man, the relief that comes over me when he says that. Yeah, I can roll with that part. "Okay, but I need y'all gone the minute it's over, real talk. I can deal with adults being there to make sure things are cool, but I need y'all to be somewhere else enjoying the night without worrying about me."

"I'm always gonna worry about you, Ya-Ya," Unk utters while helping me with the tie that I obviously don't know how to handle. "After what you told me happened at the park last night, I want to make sure that things go smoothly tonight. I don't need you getting caught up in any more drama that you didn't create."

"I feel that, but I got tonight on lock," I tell him, stepping in front of the full-length mirror on my closet door to make sure everything is in its place before I put on the coat. "I mean, there's nothing that could pop off with all the grown people around to keep us from really getting lit."

"That's a good thing, young'un, because I was concerned about whether to let you do this tonight." Unk sits on the bed, his solemn expression throwing me off a bit. "I mean, Ian and his crew are gonna be there tonight, right?"

"And I got backup, so the odds are even," I counter, not really wanting to bring Ian's name into the mix. I'm not about to let him mess up a potentially epic night. "We've called a truce, so I'm not tripping about anything popping off."

"Do you think he's gonna keep his word?"

"If he doesn't, he won't like how that ends."

"Yeah, that's what has me worried," Unk remarks. His expression hasn't changed at all, which puts me on edge a bit. "Thanks to that TikTok, the Grove knows you got hands, and that isn't exactly a good thing."

At this point, I'm irritated, and I'm trying to keep Gamba on the low. "Unk, you know there are two ways I don't go with anyone, and that's back and forth. If he tries to start anything, I'm gonna end it. Self-defense is still a thing. Good vibes only, you know?"

Unk picks up the suit coat and helps me put it on, then looks at the finished product in the mirror with a satisfied grin. "Good vibes only, I feel that. But if you get to a point where you need to handle yourself, do what you have to do. I got your back regardless."

I smooth out the coat, taking a lint roller to get rid of any dust. I do a last-minute check of it all, and I like the way the suit hangs. Yeah, this will work. "I appreciate that, seriously. Now, I need to get on the road so I can pick Z up and set this night off right."

"Yo, I wasn't expecting to see you here," Kyle says, leaning against his truck with this perturbed expression on his face. I can relate; when Kendyl and Zahra get together, things tend to take a lot longer than they should. I don't know what happened, but it can't be good. Although, I guess I can take it as a compliment… she must've really wanted to blow my mind if she asked for her best friend to come over at the last minute.

I tap fists with him and match his body language for a few moments. He's irritated, but I can tell he's not trying to look like it. "I don't know what you've done to my best friend, but she's literally frantic over the phone with my girl, getting her to sweet-talk me into coming over here to help her get ready."

I shrug. "I have no idea what I did, or if I even did anything. I haven't even talked to her today."

"Well, you're about to get the whole experience, that's for sure," Kyle says just as the door cracks open. Someone's hand motions for us to come inside the house, and I can only assume it's Kendyl because Zahra's mom wouldn't be that dramatic. "Yep, that's our cue. Time to check out the show."

I rub my hand over the length of my face as we trudge up the stairs. Only Nyati knows what's about to happen right now. If this is what I have to look forward to when prom season comes around, I'm in for a long night.

We slip into the foyer, and Kendyl stops us in our tracks. We're at the base of the staircase, and it's a curved descent from the upper floor to where we're standing. I can already feel the drama building as Kairo saunters in from the great room and acknowledges us with a handshake and a warm smile.

"Good evening, sir. I hope you've been doing well," I say to Kairo, trying to suppress my nervous energy. I know we've technically gotten all the pleasantries and "getting to know you" stuff out of the way a while back, but he is still her father. "I take it the ladies are upstairs handling last-minute preparations."

Kairo laughs as he leans against the wall, glancing up toward the second floor, and shakes his head. "Boys, you know how women are when it comes to gala events like this. Get used to it, because it does not get any better."

Great. Prom season is going to be a whole production if what he says is true. I'm all for getting dolled up and black carpet ready, but it's not like we're going to a celebrity-studded event or anything. Oh wait, maybe I shouldn't speak too soon.

"Yeah, Anniversary Week is huge for the town, bro," Kyle adds his perspective the best way he can. "The only reason that this year is so over the top is that it's the bicentennial. Next year should be much less spectacular."

That's not making me feel better. In fact, this whole thing is doing the most for no damn reason, but I can't really say that out loud. "If they want us to get there on time, we'd better get rolling in the next ten minutes, or they'll blame us for not getting a good table."

Kesi appears out of nowhere while we're talking, clearing her throat as Kendyl seemingly glides down the stairs to join us at the base of the landing. She smiles at me and makes this subtle wave before she checks behind her as though she were waiting for her cue to begin. "Ladies and gentlemen… *her*."

Okay, Mrs. Assante with the fire introduction. But that pales in comparison to what has my attention now.

The vision of pure, exquisite, radiant beauty descends the stairs, and I swear everything, and everyone, fades to black. The only thing I see… the only thing I *can* see… is as close to a real-time rendition of what I could've imagined Zahra to look like if I created a painting of her in the dress she's wearing.

My gaze never leaves hers, and I almost forget to breathe. To say she looks stunning doesn't do her justice. I'm trying to find the words, and honestly, that's not gonna happen. Nope.

Even Gamba found his way to my conscious mind to peek for himself. *"By Nyati, she is goddess-level gorgeous. It's like the goddesses put the finishing touches on her and allowed her to borrow their glow for the evening."*

Man, he takes the words right out of my mouth, and he's probably said it much better than I ever could. I've never seen her look more beautiful than in this moment, and I'm fumbling over every word that I want to say for fear that it might insult her.

I'm so frozen in space and time that it takes a sharp elbow to my side from Kyle to shake me out of my daydream. He leans over and whispers, "This is the part where you take her arm and slip the corsage on her wrist, my boy."

I blink a few times to remind myself that I'm in the here and now, and I reach out to take her hand and lead her to me. I pull the corsage from its container and—I don't remember giving the box to Kyle, okay, but I think that's what happened—I stare into her eyes for what seems like an eternity. "You look… you've taken my breath away, Z. It's like Ashanti placed her touch against your skin and allowed you to borrow her glow for tonight."

"Did you really just steal my line?" Gamba says with a laugh. *"Is that what we are doing now?"*

"You're here to help me, remember?" I remind him. *"And that line is boss-level epic."*

Zahra blushes as I finally slide the corsage onto her left wrist, then offer the crook of my arm for her to take. "I was hoping you would approve of the final touches. I begged Kenni to get over here to help with that. It was a two-person job to get what I was looking for."

I kiss her cheek, still unable to tear my eyes away from her. "All I can say is thank Nyati for the both of them. I'm… I still have no words right now."

"Oh, I have a few words. Soooooo, now that you two have had your magical moment, can we get to the ball before all the good seats are taken?" Kendyl taps her foot against the hardwood floor, giving every bit of attitude she can, much to the amusement of everyone in the room. "Mama, come on down so we can get the pictures together and get up outta here, please?"

CHAPTER SIXTY – YASIR

The moment we step into the building, the whole room shifts in our direction. The pop of so many different colors from our clique's outfits start murmurs from the crowd, and with the way I've been feeling today, I soak up every ounce of energy. I glance into Zahra's eyes, and I feel the excitement in the air.

I didn't realize how spacious the interior was, and I have to admit I'm shocked. There's room for everyone to maintain their own space, with a large buffet that includes four different punch bowls and a *lot* of food. Like, they "pulled out all the stops" type of menu. I hate to be biased, but Unk and I could've done better on the selection. We weren't working this event, though, someone else was in charge tonight. The seafood isn't up to par, the other meats are questionable, and even the vegan choices are lackluster.

Zahra cuts her eyes in Chrisette's direction, coming close to sticking her tongue out like she's ten years old or something. I can't help noticing the heated stare coming from Ian, but he's not gonna faze me tonight. He asked for a truce, so we're honoring the truce. There's nothing in the rule book that says we can't step into the spotlight and take the shine away from the competition.

Taylor and Tania, once they join us at our reserved table, can't stop laughing over the glares coming from the rest of the group surrounding the wannabe power couple of Oakwood Grove High. Taylor taps fists with me and Kyle before we take our seats, shaking his head as he continues to laugh out loud. "Did y'all have to break out the top-tier outfits, yo? People started buzzing before you came through the door."

"Good, because that's what I wanted to happen," Kendyl brags, smoothing out her dress so she can get comfortable. "I told you we needed to apply some pressure, and we did that."

Well, she's not wrong, and we aren't the only ones who notice Chrisette seething. As Zahra told me on the way here, Chrisette's family is one of the six founding families that settled in Oakwood Grove two centuries ago. I imagine that comes with a bit of unreasonable expectations and a bit of entitlement, now that I think about it. The weird part is that none of the children of the other families have been as obnoxious about things, but that's not in my circle of concern.

We all turn toward the podium on stage as Mayor Lance taps the microphone to get everyone's attention. He clears his throat a couple of times before he takes the microphone off its stand. "Welcome to the Anniversary Ball, everyone. We are so glad you could all be here for the event. I'd be remiss if I didn't offer kudos to our talented Oakwood Grove High students for their efforts over the past couple of days."

Zahra rolls her eyes as the crowd erupts in applause, and I pull her close to kiss her cheek and try to fix the irritated expression on her face. I take my index finger and turn her head to turn her attention to me, whispering, "You did that, baby, take your bow."

"*We* did that, baby, but look at Chris trying to stand up like she spearheaded the whole thing," Zahra points out. "She only focused on the things that would make her look good. I'm over it, and I'm over her."

"Don't worry about all that," Kendyl says. "Once we put this trap waltz on them, they won't know what hit them." Kendyl gives up a smirk and a wink to both of us as she continues to clap with the rest of the crowd. "They're not ready for this smoke, I promise."

Kyle and I nod along with Taylor and a few of the other boys sitting at our table, which causes the girls to collectively raise their eyebrows. Zahra locks eyes with me, leaning in close so no one else can hear her. "I know that look, Ya-Ya. What do you have up your sleeve?"

Mayor Lance continues his announcements before he gets around to the part we've been waiting to hear. "And now, as part of the Anniversary Ball tradition, our young adults will show off their dance skills with the group waltz. I can't wait to see what they've come up with this year."

Zahra keeps me in my seat while the rest of our crew makes their way to the dance floor. "I'm serious, what are you up to, pretty boy? You've been riding high all day, and I can feel it on you. What do you have planned?"

I cup her face in my hands, leaning her forward to kiss her forehead, and shake my head before I place my fingers over her lips to keep her from asking any more questions. "Don't worry, what we have planned, Ian and his crew will never see coming. We can show you better than we can tell you."

"By Nyati, that was lit!" Zahra shouts. "How cool what that?"

Who knew putting together a waltz with our own spin on the steps would draw so much attention? I mean, there were only a dozen couples dancing, but the way we were able to stay in sync with each other kept the audience clapping and cheering us on.

Not gonna lie, though, the sour expression on Chrisette and the rest of her group was so worth the effort we put in to get the routine done. I even came up with a few old school steps Unk taught me for the boys to perform that had our girls screaming in surprise. If she thinks that was something, she's really gonna burst when I spring my other surprise on her later.

The routine was only supposed to be ten minutes long, but the way we executed, it felt like we were only out there for a few seconds. By the time we glided off the dance floor, the roar of the crowd was overwhelming. And when I say we glided, I mean I couldn't feel the floor. It wasn't supposed to be a contest between the groups that danced, but the conservative versus contemporary style was on full display.

Zahra's sitting in a chair as I return with a drink for her, and she's glaring at Chrisette as she trudges over to our table. She gives her the quick head-to-toe glance, and I already know it's gonna be pressure the minute she opens her mouth to speak. "Is there something wrong?" Zahra says. "Are you lost, little girl?"

Chrisette huffs, stopping mid-stride as she regards Zahra's hostile body language. "I guess there's no truce tonight after all, huh?"

"There might be a truce between our boyfriends, but make no

mistake, I don't need you in my space under any circumstances." Zahra grits her teeth, and I know she's trying to keep her temper under control. Imara doesn't need to rise to the surface any more than Gamba needs to if I'm in the same situation. "So, move along, lick your wounds from the L you just took with the waltzes, and figure out what else you plan to do with the rest of your evening."

Ian rushes over to the table, and for a few seconds, I'm ready to react to whatever energy he's about to give. He has a concerned expression on his face, like he didn't expect his girlfriend to come over. "Whoa, okay, there's no need to pull the claws out, alright? What Chrissy meant was y'all did your thing with that trap waltz. Had we known it would've been approved, we could've come up with our own version."

"Nobody told her to come over like we're cool and everything, either." Zahra frowns as she stares Ian down. "I had to put up with her all week under protest, and I made the best of it. Tonight is a whole no."

Kendyl slips into a chair next to Zahra as she gives up her own menacing expression. "Let's make this loud and clear for the people in the back. She wants both of you—hell, we all do—to stay in your damn lane. The audacity you're coming with like we're supposed to be cordial is high comedy, I promise you."

Chrisette's about to respond to Kendyl, when she notices Zahra's index finger in the air. I don't know about anyone else, but this isn't gonna end well. "We're not friends anymore, and I'm able to tolerate you in small doses when we're in public spaces, but whatever redemption arc you think you're on, this ain't it. You're gonna have to come better than empty congratulations."

"Okay, fair enough, but you understand that things flow much more smoothly when Ian and I are at the top of the power structure."

Umm, what? She can't be serious right now.

"If we have to tolerate each other—your words, not mine—then we need to make sure the natural order of things is acknowledged."

Before Zahra can get up to take things up a notch, I hold my hand out to her, flashing the widest smile I can to distract her. It must've worked because she's caught in my stare, and it's like no one else is around us in that moment. "I know we just rocked the trap waltz and everything, but would you like to dance, my beautiful one?"

She doesn't say a single word. We still stare at each other, and her eyes switch to this shade of red, and I know what's going through her mind now. Kendyl taps her left shoulder, but I don't think she's noticed at all. She finally manages a nod, wearing a smile on her face that threatens to melt me right there on the spot.

The music kicks in before she can get her bearings as I lead her out onto the middle of the dance floor. I take as much care as I can despite my body wanting to be much more aggressive. I place my other hand at the small of her back, holding her close to me, the jasmine and honeysuckle scent on her skin sending me deeper into our shared zone.

While I'm captivated by her gaze, she's literally spellbound by whatever she's found in my stare. "What do you see?"

"Your eyes… they're this rich color of cobalt," she utters, reaching up to kiss my lips. "I can't stop staring. They remind me of the Aegean Sea, like in the pictures I saw a few weeks ago."

"You're one to talk. Your eyes have a shade of red, like they've been replaced by garnets," I remark, still unable to break from our shared gaze. "I guess I should be asking what you're thinking instead of what you're seeing."

I pull her closer, staying in the moment with her, not wanting to leave for anything on the planet. I can't resist asking the question in my mind, but it begs the ask. "I have a feeling I was saving you from killing Chrisette when I came back. You know she's trying to fight for power, and she knows she's losing."

"What is it your uncle loves to say? 'Not my monkey, not my circus.'" She leans against my chest, listening to the music swirl as we sway with the rhythm. "She's trying her best to stay on top of a hill that means nothing to me."

We spin slow and easy. Each move feels effortless even though we've never danced this closely before. I release my grip on her hand, slipping it on my shoulder so she can clasp her fingers around my neck while I lock mine around her waist. We fall in step with each other, letting the flow of the songs control our movements. It feels so perfect being in this space with her, creating the energy between us.

"Tonight is not about anyone but you and me," I declare. I study her face, and I can't avoid the smirk spreading across my lips. "And I'm looking forward to creating some more magic with you tonight with no distractions, no interruptions."

"I love the sound of that." She arches her left eyebrow, curious about the tone in my voice. "So, what's the surprise?"

I shake my head, removing one of my hands from her waist to lift her chin, and I lean down to press my lips against hers. It's soft at first, my silent request for permission. She smiles through the kisses, nodding her approval for me to kiss her the way I really want.

We deepen our embrace, and for a few minutes, the landscape changes the same way it did when we were in my studio. I have a little better control over things this time around, and from the grin on her face, she looks like she's ready for the trip this time.

Zahra wiggles her toes against the cobblestone beneath our feet, and we smell the salt in the air and the heat on our skin as we notice the sunset from the top of the island. She casts her gaze toward the buildings as they slope down the hillside and lead out to the beach.

The surprise in her tone? Worth the trip. "Wait a minute, how did you—?"

"Do you know where we are?" I ask as I press my lips against the nape of her neck. "Surprise."

"We're in Santorini, Greece. I'd know this place anywhere. I was just thinking about it when I—oh, you're gonna get it when we get back." She leans her head against my chest, tapping her hand against my arm as we take in the picturesque scenery. "How in the world did you pull from my thoughts and bring us here when we're supposed to be back in the Grove? All I did was look into your eyes and the color reminded me of this place."

"A machari never reveals their tricks—at least, not yet." I spin her around to face me, and her smile melts me in seconds. "I wanted tonight to be *special*, special, and I actually have one more surprise when we get back."

We travel back to the ball, returning to the dance floor, still swaying among the crowd as the music continues to flow. I offer the crook of my arm for her to take as I escort her to our table, where Kendyl, Kyle, and the rest of our group are staring at us like we made a whole spectacle of ourselves.

"So, you two had one of your moments again, huh, sis?" Kendyl's the first one ready to act up. "I'm gonna need y'all to keep all that to yourselves, please and thank you. Ain't nobody got time for you two to create whatever you just had out there so we can sit back and be jealous and stuff."

"Yeah, I could've sworn there was this purple glow around y'all while you were dancing, like you were the only ones on the floor," Tania remarks as she takes a fan to cool herself down. "I don't know what y'all got going on, but I'm low-key jealous that we can't get in on whatever you're doing."

Zahra can't stop laughing, giving me a sideways glance the whole time. I shrug it off like it's nothing. Sounds like a personal problem to me, real talk. "I'm sorry, sis. The next time we decide to have our moment, we'll try to make sure you're not witnessing the magic."

"Yeah, yeah, whatever. So, what else do we have left to do tonight?" Kendyl smirks like she's got something up her sleeve, and Zahra's glaring at her like she wants to wring her neck. "I know this food ain't it, so, maybe we need to head into Savannah and grab something to eat."

Unk and Ms. Lennox stop by the table for a few moments, and Unk taps fists with the boys before offering his arm for Ms. Lennox to take. "Okay, so, now that we've seen what we came to see, we're about to head out. I'm glad the steps I taught you boys flowed so well. You had the crowd shook."

"We appreciate the lessons, sir. It was a good look out there," Kyle says to him. "Maybe we'll cop a few more moves from you for next year so we'll have more time to put our own flavor on it."

"Bet. Ya-Ya, we'll see you at home later. Be safe out here, alright?" Unk advises before they pivot and stroll toward the exit. "And congratulations to you all. This week has been very entertaining and well organized. Proud of y'all."

Once they leave, Kyle and I share glances real quick, and I nod that now's the time to handle that last surprise I have in store for Zahra. We get up, kiss our girls on the cheek, and head toward the exit with all due haste. "We can roll up outta here, definitely, but there's something I gotta grab first, and I need my ace to help me with it. Be right back."

Chapter Sixty-One – Yasir

Kyle and I rush to Storm, and the first thing I do is open the cargo door and lift the secret compartment. Inside, I pull out a small box I've been hiding all week. It took forever to get here, but it's worth it on so many levels.

I turn to see my dawg furrow his brow, wondering if he missed something. "So, what's this big surprise that you've been teasing all week?"

"Nana had been holding this for me since I was little." I smile as I hold up an obsidian pendant. "She always told me that I'd know when I wanted to place this around the neck of the girl I'd fall in love with."

Kyle gives me this confuzzled expression. "I don't get it. I mean, I know you and Z are into each other, but this looks like a regular onyx stone."

"Actually, it's an obsidian crystal mined from our native country," I explain to him. "It's been blessed and charged by a Kindaran priestess, and it protects its wearer from negative energy and physical harm."

"Deadass?"

"Deadass, bro. To most people, it sounds like an urban legend, but that's not how it works for us."

"But I thought you didn't know a lot of the customs. How do you know you're not proposing marriage or something?" Kyle poses a valid question. "I ain't ready to be your best man yet, playa."

We burst into laughter for a minute, but I get where he's coming from. "I trust Nana not to steer me wrong. This isn't a promise ring or an engagement ring, but it means a lot in our culture to place this crystal around those who mean the most to us."

"Okay, that's what's up, but are you *sure*, sure about this?" Kyle asks me. "I mean, this is next level, yo. Popping the 'L' word ain't something you just toss in the air for no reason."

I don't know how to explain it to him without it sounding like I'm out of my mind. "I don't remember the last time I felt this deeply about anything or anyone. I wouldn't do this if I wasn't sure, sure. Trust."

We tap fists before I close the door. "Then let's make the grand entrance and gesture so the rest of the girls in the place can have something else to hate on your girl about."

Kyle sprints ahead of me to head into the building so he can get everything set up for the big reveal, and I lean against the back of my car and take in the moment. I can't remember feeling this good about anything, ever.

Gamba pops up, like he does when I have nervous energy. *"Are you good, kiddo? Anything I can do to settle things down?"*

"We're good, godfather," I assure him. *"There's not much to worry over tonight. In fact, things couldn't be better. I'm feeling epic."*

I move from the car to walk back to the front entrance. I slip the box in my coat pocket, making sure it's safely tucked away. "*The only thing we need to prepare for is the screaming girls when I present the pendant to my chosen—*"

Someone rushes me from behind and pins me against a truck. I force my way to face my attacker, anger radiating through me. Jordin stands mere inches from my face with one hand balled tight and the other gripping my shirt.

"Yo, are you kidding me? You're not even supposed to be here. I don't have time to deal with your foolishness," I say while trying to struggle out of his grasp.

"Well, whether you're in the mood or not, you're about to deal. You can bet that, playa."

I look around and try to find a way around Jordin and get out of there, but Mark shows up quick with Reggie, closing my escape routes.

"I guess I should thank Ian for getting you to drop your guard tonight," Jordin utters. "This beat down is gonna be easier than I thought."

Dammit. I should've known Ian would set me up. "It's not gonna be as easy as you think."

Gamba senses my fear and anger and rushes toward the door to my conscious mind. *"Keep your calm as best you can until the security patrol comes. We have a couple of minutes, just hang on, kiddo."*

"I don't know if I can hold out that long," I admit. I haven't been gone long enough for Kyle to think something's gone wrong, and the parking lot is empty. Everyone else is inside enjoying themselves. Unk and Lennox are already gone after watching the waltz we performed. I've got no help. *"It's all on us if things go sideways. Are you with me?"*

"Always, godson."

Despite the comfort of his words, those couple of minutes might as well be hours, and I have no idea what they're prepared to do to me. I expect Jordin to take whatever weapon he has and put me out of my misery.

"Man, you still talking bad, even when it's obvious you're clearly done." Jordin punches me in my mouth before I have a chance to react, and I taste blood. He split my bottom lip with ease. "Go ahead, yell for help. All those people inside can come out and witness your demise."

"Either get this over with or let me go. Time's running out." I'm doing everything I can to delay the inevitable. I'm pinned and vulnerable. I need Kyle, my crew, and any others to help even the odds. "What happens next is on you."

"Yeah, you don't know when to shut up." He punches me again, hard enough this time for me to realize he's done playing around. "I'm gonna enjoy silencing you for good."

Nope. I'm not going out bad without a fight.

Gamba yells for me in the darkness, *"Yasir, I need you to calm down, I cannot get to you. There's no way to get to you when you're in distress. You need to conjure your zamwani now."*

I'm not sure if I wanna do that, but I hear something growling in the darkness that catches our attention. *"What was that??"*

"Whether you want to or not, your zamwani knows you are in

danger," Gamba replies as the growls grow closer to the door. *"Conjure it to the surface. There is no other alternative."*

He's got a point, whether I agree with him or not. *"There's no way for me to do it without exposing what we are."*

"I understand, godson. Do you trust me?"

"Yes."

Gamba nods as we peer through my eyes to figure out how to get out of this mess. *"Then when it is time, we need to let go and allow things to happen as they are supposed to happen."*

"But what if someone sees what I've conjured to the surface?"

"We will handle it… together."

Jordin lets me go, but Reggie and Mark close in on me at the same time, Reggie from the front, Mark from behind. I get the drop on Reggie, landing a right cross to his ribcage, but Mark strikes my lower back near my kidneys, bringing me to my knees in seconds.

Mark and Jordin are on top of me before I can rise to my feet, raining elbows and fists down on me. The three of them find every inch of exposed bone and muscle that I can't protect. Every spot I cover after it's struck, they find three other spots to exploit and damage.

Then someone pops up that I don't expect to be there, and it only fuels my rage, knowing that he got the better of me, and I allowed it to happen. He just stands there, watching me get pummeled within an inch of my life, and I can hear him laughing the whole time.

I try to keep blocking, but the pain's taking over.

"You really aren't as good as advertised, my guy," Ian taunts. "I expected you to at least fight back. I guess you're more like your folks than I thought."

"Bro, what the fuck? You're gonna let these boys do this right here?" I can't hide my anger, and that dig at my parents was a low blow. "What happened to sticking up for the Grove?"

"Well, I mean, they have to get theirs, considering three of theirs were hurt, right?"

I yell out in pain, using my arms and hands to protect my head and face from the barrage of blows I take. The growling inside my head grows more intense, gets closer to my conscious mind, but it feels familiar, almost like I'm welcoming an old friend. My mind is having a hard time understanding it all, and it's confusing things.

"Now, Yasir! It is time!" Gamba screams out. I'm still trying to sort through my rage and fear but bringing my *zamwani* to the surface is the only option if we're gonna get through this alive.

Enough is enough.

I don't care who sees what happens next. I'm ready to jump off the edge and into the abyss. As far as I'm concerned, we can lay waste to everything and let Nyati sort it out. "I warned you, and now it's my turn!"

The next thing I see is a blinding flash of light, and then a blood-curdling roar I don't recognize from within the depths of my core cuts through the air.

What comes next… legit scares the living hell out of me.

CHAPTER SIXTY-TWO – YASIR

All I feel is darkness. And rage. And the desire for retribution.

And this time, I don't care.

The shift happens quicker than the blink of an eye, and I'm so dialed up, I sense everything around me. Our sight is nearly panoramic, and we hear things from so far away, we swear we can hear Unk and Lennox as they're just getting home from their night out.

We look down at our hands and see claws and how different our skin looks. It's literally a midnight black hue, and the spikes that cover our arms and the rest of our body make us look absolutely menacing. I feel… longer? I don't know how to explain it, but our line of sight is so much different from up here. When we stretch our arms out to grab Mark and Reggie, we notice our limbs are *way* longer than what was explained to me.

What in the world have I conjured to the surface?

All my senses are heightened, to the point where I'm almost overwhelmed. Everything, everywhere, all at once. I struggle to focus on anything, but I know why my *zamwani* has risen to the surface.

I've conjured its presence to protect me. Period.

We hear the screams from the boys, noticing the abject horror in their eyes. Instead of empathy, we lick our lips in anticipation of what we plan to do to them as soon as we get our claws into them. We let out a hair-raising growl, casting our eyes skyward to bay at the crescent moon, then set our attention back to them, taking delight in their fear, wishing they knew that it's *me* inside of this hulking creature.

Except—it's not me. Well, it is, but it isn't. It's like I'm piloting a drone or in an immersive role-player game or something. That's the only way I can explain what's happening to me. Everything the zamwani senses, I'm in sync along with it.

While we enjoy the hunt of our prey, I can't help but feel a little distracted the moment I hear Zahra's voice cut through the noise. She's trying to get to me, and Kendyl and the rest of the crew are trying to stop her.

"Yasir's in trouble. We need to get to him now!" I hear her say through the partying crowd around her.

"Z, what are you doing? We need to head that way, not toward whatever the hell is happening out there."

"You don't understand, Kenni, I have to get to him. Something's wrong, something's really wrong."

"Yasir can take care of himself, baby. We have to get somewhere safe." I hear Kendyl yell out. "You can't possibly do anything that won't make things worse."

"I'm telling you right now, if you want to go, then go, but I've got to see what's going on. You can let me go, or I can force my way through. Your choice." I can hear it in her tone. She's gonna get her way, whether they like it or not. "I promise I'll be okay. I'll catch up with you in a bit."

While I'm distracted, Reggie and Mark manage to escape from where we cornered them. That's okay, we can catch them with ease. We spot Reggie first, trying to hide behind a car. He peeks over the hood, and before he knows it, we're on top of him, ready to finish what we started. He screams again, running from the car just as we come close to snatching him mid-stride.

The cars become more of a nuisance, and they need to be out of our way, so we lift and flip and toss everything in our path, not realizing the ease of how we're able to do it.

The explosions from the leaking gas and engines don't faze us in the slightest. Metal screeches and glass shatters all around us, and we can't get enough of it. The carnage we leave in our wake only fuels the desire to create even more chaos.

We let out another roar that echoes through the night air, and I feel like the anger and frustration, everything I've suppressed in an effort to behave and not cause trouble, is wrapped inside of that howl. Even the horrified screams from the onlookers cowering just inside the entrance to the hall don't affect things. We won't be satisfied until they're eliminated.

"Now this is what I'm talking about." I feel so powerful, like I can do anything I put my mind to. It feels too good to stop what I'm doing. It's a trippy sensation, being in two places at once, but I'm completely connected to my zamwani. *"I should've been doing this the entire time. We need to get to them now."*

"Then let us handle this and be done with it," Gamba growls as we continue to pursue the boys. *"They need to know who they are dealing with."*

We finally track down and trap Mark against a car. There's nowhere for him to go without catching our claws, and the terror-filled look in his eyes makes us realize that he's figured it out too. We stalk him slowly, our grin widening, and growl, showing our intention to end him where he stands.

"Please don't kill me, please!" he screams, but we're fresh out of mercy. All we want is for him to suffer. "Oh my God, please, let me go!"

Our paws claw through the concrete, leaving prints behind as we continue to stalk our prey. Somehow, Mark manages to crawl under the vehicle, but he's still not safe. We grab the roof with both paws and throw the car over our shoulders, hearing it explode as it lands on top of the mangled heap of metal we've left in our wake.

We use our enhanced agility to get ahead of Mark and trap him again, this time he's in a corner and there's nowhere for him to escape. The flickering light from the damaged streetlamp above makes for the perfect backdrop for what's about to happen to him, the fear etched in his face leading to the fact that he knows his life is over.

We bare our teeth, moving closer and closer to dispatching Mark into permanent darkness.

It won't stop with him. The other two are still in the area. We can smell their distinctive scents. They won't be able to escape, either.

"Hey! Over here! Over here!" I hear a frantic voice trying to get my attention. The pitch sounds different, and I'm having a hard time making sure it is who I think it is, but after a few seconds, my senses sharpen, and I know who it is in a heartbeat.

Zahra.

We turn around, staring her down as we feel the heat swirling around us simmer down to a burn. I don't know how it's happening so fast, but I don't question it. Her eyes draw me in, even in my angered state of mind, and the strangest thing happens in that moment.

She closes her eyes, and while we don't see her lips moving, we hear what she's saying loud and clear. "*Karasu horo.*"

Hearing it sounds like a thunderclap in my ears, snapping me to attention and nearly severing my connection to my *zamwani*. We whip around to face her, and she's glaring at us, almost commanding us when she repeats the phrase. "*Karasu horo.*"

In the next instant, I've disconnected from my *zamwani*, and I look on as its teeth withdraw into its mouth, the growl turns into a low mewl, and it drops to its knees. I still can't break through my wall of anger, but it isn't as hard as before. I breathe deeply, allowing her voice, her energy, to seep into my pores, giving me every reason to settle down and take control again.

"What is happening, Yasir?" Gamba's confused over why we've stopped our rampage. *"Why are we stopping? We need to end this, now."*

"I'll explain later, trust me, it's okay," I say. *"We have to find a way to coax the zamwani back into the depths."*

I turn my attention to Zahra, who hasn't moved an inch. "I hear you, my chosen. I'm here. I'm scared. I had to get them off me."

"I know, babe. I need you to calm down," she says. "I sense your pain, but this isn't the way to deal with it. We'll figure this out together, I promise. Where are you?"

"I'm behind a car in the corner of the parking lot. No one can see me." I'm disoriented, and I'm doing my best to get my bearings again so I can get to my *zamwani* to bring it back to where it came from. "Don't try to find me, not yet. I still need to coax my *zamwani* back into the shadows. Just keep it distracted."

I'm at a loss over how we're communicating telepathically. I don't know how it's happening, but I'm grateful no one else can hear us.

Gamba grabs my arm, shaking me from the connection with

Zahra. *"I understand now. We need to take control before the beast regains strength. Zahra has it distracted, so we need to concentrate on putting it back in its proverbial cage."*

"It's not gonna want to go quietly."

"Yes, I know, which is why we need to take advantage of the distraction before—"

"On my mark, unload it all." Lieutenant Greer, Sarge's superior officer, gives the order for the officers to fire on my *zamwani.* The fear in my heart that it might die overwhelms me, and all I can think about is figuring out how quickly I can escape the bullets that are coming its way. "FIRE!"

The first of them hit its hide, and I realize they're needles, not bullets. It knocks them off as soon as they penetrate, and it from the way it slows down, I figure out they're using tranquilizer darts.

I have to get it away from here, but how?

"Focus and repeat this phrase. Kitowaku," Gamba says. "Hurry, Ya-Ya."

I do as I'm told, repeating the word as many times as I can, praying it can hear me. I close my eyes, continuing to chant, afraid to open my eyes as the needles fly through the air.

The next thing I know, I hear the other officers yelling, "Where did it go? It just disappeared."

No, I haven't. I'm right here standing in front of them.

And then I watch my *zamwani* rise, almost like its taken flight. It looks light and airy, and when I look at the group of officers, I realize it's floating over and away from them. How in the hell did I do that?

Even more confusing? I take flight with it, forgetting that I'm still tethered.

The last thing I notice before we disappear from view are all the vehicles that are overturned, most of them engulfed in flames, and a whole lot of confused people, including all the kids who have come out of the building to survey the damage. Zahra's being consoled by Sarge, and it almost breaks me that I can't be with her.

All I can do is try to find a space for us to land, coax it back into the depths, and somehow get back to Storm without being seen. I've left a complicated mess of a situation to explain.

And Nyati only knows what else.

Chapter Sixty-Three – Zahra

Panic has me in a vice-like grip as we comb through the entire park for any sign of Yasir. My heart hammers against my ribcage, threatening to burst through my chest the moment I see Storm in the parking space. I forgot that I have the keys in my purse. If he's not here, it can only mean one thing—he's on foot, lost, alone and vulnerable somewhere among the trees that surround the building.

Taylor's the first one back to where we've gathered in the front of the building. He shrugs as he's as confused as the rest of us. "There's no sign of him anywhere. We've checked the grounds, and his Jeep is still in the parking lot."

"We've got to figure out where he went," Kyle utters as he leans against the doorway to catch his breath. "Those Baytown boys broke out of there when that… thing… got distracted. They could be trying to hunt him down as we speak, and we can't leave him out there by himself like that again."

Taylor agrees, nodding toward a few other boys who were helping in the search. "We'll take a section of the park and the tree line; we can cover more ground if we split up."

I'm stuck between a proverbial rock and a hard place. I need to tell them about what's going on with Yasir. Telling Taylor is one thing, but can I trust the rest of them with something this mind-blowing? "Okay, it's obvious he's not in the immediate area. Taylor's right, maybe we should split up and search some of the other spots he might have gone?"

Kendyl shakes her head with such force, her ponytail snaps from left to right. "I'm not going anywhere until we have a clue where that… that *monster* went. Can we have a conversation about where the hell it came from? Was that thing even real?"

If only they knew how real this all actually is, they'd be looking at me and Yasir like we've really lost it. "Maybe that was a fluke sighting or something? There's no guarantee that it's still out there."

"There's no guarantee that it isn't still out there, either, Z," Taylor reasons. "I don't know about you, but if I'm gonna continue the search for Yasir, I'm doing it with a weapon in my hand, in case it shows up again."

"We might be able to find Yasir and still not have to deal with any weapons," Kyle says. He stares at me, nodding while putting his index finger to his lips. I'd completely forgotten that he and the girls know about Gamba and Imara, so I can only assume they connected the dots to Yasir's *zamwani*. "We can grab the stuff out of my truck and get on the hunt. The sooner we can find him, the better off we'll all be."

As soon as the boys take off toward Kyle's truck to grab whatever's available, Kendyl turns to me to ask the million-dollar question. "Okay, so now that we've technically had to lie to Tania's boyfriend about what might really be going on, is it a simple possibility that whatever we just saw *was* Yasir?"

I sigh, thankful that I'm not alone in my smoke-and-mirrors routine. "Yes, unfortunately, that was the beast that Yasir can conjure when he's in danger. I never got the chance to see what his *zamwani* looks like, so, I was as shocked as the rest of you when it showed itself."

"And the disappearing into a fine mist, is that a new trick that we need to be aware of too?" Tania asks. "I knew he was on a different level than the other boys in school, Z, but this whole thing takes the cake. He's a real-life Dr. Strange. How are we supposed to rock with that?"

"Right now, we just need to find him. He's gotta be scared out of his mind, and Nyati knows what other emotions could be flowing through him," I tell them. "I just wish there was another way to locate him."

"Well, you two do have a connection that you said Ms. Kynani told you about, right?" Kendyl mentions to me. "Maybe you can reach out, like, use the Force or something. It's not like we have a witch lying around to do a locator spell."

"Okay, I need you to commit to a fictional world, Kenni, either *Star Wars* or *The Vampire Diaries*, because you're confusing me right now." I allow myself a good giggle over my bestie trying to lighten the mood. "But you're right, she did say that we are connected, so maybe if I can concentrate deeply enough, I might be able to get an idea of where he might be."

Long shot? Sure. I have no idea what abilities I possess, and until I have a chance to sit down with Kynani to flesh all of that out, I'm pretty much fumbling around in the darkness. I scan the area with the girls to be sure no one sees what I'm about to do, and then I close my eyes and focus on him.

"Do not try to stress yourself, baby girl," Imara cautions me. *"We are still trying to figure things out, and I do not want you to think that something is being blocked."*

"I can't feel him. I'm trying, but I can't sense him out there."

"I need you to slow your breathing, this can't work if you don't control your emotions."

"That's easy for you to say," I reply as I focus on Yasir. *"But normally, I can pick up on his energy or something. I just need to know he's okay."*

"He is going to be okay, Zahra. We may have to find him the old-fashioned way."

The disappointment on my face tips my girls to my unsuccessful effort. They wrap their arms around me, offering as much encouragement as they can as they tighten their grip.

"We will find him, baby. Promise," Kendyl states.

"Yeah, he couldn't have gotten far on foot, even if he has a magical side to him," Tania adds. "We can check the obvious spots first. If I was off-balance, there would be at least three go-to spots to try to get my head together."

Something in what Tania explains sparks me. I take the car key out and head for Storm. "Do me a favor and call the boys off the hunt. I need you to check Palmetto Square Park and Wright Square. There's one other place he could possibly be, but unless he's developed the ability to fly, he can't be there by now."

"Where are you going?" Kendyl asks. "We can't have you heading off by yourself."

"I'll be okay, baby, trust me," I insist. "If anything comes up and you find him, call me. I'll check in on y'all in about twenty minutes."

I rush to hop in the driver's seat, peeling out of the parking lot. I'm taking a huge gamble that I may be right, but there's only one way to find out. I think I know where he could be. I just hope I can get to him before it's too late.

Chapter Sixty-Four – Yasir

My heart races as I glide through the dense forest as branches and leaves whip past me. My feet barely touch the ground as I push myself to go faster. The police could be searching for me, but they're the least of my problems. Jordin and his crew are still out there, and I can't afford to get caught out in the open when I'm at my most vulnerable. Conjuring my zamwani left me weak, and I'm functioning more on fear, anger, and adrenaline than anything else.

Finally, I reach a clearing where it's safe to land, and its incorporeal form solidifies. Feeling the ground beneath my feet is welcomed, but now that I've had to put my *zamwani* to rest, the whole process has left me disoriented and frantically scanning my surroundings to figure out which way to go to get back to the building. To my utter surprise, my tuxedo is in one piece, all things considered. It's a bit dirty, but there are no tears in the fabric, so that's a relief.

I check my pockets and completely freak out as I notice the pendant I wanted to give Zahra is gone. I must have lost it in the middle of all the chaos, when I was so focused on controlling my *zamwani*. My stomach twists in knots as I pray to the Divine Mother that I can find it once this is all over.

I glance around again in search of anyone who may be in the area before I retreat inside my mind to have a convo. *"That was intense. I know we could've hurt someone, but it was worth it to get all that out of my system. Still, that was a populated area, and we were out in plain sight. What do we do now?"*

Gamba shakes his head as I create a veranda on the shores of Kindara from one of my paintings for us to engage in a more civil discussion. *"Yes, it was worth it, but there are always consequences to our actions. If it were not for Zahra distracting it, there is no telling what else would have happened tonight."*

I tilt my head to the side, confused by the explanation. I ease into the lounger, taking a sip of water, considering Gamba's words. *"So, you mean to tell me that once I let it out, there's no way to control it? I mean, I know how my temper can get sometimes, but I'd like to think I can control my emotions."*

"Whether you want to believe it or not, everyone has a dark side," Gamba says as he joins me on the landing. *"The problem is when you deny that it exists."*

"Well, I'm not everyone." I stare off into the horizon. *"What makes you think I want to indulge that side of myself? That I want to become the monster that Ian's trying to convince the whole town that I already am?"*

Gamba exhales slow, and I feel the frustration rising inside him. "*You are not a monster. You have control over a being that is created to protect you. As much as you want to, my godson, you cannot ignore that side of yourself. To become your truest self, you have to embrace the light ... and the darkness. It is only then that you will be able to control the rage that is in all of us. No one is immune to it."*

"Do you remember what happened a few minutes ago?" I ask, allowing the bluntness of my question to land between us. *"Whether I like it or not, damn near the entire town saw my zamwani. Nyati only knows how many took out their phones and recorded everything."*

I hear a twig snap, jarring me from our conversation. My senses are still heightened, so I focus my hearing to pick up where the activity is coming from. Gamba focuses on the sound as well, using the *zamwani*'s residual energy to increase my hearing sensitivity. We hear the sheriffs cutting through the brush, realizing that they're still on the hunt. *"How far off do you think they are?"*

"Maybe a couple hundred feet, give or take," Gamba says. *"We will have to deal with the other issues later. Right now, we need to get to safety. Sounds like the sheriffs have picked up the trail."*

Voices bellow through the night air, calling for me to let them know I'm okay. Part of me wants to yell out and put an end to the search, but something from deep within urges me to remain hidden.

I keep moving, getting to the outer edge of the forest and into a clearing, heading toward another parking area. If I'm lucky, I can get there without being seen so I can find a way back to the event space and get to Storm. I left the second key fob under the wheel well, so I won't have to bother Zahra just yet.

And then I hear the one voice I don't need, immediately wishing I stayed put within the tree line. Dammit.

"I was wondering if I would run into you again," Ian huffs as he leans against his Corvette. "You and I have an unfinished conversation to work through."

"Don't you have a curfew or something, my boy? I don't have time for games or bullshit conversation." I stand still, no longer bothering to hide my irritation. "It's been a long night, you tried for a second time to take me out and failed, okay? You were the one who riled up those Baytown kids. Let's just hit the reset button, go home, get some sleep, and try it again next week, huh?"

"Nah, we're gonna do this right here and now." Ian steps in my direction. "And from the looks of your tux, I'd say you have a lot of questions to answer. Let's see if I can rile you up the way they did. Everyone's already seen what you can become, I just need the sheriffs to see for themselves and we can wrap this up, neat and clean."

"You have no clue of what the hell you're talking about, seriously," I spit. "But go off, though. Tell me more about what you think you know."

Kyle and Taylor pop out of the tree line, along with Sarge and LT. LT steps in front of Ian while Sarge shadows me. Kyle and Taylor stand with me as I try, and fail, to step around Sarge to get to Ian.

"Your girl is worried sick about you, bro," Kyle announces. "We couldn't find you when those Baytown boys ganged up on you."

"That's because he and that thing that showed up might be one and the same, Kyle," Ian shouts. "He's a menace to this town, I'm telling you. Why can't y'all see that?"

I'm desperate to find a plausible answer to throw everyone off the trail. No one saw me conjuring, so I have a chance to still cast some doubt. "That thing was chasing me too, and I barely got away from it. It managed to corner me, and when I tried to escape, it started clawing at my clothes. I was lucky to get out of there without much more damage."

"All right, boys, let's settle it down a notch. We've found Yasir, and there doesn't seem to be any sign of the beast we saw earlier." Sarge jumps into the conversation to calm things down as best as possible.

"I told you before that you're off-key, all right?" Kyle demands as he focuses in on Ian. "You and these wild theories are getting really weak, for real. You have no proof and bad blood. Any idiot can tell you got pressure against my ace."

"I got pressure alright, but that doesn't mean I'm wrong." Ian waves us off and opens the door to his car, then slides into the seat. "But as usual, Sarge and LT are here to save the damn day, so we'll have to pick this up another time."

LT inserts himself into the conversation, but he's late to the party. "What is Ian talking about, fellas? If you know something about what happened earlier tonight, you need to let us know. We'll have to keep searching for it until we get a positive ID on whatever that creature was."

That declaration sounds like a bad underground mixtape to my ears. This isn't going to go away anytime soon. I better find a way to spin this before it becomes a problem I can't solve. "It might have been a one and done, LT. Maybe it got scared off when y'all started firing at it."

"I hear you, Yasir, but we have to make sure. The public that was here tonight will have their tongues wagging on social media by morning, and we need to be on top of things," LT says. "I'm gonna need you boys to scatter, get home. If we need you for anything else, we'll alert your parents."

Ian doesn't bother to stick around, slamming the door and screeching the tires while making his exit. The boys and I are left to deal with Sarge and LT, and that conversation seems to be long overdue.

"Yasir, what did we tell you about being the bigger man and keeping out of the mess you're already in right now?" Sarge closes his eyes for a few moments. "Thankfully, there were witnesses to your earlier incident and we know you weren't the aggressor, but you have to be smarter."

"Yeah, while the golden child gets off scot-free with everything he's done, right?" I counter. "Don't worry, I'll wait."

"Okay, you've made your point." Sarge admits. "We've been treating the family with kid gloves ever since they stepped into the mayor's office." He glances at Kyle and Taylor, dropping a not-so-subtle clue on them. "And it's been extended to people who shouldn't be putting themselves in the position to have to utilize that type of clout."

"So, what happens now, Sarge? Do I get to go home too, or nah?" This whole situation irks my nerves, and I'm over it already. I have to find Zahra. She's got to be worried sick, and she's driving Storm too. "Or is this gonna be one of those types of nights where paperwork is involved?"

Sarge cuts his eyes toward LT, getting a subtle nod from his superior officer. "You're good to go, Yasir, but careful with anything you might be feeling as far as any type of reprisal. We still follow social media buzz."

I simply nod and plod toward Kyle's truck to climb inside. As Kyle and Taylor get settled, I wait for the engine to roar to life, content to get home as quickly as possible so I can put this nightmare of a night in the proverbial rear-view mirror.

"Yo, shouldn't you be calling Z to let her know we found you? She's worried sick about you." Kyle turns to check on me in the back seat. "And what about your surprise gift? You still need to get that to her."

"I don't even know where it is," I reply. "I lost it, and my tux got ripped. For all I know, it's probably in the hall in the parking lot. Anyone could've found it."

"Then we need to head back there before they lock it down and see if we can find it." Kyle tells me, holding up his hand when I launch a protest. "We need to do this. I'm not gonna let you go out bad."

"Nah, bro, I'm gonna have to reevaluate some things, and I can't do that with her distracting me. I appreciate you looking out, but I need to hit the reset button." I slump in the seat, completely exhausted. "I don't care what you have to tell your girls. I just need to get home."

ᘓᘓᘓ

We pull up to the house after leaving the banquet hall (Kyle can be really persuasive when he wants to get his way) and I'm not gonna lie, I'm glad that we were able to find my pendant, despite the area being taped off as a crime scene. I probably would've driven myself batty if I'd lost it.

That's no longer on my mind the moment I spot Storm in the driveway.

I don't know how Zahra could've known I'd be here. I made sure to tell my boys not to let anyone know I was heading home just yet, but here I am, trying to figure out what to say to Zahra before I'm ready to talk. My emotions are still all over the place.

The moment she exits the car, my heart skips a few beats. I'm happy to see her, but I hoped to get myself together first. I won't be able to tell her to go home, no matter how badly I want her to leave. Fear mixes in with confusion as she pads in my direction, flashing that smile that makes everything better, regardless of how bad I felt things had gotten.

"Are you okay? I was worried about you." She continues to check me over once I slide out of the truck. "Are you hurt? We looked everywhere for you."

"I'm still trying to figure out how to answer that question." I'm still reeling from everything I did to try to figure out what happened up to this point. "That whole scene was weird. One minute I'm eating fists and elbows, and the next minute, well… you saw what happened."

I lean against Storm's driver side, still sorting through my feelings, barely keeping eye contact with Zahra. I want to reach out to embrace her, but my thoughts are dominated by the images of the people who saw my *zamwani* and reacted with such fear and aggression. It's gonna be a minute before I forget how it made me feel.

I ignore Gamba as he tries to catch my attention. I'm not in the greatest headspace, and the overwhelming desire to isolate myself from everything and everyone races to the surface.

Zahra slips her fingers over mine, placing soft kisses across my lips. "I'm glad the boys found you. We'd been looking all over for you after… well, after all the confusion at the ball."

"Yeah, we managed to catch up to him without incident," Kyle mentions. "It's been a wild night, to say the least."

Taylor adds, "Bro, we've had wild nights before, but tonight was a whole other level of weird. I'm still trying to wrap my head around what we saw tonight."

I drop my head, kissing Zahra's shoulder as I make every effort to calm down. "I had hoped to have a normal night with you, babe, but as usual, that jackass Ian had to find a way to screw it all up. I'm beginning to wonder if there's a such thing as a normal night."

"What's important right now is that you're home safe," Zahra tells me. "And I'm sure we can find a way to salvage the night."

Kyle taps my fists as he and Taylor head back to his truck. "Kenni just hit me up. She's on the way to drop your car off before we jet, Z, so we'll stick around until she gets here."

"Yo, Kyle, TK, thanks for having my back. It means a lot to me, more than you know." I tap fists with Taylor, feeling the overwhelming urge to express my gratitude.

"That makes two of us, Yasir," Taylor utters.

"We'll leave you two to your privacy, I'm sure you have some catching up to do," Kyle says before they leave us alone. "And take care of that *other* thing you were planning, all right?"

"What's Ky talking about?" Zahra moves closer to me as the others pull out of the driveway, finally leaving us in some peace and quiet.

I sigh as I consider my words. There's no easy way to say it, so I blurt them out before I lose my nerve. "I'm not safe to be around anymore."

Zahra raises an eyebrow. "What are you talking about? You're not making sense."

"You saw what happened earlier, Z, stop pretending that it didn't happen," I snap. I don't want to react that way, but the flood gates are open. "All that rage, all that anger, all because Ian and the rest of those boys triggered me."

Zahra grips my hands tight, pulling me closer. By Nyati, she feels so good in my arms. "We will figure this out, Ya-Ya. You're not alone in this, I'm right here. I already know what's going on with you, babe."

"Wait… what? How is that possible? You never got the chance to see what I can conjure before tonight."

"There's a longer conversation that we will need to have when we're with Ms. Kynani again, but I know what's going on with you, and I'm not afraid."

"No, I need to stay away from all of you until I can get a better grip on whatever *beast* keeps taking over me," I counter, struggling to keep my voice from cracking. "I'll never forgive myself if I use my powers and you get hurt."

"I'm a big girl, and I can handle whatever you think you have going on in there," Zahra shoots back as she taps her manicured finger against my temple. "Even when it was out and acting on all your rage and fear, the minute it saw me, it recognized me because it's a part of you. Don't you dare push me away. We'll get through this."

"Until I get triggered again, right? I don't care that you were able to get it to settle down for a few seconds. You can't be everywhere, and if someone sets me off again, I can't be sure that I can calm down." I'm no longer sure I can stop the tears from falling this time. "I can't take that chance. I've got to figure this out alone. It's better for everyone."

"Is it better for us? Shouldn't I have a say in this?" Zahra scoffs, shaking her head in defiance over what she's hearing. "You're giving up on us? Tell me that's not what you're saying."

"I don't have a choice, Z."

"You do have a choice, dammit. Do you love me?"

"Don't you hear what I'm telling you? I can't have someone's death on my hands," I tell her. I step away, creating space between us. "I'm scared of what's happening to me, but I need to get a handle on this."

Her eyes never leave mine. "Do… you… love… me? I know you do. There's nothing you can say that will convince me that you don't. Tell me you love me."

I take a breath. I gotta get my emotions under control, period. I didn't mean what I was saying, but I can't have her harmed because of something I did. I cut out all the noise, searching for a voice of reason, anything to help me figure out what to do next. How am I supposed to explain to her the rage I'm feeling? She knows about Gamba, but my *zamwani* is another matter entirely.

"Yasir... do not let her go, my love."

The voice shoots through me, stopping me cold. Hearing it unlocks something inside me, almost compelling me to listen. Even after all this time, it soothes me, its warmth feeling like a thick blanket. Mom. Like before.

I don't even question how she's able to reach me. But I'm gonna put her advice into action before something else goes left.

I reach out to pull Zahra closer without any hesitation, cupping her face in my hands and kissing her with every ounce of energy I have left. I pick her up and sit her on the hood, watching her eyes as they switch from a fiery red to a calming ice blue. I don't care about anything else. I just need her right there with me. I ignore the eye color changes for now. We'll have time to figure all of that out later.

Like she said, we have a different conversation to have with Ms. Kynani.

Without wasting another second, I pull out the box that holds the pendant, take it out, and drop the box on the ground. I hold it in my hands like my life depended on clasping it around her neck.

"I love you. I love you." I keep kissing her face, convincing myself that this isn't a dream. "Forget what I just said, I didn't mean any of it. I can't do this without you. You're my chosen. Please, say you won't leave me?"

"I never left, my chosen. I love you too. I just found you, and you're not getting rid of me that easily." She wipes the tears rolling down her cheeks. "I know this is scary, but we'll figure this out … together. Promise. Now, what's this in your hand?"

I smile wide as I glance down at the small, but significant, piece of jewelry that has the power to change everything between us. "This was something Nana wanted me to give to the one who means the most to me in this world. *You* are that one."

She starts trembling the moment I place the necklace around her neck, pulling her hair up so I can connect the clip. "Is this what I think it is? Is this an obsidian stone from home?"

"Yes. Do you know what it means?"

She nods excitedly, planting more kisses across my lips. "I know what it means. Do *you* know what it means?"

Kendyl pulls into the driveway with Raiden before I can answer her. I keep Zahra right there on the hood, refusing to let her out of my sight.

Kendyl slows her pace, reading the body language between us. She gives Zahra a head-to-toe scan as she wipes her face, and her bestie is ready to read me up one side and down the other. "Is everything okay? Z, you look like—Yasir, what did you do?"

Zahra takes one look at me and closes her eyes. The smile she offers reflects the fatigue we both feel after such an emotionally exhaustive night. "It's been a long night, chica, but we are okay. We are better than okay. There's a lot that we have to explain, but it will have to wait until morning."

I don't have much else to add to that. I'm tired from everything over the past two nights. "Yeah, we'll see y'all in the morning. We can talk once we've had a decent night's sleep."

Zahra and I watch as Kendyl and Tania get into vehicles and pull out of the driveway. Then I escort her to Raiden, tucking her into the driver's seat, slipping a few more kisses before I wave and wait for her car to disappear around the corner.

I don't have it in me to explain to Unk and Lennox about what happened tonight. I'll have to deal with that in the morning. I take the remaining energy I have to climb to the studio window so I can avoid them altogether, thanking the gods that the alarm system only covers the first floor and the basement levels. I deftly slip inside and slowly descend the stairs, hoping I'm not making too much noise along the way.

When I make it to my bedroom, I plunge head-first onto the bed, screaming into the comforter and hoping neither Unk nor Lennox can hear me. So much has happened tonight, and there's no telling what tomorrow's convos will reveal. There's no way I can keep this from those I care about the most anymore. They need to know what they're getting themselves into, and what we're asking of them.

No matter what happens, I have Zahra by my side. I can handle anything.

"It will be okay, kiddo. This is a bump in the road." Gamba cuts through the fog in my mind, trying to balance me as best he can. *"We will have the chance to sit down and talk things out with everyone in the morning. Just rest for now."*

"I will, but there's one more thing that I need to do."

In a last-ditch effort to grasp at whatever sanity I have left, I pull my phone from my pocket and tap on the number… outside of Gamba… of the one person who could possibly help me climb out of the darkness and possibly unlock my memories so I can put everything together. "Ms. Kyani? I'm scared. I really need your help."

ACKNOWLEDGEMENTS

2 August 2025
2314hrs (11:14PM)

When I first began this journey to where we are now with *Sageborn*, it was under different circumstances. Different name. Different powers. A lot of rewrites. And a lot of heartbreak.

My mom transitioned in the middle of the rewrites, and I'd lost my energy and passion for the project. Hindsight is 20/20, and if I had it to do all over again? Maybe I'd have done the same thing, who knows?

What I do know is that sometimes in life, you get a second chance to make a first impression. They don't come very often, and with this book, I'm hopeful that you'll give me the second chance to make a first impression with how I wanted this book, and Yasir's journey, to progress.

The added bonus of adding Zahra's voice back into the story was something that I originally gave up in the interests of getting the story in front of eyes that might have taken the book into other rooms I'd otherwise not be able to enter.

Now, you get to hear from my other fictional niece too.

If I play my cards right, there might be a crossover in the future between my fictional kids, but I'm not gonna force it if I can help it. But if you've ever had teenagers, you know they can surprise you daily. LOL!

Enough of my rambling, you know what comes next, so let's get down to the brass tacks.

To my parents, and my maternal grandparents… this book started out in one direction and took me through memories that I never, ever took for granted. Thank you for providing the safest spaces a kid with the wildest imagination could've ever asked for.

To my sister, I love you. Watching you reclaim a piece of you earlier this year was probably the best thing I've witnessed so far. When you're ready to pick the pen up again, I got your back. Always.

To my Beloved, I love you always. Thank you for indulging my eccentric and quirky ways and the worlds that I conjure as a result of it. There's more where that came from, and I'm blessed to have had you on this journey with me.

To babygirl, another promise kept. Despite your penchant for dramatics, you still surprise me every day. Daddy loves you.

And to my sixteen-year-old self, who mixed basketball and reading and writing fantastical stories because an English teacher at Frederick Douglass High School told you during your sophomore year that your imagination knows no bounds, and that all you have to do is follow the path and let it lead you to unimaginable places?

She was right the whole time. All we had to do was follow the path, no matter where it led us.

Finally, I'd like to thank you, dearest reader, for your support throughout the years. I've still got a lot of stories rattling around in my head, and hopefully, you will continue the journey with me. I'm forever a grateful prince.

May the gods smile upon you always,

Shakir

www.ingramcontent.com/pod-product-compliance
Lightning Source LLC
Chambersburg PA
CBHW020451310726
48979CB00016B/2607/J
* 9 7 9 8 9 8 6 6 6 8 8 1 9 *